WITH A YANKEE YELL

"Ration the watehe
knew it was futile. rily
from the little bit

Ryder looked for ath
the actual crest an ce
their defenses. He was about to order a patrol farther
downhill when shots rang out. Puffs of smoke showed
from trees only a little more than a hundred yards away.
Brief flashes of white Spanish uniforms could be seen
through the foliage. Without orders, his men dropped to
the ground and returned fire. More Spaniards could be
seen joining the first group and he realized that they'd
made the top first by only a few moments.

Someone screamed. One of his soldiers had been
hit. Haney dropped down beside Ryder. "I don't think
there's all that many of them, sir. I think if we rush
them all shooting and screaming they'll run away. At
any rate, clearing the hill's a lot better than sitting here
and shooting at each other."

"Agreed," said Ryder. He sent runners to the company commanders and impatiently bided his time until
he got word that everyone understood.

Now came the truly dangerous part, he thought.
"What the hell," he said to no one in particular. He
stood and blew hard on a whistle. Responses came from
either side of him and he could sense rather than see
several hundred soldiers emerging and moving forward.

Ryder drew his pistol and waved it, "Faster, men,
faster! And yell, damn it!"

Four hundred men screeched and hollered and ran
towards the Spanish, shooting as they went...

BAEN BOOKS
by
ROBERT CONROY

Himmler's War

Rising Sun

1920: America's Great War

Liberty: 1784

1882: Custer in Chains

Germanica

Storm Front

To purchase Baen Book titles in e-book format, please go to www.baen.com.

1882

CUSTER IN CHAINS

ROBERT CONROY

1882: CUSTER IN CHAINS

Copyright © 2015 by Robert Conroy

A Baen Book

Baen Publishing Enterprises
P.O. Box 1403
Riverdale, NY 10471
www.baen.com

ISBN: 978-1-4767-8142-6

Cover art by Kurt Miller

First Baen paperback printing, May 2016

Library of Congress Control Number: 2015006166

Distributed by Simon & Schuster
1230 Avenue of the Americas
New York, NY 10020

Pages by Joy Freeman (www.pagesbyjoy.com)
Printed in the United States of America

Introduction

IN ORDER TO BE SUCCESSFUL, AN ALTERNATE HISTORY novel has to be plausible, accurate, and relevant. While plausibility and accuracy are more or less self-explanatory, relevancy might not be. For instance, had I studied harder in high school (or at all when I first started college) my life might have turned out significantly different, although not necessarily for the better. The world, however, would have neither noted nor long remembered my changed efforts, to misuse Lincoln's immortal words at Gettysburg.

Thus, I had always felt that if George Armstrong Custer had somehow survived his very bad day at the Little Big Horn, the world wouldn't have given it—or him—a second thought. Like many old soldiers, Custer would have simply faded away, eking out an existence on his miserable pension. In sum, not much would have happened to change the world had he snatched victory from the jaws of defeat.

But would that really have been the case?

First, victory over the Sioux was always within his grasp. He underestimated his enemy and had foolishly split his forces. And he also had a pair of Gatling guns that he refused to take with him because he felt they would slow him down. This was a problem that could have been solved simply by using decent horses to pull them instead of the sickly nags he did use. My own feeling is that he didn't want to bring the Gatlings because they weren't glamorous enough for the hard-charging Seventh Cavalry.

Second, Custer and his wife Libbie were ambitious to a fault. They also loved each other deeply. The very lovely Libbie Custer was far more cunning and politically attuned than he, and, after getting a medal for his heroic achievements in defeating the Sioux, I believe she would have urged him to run for the presidency in 1880 as the Republican nominee. With her backing and conniving, he would likely have won.

And how lovely was Libbie? Photographic technology of the period often resulted in people looking stark and severe, and this is the case with most photos of Libbie. However, there are a few that can be viewed on the internet in which she looks absolutely stunning and sensual.

What would have happened to the United States if he, the nation's newest war hero, had won that election?

Custer was no dummy. He had graduated from West Point and had risen in rank through his courage and his abilities to become a very young brigadier general in the Civil War. Nor was he a coward. His exploits in battle prove that he was brave. He was, however, headstrong, impetuous, and heartily disliked by many of his peers. What mischief would President

George Armstrong Custer have brought us? In my opinion, Custer would have gone looking for another war not just to get reelected for a second term, but make him a major historical figure and not just a peacetime caretaker. I think he would have found peacetime very boring.

One historical note: What we now call the White House was called a number of things back then. The term "White House" was just beginning to become common. I have used it for simplicity's sake.

1882

◇◇◇◇◇◇◇◇◇◇◇◇◇◇◇◇

CUSTER
IN CHAINS

◆ Chapter 1 ◆

THE SPENT BULLET SLAMMED INTO CUSTER'S SHOULder, spinning him and dropping him face down on the ground where he tasted dirt and blood through split lips. He staggered to his knees. Blood streamed from a cut in his scalp, which, he thought ruefully, might not be his for very much longer. At least the redskinned savages would have a difficult time lifting it. He'd cut his hair short in anticipation of the fight, although not his death. His long golden locks, now graying slightly, had been thrown away and were blowing around the Dakotas. The Indians would never get them.

Custer snapped an order and Sergeant Haney helped him to his feet. If he had to die, Custer thought, he would do so standing up. "What the devil are they waiting for, Haney?" The blood from the cut was dripping into his eyes and he couldn't see very clearly. Being blind, however, was the least of his problems.

"Fucked if I know, General dearest," muttered the short, stocky sergeant who'd been with him since the

1

Civil War. Custer usually yelled at him when Haney referred to him as "General" dearest, but it didn't seem to matter this sunny day of June 25, 1876. And the hell with him if it did, Haney thought. He'd been wounded several times this day and the next could finish him. Custer, the stupid bastard who commanded the Seventh Cavalry, had just gone and gotten all of them killed. Why the hell hadn't Custer waited for General Terry and the rest of the army to come up before attacking? Because he wanted the glory of victory and he was afraid that the Indians would flee before he could be reinforced.

Custer's vision cleared a little. The Sioux were riding their ponies in swirling clusters, whooping and shooting wildly at the small number of men still alive on the grassy knob. He looked around and counted only a dozen of his men still standing with him. Several others lay prone on the ground along with an almost equal number of Indians. He had taken five companies of his Seventh Cavalry to attack the main Sioux camp while other units hit them from the other side of the river. He'd figured that two hundred and ten soldiers were more than enough for this part of the attack. The savages wouldn't stand up to an assault on their homes. In previous battles, they'd broken up in attempts to save their families and had fled. Custer had laughed when planning the assault. Only fools would take their women and children along on a war. His own wife, Libbie, along with a number of others, was safely ensconced on a steamer in the Missouri.

Only he hadn't counted on there being so damned many of the Indians. There must be at least a thousand warriors, not the few hundred he expected to find on this side of the Little Big Horn. He'd also anticipated that Reno, with the rest of the regiment, would support him by attacking from the other side of the river. Caught in a vise, the Indians would break. But where the hell was Reno? And where was Benteen? Reno was just across the river, so why didn't he come and help? Benteen was farther away, but he too should be arriving soon. Benteen was junior to Reno, so maybe he was coming with Reno. But where the hell were they? If they didn't arrive in the next few minutes it would all be over.

Custer swore and called Reno a son of a bitch. Reno hated Custer but he always obeyed orders. Custer rarely swore, even to himself, but this day was an exception. Of course, he laughed ruefully, being surrounded by a thousand angry Indians will do that to a man.

Custer checked his pistol. He had two bullets left. Should he save one for himself? Yes. If taken prisoner, they'd cut him into little pieces and then roast what remained of his still living carcass over a small, slow fire. Or maybe they'd parade him naked all throughout the Great Plains and defer cutting him into those little living pieces for agonizing, humiliating weeks. No, he'd rather be dead this day.

"Haney, if I fail, kill me."

Haney snorted and checked his Springfield. It was loaded and wasn't jammed.

Bullets fired from a long distance rained down on the knob, kicking up dust and only occasionally hitting someone. Only the fact that many of the Indians were unused to rifles and, therefore, poor shots, had kept them alive for this long. Haney had one of Mr. Colt's big revolvers stuck in his waistband and a bullet was intended for himself—Custer could go to hell. After all, hadn't the arrogant son of a bitch gotten them into this mess? Let him solve his own damned problems.

"Look, General, they're gathering a lot of them together. They're going to ride right over us and there isn't a damn thing we can do."

"We can die well," Custer announced. Haney looked away and almost fell over. He'd taken three arrows and one bullet already. Fortunately the arrows had barely penetrated flesh and the bullet had gone through the meat of this thigh without hitting an artery, but fatigue and loss of blood were weakening him. He didn't want to pass out and be scalped alive. Or worse, be taken by the savages for their sadistic entertainment.

Nor did Sergeant Haney particularly wish to die well. If given a choice, he'd choose to live poorly rather than die in any way. It was all well and good for an Irish Catholic to believe in the afterlife, but did it have to begin today? Besides, he hadn't been to Confession in several months of Sundays.

"They're coming," a trooper said. The Indians were moving slowly towards them. Haney estimated maybe two hundred horsemen in the bunch, including some leaders. It would be more than enough to trample them into the dirt beside the Little Big Horn River.

The Indians were howling and picking up speed. They were only a few hundred yards away. Haney shook his rifle at them. "Come on, you fuckers! Mike Haney ain't gonna die all that easily. Some of you are going to die as well."

Custer laughed, his voice a cackle. He was about to say something when a harsh screeching sound erupted.

Suddenly, the Sioux horde seemed to shudder as if it'd been punched. Warriors and horses tumbled and fell. Screams of fear and dismay, mingled with pain, came from Indian throats. Horses screamed in agony and there was chaos.

More bodies fell and formed ghastly piles. Some Indians tried to get up and were trampled by their panic-stricken horses.

"Bloody fucking hell, General dearest, would you mind telling me just what is happening?"

Custer turned to his left and began to cackle even more loudly. At first he couldn't see because of the gunsmoke, but then it cleared. "Gatlings. Somebody disobeyed my orders and brought the Gatling battery along. It must be Lieutenant Low."

Despite his wounds, Haney's eyesight was much better than Custer's. "No sir, it ain't Low. It looks like that young pup, Lieutenant Ryder."

The two hand-cranked machine guns were several hundred yards away and each was firing at three hundred and fifty rounds a minute, spraying the close-packed Indians like watering a lawn with a hose and dropping the Sioux warriors into piles of bodies.

It was enough. The Sioux began to pull back, slowly at first and then at a gallop as the Gatlings' bullets followed them.

Custer sagged to his knees. "We're going to live."

"Indeed we are. At least for a while, General dearest."

Custer swung his good arm and hit Haney on the thigh. "Then quit calling me 'General dearest' you bow-legged shanty Irish bastard."

◆　◆　◆

Second Lieutenant Martin Ryder, Seventh U.S. Cavalry, walked among the dead and was appalled. So many of them were men he'd known and now they were mere lumps of meat. A number had already been scalped or mutilated by the Indians before the rain of death from his guns had chased them away. The Indians liked to disembowel their victims as well as slicing the muscles of their arms and legs. He'd heard that it was supposed to hamper them in the afterlife. Whatever the reason, the wounds were hideous. General Terry had arrived with the rest of the column and men were just beginning to gather up the dead. They had bloated in the sun and already stank to high heaven.

Among the dead, Ryder had recognized Custer's two brothers and he'd been informed that all of Custer's officers had been killed. The death total was one hundred and eighty seven out of the two hundred and ten men who'd accompanied Custer, and it was likely to go higher, since some of the survivors were severely wounded. There were additional casualties from the two detachments commanded by Benteen and Reno that had fought desperately on the other side of the Little Big Horn. They too had almost been overrun by larger than expected numbers of Indians.

"If I'd arrived an hour earlier, how many others would still be alive?" Ryder wondered out loud.

"The survivors are lucky you arrived at all."

Ryder wheeled. He hadn't noticed the man in civilian clothes who was slowly walking up to him.

"Who the devil are you?"

"James Kendrick," the other man said with a warm smile, "and I'm a freelance reporter who's been following the campaign. I'm attached to General Terry's headquarters. I'm surprised you didn't notice me."

"My mind was elsewhere, Mr. Kendrick. I was thinking of so many dead friends. I've never seen anything like this in my life."

Kendrick shook his head sadly. "I'm a decade older than you and I haven't either, and the reporter in me says I have to find out what happened. For instance, why the devil did Custer divide his forces when confronted by a vastly superior enemy? For that matter, why did he attack in the first place? Then why didn't Benteen and Reno come to his assistance sooner instead of waiting until you arrived with your guns?"

"Have you talked to Custer?"

"He's still recovering and dictating a report to his aide. His physical wounds will heal, but I fear the loss of his brothers will be harder for him. I also feel that the official report will show General George Armstrong Custer in a most favorable light. I want the truth, Lieutenant. For instance, is it true that your guns were left behind because only miserable nags were assigned to pull them?"

"Cavalry always gets first crack at the good mounts. Cavalry is supposed to ride ahead of the army; dragging artillery—and Gatlings are defined as artillery—would definitely slow them down. I did convince Lieutenant Low and General Terry that, with better horses, I would be able to keep up with Custer. Terry agreed after Custer left and he gave me good mounts, some remounts, and a total of fifty men. Low didn't want to do it. He felt that he had to obey Custer's orders and leave them behind. Riding hard and alternating horses, I was able to make up the lost time. I only wish I had gotten here sooner."

"As do the almost two hundred men of the Seventh Cavalry who are now dead. The savages aren't stupid, Lieutenant. They retreated because it was obvious they were going to suffer heavy casualties if they didn't, and that's something they don't want to do. The Indians realize that there are far more white men than red and they don't want a stand-up fight if they can possibly avoid it. Every dead white man can and will be replaced but that's not true for a dead red man. By the way, it looks like your guns managed to kill Crazy Horse, which further demoralized them."

"Another good reason for them to pull back," said Ryder.

"I'm going to do you a favor and give you some information for free. Custer's first draft of his report indicted you for dereliction of duty. It said that the reason you were late was because you were responsible for the poor horses and then took your own sweet time getting to the battle. You're not alone. He also condemned Benteen and Reno."

Ryder was stunned. "You can't be serious. He was the one who insisted on the poor horses. It was a joke around the regiment that he hated the idea of machine guns taking the glory away from his cavalry."

"He felt you should be court-martialed."

"Son of a bitch!"

Kendrick laughed. "Don't worry, it won't happen. That report will never leave the camp. Terry knows the truth, as do a number of others. A sergeant named Haney told them what was happening and they put a halt to that nonsense. The only one in trouble is Reno and that's because there are rumors that he was drunk. In the new and latest official version, you will be commended for recognizing the problem with the horses, replacing them, and riding like a bat out of hell to rescue Custer and what remained of his men. Along with a commendation, you will likely be promoted."

"So why are you telling me all this?"

"I'm a reporter and I like to report the truth, and the truth is that Custer's responsible for all the dead and wounded currently rotting on this hill. I'm going to write articles and perhaps even a book on this battle, only with my version showing the world just what a headstrong bastard Custer is. And I wouldn't mind making a lot of money and a name for myself with it. On the other hand, I'm going to have to move quickly. Some very important people want him to run for president. If he becomes too powerful politically, his friends will protect him and the truth will never come out."

"Thank you, I guess, but any early promotion will be resented by others."

"Christ, Ryder, they're not making you a general, just a first lieutenant. Even Sergeant Haney thinks you deserve it for saving his Irish ass. He's recovering nicely and sends his regards."

Ryder laughed. The last he'd seen of Haney was on the knob where Custer was making his final stand. He'd had arrows sticking out of him and looked like a human pincushion. Haney was highly regarded and it was good to have the older NCO's concurrence with his actions.

"Assuming I actually am promoted, what will happen to me then?"

"If the political part of this gets as messy as I

think it will, the Army is going to circle the wagons to protect one of their own, Custer, and you will be sent far, far away so nobody can ask you difficult questions. My guess would be Oregon or even Alaska, at least until things settle down."

Oregon? Alaska? Ryder's mind whirled. They were at the end of the world. What the hell had he done to deserve this? Why not just send him to Siberia? So much for being rewarded for doing the right thing, he mused. What the hell, at least he'd be promoted.

◆ Chapter 2 ◆

LIBBIE CUSTER STRETCHED HER BARE LEGS UNDER the silk cover and listened to her husband snore. It was comforting but also worrisome. He'd returned to the White House late after a meeting at the Willard Hotel with some political allies. As usual, since it was a political meeting where women weren't welcome, she hadn't been with him and she didn't like that. She worried about what he might have agreed to. He was still so naïve when it came to politics and she didn't want his presidency to become a national disgrace like Ulysses Grant's had become. She accepted that she was by far the smarter of the two very ambitious people and that George needed her to control him as well as lead him. She and George were a team and a team should not make decisions without both members being present. She was not yet forty and some said she was even lovelier than she had been when she was twenty.

She and George were also still passionately in love and there were many times when they laughingly thought their White House lovemaking would wake the servants.

It could have been paradise, but it wasn't. She acknowledged that George was in well over his head. If power corrupts, then he was also being corrupted. He'd begun drinking heavily and he seemed distracted by events he didn't quite understand. She didn't think he had a woman on the side, or, she laughed softly, on her back. However, if he did, she would exact the only form of revenge a woman could. She would betray and humiliate him as well, and he understood that.

Until and if that unlikely event occurred, she had two goals—protecting him and advancing his presidency.

Beside her, Custer stirred and yawned. "Libbie, I'm bored."

"That, sir, is a terrible thing to say to a woman you just had your way with. Did my ripe and lovely naked body not please you?"

Only an hour before, she'd been awakened by the familiar feel of his hands roaming her body. He'd gotten her nightgown up to her shoulders and had discarded the silk pajamas from India that she'd given him for his birthday. She'd responded eagerly and matched him stroke for stroke after he'd entered her. When they were finished and he seemed to be dozing, she wondered why so many of her married friends felt uncomfortable with sex. Why did they feel that it was a chore to be endured instead of a pleasure to be savored? For all his faults, she immensely enjoyed having sex with him.

Still, she wondered at his comment.

"How can the President of the United States and master of all he surveys be bored?"

"Because it's a boring damn job, that's why. Nothing has happened since I was elected, and nothing will. I also had that damn dream again. Once again I was lying on the ground with a bunch of Sioux standing there and laughing at me. Then one of them reaches down and starts scalping me."

She stroked his head. "And that's when you awake, because it is only a dream."

His notoriety as the man who had subdued the Sioux, as a reporter named Kendrick had put it, had carried him all the way to the White House. He had been nominated as the Republican candidate for president, defeating the other Republican nominee, James Garfield, in the primaries. And later he had narrowly defeated former Civil War general and Democratic candidate, Winfield Scott Hancock, in the general election of 1880.

Yet George, or Autie as his family had sometimes called him before his brothers were killed, was correct. He was serving at a time when not much was occurring in the United States. The Indians had been reduced to a minimal menace and there was peace in the land. Europe might be in turmoil with the Prussians trying to gobble it up, but those wars were far away. The Reconstruction Era of the south was over and those former Confederate states were now free to do whatever they wished. That this meant suffocating the desires of the newly freed Negroes was of no concern to him, or most other people for that matter.

"Libbie, I am terribly afraid that my four, or, God forbid, eight years as president, will be as little more than a night watchman. I'll become a footnote in history like some other presidents such as Fillmore or Pierce or my own predecessor, Rutherford B. Hayes. I need something exciting to fulfill me. I need to accomplish something important. I need to start a war."

Libbie sat up. Her nightgown was still above her waist and he grinned at the sight of her exposed body. "You can't be ready again," she chided him playfully as she saw his eyes widen. If he was indeed ready she would be as well. "Now, let's talk about a war. Who would you want to fight? Clearly, it can't be the Indians again."

She got up and walked barefoot across the bedroom. "Nor can it be the Mexicans. They've done nothing to provoke us and Congress will not let you just up and invade them. We did that once already. Somebody has to start the war and it can't be the United States. The nation is still recovering from horrors of the Civil War."

Custer yawned. "And that also leaves out the nations of Central and South America. They're all too helpless and too far away and besides, they'd never start anything against us."

"Agreed, George. Therefore, it must be a European power. However, we must choose carefully. Great Britain is out. Not only is she too powerful, but our economic ties with her are too close. War with Great Britain would be a total disaster. France is too powerful as well, although we very nearly did fight them at the end of the Civil War. They do hate us, so let's keep them in mind for the future. But right now, they are too mighty. Their navy is second only to Britain's."

George smiled at the memory. The French had backed a puppet emperor in Mexico—a pliant fool named Maximilian—and sent troops to support him in violation of America's Monroe Doctrine. With the Civil War raging, Lincoln did nothing. After the war, an army under General Phil Sheridan was sent to the Rio Grande with the clear message that the French Army in Mexico had to leave. They did and poor Maximilian wound up in front of a firing squad while his mentally ill wife fled to Europe. Neither George nor Libbie would mind rubbing France's nose in the dirt, but, again, would the French oblige by starting a conflict that the U.S. could win? Probably not, they concluded. The French had their own internal conflicts tormenting them. Their Third Republic had begun with a massive bloodbath.

Germany was a newly created nation dominated by the always belligerent Prussians. She was still trying to get organized, although she might be a possible combatant in the future. But Germany too was doubtless already too strong for America to fight after she'd defeated both France and Austria. Also understood was the fact that Germany and the United States were almost half a world away and couldn't reach each other.

Italy, an equally new nation, was immersed in internal problems and was also far, far away.

They decided that the Ottomans would make marvelous enemies and not just because they were Moslems who'd abused Americans decades earlier. But they too were far away and doubtless cared nothing about starting a war with the United States. Ottoman ships in the Mediterranean had captured American merchantmen and held their crews as hostages, but that was in the past.

The lands of Asia were already being carved up by the Great Powers. Perhaps the U.S. could slice off a piece of China or Japan, but for what purpose? No, Asia was out.

"Russia?" he asked. "Maybe we could get them to attack us because they want Alaska back."

"I don't think so, George. And besides, they are almost our allies."

He laughed. "You're right, and who would ever want Alaska returned to them?"

Libbie smiled like a cat. "That leaves Spain."

"Yes," he said thoughtfully, "Spain. Her remaining possessions in the Caribbean are close by and always on the verge of exploding. The Spanish are corrupt and keep slaves, even though they've begun to abolish slavery. We can provoke something and a war can easily follow. The Spanish are nothing militarily and we'll have an easy victory."

She pulled the nightgown over her head and watched him revel in the sight of her naked body. Even though it was mid-morning, the servants knew enough not to enter without being invited. She saw that he was aroused again and it pleased her. Controlling him with her sex was so easy. It was even better because she truly loved him and wanted him to be a great man.

She ran her hand down his chest and belly and began to stroke him. "First, George, you will finish what you are obviously about to start and then we'll go about provoking Spain. When we're done with Spain you will have become one of America's great presidents."

Custer laughed and pulled her body to him. What a hell of a woman, he thought. I am the luckiest man in the world.

◆ ◆ ◆

The *Eldorado* was a decrepit wooden steamship of about fifteen hundred tons and she was stuffed with military supplies for the insurgents fighting Spanish oppression in Cuba. At least that's what journalist James Kendrick had written in his notebook. Unfortunately, he hadn't gotten much farther in his writing because he didn't quite believe it. The peasant revolution in Cuba was in a quiet phase, so why the rush to arm a population that wasn't doing anything? There had been a long revolutionary war in Cuba that was now quiet, with both sides suffering from severe exhaustion.

Along with the guns and ammunition, about a hundred men, mostly Americans, were coming along as volunteers. To do what, Kendrick wondered. At the moment, that question was a minor concern. A Spanish gunboat was approaching them and gaining quickly. The *Eldorado*'s captain had his ship fleeing as fast as it could, but it was a sick turtle racing against a rabbit. Kendrick thought that was clever and wrote it down.

Worse, the crew and passengers had nothing but rifles and sidearms to protect themselves and those they'd taken from the ship's hold. They'd been disgusted and dismayed to find that the weapons being shipped to Cuba were rusty and most didn't work. Some even dated to well before the Civil War. It was clear that someone had unloaded a large quantity of junk for a huge profit. Some of the young American warriors now looked frightened. It occurred to Kendrick that he should feel that way too.

When the Spanish gunboat was less than a hundred yards away, she pulled alongside and ordered the *Eldorado* to heave to. Faced with a pair of cannons and a host of armed men lining the rails, the *Eldorado*'s captain was about to surrender when shots rang out. Some of the undisciplined American volunteers had begun shooting and others followed suit. Kendrick watched in horror as several Spanish soldiers were hit and fell, with one dropping into the water and disappearing.

The Spaniards returned fire almost immediately. Their cannons were loaded with grape and their shells swept the deck of the Eldorado with flying metal, while the Spanish soldiers fired into what was now a confused mob of Americans. As shells struck the ship, Kendrick threw himself on the deck and tried to make himself invisible. Shells ripped the wooden hull and deck, sending knife-like splinters through the air. He screamed as one imbedded itself in his cheek. He pulled it out and blood began to pour down his face and chest.

Only a few moments later, armed Spaniards climbed over the gunwale and killed those foolish enough to still be carrying weapons. The others, including Kendrick, were gathered in a bunch by the bow. The reporter in him estimated maybe thirty survivors. The *Eldorado*'s captain was not one of them.

An officer approached the group. "Which one of you is the journalist named Kendrick?"

Kendrick was surprised. He stepped forward and tried to look as unconcerned as he could. "I am James Kendrick, sir, and you are?"

"My name is Gilberto Salazar. I am a major in the Spanish Army. I am delighted that you were not harmed," he said with thinly veiled sarcasm. "We have been following the course of this wreck since it left

Charleston several days ago. You Americans think we are stupid and ignorant of the ship's intentions, but we are not. Our spies have been well informed about this stinking ship and its cargo, both human and otherwise. You have come to start another civil war and to free the slaves who are already being freed." He waved his arm at the other prisoners. "These men will be executed for their efforts."

Kendrick's mind worked quickly. "You are not counting me among the invaders?"

Salazar laughed. "I would like to, but men more important than I want you to witness the justice we will be handing out."

"A small point, Major, but aren't we in international waters? Should you have stopped an American-flagged ship in international waters, or any other ship, for that matter?"

Salazar looked about dramatically. There was no sign of land on the horizon. "You are that good at judging distances? I assure you that we are well within Spanish territorial waters. I suggest that you accept that declaration as a fact and not annoy me."

Kendrick decided that it was an excellent idea. Just as important, he wondered how Salazar knew his name along with all the information about the ship. Obviously, the Spanish had spies in the group that had chartered the *Eldorado*.

"What will happen to these men, and me, for that matter?"

"Watch," Salazar said.

He gave a signal and his soldiers pushed the men, now screaming in terror, into the ocean. Kendrick watched in horror as their heads bobbed in the waves.

Soldiers lined the ship's railing and began shooting at them. In a few seconds there were no more heads bobbing in the water, just an occasional red stain that was being swallowed and erased by the sea.

Kendrick was so stunned that he nearly fell to his knees. Laughing soldiers held him upright. Finally, he regained some of his composure. Salazar stood in front of him and slashed him across the face with the flat of a short sword, splitting his cheek and adding to the blood from the splinter.

"I was ordered to bring you back alive. Nothing was said about keeping you unhurt. You are far from innocent, Kendrick, and while I would like to throw you overboard as well, Spain has uses for you. We will scuttle the *Eldorado*, after first taking anything of value, of course. Then we will steam to Florida and drop you off at St. Augustine. I urge you to write a full and accurate report of what you have seen this day. Let your foolish and arrogant people understand that Spain is a great power and we will not be insulted by your sending miserable abolitionist revolutionaries into Cuba."

Alfonso XII, King of Spain, was shaken by the news of American outrage over what they were referring to as the "Freedom Ship Massacre." Away from the crowds of courtiers and sycophants who roamed the halls of the Palacio Real in Madrid, he had directed both his current and former prime ministers to meet with him in secret. There was so much emotion in Madrid that any open meeting might cause an explosion of panic.

The king was young, only in his mid-twenties, and his family had only recently taken power after a bloody civil war that had ripped Spain. This made him feel insecure. As the leader of the Spanish empire, he had to show strength in the face of this crisis with the United States. The Spanish empire might be only a shadow of what it had been in the past, but it could not be trifled with.

Nor was the king particularly healthy. He suffered from a number of illnesses which weakened him. The king was considered a liberal and had planned reforms to make Spain a freer country, but the news from the United States had pushed those thoughts aside. Spanish honor and its empire had to be protected. And he had to maintain his tenuous hold on the throne. Showing weakness was not an option.

Thus, he had chosen to meet with the two most important men in Spanish politics. They were his current prime minister, Praxedes Sagasta, and Sagasta's predecessor, Antonio Canovas. Of the two, he was confident that Canovas would be the better war leader. The man had helped crush a previous coup and had done so with great brutality. It was rumored that many hundreds of Spanish men and women had emerged barely alive from weeks or even months of horrific tortures in his prisons. That is, if they emerged at all. Canovas' brutality sometimes made the king shudder, but he did what had to be done.

"Sire, the situation is intolerable," Canovas said and the king was pleased to see Sagasta nod in agreement. "What the Americans wish we cannot give if we are to be still considered an important nation in the eyes of the world."

The king looked at the document on the table, wishing it to go away. It was the message from the

President of the United States, George Armstrong Custer, although they strongly suspected that the actual author had been his secretary of state, James Blaine.

The American demands were many. First, they required an apology for what they referred to as the murders of innocent Americans. They professed horror that there had been summary and brutal executions but no trials. Second, they demanded reparations in the amount of one million dollars per person killed.

Canovas had pointed to that paragraph and sarcastically said that no one man is worth a million dollars, especially not an American pirate.

The American demands then included the establishment of naval bases in Cuba at Santiago and in Puerto Rico at San Juan. They demanded recognition of the still-quiescent rebels as the legitimate government of Cuba.

And finally, they demanded that a Cuban-born Spanish officer named Gilberto Salazar be sent to the United States for trial. He would be charged with nearly a hundred counts of murder.

All of these had been categorically rejected by the king and the Spanish government, although the official notice of rejection had not yet been sent.

Canovas was predictably outraged. "They send a pirate ship full of rebels and weapons and we are supposed to do nothing? What arrogance. We cannot apologize or pay for their criminal actions. Nor can we allow the Americans to get a foothold on either Cuban or Puerto Rican soil. The Spanish empire has shrunk and can shrink no longer. Cuba is the crown jewel of what remains and we cannot even begin to let it go. If the Americans get a base in Cuba, they will use it to arm and train the rebels and then take over the whole island. Cuba will become a colony of the United States."

It was an ugly fact that the once-proud Spanish empire in the new world, first begun by Christopher Columbus in 1492, had been in decline for more than two centuries. The colonies of South and Central America had successfully rebelled and discarded Spain. Only Cuba and Puerto Rico remained as Spanish outposts in the Atlantic, along with the Philippines in the Pacific. They also recalled the ugly fact that some in the southern United States had wanted to add Cuba as another slave state before the American Civil War. Ironic was the fact that a number of unrepentant Confederates had moved to Cuba and now made it their home.

The king stood and gestured for the others to remain seated. "It is my understanding that not even the rebel Cuban leaders, such as Jose Marti, fully trust the Americans."

Prime Minister Sagasta agreed. "The Americans are greedy, rapacious, ambitious, and worse, not Catholic. Almost all of them are heretics who hate the Catholic Church. This is obvious from the way they treat their Irish immigrants. They cannot be allowed to gain any advantage in Cuba. Their secretary of state, Blaine, has stated his belief that the United States should continue to expand wherever it can, so this incident with the *Eldorado* does not surprise me. Their President Custer appears to be the same kind of man—rapacious and ambitious. The Americans will attempt to take advantage of us no matter what we do. Therefore, we must reject everything and especially decline to arrest Gilberto Salazar, a man many consider to be a true patriot and hero."

Canovas added, "And let's not forget that he is not only a patriot, but also a Catholic who commands a legion of more than a thousand loyal, well-armed and well-trained soldiers that he is supporting with his own considerable fortune."

"Still," the king said wryly, "it would have been so much easier if Salazar had brought his prisoners into port where they could have been interrogated and then put on trial. His summary execution of so many men was a tactical mistake."

"Agreed," said Canovas, "I would have liked to have had them in my prisons for a couple of weeks. I guarantee you that they would have confessed to just about anything, including fornicating with their mothers and barnyard animals."

Alfonso shuddered but dismissed the comment. "Their message is phrased quite cleverly. They are saying that if we do not accept everything they've demanded, Spain will have declared war on the United States. In effect, we're damned if we do and damned if we don't."

Canovas shook with righteous anger. "Then let's give them what they want! If they want war then they shall have it. We shall either win back our empire or die with honor. We will never let them forget that we are Spaniards with centuries of empire behind us and they are nothing but barbarians."

Sarah Damon and Ruth Holden watched and cheered as yet another band marched down Pennsylvania Avenue and past the White House. Sarah, the younger of the two at twenty-five, could barely bring herself to call it the White House, instead of the President's House, as most people were now doing. She thought White House sounded too common.

Sarah wondered when she would see her brother's regiment. He was a captain in the newly formed First Maryland Volunteers, one of a number of units springing up all across the nation and forming to fight the Spanish should a war actually come.

Finally, the First Maryland came in sight and marched past them. "They're almost in step," laughed Ruth and Sarah agreed. "Of course, they have been training for the last few weeks."

"But look at Colonel Fowler," Sarah said and pointed at the overweight older man who led them. He was clearly in distress. The fifty-year-old Fowler's face was beet red and he was having a hard time walking. "Someone should help him. He might be about to have a heart attack or even a stroke."

"Dear God, you're right. It shouldn't take a doctor's daughter like you to recognize that the man's in trouble. However, we both know the man. He is stubborn and unmovable as a large boulder. As long as he can, he will lead his men."

"Right into the grave," Sarah said. "Just like my late husband."

Ruth reached over and patted Sarah's hand. "Are you getting through it?"

"My husband was a good man and he was good to me in many ways. His death was senseless."

Ruth did not respond. Sarah's husband had been fifteen years older than she, a hard-working and prosperous businessman and farmer and, one day, he'd simply and unexpectedly collapsed and died at his desk. He had left two large farms and a shoe factory to Sarah, along with several other businesses. Recognizing her own limitations and the restrictions of what she thought was a near-feudal society, she sold them and had invested the proceeds in strong stocks and bonds. She was particularly enamored of Mr. Bell's telephone company.

Two hours later, Sarah's brother Phil Barnes met them in the restaurant of the Hay-Adams Hotel. He looked distraught. "The colonel's in the hospital. The march was too much for him. We tried to tell him it would be but he'd have nothing of it."

"How bad is he?" Sarah asked. She wasn't fond of the argumentative and stubborn Fowler, but that didn't extend to wishing him ill.

The waiter brought a glass of cold water which Phil downed in one long swallow. The waiter grinned and brought him another. "They think it's a heart attack and, if that's the case, he won't be returning to the regiment anytime soon and that scares the heck out of me."

Ruth smiled. "You can say hell. I've heard the word and so has Sarah. Now why does it scare you?"

"Because right now I'm the acting major and that makes me second in command. If Fowler doesn't return, then I'm in charge of the regiment."

"God help the First Maryland and the United States of America," Sarah said while stifling a smile.

She did understand much of what he meant. The regiment had been organized only a few weeks earlier and consisted of close to eight hundred men, and most of them had never been in uniform before. Worse, the handful who had had military experience had not been officers and had forgotten what they'd learned in the sixteen years since the end of the Civil War. All the regiment had were uniforms, old weapons, and little else. Fowler, who had served in the Union Army had fought in several Civil War battles and had been attempting to impart his knowledge and experience to his raw unit.

There was no way on earth that her brother could lead a regiment. The War Department would have to do something about this tragic circumstance. Sarah and her brother thought President Custer was wrong in pushing for war, but they had confidence in Generals Sheridan and Sherman. Yes, those two would do the right thing for the First Maryland.

Captain Martin Ryder waited for the command that would send him in to see Lieutenant General Phil Sheridan. To Martin, Sheridan had been a true hero of the Civil War and was now the man rumored to be the heir apparent to the current commanding general, William Tecumseh Sherman.

Ryder had been ordered to report to the War Department and wondered what he might have done wrong. No explanation had accompanied the summons and that concerned him. The War Department was located at 17th Street and Pennsylvania Avenue NW, almost adjacent to the White House. Ryder could imagine a beleaguered President Custer looking out a window and wondering just what he'd gotten himself into with a war with Spain close to a reality.

Ryder was still young for a captain. He was only twenty-seven, although some said he looked older. His light brown hair was thinning and his clean-shaven face was weathered. At least he was still lean and wiry. A lady friend once said he had a nice smile if he'd only ever use it. She was right, he thought, but there was so little to smile about. His military career might have peaked even though there was war on the horizon. He was afraid that he might be assigned some backwater job while others got promotions. Of course, a backwater would be safe, but he hadn't joined the army to be safe.

Since that momentous day on the Little Big Horn some six years earlier, he'd been stationed at a number of places in the Pacific Northwest and California. He'd spent two years rounding up drunken Indians who'd left their reservations, and another two stationed in a small post outside San Diego. There he had to deal with drunken and sometimes lethal Mexican bandits who kept slipping across the border to rustle cattle and steal anything that wasn't nailed down. The years had been dull with moments of sheer terror as life and death had sometimes been only a matter of inches apart. Sometimes luck determined who lived and who died. There had been a number of skirmishes with the Mexicans and he'd again seen men die bloodily and horribly. Ironically, since devastating the Indian attack on Custer, he'd never actually killed a man.

He recalled the long-ago conversation he'd had with the journalist, James Kendrick. The man had been right. Custer and the Army had wanted him out of the way. The future president could not be embarrassed by anyone contradicting the official version of the near-massacre at the Little Big Horn.

He'd thought things had been turning around for

him when he'd recently been assigned as an aide to the commandant at West Point. He'd even been permitted to give some lectures, although he never spoke about his experiences with Custer. Some thought it odd, while others put it down to modesty. He didn't much care what other people thought. He was seriously thinking of resigning his commission and getting on with life as a civilian, but he wondered if his resignation would be accepted with war clouds darkening.

He also wondered if he wanted to resign at this moment. If war came, he felt duty and honor bound to use his skills to help his country and the Army.

"You may go in, Captain," said a boyish lieutenant whose attitude told Ryder that he was not impressed by mere captains. Ryder felt like giving him a quick punch in the groin just to hear him squeal.

Ryder entered Sheridan's office and saluted the short, stout man seated behind the desk. Lieutenant General Phil Sheridan, he noted, had gained a lot of weight. He was no longer the trim cavalryman who'd given the Rebels fits. He was only in his early fifties and looked decades older. Ryder could not help but think that that if Sheridan represented the best of the Army, the Army was in trouble.

Sheridan waived him to a chair. He was breathing heavily. "You've had an interesting few years since saving Custer's tail, haven't you?"

Ryder flushed. Like many senior officers, Sheridan did not hold Custer in high esteem. "It hasn't always been interesting, sir."

Sheridan snorted, but did not appear angry at the comment. "Your superiors have always given you high grades and you have the respect of your peers.

Rumor has it you might have risen quite high if you had not been held back by that Custer debacle. Damndest things happen when you try to do your duty, don't they?"

"Yes, sir."

"That's right. The road to hell is sometimes paved with good intentions. But now there's about to be a war and nobody's going to remember that strange day on the Little Big Horn. Do you speak Spanish?"

"Pretty well, sir. Learning it was almost essential while I was stationed by the Mexican border." He declined to mention that it had been a lovely young señorita who'd been his tutor and that much of his lessons involved a detailed study of her anatomy.

"You're to be commended. Too many young officers would have pissed away their time drinking and screwing Mexican women. You didn't do any of that, did you? Don't answer. Do you want coffee?"

Before Ryder could respond, a mug of black stuff was in his hand, courtesy of the smirking young lieutenant. "Captain, we are going to have to rebuild the Army if we're going to fight Spain. We will need experienced officers who can be promoted to higher positions so they can command what is now little more than a rabble with mostly ancient weapons and using even older tactics. That is if they're lucky and they have any weapons at all. A need for a man of your talents just opened up. The colonel commanding the First Maryland Volunteers collapsed and nearly died while marching down Pennsylvania Avenue in the extreme heat. Even if he survives, he will not ever return to his regiment. To say that the rest of the officers in his regiment are inexperienced would be a gross understatement. They need a younger commander with combat experience and common sense. They need you, Captain. Effective immediately, you are to take over the First Maryland with the brevet rank of colonel."

"Sir, I'm at a loss."

Sheridan smiled, "Don't be. You deserve it; just don't make too big a mess of things."

Ryder was almost giddy. He'd gone from captain to full colonel in less than five minutes. Granted it was only a temporary rank, but it might become a permanent opportunity if he didn't screw up. At the very least, there was the possibility that his new permanent rank would be major when the war ended. Of course, there first had to be a war. It was considered probable, but the Spaniards might act sensibly and negotiate a settlement. Would that change his thinking? Would he want to stay in the Army?

Sheridan continued. "The regiment is here in Washington, so take over as soon as you can get your new rank sewn on your uniform. Also, I'm sure you remember Sergeant Haney. Well, he's Master Sergeant Haney now and he's just out of the hospital where he'd been recovering from a broken leg. He says he fell off his horse, but I think he fell out of some woman's bed. He'll be joining you and, between the two of you, you ought to be able to whip nearly a thousand volunteers into shape."

The lieutenant knocked on the door and reentered. "Sir, we've gotten a response from the Spaniards."

Sheridan looked forward eagerly. "Well, out with it, damn it."

"They reject all our demands and, in turn, demand

that we send the man they say is the chief pirate, President Custer, to Madrid in chains."

Sheridan's jaw dropped and Ryder thought his did as well. The general recovered quickly and laughed hugely. "Custer in chains? My, my, what an intriguing possibility that is. I know a lot of people who'd pay money to see that picture."

Gilberto Salazar lay in the mud and tried not to show his men how uncomfortable he was. Leadership often came with a price and getting muddy water down his shirt and into his pants was a small one to pay.

Nearly a hundred of his legionnaires were arrayed in a line to either side of him and were as well hidden as he. His only regret was that they were not able to wear their splendid white uniforms. Instead, they were dressed as the rabble they were out to kill.

He chuckled to himself. One of the side benefits of going to war with the United States was that the rebels, quiet for a few years, had emerged from their rat-holes and again begun fighting for freedom from Spain. It was not lost on Salazar and other Spanish leaders that many of the rebels were slaves who were beginning to get their freedom as the result of the treaty ending the war in 1875. However, slavery in Cuba still existed and would until the year 1888. The idea was that the slaves would somehow be able to buy their freedom from their masters.

Salazar shifted slightly, thus allowing a fresh stream of dirty water to enter his clothing. He hoped he wasn't getting bugs or leaches in his crotch. Some people, he thought, deserved to be in bondage and that included the poor blacks who were now rebelling

against the Spanish empire. Of course, not all of the
rebels were Negroes, but a lot of them were. The
group he'd been tracking fell into that category.

The sound of gunfire interrupted his thoughts. A few
seconds later, he heard screams. The other company
of soldiers he'd brought with him had begun pushing the rebels in his direction. In effect, they were
beaters sending animals to be slaughtered. All he had
to do was make sure that his men didn't shoot their
fellow legionnaires.

"Hold steady," he said as he saw motion. As expected,
the fleeing rebels were taking the path of least resistance
through the thick underbrush and would emerge into a
field where they could be cut down like weeds.

The first to come into view were a couple of dozen
women and children. A few seconds later, their men
followed, looking fearfully behind them and not to
the front where the real danger lay. Only a handful
of the rebels had rifles. Most were armed only with
machetes that they held nervously. They began to run
faster. They had to leave the field and hide in what
amounted to a jungle. Some were wounded and were
being dragged by their companions.

"Now," Salazar yelled. He stood and opened fire
with his pistol and was delighted when a woman he'd
aimed at staggered and fell.

His men responded with well-disciplined fire that
ripped through the rebels, throwing them around like
toys. They howled and tried to escape to their right
and left, but his men followed them with their rifles,
cutting them down.

In less than a minute it was over. Salazar figured
that a few had made it to safety, but that was not

a major concern. Let them tell of the punishment Gilberto Salazar could inflict on the enemies of Spain.

His men had commenced picking through the dead and the wounded. The men were executed immediately, as were the young boys. His philosophy was that pups could grow up to become wolves, so they needed to die. The few surviving women and young girls were handed over to his men who had already stripped them and were raping them on the ground. They would not survive their ordeal. His men would make sure of that.

He would not take a woman from this group. Not only were they black, but they were filthy. He had a wife and a mistress and his choice of the many Spanish ladies in Havana, should he desire it. What he would like to do now was go home, bathe, and put on a uniform as befitted his rank and his victory.

He thought it would also be nice to be able to advertise his successes. He had been thinking it would be advantageous for Spain to have these printed in American newspapers where they would doubtless be misinterpreted as atrocities. How difficult, he wondered, would it be to have an American reporter on hand to witness them? He quickly thought of Kendrick, the man he'd permitted to live after the others on that pirate ship had been thrown to the sharks. Would Kendrick come to Cuba? Of course he would, Salazar decided. All reporters lusted after good stories. He could provide one—and a war to boot.

Across the field and well hidden in the dense growth, Diego Valdez watched as the massacre played out. He'd been one of the fortunate ones. He'd been on the far right flank and had quickly seen that safety lay in running in that direction. He'd been slightly wounded in the leg, but was otherwise unhurt. He'd told the fool in charge of the group that they were being pushed to an ambush, but that man, now dead, would hear nothing of it. His idea of an escape plan was to have everyone run as hard and as blindly as they could.

After a while the screams died down and only a few moans were heard as the soldiers finished with the women. When done, they slashed the women's throats and left them. Diego would not go out to check on them until later, if at all. Even though one of the women was his sister, he couldn't risk looking for her until it was truly safe. He would have to save his grief for later. He wouldn't put it past Salazar to leave men behind to look for survivors and those wanting to help them. Being lighter skinned had helped him in the past, but he doubted there would be any advantage today. No, he would return to Havana, swallow his anger and shame, and try to earn a quiet living, all the while thinking of a way to win freedom for Cuba.

◆ Chapter 3 ◆

CUSTER WAS ANNOYED AND SHOWED IT BY ANGRILY tapping his fingers on the highly polished table. The response among his cabinet had been less than enthusiastic, and there was actual resistance to his ideas for the prosecution of the war. Congress had just passed the declaration of war with a vote that was far from unanimous, and he wanted to move on it quickly before enthusiasm waned even farther. But now his secretaries of War and the Navy were telling him that quick action was impossible.

The president accepted the fact that there would be logistical problems, even nightmares. He already knew that from his prior military experience. An army "moves on its stomach" was an oft-mentioned quote by Napoleon and it was still true. Neither the Army nor the Navy was large or well-equipped. The massive forces that had been built to crush the Confederacy were but fading and rusting memories.

Equally important, Libbie wasn't with him at the

meeting and he felt uncomfortable without her incisive comments. The world was not ready for a woman assistant to the president. She was, however, listening in the next room and they would talk about it later as they always did.

Robert Todd Lincoln, son of Abraham Lincoln, was the secretary of war and the first bearer of bad tidings. "Sir, as an Indian fighter, you well know that the Army is small and scattered all over the west. There are barely enough men to keep the Indians in their reservations. We cannot take that army and send it east to either protect our coast or invade Cuba without putting just about every city west of St. Louis at risk."

"But it will have to be done," Custer replied testily. "If we are going to develop our volunteer units, then their senior officers must come from the pool of officers and even senior enlisted men we currently have out west. Perhaps we shall require the western states and territories to supply their own volunteers. If they won't send them to fight the Spanish, perhaps they will use them to protect their homes against the Indians."

Lincoln continued. "Do you have any idea how many men will be needed to invade and conquer Cuba? General Sheridan's estimate is at least a hundred thousand, and all of them will have to be fed, clothed, housed, and provided with weapons and ammunition. This is based on our estimate that the Spanish have at least fifty thousand of their own soldiers in Cuba along with an unknown number of loyal militia. We can assume that Spain will quickly reinforce their garrisons both in Cuba as well as Puerto Rico. We can also assume that reinforcements are on their way from Spain or North Africa as we speak. A successful invasion of Cuba will not be easy. If done halfheartedly or ineptly, it could be a disaster."

Custer growled something and Lincoln continued. "Sir, it is highly unlikely that we will get that many volunteers, maybe half that number. Then, we will have to supply and support those troops in Cuba and we simply do not have the resources to do that."

Custer glared at him. "Then we will make do with what we can."

Lincoln was shocked. "Surely you're not suggesting that one American is worth ten Spaniards or anything like that."

"Of course not," Custer said angrily. "I learned that on the Little Big Horn. But I will say that one American volunteer is worth more than one poorly trained, poorly armed and poorly led Spanish conscript."

William H. Hunt, the fifty-eight-year-old secretary of the Navy, decided it was his turn to comment.

"Mr. President, as I have been trying to inform you since your inauguration, the Navy is in even worse shape than the Army. The mighty fleet of ironclads and other ships we had during the Civil War has either been scrapped or else the ships are little more than barely floating piles of rust. Worse, those few that remain afloat are obsolete. Naval technology is increasing at a rapid rate while we have been either standing still or moving backwards. We have a number of ships, but they are all either small, old, obsolete, or all of the preceding. In fact, many of our so-called warships are wooden sloops and schooners that were inadequate before the Civil War commenced. Simply put, we have no ships capable of defending the troop ships and supply ships that we might send to Cuba."

"Damn it to hell," Custer muttered.

Hunt continued, undeterred by the comment. "Spain, on the other hand, has a handful of what are now being categorized as battleships and cruisers. Their navy might be laughably small when compared with Great Britain's or even France's, but it could easily overwhelm ours."

Custer glared at him. "Then we will build a navy, just as we are building an army."

Hunt glared back, "And that is much easier said than done, sir. Starting from scratch, it will take possibly two years to build a good-sized warship of, say, eight thousand tons, and another year to get her crew trained. And obviously, we must have a number of these to fight Spain. We have the ability to create a fleet, just not the time."

Robert Lincoln laughed harshly. "If we're not careful, Spain and the United States will be likened to two chained dogs who cannot quite reach each other because of the lengths of their chains. They just sit there barking and growling at each other in impotent fury. Instead of this war serving to create an American empire, or fully reunite the North and South, or even free the slaves in Cuba, we could become the laughingstock of the world."

Custer stood and began to pace. Uniting the North and South was a secondary consideration and freeing Spain's slaves was not even on his agenda. He wanted the glory that would come from being victorious over Spain. He wanted to take that giant step in creating an American empire. He wanted to cement his place in history as a great president.

"That cannot happen," he snapped. "We must get our men to Cuba. My goal is to have an army at the gates of Havana within a month. I think we can hire or commandeer enough civilian transports to send a good-sized army to Cuba before the Spanish fleet can gather in strength."

"I do have a few suggestions," said Hunt.

"Let's hear them," snarled Custer.

"First, regardless of what other steps we might decide, we must begin building proper and modern warships, even though it will take time and money."

"Agreed," said Custer.

"Second, we must arm merchant ships, just like we did during the Civil War. These ships must be listed as regular navy ships and not privateers, which are, of course, illegal according to international treaty. While these ships would not be able to take on large regular warships, they should be able to blockade Cuba and Puerto as well as interdicting Spanish commerce. They should also be able to defend themselves against smaller Spanish warships."

Custer rubbed his hands together. "Excellent."

Hunt smiled, "And finally, sir. If we cannot build a navy, may I suggest that we rent one?"

Brevet Colonel Martin Ryder arrived unannounced at the encampment of the First Maryland Volunteers. An astonished sentry did nothing more than salute him and let him pass.

It was before reveille and no one was stirring, at least not anyone he could see. He noted approvingly that the camp was well laid out and well kept. The tents were all in straight lines. There was no trash or debris in sight. And there was no stench from improperly dug latrines. He quickly found the commander's tent and entered. Inside were an old folding cot and a desk. Even though he was tired, the cot did not look inviting. What the hell, he thought, he'd slept on the ground often enough. He'd get used to the cot. He decided he'd been corrupted by sleeping in a real bed for the last few months at West Point.

He lit the oil lamp and began reading some of the correspondence on Colonel Fowler's desk. Most of it was old, so he assumed that other officers were taking care of pressing matters.

There was a knock and a clearly flustered young major entered and saluted. "Sir, I'm Major Jack Barnes and I apologize for not being here to greet you."

Ryder stood, returned the salute and shook the major's hand. "Don't worry about it, Major. If I'd wanted a ceremony I would have told you in advance that I was coming. I assume that sentry did his duty and reported upward."

"He did sir. Now, what can I do to assist you?"

"First, Major, you can get us some coffee and then you can sit down and we can talk."

Mugs of coffee arrived almost as quickly as they had at General Sheridan's office. It was hot, dark, and thick. "Excellent," Ryder said after a swallow. "Now, after reveille I want all officers assembled. I'm sure they've got some concerns and questions and I'm going to answer them to the best of my ability. To set your and everyone else's mind at rest, I have no plans to change command assignments or demote anyone. Everyone will stay as is until proven incompetent or until we need them elsewhere. And that includes you, Major, even though I've noticed that your military experience is somewhat less than negligible. Has Sergeant-Major Haney arrived yet?"

"He came yesterday and informed us that you were on the way. He just didn't know the details as to when."

"Good. Now let me be blunt. Haney knows more about the army than all of you in the regiment put together. I strongly—*strongly*—urge you to take solemn heed of anything he suggests. He may not be an officer, but, trust me, I will back him fully."

Barnes grinned. "I already came to that conclusion."

Bugles sounded and men stirred. Word that their new commanding officer had arrived was spreading quickly.

"Barnes, we are going to train hard and fast. This regiment is going to Cuba a lot sooner than anticipated. We might have only a month before we depart."

"Jesus. Can we be ready in that short a time?"

"I don't think we have a choice."

James Kendrick presented himself to the White House usher and was told to wait in the first floor Green Room. A few moments later, Libbie Custer arrived. She was dressed in a blue silk gown and smiled radiantly. The dress was cut to show her shoulders and a significant amount of her exquisite bosom. Kendrick could easily see how the very lovely Mrs. Custer could melt anyone. What really struck him was the wit and intelligence behind her eyes. She would be a helluva woman to conquer, he thought, and then wondered just how her husband had managed that task. Perhaps there was more to the president than he thought. Or

maybe *she* had conquered *him*. After all, it was widely
rumored that she was the power behind the throne.
Women could neither vote nor hold office, but Libbie Custer was clearly in charge of the President of
the United States.

They sat in facing chairs and sized each other up.
Finally, she spoke. "Are you satisfied with what you
see, Mr. Kendrick? Or have I changed so much in
the last few years?"

The last time he'd laid eyes on her, she was taking
her wounded husband away from the Dakotas down
the Missouri on a flat-bottomed steamer. She'd been
anguished but firm. Her husband would survive his
wounds and the reports of the battle would paint
him as an American hero. Any attempts on Kendrick's
part to tell a different version of the story would be
quashed, and, for the most part, they had been.

"I wouldn't be lying if I said you have become
even lovelier, Mrs. Custer."

"You're too kind to be a reporter. Now, why did
you ask to see my husband?"

"Madam, we are either fighting or not fighting a
very curious war. Despite a declaration of war, there
has been little fighting and even the telegraph lines
between Cuba, Spain, and the United States are still
operational."

"And they are likely to stay that way. It serves
everyone's purposes to keep lines of communication
open. It is also possible that some in Spain and Cuba
are so technologically backward that they are unaware
of the potential of the telegraph."

Kendrick wondered if President Custer would have
thought that way. "I thought you should know that I

received an invitation from the Cuban General Gilberto Salazar to be his guest in Havana so I can report accurately on events in Cuba."

Libbie looked momentarily astonished, but recovered quickly. "Isn't Salazar the filthy little man who massacred the Americans on the *Eldorado*? Yes, of course he is. Do you want to go, and why are you, in effect, asking our permission? You journalists seem to go and do as you wish."

"I do want to go. It could be a wonderful story. I might also be able to maintain very personal lines of communication between our countries."

"While getting rich and famous in the process?"

Kendrick grinned. "Of course, and I would not like to be painted as a traitor for my efforts in writing an unbiased report."

Libbie stood and Kendrick did as well. She was a little taller than he recalled. She exuded a hint of some perfume and he was acutely aware that the president's wife was as sensuous a woman as he'd ever met.

"Mr. Kendrick, both my husband and I are of the opinion that the coming war will be short and will result in a great victory both for us and for the country. It has been years since the Civil War ended and it is time for a major reconciliation between the North and the South. A victorious war against a common foe will go a long way towards accomplishing that goal."

Kendrick agreed with that, but with one caveat that he kept to himself. The Spanish had had their own civil wars, the last ending with Alfonso XII becoming king. The Spanish needed a unifying war against a foreign enemy as much as the United States did, perhaps even more.

He also wondered if members of his own government wanted war so badly that they would have betrayed the men on the ill-fated *Eldorado* to the Spanish, thus precipitating the crisis. No, he thought, no one could be that duplicitous. Of course, perhaps no one had intended it to go that far. From what he'd seen of the government's reaction, the shock of the massacre had been very real.

"May I ask a favor from you, Mr. Kendrick? First, I would like your promise that you will give us any information that might help our nation before you submit it for publication. That will be at your discretion, of course. I don't want you to either get fired or killed."

"Agreed, Mrs. Custer, although I'm not totally certain how I'd work that out."

Libbie smiled radiantly. "Excellent, and I'm sure you'll think of something. Now let's have some sandwiches. I'm famished."

She took his arm and steered him to a table where a servant dashed in with some small sandwiches. He was acutely aware of the light feel of her breast against him. Jesus, he thought, she really is something.

When they were again seated, she smiled warmly. "Now, I would like a favor from you."

"Just ask."

"Since we're going to be such good friends, please call me Libbie."

Waves of blue-uniformed soldiers moved up the low hill while other soldiers awkwardly tried to maneuver a pair of brass twelve-pound cannons commonly known as Napoleons, and another pair of Gatling guns into position. This was the first time he'd had the entire regiment try a maneuver like this and it was apparent that they all had a lot to learn. The men were enthusiastic but untrained. Ryder had forbidden them to fix bayonets to their new to them 1873 Trapdoor Model Springfield rifles. There was a real fear that they would skewer themselves and that, as Haney said, would be bad for morale.

These rifles were improvements over the ones used by the Army during the Indian Wars and had largely solved the problem of jamming caused by overheating during prolonged firing. When the old rifles overheated, the spent cartridge might expand and get stuck and that would be disastrous on the battlefield. Unconfirmed rumors had it that some of Custer's men had suffered from that problem and lost their scalps as a result.

The soldiers reached the summit of the hill and lustily cheered their victory over a nonexistent foe. The men dragging the cannons and the Gatlings were too tired to cheer.

"What do you think, Sergeant Haney?"

Haney snorted. "I think they look like a thousand little kids running for free ice cream. At least they didn't bunch up until the last minute."

Ryder agreed and dismissed them to their ice-cream reward. Despite all the good work done by Colonel Fowler, their former commander had trained them in Civil War tactics that included massed forces slowly approaching an enemy. With current weapons that fired more rapidly and more accurately and at greater ranges, the tactics used at Gettysburg were a recipe for disaster. The men had quickly learned that spreading out and shooting and reloading from a prone position, which the Springfield permitted, was a potential lifesaver. During the Civil War, soldiers generally had to reload while standing, which made them excellent targets.

The two battalions of five hundred each were only part of his regiment. A third battalion of almost totally untrained men was being formed. They were mere spectators to this show, although they looked as if they'd like to join in what appeared to be a lot of fun.

Ryder looked at the large number of civilians who'd showed up to watch the maneuvers. It reminded him of what he'd read about the First Battle of Bull Run when thousands of civilians had appeared thinking that war was a spectator sport. They'd quickly had their illusions dashed when they saw the bloody reality of battle. They'd fled in panic for the safety of Washington after the Confederate victory.

"Sergeant, we are going to keep doing it until we get it right. We are going to keep teaching these farm boys and mechanics how to attack and shoot without hitting themselves in the rear and we are going to whip them into shape."

"Indeed, sir. By the way, I see young Major Barnes approaching with two ladies. With your permission I think I shall disappear and leave you to charm them."

"Go to hell Sergeant Major," Ryder said with a laugh. Barnes was only a couple of years younger than he. "And did I ever tell you how good you looked with a thousand Sioux arrows sticking out of your body?"

"Several times, sir. A bloody pincushion I was, although there were only three of them and not a thousand and they hurt like the devil," Haney said and quickly walked away.

A slightly flustered Barnes approached. "Sir, may I present my sister, Mrs. Sarah Damon and her friend, Mrs. Ruth Holden."

"A pleasure," he said and wondered why Barnes had hesitated slightly before announcing Mrs. Holden. Barnes' sister was a small slender woman who had intriguing features. No beauty in the classic sense, she had dark hair, large expressive eyes and looked intelligent, although quite prim and solemn. The other woman was older and a little more, well, robust and earthy.

Sarah Damon took the lead. "My brother has informed me that you are living a Spartan life in a tent and eating miserable canned food while you try to turn these poor boys into soldiers."

"It's not quite that awful, Mrs. Damon."

"But it could be better. My brother is still too much of a civilian to understand military protocol and I know even less of it. So unless I am making a huge faux pas, we would like to invite you to dinner tonight. I can guarantee you that the Willard Hotel's cuisine will surpass the tinned food you've been eating."

"To tell you the truth, I think that anything that had once been alive would be better than the tinned food supplied by the Army, and, yes, I'd be delighted. Other than you two ladies and your brother, will your husbands be in attendance?"

Ryder noted a flicker of dismay before Sarah responded. "Both of our husbands have been dead for several years. I'm afraid you'll have to make do with the three of us."

"Please accept my condolences. Again, I'm delighted."

His acceptance was greeted with a radiant smile that totally changed Sarah Damon. Yes, he would very much like going to dinner with the two widows and the young Major Barnes. Maybe, he thought wickedly, he could get rid of the young major.

Ryder was enjoying that last thought when a portly middle-aged man in a civilian suit approached him. "May I speak with you for a moment, Colonel?"

The man had a heavy accent and he wore his clothes like they were uncomfortable and that he would rather have been in a uniform. "Of course, and what embassy do you represent? From your accent, I would guess that it is either Germany's or Austria's."

The man blinked and smiled. "Well done. I am Adolf Helmsdorf and I have the honor to be a colonel in the army of Imperial Germany. I am further honored to serve the Emperor Kaiser Wilhelm, whom, it is hoped, will be the first in a long line of German emperors ruling the new nation of Germany."

Ryder nodded politely. "I'm honored to meet you. May I assume that you are assigned to the German embassy, which means that you have diplomatic immunity and are not a spy?"

"Colonel Ryder, why stoop to spying when all I had to do was follow the crowd to a very public event and observe to my heart's content? And yes, I do have diplomatic immunity, for all that's worth. All I wanted to do, Colonel, was congratulate you on the efficiency shown by your men. I've watched other volunteer units and many of them would give a mob a bad name. Your army has a long ways to go before it can take on even an enemy as inept and corrupt as Spain's. However, your regiment is off to a very good start, although I'm not sure I would recommend ice cream as a reward for a battle well fought." That last comment was said with a small smile.

Ryder shrugged. He could not argue with that observation or its source. The new Imperial German Army, which previously had been the Prussian Army, was considered to be the finest in Europe. The Germans had defeated France and Austria-Hungary along with a number of smaller countries as Prussia became Germany.

Helmsdorf continued. "I was pleased to see that you took Gatlings with you up the hill. The machine guns are excellent defensive weapons, but not too many officers try to use them as offensive weapons. You, of course, did that when you saved Custer, and we in Germany have been trying to find offensive uses for them as well."

Ryder was both surprised and pleased that the German knew about this exploits on the Little Big Horn.

"On the other hand, Colonel Ryder, I would strongly urge your government to find lighter weight uniforms. Your men will be weak and uncomfortable in what they are wearing. The British have begun wearing something called 'khaki' in warmer climes. I will be leaving shortly for Havana and a new assignment on the German consular staff. Of course I'll be a military attaché and will be doing a lot of snooping. Assuming your country wins, I look forward to seeing you again some time."

Helmsdorf bowed and departed. The German did not offer to shake hands. The Germans, Martin recalled, were too formal for that sort of thing.

◆   ◆   ◆

Later as they walked from their horses to the Willard Hotel to meet the two widows, Barnes decided that some explanations were in order.

"Neither of the two women is in mourning, so please don't let that be a concern. My sister's husband died of a sudden heart attack almost five years ago. She inherited his substantial property, most of which she has sold and is living off the investments. She handles them herself and is doing quite well. The other widow is similarly well off, although I'm not totally certain of the source of her funds. I tease them about being the two richest widows in Maryland, although I believe that Mrs. Holden's past has been a little more, shall we say, colorful? She actually lived in France and was in Paris when the Prussians attacked and when the French had their own bloody mess of a civil war. It is my understanding that her husband got himself executed for his part in it."

Interesting, Ryder thought. A woman who handles her own investments and another who saw and survived the horrors of the fighting in Paris in 1871.

They entered the Willard Hotel and were informed that dinner would be served in the women's suite. Yes, Ryder thought, the ladies did have money. He liked the idea of a private dinner more than being in the Willard's large, gaudy, crowded and ostentatious dining room where it was sometimes necessary to shout to be heard. Too many people who thought they were important liked to see and be seen at the Willard. This made private conversations almost impossible.

In the women's suite, Ryder found himself essentially paired with Sarah, which he didn't mind at all. He confirmed that his first impressions that she was quiet and reserved were totally wrong. Sarah was vivacious and delightful. Either that or he'd been away from women for far too long. No, he decided, she was both attractive and pleasant.

Dinner was extremely pleasant as well. He decided that the ladies must have thought he hadn't eaten in weeks and had ordered a full menu of beef, fish, and chicken, all cooked superbly by the Willard's staff. Wine was served, and since they were in private, no one looked askance at mixed couples enjoying themselves, as sometimes still happened.

In short, Ryder was soon as stuffed as a Thanksgiving turkey. A walk was in order, they decided. Again, he found himself paired with Sarah while Barnes and Ruth Holden went in another direction. Part of him wondered if this had been planned. Another part decided he didn't much care.

The Willard was only a block from the White House so they decided to walk to it and then around the mansion where George and Libbie Custer lived.

In response to her question, Ryder gave her a brief personal history. "We lived in Ohio and my father owned a store. He had political connections so I was admitted to West Point at the tender age of sixteen, which meant I graduated at twenty. I think a mistake was made in admitting me at such a young age, but I also think the Army decided to live with it once they found out.

"After graduation and being commissioned, I was immediately sent out west and you already know the story of me allegedly saving Custer from the Indians."

"Allegedly? Colonel, everything I've read and heard said that if you'd arrived a few minutes later, Custer and the remainder of his men would have been killed."

Martin grinned. "And do you know how many people have told me I should have waited another half hour before showing up? Or maybe stopped for lunch and a beer? Custer is not overwhelmingly popular among the military."

Sarah smiled at the thought. "And after that, my brother says, you had a number of postings in the west and helped keep the Indians pacified."

"Let's just say I tried. Many Indians hate us and don't want to be pacified. To them this means being confined to those open air prisons called reservations, all the while being swindled by government agents who are supposed to distribute food and clothing to them. I tried to put a halt to that but was singularly unsuccessful. The agents have too many powerful political connections here in Washington. It's another reason I'm not all that popular here."

"It sounds like you sympathize with the Indians."

"I do. They've been treated brutally and I hope that the country someday realizes the shame of it. Now please tell me something about yourself."

They had walked more than a mile so she steered him to a bench in a small park. They could still see the White House from where they were seated.

"I was married at seventeen and widowed at twenty. My parents loved the idea of my getting married. They were afraid I'd become an old maid. My husband wasn't much taller than me and quite possibly just as skinny."

"If I may be bold, I don't think you're skinny."

She smiled and flushed. "Thank you. At any rate, Walter was an incredibly hard worker and, shortly after our marriage, his parents died in a train accident and left their businesses to him. He tried hard to run them, but it was overwhelming. I helped him and learned a lot. In fact, I think I ultimately knew a lot more about the world of business than he did. Then one day he simply keeled over at his desk and died. The doctor said it was likely a heart attack."

"I'm sorry."

"Again thank you, but it was five years ago and, while I was fond of him and have warm memories, that part of my life is over. I sold off most of his properties except a house and small farm in Maryland, and formed my own investment company with the proceeds. I buy stocks in companies I think will do well in the future and, so far, I've won far more than I've lost."

"I'm impressed," he said truthfully.

"Sometimes it's so annoying when I find that some laws do not permit women to do certain things in the world of business, while some men flatly refuse to deal with a woman regardless of the law. Fortunately, I do have a brother and a father who front for me when the occasion arises. Please don't tell me that you believe women have no brains and should be confined to the kitchen."

"Not anymore," he said with a laugh.

"I also have vices, although I don't think they'll consign me to hell. I like an occasional cigarette and a nice brandy is a delight. I also like horseback riding, but I cannot abide riding side-saddle. If circumstances permit, I like to wear men's clothing and go out in the country where I can ride like a man. Since I am small I can wear a hat and most will think I'm a boy."

"I would never make such a mistake."

They stood and began the walk back to the hotel. Ryder realized that he would have to go back to his damn regiment and he didn't want to. He wanted the evening to continue.

"Do you consider Washington a great city, Colonel?"

The question surprised him. "No. Our nation's capital in no way compares with New York or Boston or Philadelphia."

"What about Paris, London, or Rome?"

"If I'd ever been to them, I might be better able to answer the question. From what I know and have read, Washington is nothing compared with them. Quite frankly, Washington is still very squalid."

"Agreed," she said. "President Custer wants us to be a great country, but we can't be one until our capital is a great one as well. Look around you. The White House is lovely, but it is miniscule compared with the palaces of Europe or even the new palaces of the wealthiest Americans. Our Washington Monument has been under construction for almost forty years and still isn't completed. And the original city plans called for a park in the mall running from the Capitol Building to the Potomac, but what exists there now is a weed-choked field with the remains of a canal off to its side that has become a sewer. Worse, there are slums all around the city and most of the roads are muddy tracks. And yes, I know that all cities have slums, but ours are terrible and they are so close to the center of government. Something should be done," she said and laughed at herself. "Oh dear, once again I've begun a lecture."

Ryder thought about suggesting that the two of them tour Europe someday, but decided to wait for another time and place. "May I ask you a question, Mrs. Damon?"

"Only if you call me Sarah and I will call you Martin."

Ryder grinned like a little kid who had just passed a test he hadn't studied for. "I would love to take you riding in the country and I would not be offended or shocked if you dressed as you wished."

"Then give your men Sunday off and pick me up in the morning."

They were almost at the hotel. They'd been so wrapped up in themselves that they hadn't noticed that it had gotten dark. Washington in the night was not the safest place in the world and Ryder was suddenly concerned that he'd made a mistake by suggesting that they walk so far.

They were only a dozen or so yards from the hotel door when two men jumped out of an alley and grabbed at Sarah's purse. She screamed and pulled back. An astonished Martin was staggered by a punch to the top of his head from the second man who pulled a knife and lunged at him.

Ryder regained his balance as best he could and ducked as the knife man lurched past him. He punched the man hard in the kidneys and he dropped to the ground but did not let go of the knife. Ryder stomped on the man's hand and heard bones break. The man who'd grabbed Sarah's purse jumped on Martin's back and began to claw for his throat and eyes.

Suddenly, the attacker screamed and let go. He staggered backwards and Ryder saw Sarah standing there with a long metal hat pin that was nearly a stiletto held tightly in her hand. The man grabbed his crotch and Martin realized just where Sarah had jabbed him.

They'd had enough. The two would-be robbers ran and limped down the street. It had taken only seconds and the few other pedestrians hadn't had time to react.

Sarah smoothed her clothing. She had begun to shake and was trying to hide it. "Well, that was exciting. Are dinners with you always like this? You are all right, aren't you?"

"Yes, and are you?"

He reached over and touched her hand. She put her other hand over his. She took a couple of deep breaths and smiled.

"Of course. I may be petite, but I do know how to protect myself. Things like this have happened to me before, as they have to so many women. Now, will I see you Sunday or has this little incident alarmed you?"

◆ Chapter 4 ◆

THE HMS *SHANNON* WAS CLASSIFIED BY THE ROYAL Navy as a First-Class Armored Cruiser. She displaced almost six thousand tons and was armed with two ten-inch and seven nine-inch muzzle-loading cannons, along with a miscellany of smaller guns. Her top speed was only twelve knots and, even though she had a steam engine, she still carried masts and a full complement of sails.

Although only constructed in 1875 and recently refitted, the *Shannon* was considered a poorly designed warship. She was slow, had chronic engine troubles, and her coal bunkers were considered inadequate. The *Shannon* was considered a poor investment by the British government. She was, therefore, expendable.

All of this was why Great Britain was interested in either selling her or leasing her to the United States Navy. As bad as the *Shannon* was, she was better than anything in the United States Navy. Nor was the *Shannon* the only warship the British were willing to unload. Several other of her obsolete sister ships were on the market to the highest bidder. James Kendrick was hopeful that the high bidder would be the United States Navy.

Kendrick had come aboard in Baltimore only a couple of days after his White House visit with Libbie Custer. Somehow, the Custers had convinced the Royal Navy to ferry him to Havana. Nor was he the only American on board. Navy Commander George Dewey was also on board along with a young ensign named Paul Prentice who served as his aide.

Relations between the Americans and the British skipper were frosty. The captain didn't like the idea of turning over his command to a bunch of damned Yankees and made no bones about it. Even though the decision hadn't been made official or announced, it was pretty much a foregone conclusion. Kendrick and Dewey and the young Prentice stayed out of his way. Kendrick watched as Dewey quietly learned everything he could about the ship that might just be his to command.

"Amazing," said Dewey. "This ship is only seven or so years old and she's already obsolete. Naval technology is changing at breakneck speed. Even so, we will still buy her. She's far, far better than any of the ships we have."

"How long before we can use her against the Spanish?" Kendrick asked.

"If we bought her yesterday, it would still take several months before she was ready. Logistics is the curse of war. We would have to find and train officers and men to form a crew and then steam about in order to find and resolve all her idiosyncrasies, and I understand she has many. That and gunnery training will all take time. Additional time will be required if we are to sail with other American warships and not get disastrously in each other's way."

"Why can't we rent the crew as well as the ship?"

Dewey laughed hugely. "Believe me, it was considered. Then cooler heads realized that there would be hell to pay in England if any of her sailors got killed fighting under an American flag."

"I can't believe she still has a supply of sails."

"Even in modern ships, sails are needed for two reasons. First, a ship like the *Shannon* can carry only so much coal and supplies of coal are often not readily available. Therefore, she will use her sails and conserve fuel every chance she gets. Second, the engines of a modern ship are picky things. Sometimes they simply break down and, since there are no telegraph lines from ships to other ships or the shore, there must be a means of moving a crippled ship. If not, a ship could become a hulk filled with starving men."

"Makes sense," Kendrick conceded.

"There is a third reason I neglected to mention and that is tradition. Far too many senior officers think that a ship without sails is repugnant and they absolutely hate to see the clean lines of a sailing ship spoiled by black coal smoke spewing from a stack. Some days I agree with them."

There were still clipper ships sailing and Kendrick fondly recalled how graceful and lovely they looked. "Sadly, sailing ships will be either for pleasure or be relegated to a museum."

"And the world will be less for that," said Dewey, "yet no sailing ship should ever be in a modern naval battle. Now tell me, what will you do when we arrive in Havana? After all, you are an American."

Dewey laughed. "We will be in Havana for only a day. It will be a brief courtesy call and the ship's crew won't even get liberty. As for me, I will be trying hard to stay out of sight. While they may suspect my presence, I am confident the Spaniards will turn a blind eye to my being here."

And so it happened. The *Shannon* steamed slowly through the narrow entrance to Havana Harbor and under the guns of the fortresses of Morro Castle and La Cabaña.

"What are you thinking, Commander?" Kendrick asked as they looked at the Spanish fortifications.

"That the forts are centuries old and in disrepair and that the guns are largely rusted relics. Still, they could cause a great deal of damage to any ships trying to navigate the narrow harbor opening before being blown to pieces by modern naval guns."

The forts were symbols of a bygone age and an empire that had decayed and almost disappeared. But Dewey was correct—even ancient cannons could kill.

They anchored in the harbor only a couple of hundred yards off the city's waterfront. The buildings were mainly stone and were painted many colors. Havana was a bright and lively city, Kendrick concluded. He said goodbye to Dewey and, along with the *Shannon*'s captain, was rowed in the captain's boat to the dock. Several political types and one man in what Kendrick presumed was a naval uniform waited for them. Kendrick was nudged away from the short receiving line. Officially, he wasn't there.

He picked up his one suitcase and looked around.

Finally, he saw Salazar standing beside a man in the uniform of a Spanish general. Christ, he thought, who is that?

He approached the two men. Salazar greeted him formally. He seemed slightly uncomfortable with the other man beside him. "Welcome to Cuba, Mr. Kendrick," Salazar said, "and may I introduce you to Major General Valeriano Weyler, the recently arrived commander of all the Spanish army forces in Cuba."

Sarah was a superb rider. She took the uneven ground with ease and directed her horse to confidently jump small obstacles. She and the mare she'd chosen seemed to flow across the ground as one. Better, she looked delightful in the specially made denim jeans she wore. They were designed for her by the Levi Strauss and Company and fit her well. Ryder happily concluded that no one would mistake her for a boy.

It occurred to him that she was likely a better rider than he and she commented on it when they paused to give their horses a rest.

"You ride for pleasure," he said, "while we in the cavalry ride for work. We use horses to get to our destination and generally dismount to accomplish our goals."

"Such as when fighting Indians?"

"Precisely. Fighting on horseback largely went out when someone invented the rifle, and certainly diminished further when Mr. Gatling invented the machine gun. Most of the men in the Seventh Cavalry at the Little Big Horn hadn't known which end of a horse was the front when they enlisted and that had been only a few months earlier. Even though they were listed as cavalrymen, they were not expert riders. Few soldiers are. As for me, even though West Point taught me to ride without hurting myself, my specialty was artillery and now I'm an infantry officer. I defer to your skills as a rider as well as your charm."

She laughed and decided it was time to eat. They had brought sandwiches in their saddlebags and were pleased that neither the meat nor the cheese tasted too much like horse after their ride. A bottle of a local and mediocre white wine had been packed in ice and hadn't gotten too warm, and they drank from small pewter glasses that had also been carefully packed.

"I'm enjoying myself," she said and Ryder beamed. They were sitting in the shade of a large oak tree while their horses grazed and rested. "I just wonder how much longer it will be before you and my brother and all those other young men go off to war."

"I hope it's not too soon," he answered solemnly. "First, we're simply not ready although we're one of the better trained regiments and, second, I rather like getting to know you."

"Some women might think your comments very bold, Martin."

"Do you?"

"No. Like you, I'm enjoying all this. But you didn't answer my question—when do you think you'll be leaving?"

"At first we were told a month at the most, although the dates keep changing as reality sets in. The truth is, nobody really knows when we'll depart. Someday the Army will tell us that we should have been there yesterday. The Navy is gathering ships and some units have begun moving towards Florida. Since rail connection to most parts of Florida is miserable at best, those already heading to Florida are southern units. My regiment will depart by ship from Baltimore."

"And where will you land, and please don't think I'm a spy. I'm no Rose Greenhow."

Martin laughed at the idea of her comparing herself to the notorious Confederate spy. "I didn't think you were, and it doesn't matter. I can't tell you because I don't know. I don't even know who is going to command this army, much less where we'll land. I sometimes wonder if anybody has a clue."

President Custer slammed his fist down on the desk in his office. "There is no way in hell that that goddamned son of a bitch Winfield Scott Hancock is going to command my army."

Army Secretary Robert Lincoln shook his head. "Even though he is not now in the Army, Hancock is head and shoulders above anyone who currently *is* in the Army. He's commanded large forces and many people feel he was the man responsible for our victory at Gettysburg, and not Meade."

"I don't give a rat's fart what people think. Hancock ran against me in the last election and damn near took it. I am not going to give him a chance to do it again and next time win just because he's the country's latest war hero. No, the Army will be led by Nelson Miles."

"Miles is a good Indian fighter, but that's about it," Lincoln said. "He's never led a large force, and he doesn't seem to inspire confidence in those he commands. Admittedly he's brave, but he's vain and stubborn, while Hancock is a proven fighter."

"I don't care what he inspires. Look, if I can't have Miles, then I will command in person."

With that, the others in the room looked aghast. Navy Secretary Hunt was the first to protest. "Sir, you know it is against tradition, perhaps even law, for a sitting president to leave the United States."

"Maybe it's time for the tradition to change."

Secretary of State James Blaine decided it was time to intercede. "Mr. President, if you leave the country, who will be in charge? Vice President Arthur? You cannot be two places at once and even with the telegraph, you cannot deal with the problems of Congress and the nation."

"Shit," muttered Custer, accepting defeat. "But I want Miles and that's that."

Reluctantly, they agreed that Nelson Miles would command the invasion force and the discussion moved to the subject of the Navy. Secretary Hunt was more than a little pleased at the progress he'd made.

"Gentlemen, the three warships we bought from Great Britain are currently being refitted at Baltimore. They have been renamed the *Atlanta, Boston*, and *Chicago*. The *Atlanta* is ready to sail and will escort a number of troopships that are gathering there. We will utilize several of the smaller steam sloops to also protect the convoy. We are also arming and commissioning a number of civilian ships and have chartered several hundred other civilian ships as transports. I am confident that we can land upwards of fifteen thousand men in a first wave against the Spanish in Cuba. The only question I have is precisely where shall they land?"

"Well, it can't be right at Havana," said Lincoln. "That place is too heavily fortified. Our men would be slaughtered. Nor can it be Santiago. It's too far away, several hundred miles, in fact. We would have to fight our way across the length of Cuba and that's a very long way. If we want to get the campaign over before either the hurricane or fever seasons strike, we have to get closer."

"Matanzas," said Hunt. "It's a small city about fifty crow-fly miles east of Havana and it has a decent harbor. Not a big harbor, but one that can handle a number of ships at a time. The troops can land outside the harbor while the ships carrying supplies can use the docks in the harbor."

Custer nodded. "I like it, but is it well defended?"

Hunt winced. "We've just established a naval intelligence unit headed by one Lieutenant Theodorus Mason, but I'm afraid we know very little about the defenses at Matanzas."

"Who would?" asked Custer.

Secretary of State Blaine smiled. "Why, I suppose the Cubans would."

James Kendrick rapidly came to the conclusion that Salazar was serious about having Spain's side of the story told. He was put up in a small suite of rooms at one of Salazar's mansions on the outskirts of Havana. He was only a few minutes ride from the harbor and wasn't particularly surprised when, the day after his arrival, his host practically ordered him to ride with him to the harbor. The Spanish fleet was arriving.

They left their horses a few blocks from the waterfront and walked the rest of the way, along with just about everyone in the city. What they saw truly was impressive. Both of Spain's battleships had made port and they were accompanied by a number of steam sloops and smaller gunboats. The battleships were the *Vitoria* and the *Numancia*. Salazar proudly informed him that they displaced more than seven thousand tons and had a number of cannons that fired shells of more than six inches. He added that four cruisers were also en route to reinforce the Spanish fleet.

Kendrick had to admit that the grey bulk of the warships was menacing. The ships were functional and, in his opinion, ugly. They had none of the graceful lines of the sailing ships that had become obsolete. A pity, he thought, but why should the instruments of war and killing be graceful and lovely?

More important, the Spanish warships had escorted several transports that were disgorging a large number of soldiers. A second convoy, this one escorted by the cruisers, would dock tomorrow or the next day.

Salazar was practically giddy with happiness and pride. "I hope you do not take offense, Kendrick, but you will see how the pride of Spain will crush the United States."

"It is very impressive indeed. I wonder how long it will take for President Custer to find out about this."

Salazar laughed. "I would say about ten minutes. The telegraph lines between here and Florida must be burning up. If you'd like, you can write a story about your impressions and I'll see to it that it is given priority."

"Would you want to clear it first?"

"Of course not. There's not much to hide, is there?"

Kendrick agreed. He didn't add that the two Spanish battleships were on the small side in comparison with most of the battleships of the Royal Navy. Nor did he add that the U.S. was attempting to buy some

British ships of roughly similar size. He was fairly certain that the Spanish knew all about it. He now believed the rumors that Spain was attempting to buy warships from France were true.

Salazar took his arm. "Come, we shall go back to my home and have a good meal along with some excellent wine, perhaps a lot of excellent wine. I will introduce you to my family and you will see that I am not a total barbarian, merely a devoted Spanish patriot."

Yes, Kendrick thought, and a Spanish patriot who murders prisoners and slaughters innocent Cubans. In preparing for the trip, he'd done some more homework on Salazar and found a number of stories in which his personal army had killed numbers of Cubans that he'd arbitrarily named as insurgents.

It occurred to him that Salazar might just become an embarrassment to the Spanish government. But not just yet, he thought.

Ryder laughed at the surprise on Sarah's face. "It's true. Since we're at war, President Custer no longer wishes to be called president. He'd directed everyone to call him general."

"That is incredibly pretentious."

"Agreed, but I'm not going to be the one to tell him. I like being a full colonel. Perhaps I'll even become a general before this is over."

"How many would have to die for that to happen?"

He winced at the thought. These men were either his friends or those he respected. "Only a couple."

They were seated on a couch in the living room of her country house. It had belonged to her late husband and, she'd informed him, it had six bedrooms on two levels. Even more important, her husband had installed indoor plumbing and a means for having hot flowing water. It occurred to Ryder that her husband must have truly loved her.

On her own, she had installed a sanitation device called a septic tank that had recently been invented in France.

Sarah had a staff that consisted of a cook, a woman who kept the house clean and did the laundry, a gardener, and a man who looked after the animals, including the horses and a handful of cows.

"They are all very loyal to me," she said, then grinned. "Of course they are also very concerned that I'll remarry and they'll be out of a job. This is at least partly why they are protective of me and very concerned about any man I see."

"And how many men do you see?" he teased.

"Not as many as you might think. I'm afraid I've discouraged most of them. They all seem to think that I would be happier and much better off if only I would let them handle my wealth, and that is simply not going to happen. I know that some men in business are shocked to find that they are dealing with a woman and others simply refuse to, but enough are concerned only with making a profit that I'm able to function. When things get difficult, I generally use my father or my brother as a go-between. They are both listed as vice presidents in my company."

"Are you implying that you don't think I'm after your money?"

She reached over and tapped him on the arm. "I'm usually a good judge of character and, no, I don't think you'd try to seduce me for my wealth."

She stood and walked to the window. "So now can you tell me when you're leaving for Cuba?"

"It's still vague and subject to change, but a couple of weeks at the most," he said softly, and he saw sadness in her face.

He stood by her at the window and she put her head on his shoulder. He would not tell her that his regiment was going to be the spearhead of the invasion. She didn't need that worry. Then it dawned on him that she actually would be worried.

Secretary of State James G. Blaine was convinced that someday he would be President of the United States, replacing George Armstrong Custer, the man he considered to be a flaming horse's ass. Blaine was also convinced of America's future in the world. The United States would become an even greater power than she currently was and the only way to do that was to explode beyond the limitations of her continental boundaries. Thus, the first steps in developing an overseas American empire involved taking Cuba and Puerto Rico from the rotten Spanish empire.

When those lands became under American control, it would be time to look farther afield, to such places as the Philippines, or Hawaii, or even lands near the Isthmus of Panama where a canal might someday be built. Since everyone in Europe was taking chunks out of China's carcass, he thought that an American equivalent to Hong Kong on the Chinese coast might be feasible.

Blaine sighed. He was thinking big, perhaps too big. First Cuba had to be taken. Thus, this day he was quietly and secretly meeting with a representative of the Cuban insurgents.

"Señor Cardanzo," he said with a look of warmth he didn't feel. "It's a pleasure to meet with a representative of those also fighting Spain."

Cardanzo was a small dark man in his forties. Blaine was not comfortable dealing with black men as equals and Cardanzo sensed it.

"I'm proud and honored to meet you, Mr. Blaine. Now, to be blunt, how can we help each other?"

Good, Blaine thought, let's get this over with. "We need information, and you and others in your movement are in a position to provide it. We would like to know the disposition of the Spanish army and the strength of the Spanish defenses."

Cardanzo was puzzled. "Why are you asking this and not representatives of your army or navy?"

"Let's just say that our intelligence-gathering resources are not what they should be. Also, I am in a position to offer you something after the Spanish are expelled."

Cardanzo smiled. "Independence?"

"Perhaps in a while, a very short while, we would be able to support Cuban independence. We would have to remain in charge to ensure a peaceful turnover to the Cuban population."

"Would you feel that way if we were white?"

"Your candor is appreciated and you are correct. If you and your compatriots were white we would not have many of the concerns we have. Let's face it, Mr. Cardanzo, the only successful nations in the world today are those governed by white people. If you want to see what could happen if unprepared non-whites are in charge, you have to look no farther than the bloodbaths that took place in Haiti and the constant revolutions that are occurring in those Central and South American nations that were once the property of Spain."

Cardanzo was not impressed by that logic. "You realize, of course, that if the tyranny of Spain is replaced by the tyranny of the United States, there will be continued fighting."

Blaine leaned back in his chair. "Is that a threat, sir?"

"Hardly. My people would not ever want to fight their liberators. But it could be a statement of reality. My people want independence, not simply a change. However, being controlled by America would be far better than being the enslaved property of Spain. Yes, we will provide you with what information we can glean and we will trust you to do what is right for the people of Cuba. After all, I'm certain that you would not want an army in Cuba during the fever season. Thousands of your soldiers would likely die if that should happen."

"Wouldn't that happen to the Spanish army?"

"Of course, Mr. Blaine, but Spain doesn't care about the poor creatures in its army, while the United States does."

With that they shook hands and Cardanzo departed. He had barely left the room when Blaine muttered "nigger" under his breath.

Outside, Cardanzo met with a couple of his compatriots. "It is as I feared," he said. "The United States wants us to be their colony. The only question is for how long. Forever is a possibility. But waiting for a new president to be elected and replace Custer is more likely. If we make it difficult for the Americans, perhaps they will let us go sooner. First, they have to defeat the Spanish and we will help them. Then, if necessary, we will deal with the Americans just as we are now dealing with Spain."

Master Sergeant Haney spoke very little Spanish. Thus, he was somewhat surprised when he was chosen by Colonel Ryder to scout the lands and bays near the city of Matanzas.

He was slipped into Cuba by a small and foul smelling fishing boat. When he got off in the middle of the night, he was greeted by another man who told him in surprisingly good English that his name was Diego. Diego added that he was a member of the rebellion, which Haney hoped was the case. If not and he was a Spanish army officer, Haney was likely to spend several years in a miserable prison if he wasn't hanged outright. What happened to the men of the *Eldorado* was on everyone's mind.

Diego led him inland, carefully staying off the dirt paths he called roads. "I think this is want you want to see," he said as they breasted a gentle hill just a mile or two inland from the city.

Haney nodded and looked around. The hill was only a few hundred feet high. It wasn't much of a vantage point, but it would do. From it he could see the city of Matanzas itself. He estimated the population at about ten thousand. The bay looked like it could handle a number of good-sized ships, but it also looked like it was silting up. That, he concluded, would severely limit the number and size of ships that could unload at any one time.

He also wondered why the Navy hadn't sent some-one along with him. He'd asked that question when

Colonel Ryder suggested that he volunteer and was told that the Navy was too busy trying to round up ships to spend time scouting inland Cuba. They said it was the Army's business.

"I don't see any fortifications," Haney said. Even though it was night, the moon and stars allowed him to see that the land was undisturbed. What he assumed were sugar cane and tobacco were growing in fields, but no entrenchments or cannons could be seen.

"That's because there aren't any. All the work being done to protect Cuba is happening just outside Havana. There they are digging in like beavers, building fortifications that will stop any army. I understand the Spanish are now bitterly regretting tearing down Havana's defensive walls only a few years ago. Little places like Matanzas have been left to their own devices."

Haney didn't like hearing about the fortifications around Havana, but his job was to scout out the Matanzas area. "Are you telling me there are no troops here?"

Diego laughed. "Of course there are soldiers, just not too many of them. I estimate several companies, perhaps a battalion. You should be able to crush them when you attack."

Haney was too much of a realist to accept such optimistic estimates. After all, hadn't Custer said the Indians would run when the Seventh Cavalry approached? Unconsciously he rubbed a scar on his shoulder where a Sioux arrow had stuck in his flesh. He still remembered the pain when a surgeon pulled it out.

Haney was about to comment when he heard voices. They were close and getting closer. Shit, he thought. The two men quickly tried to make themselves invisible in the dark.

Three Spanish soldiers passed them only a few feet away. They were talking loudly and not paying much attention to the world around them. Garrison duty and going out on the occasional patrol were not too arduous despite the war, Haney concluded.

He was about to exhale and thank their lucky stars when Diego suddenly screamed, bolted from his hiding place, and slashed at one of the soldiers with his machete, ripping the man's throat.

The wounded soldier fell while the other two wheeled in disbelief. Christ, thought Haney. What the hell had just happened? He pulled his revolver and a Bowie knife and joined in the assault. Diego was wrestling with a second soldier while the third tried to bring his rifle to bear. Haney plunged his knife into the belly of the third and ripped upwards. The man screamed and fell back. Haney waited until he had a chance and then used the handle of his revolver to crack the skull of the man wrestling with Diego. He hit the man several more times before the soldier let go and went limp. Haney checked to see if any were alive. None were. Even the man he'd stabbed had stopped breathing and was gazing at the night sky with blank eyes.

Diego staggered to his feet. He was covered with blood, but most of it wasn't his. "Thank you, my friend. You saved my life."

Haney wiped his knife on the shirt of one of the dead soldiers. "Yeah, and your bullshit action might have gotten us killed."

"You are right," he said contritely. "But when I saw their uniforms I couldn't help myself. They are from a regiment formed and led by Gilberto Salazar. They are the ones who massacred your fellow Americans on that ship. More important to me, they are the devils who slaughter Cubans they think are rebels just because they are wandering and looking for food. A while back, they killed my sister, but not until many soldiers abused her. When the soldiers were through with her, they cut her throat and left her to bleed to death on the ground. She was fourteen."

"I'm very sorry," said Haney as he looked around nervously, "but these guys' comrades are going to be looking for them very soon. You better get me back to that dinky boat so I can get the hell out of here."

"You're right that we must move, but there is no hurry. They won't be missed for several hours and we will be many miles from here by then."

"Diego, where do you want to go?"

The Cuban laughed. "I want you to see Havana. But before then, tell me what a sergeant major does in the army. I have a lot I need to know."

Haney thought for a moment before responding. Screw it, he decided. "A sergeant major beats the shit out of untrained recruits until they get it in their heads that they have to obey orders and can't go and do what they want. And sometimes I have to talk very firmly to undisciplined officers, too."

Diego flinched. "I understand your message. What I did was unforgivable and it will not happen again. Unfortunately, this lack of discipline is common in our army. Every man seems to think he is a general and, therefore, enabled to lead. Sometimes there is chaos. May I borrow you to help instill discipline?"

"Let's get back from Havana first."

◆　　◆　　◆

Sarah yawned. She'd had at least one glass of wine too many. She wondered if she was slurring her words and decided she didn't care. Sarah and her good friend Ruth Holden were on the second floor of Sarah's house in the country, residing on couches in the large master bedroom. Ruth was going to spend the night in her own room down the hall.

The two women had changed into their nightgowns and were also wearing light robes. No servants were present. They could talk candidly without a housekeeper's sometimes very large ears picking up gossip.

"Do you miss marriage?" Ruth asked.

"Sometimes very much. Walter was a good man, considerate and kind. He made me feel secure and he genuinely cared for me. I was genuinely fond of him." Although, she thought, that fondness had not necessarily translated into love.

"That isn't what I meant. Do you miss the physical part of marriage?"

Sarah felt herself flush. "Sometimes. Despite the fact that he was older, neither of us was all that experienced as lovers; but we both learned quite rapidly. We enjoyed each other immensely. What about you?"

"I miss it as well. You are aware, of course, that I was never actually married. Jean was a lover, nothing more. And yes, I do miss the exciting physical part. You are aware that he was a thief, aren't you?"

Sarah giggled. The wine was winning. "I thought there might be something like that from statements you made."

"Yes. When we weren't romping in bed, Jean would go out and rob rich Parisians. He stole money, usually negotiable securities, and, rarely, jewelry. Jewelry was too special and unique and he could only sell it for a fraction of its real value. Sometimes he would melt it down for the gold, but that was too risky. Money and negotiable securities were a different matter. The chaos of the war with Prussia and the later revolution permitted him to steal almost at will. I don't think he ever hurt anyone. He didn't have to. My job was to take the plunder to Switzerland and convert it to Swiss or British money."

"That's a lot more exciting than farming," Sarah said as she poured them each some more wine. She had to concentrate on not spilling any.

Ruth continued. "It got *too* exciting. Jean got swept up by the police and was executed along with several thousand others. Those were terrible, horrible, days in Paris. I know he was killed because I portrayed myself as the grieving widow and they let me identify him. Of course, they had no idea he was anything more than a low-ranking rebel, so they let me take his body and have him buried. Ironically, he was never a rebel, just a thief.

"When he died, I went to Switzerland and got a number of bank drafts and traveled to Italy. From there I took a ship from Naples and came to the U.S. I opened a number of accounts in my name and here I am, a very rich but lonely widow.

"I can't imagine you being lonely too long."

"Nor can I, but I too am going to be choosy. As you've found out, there are too many men who want only money. Still, I do very much miss having a man in bed with me. Have you ever thought of inviting Colonel Ryder to your boudoir?"

"It's crossed my mind," Sarah said with a smile. "It may happen but not just yet."

"When you fantasize, is it with Ryder? When I think about doing it with someone, I often think of being in bed with that charming but rough Sergeant Haney. It may surprise you but I've managed to speak with him on a number of occasions. We have a lot in common. He comes from a country that is enslaved, Ireland, and I come from a country that people insist doesn't exist, Poland."

Ruth poured herself some more wine. "Haney reminds me of a reasonably honest version of Jean. Since I can't have him just now, I usually just pleasure myself or use one of the delightful toys I brought back from France. Once I even did it with a woman."

"Dear God!"

"It was pleasant enough from a physical standpoint but totally unsatisfying emotionally. And no, I am not going to suggest that we even think of trying it."

Sarah just laughed and shook her head. "Good. I'm not that desperate and hopefully never will be."

The conversation was getting entirely too personal, but Ruth did have a point. In the past she'd thought of Walter being in bed with her and how they used to please each other. Lately, however, her thoughts had turned to wondering how Martin Ryder's hands might feel on her body. On rare occasions she had indeed pleasured herself and, now loosened by alcohol, thought that tonight might be another one. Since Ruth would be sleeping down the hall, she would have to make sure she was quiet. On the other hand and given the amount of wine they'd drunk, it was possible that nothing would awaken Ruth.

She also wondered what kind of toys Ruth had brought back from Europe and precisely what they did. She decided she really wasn't ready to find out.

Even though the nearly impoverished village was only a little more than a day's walk from Havana, it took almost a week for news of the coming war with the United States to reach it. As soon as their work was done, the people gathered before the small church to discuss what it all meant. They had heard of the United States, but other than the name, knew nothing about it. Nor were they in the slightest bit thrilled at the thought of a new war. A truce had been called in the long and savage war of liberation between the rebels who wanted independence and the loyalists who wanted Spain to remain in control of Cuba.

The village did not have a name. It was nothing more than a cluster of several dozen huts and hovels and a small church large enough to hold the women and children. This was satisfactory, since the men never went to mass anyhow, at least not before their own funerals. The road through it was little more than a dirt path.

Cuba was exhausted. Both sides had been bled and mauled. Rosita Garcia had lost two cousins in the bloodletting. She had always been afraid that her one son would be conscripted by one side or the other or, worse yet, foolishly volunteer to fight. So far he had resisted that temptation.

"What side are we going to be on?" asked one field worker.

"It doesn't much matter," answered one of his friends. "Whatever side we're on will be the loser."

Rosita thought she understood. Most of the people in the village sympathized with the rebels. Spain was a far-off land that had mismanaged Cuba with cruelty and indifference. The rebels represented the future, but when would the future arrive? What would happen if the Yankees and Spain patched up their differences and there was no war after her village and thousands of others like it declared for independence? Why, it would be a bloodbath, she answered herself.

Two priests were present and they'd begun screaming at each other. One was pro-independence while the other felt that Spain ruled Cuba through the grace of God and Holy Mother Church, and that any act of defiance would be a grievous sin.

Others were more pragmatic. "Will we have enough to eat?" asked Rosita. "What will we do if either army comes in and takes what little food we have."

"Then we will starve and die," and old man said and grinned toothlessly.

Both priests agreed that the people should store and hide their food from whoever their oppressors might be.

"Will it ever end?" Rosita asked the priest who was pro-rebel. She could not recall his name.

"Only God knows."

Rosita persisted. "We are so close to Havana. The armies will have to come this way, won't they?"

The priest shook his head sadly and didn't answer. It was all too obvious. The Cuban people wanted no part of any war between Spain and something called the United States of America. As usual, however, the poor, ragged, dirty, and hungry peasants would be ground under the heels of others. As usual, each side would blame the peasants for siding with the other and punish those they thought to be guilty. The Spanish would be the most savage, because they were so far away from home. They were oppressors without inhibitions.

"We must hide everything, like we used to do," the priest finally said. "And that includes our women."

There was no disagreement. Rosita herself had been raped a few years ago by a Spaniard. She had endured. That's what women were supposed to do. At least that's what another priest had told her.

As would any mother, she feared for her son. This night she would sneak into his room while he was sleeping and pray over him. If he caught her, he would be embarrassed. Then she would pray that the war didn't come. But she knew it would.

◆ Chapter 5 ◆

ACTING MAJOR JACK BARNES SMILED AND DRAMATI-
cally swept his arm over the crowded harbor.
They were on the ramparts of historic but obsolete
Fort McHenry. Below them was a horde of ships of
all shapes and sizes. He pointed at three in particular.
"There, Colonel, are the three ships that are going to
take the regiment to Cuba."

Ryder shook his head sadly. "Please don't tell me
their names are the *Niña, Pinta*, and *Santa Maria*."

Barnes laughed nervously. "They're old, sir, but
not that old."

Ryder reluctantly agreed. The ships assigned to the
First Maryland looked like old tubs with rust and dirt
streaks on their hulls. But he'd been assured that they
were seaworthy and had steam engines, although two
of them were paddlewheelers. They'd been chartered
by the Navy, and he presumed the Navy knew what
it was doing. Each ship would carry one battalion
of infantry along with as much supplies as could be

stuffed in her hold. After the men were loaded, food and ammunition were the highest priority. No, he corrected himself, the *only* priority. And water, he added.

The waters around Fort McHenry were filled with steamships of all sizes. Barnes said he'd actually counted over two hundred before giving up. Additional ships continued to arrive. U.S. Navy warships were further down toward the mouth of the Chesapeake and would escort the ragtag armada to Cuba when the time came. These consisted of the recently renamed cruiser *Atlanta* and a number of armed sloops and converted merchantmen. The *Atlanta* had been the HMS *Shannon*. It was felt that her ten-inch guns were powerful enough to handle anything the Spanish had, including her two battleships. Ryder again hoped that the Navy knew what it was doing.

"Major, I have a sneaking suspicion that there is going to be a real circus when the order is given to embark. Therefore, I want an armed platoon on each of our ships to protect them from being stolen out from under us."

"Do you think that's really necessary?"

"Yes, I do. You've seen some of these units. I was recently told that to call them mobs would be to insult a true mob, yet they all want to be in the first convoy and get all the glory. Since there aren't enough ships to take everyone, it's possible that some of these so-called warriors will try to steal our transports. Look, we've been training hard and it shows. However, some of our sister regiments have been acting like this is a picnic with rifles."

Barnes laughed. "You're right. I'll have men on each ship and they'll be armed and ordered to use force to repel boarders. By the way, Colonel, what have you heard from Haney?"

"Nothing, and I don't expect to, at least not for a while. If he can, he is going to meet us off Florida. If not, we'll wait until we land at Matanzas. Right now he's probably running around Cuba with a pack of rebels and having a wonderful time killing Spaniards."

For Kendrick it had been one of the most awkward dinners in memory. Gilberto Salazar had tried being a gracious host, but had showed up drunk for the meal and continued to drink throughout it. His wife, a stern and plain woman named Juana, had been there as well and had glared daggers at her husband. There was clearly no love lost between them.

To make matters even more awkward, Salazar had brought a German woman named Helga to sit beside him, and she was obviously his mistress. Helga was blond, plump, and looked vacantly around the room. It was clear that she'd been drinking as well and, with each deep breath she took, her ample breasts threatened to spill out of her dress. That Juana wanted to kill both of them was evident. Kendrick found himself feeling sorry for the slighted woman. Salazar's wife was thin, had a hook nose, and wore her dark hair pulled back in a severe bun. She was dressed in black like a caricature of a nun and said little throughout the meal.

Just as the dinner was grinding to an end, a messenger came with information that enraged Salazar. He crumpled the note and threw it across the room before announcing that rebels had attacked a patrol and killed several of his men. He would have to leave immediately. He lurched to his feet and ordered his horse saddled and a troop of cavalry to accompany him. Kendrick had no idea what use Salazar's presence would be, since, by his own admission, the rebels would be far, far away from the site of the killings by the time he got there. Kendrick was delighted that he was not invited to accompany him.

Just before departing, Salazar turned on his wife. "I brought you to this meal to meet the American," he snarled. "I thought you would at least be civil."

Juana was not intimidated. "How can I be civil in the presence of your whore? Why do you insist on flaunting the simple creature? Why don't you just leave her in bed where she belongs?"

Salazar grabbed Juana's arm and pulled her to her feet. She showed no emotion while Helga commenced to blubber. "See what I have to put up with, Kendrick? My own wife, a woman who should be submissive, shows no respect for me. Do you like women, Kendrick?"

"Of course," he answered softly, wondering what the hell kind of trouble any answer would result in.

"Excellent," Salazar said as he roughly pushed Juana back into her chair. "Tonight she will come to your room and you have my permission to fuck her. No, I insist that you fuck her."

With that astonishing pronouncement, Salazar left. Kendrick figured that Salazar would be gone the better part of a week. With his angry departure, the diners abruptly left for their respective rooms.

As was customary in Cuba, they had eaten late and Kendrick had not gotten to his suite until midnight. He stripped to his cotton underclothing, sat on the bed, and lit a thin cigar. He normally enjoyed a good

Cuban smoke, but not this evening. He was too tense to fall asleep so there was no danger of fire from smoking in bed.

He heard a noise and watched as the doorknob turned and the door opened. To his astonishment, Juana entered. She was wearing a long nightgown and carried what looked like a robe over her right arm.

She stood a few feet in front of him and dropped the robe from over her arm. She had a derringer in her hand.

"My husband commanded me to come here and submit to you. If I don't, he will beat me. The servants have seen me enter your room and will believe that you and I will have done what he wished."

This is incredible, Kendrick thought. "You don't have to worry about me, Juana. I would never hurt you or take you against your will."

She blinked and nodded. "I'd like to believe you, but I don't. Gilberto has been cruel and brutal, but he's never done anything like this before. I think he has been slipping further into madness each day. Regardless, if you try to force me, I will kill you."

"No, you wouldn't."

"And why not?"

He noticed that her hand was shaking. "You didn't cock the pistol."

She looked bewildered. "What?"

"With that model, you have to cock the hammer to make it fire. Are you even certain it's loaded?"

Her jaw dropped. He reached over and took the derringer from her unprotesting hand. She hadn't cocked it, but it was loaded. He removed the bullet and handed the pistol back to her.

"If you'd like, you may hit me over the head with it. However, you will have no reason to."

Juana smiled wanly and sat down in a chair across the room. "In truth, I was never too worried. Some of Gilberto's friends are as monstrous as he, but you did not strike me as one of them. Now, however, I must stay here long enough for the two women who spy for him to be satisfied that we have consummated his command. Someday I think I will delight in having those two shrews whipped within an inch of their lives, but that would mean I would sink to his level."

"Would he really beat you?"

Juana shrugged. "He has in the past. Nothing serious, just a few slaps and punches to places where the bruises won't show. He's a very cruel person who has had people who offended him whipped and mutilated, especially the peasants. Some he's even had killed. He will do nothing like that to me. My uncle is a bishop here in Havana and Gilberto fears for his immortal soul in his own strange way."

Kendrick knew many men who beat their wives. It was quite common, although, as a bachelor, he didn't know how to judge someone who did. He was no saint, but he had never struck a woman and couldn't imagine circumstances where he would. Self-defense, of course, was another matter and a woman with a pistol was a clear threat. He was glad that Juana was so inept with guns.

"How can I help you, Juana?"

She smiled again and this time it was with a measure of warmth. "Since we are going to be together for a while, you might get me one of those cigarillos."

◆　　　◆　　　◆

President Custer read the latest intelligence estimates and was appalled. "Are you telling me that as of only a few years ago, the Spanish had a quarter of a million soldiers in Cuba? Dear God, I didn't think they had a fifth of that."

Secretary of War Robert Todd Lincoln was equally dismayed. "This information only came to light recently. The large numbers of Spanish soldiers was a result of their long war against Cuban insurgents. We have no idea how many of them remain. We do know, however, that significant reinforcements have landed and that others are en route."

Lieutenant General Phil Sheridan shifted his bulk in a chair that was far too small for him. "These are only numbers, General Custer. What they don't say is how well trained, equipped, or led the Spanish army is. It is also very likely that many of their soldiers are Cuban militia of dubious quality."

"There are still far too many of them. Dear God, what have I gotten us into?"

"This is the war you wanted," Sheridan said, stifling a laugh. "However, there is some good news. Many of the Spanish troops are not in the Havana area. We estimate there are about fifty thousand in and around Santiago, with other sizeable garrisons protecting other cities from the rebels. That and the sheer size of Cuba means that the Spanish will not be able to easily reinforce Havana, although they will doubtless try once we land and commit ourselves. We will always be outnumbered, but we should be able to outfight them, even though they will be based in a heavily fortified city."

Custer wiped his brow. He was sweating profusely. "What will the Spanish do when we land?"

Lincoln was about to respond, but Sheridan beat him to it. "General Valeriano Weyler commands the troops around Havana. He is a young, fiery, aggressive and cruel commander. He will attack as soon as he can and will attempt to drive us into the sea around Matanzas. He will not permit his army to become a punching bag for us to wear down and destroy."

Custer stood and paced his office. "When will we attack?"

"It's somewhat up to the Navy, but their plans say there will be no more than two weeks before embarking. It will also take a good week to steam to Matanzas. Then figure another week to disembark the troops, unload supplies, and get organized."

"That's too long," Custer said in a whisper.

"We could call it off," Lincoln said hopefully, "and give negotiations another chance."

"No, damn it! We'd look like bloody fools. We have to fight them and beat them. We must have this war and we must take Cuba. Just as Blaine says, our country's future as a great power depends on it. We can't back off and let a third-rate pissant country like Spain humiliate us. I don't like what I've heard, but I have to accept the reality of the situation."

"It doesn't matter how the Spanish split their forces, our boys will still be outnumbered many times over," said Sheridan. "We haven't been able to enlist anywhere near the number of men we thought we'd need. You could be looking at a bloodbath if things don't work out."

"All the more reason I should be in command," Custer snapped. "It's going to take a brave and resource-ful commander to lead the Army to victory and I'm not certain Nelson Miles is that man."

Sheridan laughed. "Then replace him with Hancock, but you cannot leave this country and remain president."

Custer bristled. "Winfield Scott Hancock can go straight to fucking hell. He will never command a thing while I am president."

Custer rose and stormed out of the room. He went directly up to his personal quarters to find that Libbie had beaten him there. She had been in an adjacent room and been listening to every word through a speaking tube held against the wall.

"Libbie, they want to destroy me," he said as he pounded his fist on a dresser.

"Of course they do," she said calmly. "Jealousy from insignificant others is the fate of all great men." She sat down on a couch and he sat beside her. She smiled and pulled his head down to her lap where he could rest against her bosom.

"You will win, George. You will prevail against both Spain and the small minds who conspire against you. They can never stop us."

Two nights later, Kendrick and Juana had a glass of brandy and another cigarillo in his room. As before, she was dressed in a nightgown while he had discreetly put a robe over his underclothing. This time their meeting was far more cordial—she did not bring a pistol. It was a point they both found amusing. Salazar was still looking for rebels and would be gone for at least a week longer.

"What are you going to write about my husband?"

"The truth. I'm a reporter and I like to do that as often as possible."

"Will you say that he is a monstrous maniac?"

"If that's the truth, yes, and I am investigating that possibility. My readers in America are fascinated by the type of person who would massacre the innocent men on the *Eldorado* and feel no qualms." When she started to respond, he hushed her with a wave of his hand. "I know that Spain considers them to have been criminals and pirates, but they deserved a trial. Perhaps some or all could have been sentenced to jail and not executed. That would have been justice in accordance with established law. What your husband did was nothing short of murder. As a result of your husband's actions, we now have a war between our two countries and people wonder why he did what he did."

She took a deep drag of her cigarillo. "I could tell you but you would never print it."

"Try me."

"All right," she said with a sigh. "Gilberto Salazar is not a truly brave man. He is inadequate and a coward with women and a man who hides those inadequacies with brutal acts. He's never been in a real battle, only skirmishes with runaway slaves. He fears that he will fail in front of others in the event of a real fight. On a different level, he has never consummated our marriage, although he did try at first. For some reason, he's afraid of me; perhaps he's unable to perform with all women."

Kendrick was shocked by her blunt admission. "Jesus. You're right, though. I have no idea how my publishers would ever print this. Juana, are you telling me you're still a virgin after being married to him for *how* long?"

"Ten years, and my so-called virginity is highly debatable. He did try for the first few months, but it turned out that his sword is small, blunt, and not made of good metal."

Kendrick didn't even try to stifle a grin, "But what about Helga?"

"Oh, I'm sure she satisfies him, but not in a way that I ever would with him. Besides, she's more of an ornament than a true mistress. Now do you see why I am so bitter? I've wasted my youth on that fool just like he's wasting his time trying to save Spain's presence in a land that doesn't want her. I cut my hair short because he likes it long and I keep myself thin because he wants his women more robust. It pleases me to anger him and everything he stands for."

"Are you saying that you are a rebel?"

Juana smiled and this time it lit up her thin face. "Yes, and I'm proud of it. Since it's widely assumed that you are a spy as well as a reporter, I propose to show you everything I can about Spain's strengths and weaknesses around Havana. To help accomplish that, I propose we go riding around in Gilberto's carriage and let you see everything."

"That would be marvelous for several reasons, so, yes, I accept your kind offer."

"Good. And I hope you have plans to leave this place before the war actually starts."

"When I decided to come here, I believe I had two choices. One was to stay and write a journal about the war and publish it later. The second was to get out of here as soon as it became dangerous. I'm no coward, but I do think leaving discreetly is the best option and, yes, I do have plans to do so."

"Excellent."

"But what will happen to you, Juana?"

She rose and walked to the doorway. "I can protect myself, although the next time I need to I'll have the pistol cocked."

"Morituri te salutant," whispered Sarah as they joined the gaily dressed throng swarming into the White House.

"I am not a gladiator and this is not Rome," Ryder said with a smile. "However, if you like, I will go up to General Custer and tell him that we who are about to die salute you."

She playfully tapped him on the arm with her fan. "I keep forgetting you're partly civilized."

The invitation to the White House had come as a surprise. The Custers had decided to invite just about anybody in Congress and the government and all military personnel of significant rank to attend what was a grand going-away party. As commander of a regiment, Ryder qualified on the low end of the list of important people. He mentioned to Sarah that he thought it might be similar to the ball held by the British before they marched out to fight Napoleon at Waterloo. At least that battle ended well for the Brits, he thought. How would this coming campaign fare for the United States?

This was the first time inside the White House for either of them and each was dressed for the occasion. Sarah wore a gown of deep green that exposed her bare pink shoulders. The cut of the gown emphasized her trim figure and very slender waist. Ryder wore a dress blue uniform and, since he felt that many were staring at Sarah, thought that he was fairly inconspicuous. There were scores of colonels present and a fair number of generals, including Sheridan and Miles. His divisional commander, General Terry, looked exhausted and older than his actual late fifties and Ryder wondered if he was up to the coming task.

If there had been a receiving line to see the president, it had disintegrated into chaos. Thus, he was surprised when Libbie Custer stood smiling in front of them.

"It's good to see you, Colonel. I believe the last time was somewhere near the Little Big Horn and I was thanking you for saving George's life."

Ryder remembered no such incident. He'd seen her at a distance before the wounded Custer was evacuated. He did not contradict her. He introduced Sarah to her and they chatted politely for a few seconds before Libbie wandered off.

"I can see why men fall in love with her," Sarah said. "She is exquisitely lovely and has a splendid figure. That and she has a wry smile that is quite engaging. And to think she's forty years old. Goodness," she giggled, "am I ever being cattish and spiteful?"

"But did you notice her eyes? They were evaluating you, Sarah."

"For what, I wonder?"

"Because I'm one of a diminishing number who know that Custer nearly destroyed the Seventh Cavalry and that it was not his brilliant idea that had me there with the machine guns. I think she wonders if you too are a potential threat to her husband."

Sarah was about to respond when the subject of their discussion suddenly appeared before them. "Colonel

Ryder," Custer said genially. His eyes were red and his face was flushed. The president had been drinking. "I envy you and everyone who is going with you to Cuba. The old ladies in the government insist that the United States cannot get along without my presence here in Washington. Utter nonsense if you ask me."

Ryder introduced Custer to Sarah. The president bowed deeply and made an obvious attempt to look down the front of her dress. She flushed and smiled tightly. She thought about saying to Custer that there was more than a touch of gray in his once golden hair, but decided against it. She noted that Martin was grim and angry so she squeezed his arm tightly. He got the message and turned away. Punching the President of the United States in the mouth while in the White House was not a good career move even if the man was being a boor.

Custer reiterated his desire to join in the invasion of Cuba and wandered off. "Is he always like that?" she asked.

"Obnoxious and crude? Only when he's awake. It's the first time I've seen him in years and he never used to drink the way I hear he does now. Perhaps power has changed him, or even frustrated him. It's rumored that Libbie generally does a lot of his thinking for him. That's probably only partly true. The man is impetuous and reckless, not stupid."

She steered him outside where it was cooler. And safer for Martin's career. It would not have done for Martin to have made a scene in front of several hundred of the most powerful people in the country.

"Would you like me to do your thinking for you, Martin?"

"No, and I don't want to do yours, although I would definitely want your advice."

"As I would yours. Now tell me why you never grew a beard like so many of those very important people have?"

He grinned at the memories. "First, I did try on several occasions, but the thing always came in scraggly. Frankly, I'm very glad that having a great bushy beard is going out of fashion. But why?"

She smiled sweetly. "Because I'm thinking of letting you kiss me tonight, and I'm glad your beard won't scratch my face."

"Then that makes two of us."

Sarah was glad it was dark out so Martin couldn't see her face suddenly turn red. She had just recalled what her good friend Ruth had said about men's beards itching and scratching. When Sarah had mentioned the harsh feel of whiskers on her cheeks, Ruth had said, "Oh no, I'm talking about my thighs."

The open carriage wound its way through the streets of Havana and out into the countryside. A trusted servant of Juana's drove while she and Kendrick sat in comfort and talked quietly. Juana held a parasol, which she used to try and shield both of them from both the sun and the prying and angry eyes of the Cuban people.

Kendrick was astonished at the large number of Spanish soldiers and sailors wandering around the town. Outside of Havana proper, hundreds of civilian workers were digging trenches and building up fortifications. Even though he considered himself a novice when it came to military matters, it was apparent that any attempt to storm Havana could result in a bloody catastrophe.

On the positive side, the soldiers and sailors he did see were, for the most part, slovenly and seemed uninterested in the possibility of the coming fighting. Of course, they might react differently when the shooting started and their lives were in danger.

Nor were the officers any better. Many of them appeared to be dandies and fops. Some were nothing more than boys. He decided that Spain had superiority in numbers, but not in the quality of her troops. He would send a coded message to that effect to Washington. Of course, even poor soldiers might fight well from behind the protection of a defensive wall or the security of a trench.

Juana read his mind. "What will you tell them?"

"As I said before, the truth is often useful. I still think it's incredible that Spain hasn't shut down the telegraph lines running from Havana to other countries, and that includes the U.S. They appear oblivious to the fact that most of the Western Union workers are American. They seem to think that modern technology is irrelevant. Of course, if they do shut it down, they would have no way of communicating with Madrid. It's an incredible dilemma for them."

They continued on their ride and she showed him one of several large prison camps. "General Weyler has organized these atrocities. If he feels that the locals are not trustworthy or have harbored guerillas, he's had entire villages uprooted and the people sent to these camps where they are poorly fed, inadequately housed, and abused. People are dying by the hundreds and Spain doesn't care. Spain should not be in charge of any country."

A wooden stockade surrounded the camp. Inside were at least a thousand men, women, and children. All were jammed together tightly. Most had dark skins, but a number were lighter. All of them were dressed in rags and were filthy and thin to the point of emaciation. Many bore bruises and those that they could see through the walls of the stockade looked at Juana and Kendrick with eyes that were filled with hatred.

"I guess they don't realize we're on their side," Kendrick said.

"Are we?" Juana asked. "What have we done for them? General Weyler calls these places 'concentration camps,' because he has concentrated all of these so-called enemies together where they can be watched. While here, they are given minimal rations, no water for cleaning, and the more attractive women are either abused or allowed to sell themselves for additional food. This and other places like it are nothing but hell."

"I'll write about it."

"You might want to add that many of these imprisoned souls are recently freed slaves who have traded one form of bondage for another."

Kendrick simply nodded. What was happening to so-called free slaves in Cuba wasn't all that different from what was happening to freed slaves in the United States. With Reconstruction over, the Negro was being pushed farther and farther down the economic ladder, particularly in the South. Perhaps his editors wouldn't like reading such an interpretation. He would be discreet and write about the camps, but not that they were filled with freed slaves.

Juana came to him again that night. She walked to an open window and looked up at the stars. "Gilberto

will be back tomorrow evening. I strongly urge you
to be far from here when he arrives."

"I thought I was his guest," he said jokingly. She was
again wearing the long and shapeless cotton nightgown.

"I have people keeping an eye on him and they say
he is furious that he hasn't caught the rebels who killed
his men. At some point he will recall that he sent me
to you and realize that his honor has been insulted and
he will feel compelled to take action. It won't matter
that he was the one who suggested it. It's contradictory
and doesn't make sense, but that is the way he thinks.
He is often far from logical or rational."

"Then I can't leave you. He'll hurt you."

Juana laughed. "No he won't. I told you he's afraid
of me and my family. He'll scream and rage and then
ignore me, which I find quite acceptable." She reached
out and patted his cheek. She didn't tell him that he
would likely slap her and even punch her. He didn't
need to know that. "Don't worry, I'll be fine. And
when you leave you'll go with one of my men and
a companion of his who arrived a day ago and has
been living in the servants' quarters."

She stood and walked to the window. The nightgown fabric was light and he could see the outline
of her thin body through the moonlight. She caught
him watching.

"Am I that ugly, James?"

He took a deep breath. "No, my lady, far from it."

His initial impressions of her as a stern and plain
woman had long since disappeared. She was a classic case of the more he got to know her, the more
attractive she became. He thought it amusing since
he generally liked his women a little on the plump

side and a whole lot more bosomy. Juana had small breasts at best.

"Well then, he sent me here so that I would be punished and humiliated by having sex with you and that hasn't happened. Nor has he been cuckolded. Yet."

Juana carefully and slowly unbuttoned the front of her nightgown and gracefully stepped out of it. "You are absolutely lovely," Kendrick whispered. She smiled and blew out the one candle that had been illuminating the room.

He was sitting on the edge of the bed. He started to rise but she pushed him back down. She took his head and held it to her breasts. "First things first," she said. "We have all night, so we will take all night. You will now kiss my breasts lovingly and slowly like I've always wanted and imagined and then we will move on to other things."

He wrapped his arms around her and squeezed her so tightly she gasped. "My dear Juana, I exist to please you," he said and realized that he meant it.

Clarissa Harlow Barton was in her early sixties. Better known as Clara Barton, she had recently founded the American Red Cross. She had tended the sick and wounded in the Civil War and seen the results of the most horrific fighting. She'd also come under fire and nearly been killed. After the war, she'd traveled to Europe and helped during the Franco-Prussian War. To Sarah, she gave the immediate impression that she was a stern and demanding taskmistress.

The unmarried Clara Barton was in Baltimore to oversee the shipment of medical supplies to the south when the army finally embarked for Cuba.

"You and your friend will not be permitted to serve on the battlefield," she said sternly.

"May I ask why not?" Sarah enquired. "I have experience with terrible wounds. My father is a doctor and I assisted him on many occasions. I've seen men bleeding and mangled from wounds and injuries and, yes, even shot. I did not flinch then and will not in the future. Not that it matters, but I've also assisted in childbirth, and I've even watched as people died.

"And as to my friend, Ruth Holden spent many months as a volunteer nurse in Paris during the terrible fighting. If anything, she has far more experience than I do."

"Who is he?" Barton asked.

Sarah was perplexed. "Who?"

Barton smiled slightly. "The man you wish to follow, that's who."

"Am I that obvious? I guess I am. His name is Martin Ryder and he commands the First Maryland Volunteers."

Barton shuffled through papers on her desk until she found the one she wanted. "According to this, your young colonel is highly regarded by his superiors, his peers and his men. His men are well disciplined and well behaved. I understand that he is concerned about their hygiene. The next time you see him tell him to make sure his medical personnel keep themselves and their tools as clean as possible."

"He will be leaving in a couple of days. When I see him next, I will tell him what you said." Of course it would be in between desperate and passionate kisses.

Barton nodded. "As to you and your friends, you will accompany us to Jacksonville and, if circumstances warrant, perhaps down to the Florida Keys. We will be going by train to Charleston, which is as far south as decent rail lines go. There is a narrow gauge track running from Charleston to Jacksonville, and if possible we will use that. It's a shame that the Confederate railroad tracks were so miserable during the war and that there have been only minimal improvements since then."

It was common knowledge that the U.S. government was trying to widen the gauge and extend the line south to Daytona, but that was not going to happen overnight. There was resistance on the part of the railroad lines to building farther south since there was little in the way of civilization and customers in that direction.

Sarah nodded politely. She was delighted that the redoubtable Clara Barton was going to let her at least go to Jacksonville. Once there she and the others could prove their worth, and, if the war lasted as long as some people thought it would, she was confident that hospitals would be established on Cuban soil. It only made sense. Wounded soldiers had to be treated by skilled medical personnel as soon as possible; therefore, they would have to be close to the battlefields. Shipping them to Jacksonville or even the Florida Keys made no sense. She would take one step at a time.

She profusely thanked Miss Barton and left before the woman could change her mind. On the train back to Baltimore, she considered how much her life had changed and how much Martin Ryder now meant to her. The kiss she'd promised him at the White House for not punching President Custer had quickly turned into a number of them and all given joyously and passionately. She found herself worried sick that he might not return from the war or that he might be terribly maimed. She recalled helping her father operate on a man who'd lost his legs in a train accident. That such horrible wounds could happen to Martin as well, would soon be a terrifying reality.

She had not given herself to him nor would she, at least not yet. However, she thought it was time to permit just a few liberties that would let him know just how much she cared for him.

Sarah smiled to herself. One nice thing about being a widow, she thought, was that she now knew so much about what pleased a man.

Maria Vasquez peered through one of the small gaps in the rough wooden stockade that kept her a prisoner. She was twenty-five and a widow. Her husband had been killed by a Spanish firing squad. They thought he'd been a guerilla. He hadn't been but Maria was now. She had worked hard for the revolution, carrying messages and supplies. Even though she never carried a gun, she still could have been executed. It was ironic that she had been condemned to spend God knows how long in the prison camp because she had protested the lack of food that had claimed the life of her small son. Then she had been hungry. Now she was close to starving.

Some of the gaps were wide enough for her to stick her hand through and beg for food. Sometimes she actually got some from sympathetic Cubans. They were careful, though. They didn't want to attract attention and wind up in the camp themselves.

Several priests routinely passed out charity along

with a few civilians. In particular, an old man named
Luis would bring her pieces of cheese and chunks of
stale bread. She could not count on Luis, however.
He was old and scrawny. He would talk to her in a
respectful manner and she loved him for that. He had
a shoe repair shop a mile from the camp. She knew
where it was and he had told her to run to it if she
could ever escape from the hell she was in.

Maria was afraid that she would spend the rest of
her life in the camp. People came in but the only
ones who left were carried out as cadavers. She could
see happy people walking by the camp and a number
of wealthy men and women riding in carriages. She
had never seen a zoo, but she knew what one was.
To the rich Spaniards, she and the others were little
more than animals in a zoo. Somewhere, life was
normal. Just not here.

Luis was not the only man in her life. One of the
guards, a heavyset man named Ramon, had made it
plain to her that she would have a much better life
if only she would become his mistress or at least let
him fuck her every now and then. His comments told
her that she was still reasonably attractive. She was not
light-skinned like a Spaniard or dark like a Negro. She
was somewhere in between and she knew that men
found her color fascinating. As a child she'd asked her
mother whether she was Mexican, Indian, or Negro
and her mother had laughed and said everything.

A lot of the women in the camp had succumbed
to Ramon and other guards. So far, she had not given
in, although every day in the camp made it more
and more difficult. At least what Ramon wanted was
straightforward. There were two other guards who took

great delight in watching the women relieve themselves in the disgusting latrine trenches. She and some of the others shuddered at what they might want to do with a woman.

By telling her he would provide a place of refuge, Luis had given her the germ of an idea. Even though the thought of it disgusted her, she would use Ramon's lust to gain her freedom. She turned away from the stockade and went to her sleeping mat. The old woman who had been sleeping beside her had died during the night, which was a further shame. For the last few days, when the woman had slipped into a coma and death was inevitable, Maria had been using her food ticket. The thought that she was depriving the old woman of a little nutrition disturbed her only a little. The woman was unconscious and dying. Perhaps a doctor could have fed her and saved her, but there were no doctors available.

Maria made up her mind. She walked over to the guard shack. It was by one of the several gates that led to the outside world. Ramon saw her and smiled. She gestured for him to come closer.

"You win," she said. "I want food. You can have me tonight and any other night if you will keep getting me food. And yes, I will do whatever you want, but for you and you alone."

Ramon grinned hugely. "Come into the shack and we'll close the deal."

She smiled, hoping it was warm and seductive. "No. I am not a street whore who will do it standing up in that shack. And I will certainly not do it where people can see. You will find us privacy. I will come tonight when it's dark and you will take me out of this stockade and into the fresh air. Bring a blanket and we will do it on the ground where no one can see us, and you can have me as often and any way you wish."

Before he could answer, she undid the strings on her blouse and exposed her breasts. They were still full enough to make his eyes widen. "All right," he stammered and she almost laughed in his face.

It was dark when she made it to the guard shack. Ramon was waiting and he took her by the arm and through the gate. True to his word, he had found a secluded spot. Another guard, Carlos, was watching to make sure that no officer came and interrupted their fun. She sucked in the clearer air of the world outside the prison. She would not go back to the camp alive.

Ramon turned her and kissed her on the lips. He was aroused and in a rush. "Slowly," she said. "Take off your shirt and kneel on the blanket. You can watch me."

He did as he was told. He had even taken steps to clean up. He didn't smell quite as bad as he normally did. She glanced around for a package of anything resembling food. There was nothing and she was convinced that he was not going to pay her and would even force her to service the other guard, Carlos.

Ramon saw her looking. "Don't worry, Carlos will bring the bag of food when we're done. Now it is your turn."

She forced a smile and again exposed her breasts. She guided his mouth onto them and made pretend sounds of pleasure. She pushed him on his back and climbed on to his chest. "Close your eyes," she said and he complied.

She took the small sand-filled sack from behind her waist. She wished she had a knife, but the sand would have to do. She whipped the sack quickly and smashed it against the side of Ramon's head, just as he opened his eyes to see what was happening. The thud made by the sack's contact with Ramon's skull was sickening. His eyes widened for a second and rolled back into his head. She checked for a pulse. There wasn't one. She had just killed a man and she wanted to throw up, but there wasn't time.

Maria dressed quickly. In a few minutes Carlos would become curious, wondering how soon his turn would come, and check on them. She tucked the sack back in her waistband.

She smiled as thunder rumbled and it started to rain heavily. The sudden shower masked her dash across the road and into the streets of Havana. She ran down the streets to where Luis had his shop. She was about to pound on the door when she saw him looking at her through the glassless window. "It's about time," he said as he let her in.

Maximo Gomez was sick of war. Gomez had been born in the Dominican Republic in 1836. He had been converted to the cause of Cuban independence shortly after his arrival in 1868. Prior to that he had served as an officer in the Spanish Army and was now a major general in the Cuban rebel forces. His unfulfilled goal was to drive the Spanish out of Cuba.

Unless the military situation changed dramatically, this would not happen anytime soon. There was a truce in effect between the Spanish and the rebel governments that was based on mutual exhaustion.

Unless the balance of power changed, nothing decisive would occur.

Gomez greeted his guest at his headquarters outside the city of Camaguay, which was located east of the middle of the island. His guest was Jose Marti, the young firebrand who was considered by many to be the soul of the revolution. Gomez was not so certain. Yes, the well-educated and highly articulate Marti attracted many followers, but they were not always fighters. Marti himself had never been in battle, while Gomez had seen many, perhaps too many. He fully understood the weaknesses of his rebel army. They had few weapons and precious little ammunition. They also lacked discipline. The only weapon they were skilled in was the machete and he'd ordered them to use it as effectively as possible. On several occasions, hordes of Cubans wielding machetes had panicked Spanish regulars, letting the rebels swarm their ranks, hacking and chopping.

"Will the Americans fight for us?" Gomez bluntly asked as he twisted his trade-mark handlebar mustache.

Marti shook his head. "The Americans will fight for themselves. If we are useful, then they will support us. Our friend Cardanzo spoke with their secretary of state and it is his impression that President Custer's government would like to drive Spain out of Cuba and annex it themselves. Their Secretary Blaine hinted at Cuba being the foundation of an overseas American empire."

"Then why should we help them?"

"Custer and Blaine do not necessarily have the support of their Congress in this endeavor. There are many in that body who do not want to acquire any territory outside America's continental boundaries. There was concern when the U.S. bought Alaska from the Russians and that was only fifteen years ago. Nothing has changed. Custer and Blaine have gotten their war and it is likely that they will expel the Spaniards, but it is not certain that they will replace them permanently."

Gomez nodded. "Then you're saying we should fight on the side of the United States and gain their undying gratitude."

"Yes, General. It will definitely strengthen our hand with their Congress if we are perceived as the brave independence fighters. Actually, General, we don't have much of a choice. I do not see us standing aside while two powers fight over Cuba. Nor do I see us fighting for Spain to keep the Americans out. Even if we exchange Spanish sovereignty for American, I do not think it would be for very long. Besides, the Americans would definitely be the more gentle overlords."

Gomez snarled. "I do not want any foreign overlords in Cuba. But you're right. We must be pragmatic. Yes, my forces will ally with the Americans if and when they arrive. May I assume that you will be active in Washington instead of here in Cuba?"

Marti smiled and ignored the implied slur on his lack of military experience. "I will do what I do best and that is to be an advocate for a free Cuba."

◆ Chapter 6 ◆

RYDER GOT HIS MEN UP AND MARCHING ON THE ROAD to the harbor well before dawn. Breakfast was a few swallows of bad coffee and a stale cold biscuit along with plenty of grumbling from the sleepy troops who openly wondered just what the hell was the hurry. It was Ryder's goal to beat the rush to the ships and avoid the chaos that embarking so many men at the same time would entail.

Unfortunately, a number of other regiments had the same idea. Thousands of men converged on the limited number of places where small boats could tie up and send men out to the transports. Instead of trying to use one of the few inadequate docks, Ryder had arranged for the men to wade out to where their three ships' boats had been anchored and guarded, and then to be rowed to the transports. They grumbled some more about getting wet, but their complaints were ignored and all were on board by noon.

Sarah's brother had done an excellent job maintaining

control of the ships assigned to the regiment. A steady stream of boats took his now fifteen hundred men out to the vessels that would carry them to Cuba. They'd be cramped and uncomfortable, but the ships were sturdy and as safe as they could be.

The ship that would carry Ryder was the *Aurora*. She'd been chartered by the Navy, and her skipper and owner was a Baltimore native named Wally Janson. Janson was a stocky middle-aged Swede with thinning white hair. Barnes said he had a reputation as a firm but fair disciplinarian and had done an excellent job of allocating space for men and supplies. Once again, young Major Barnes had done good staff work.

Janson invited Ryder to join him on the cramped bridge. "Colonel, insofar as this regal craft is leased to the Navy, I'm supposed to obey Navy regulations. However, some of them are nonsense. If you want to come up here, you don't have to ask permission. Just try not to break anything and definitely don't spit on the deck."

"Much appreciated," said Ryder who found everything on the ship fascinating.

"Are you going to spend the night on board or are you going ashore to make goodbyes?"

Martin grinned. "Ashore sounds like a wonderful idea. Obviously, this armada isn't going anywhere tonight and rank does have its privileges. However, if everyone can't sleep ashore then I won't either. I will go ashore for a few hours but will be back well before midnight."

"You going to say hello to Custer? I understand he's going to be at Fortress Monroe and will wave bye-bye to the ships as they pass."

"I'll let you have that honor, Captain Janson."

As they talked, rioting had broken out as some of the later arriving units tried to bull their way onto ships that had been assigned to others. Several soldiers had been either been pushed or thrown into the Chesapeake. Ryder was certain that not all of them had been pulled out. What a hell of a way to start a war, he thought.

Protected by armed soldiers, the *Aurora's* boat took Ryder back to shore and he walked the couple of miles to the hotel where Sarah and Ruth had rooms.

Sarah met him in her suite. Ruth was there as chaperone, something that both thought was silly considering that they were all adults and that the women were widows. Sarah greeted him sedately but her smile was warm and her eyes were moist. "I don't want you to go. This is just beginning for us and I don't want it interrupted."

"I think I'll go for a walk," Ruth said with a knowing grin. "Don't do anything too terribly foolish," she added as she left.

In an instant they were in each other's arms and kissing passionately. She could feel him aroused against her and smiled to herself. She recalled the first time she had realized what effect she was having on her husband and how confused she'd felt by both his and her reactions.

"I'm tired of being a good girl," she said as she pushed him down onto the couch. "Tonight, I would like to be just a little scandalous."

Ryder grinned as he pulled her down on his lap. "Fine by me," he whispered in her ear as he slid his hand beneath her dress and up her leg. She gasped with pleasure as he found a tantalizingly bare spot.

◆   ◆   ◆

Spanish generals Weyler and Villate looked up as Major Gilberto Salazar entered their office in Havana's ancient and gloomy Morro Castle. Villate commanded all of Cuba while the younger Weyler was in charge of the army and the defenses of Havana.

"We have read your report," Weyler said after returning Salazar's crisp salute, "and, while it is interesting, we cannot necessarily agree with your conclusions. Yes, the Americans may land near Matanzas, but they may also land at a hundred other spots along the very long Cuban coast."

"Three of my men were killed at Matanzas," Salazar said stiffly. "That must count for something."

Villate, much larger and older, sighed. "Cuba is again in a state of turmoil. Rebels are attacking isolated posts everywhere. It is entirely possible that this is what happened to your men and that it has nothing to do with the Americans. Neither you nor your men are popular with the population. In fact, they hate you. It's possible that they were merely targets of opportunity and do not imply the likelihood of an American landing."

"Sir, under intense interrogation several people said they witnessed an American in the area."

Weyler shrugged. "We don't doubt that the Americans are checking out a number of places as landing spots. We also don't doubt that your methods of interrogating people would result in them admitting to murdering their own mothers and eating the remains in order to stop the agony. There might have been an American or two around, and they might have killed your men, but that does not necessarily mean that the Yankees plan on attacking us at Matanzas."

Villate concurred. "Cuba is an island almost seven hundred and fifty miles long. Its coastline is more than double that and is impossible to defend. The Americans can land anywhere they choose; therefore, we must keep our soldiers close to Havana, where they can respond to the invasion when it occurs. We can rule out nothing, not even Santiago, which is five hundred miles away. We have nearly fifty thousand men at Santiago, which means that they are effectively out of any coming campaign for Havana. Yet, if we draw them closer to Havana, the rebels under Gomez will seize Santiago. And yes, the Americans can land there, take the damn place, and force us to either negotiate a treaty or send an army five hundred miles to liberate it."

"The Americans will not land at Santiago," Salazar said, barely controlling his anger. "Their President Custer is an impetuous fool who will attack where we are strong in order to go for the jugular and end this war quickly and gloriously. Just consider what he did when he nearly got killed by the Indians."

"We agree with your assessment of Custer," Weyler said with a laugh, but quickly turned solemn. "And that is why we have nearly a hundred thousand men in the Havana area. As you know, however, our soldiers are far from the best. They are poorly trained and equipped and very far from home. To counter that, when the Americans land we will attack them with overwhelming strength. If we win, the Yankees will either surrender or withdraw. If we lose, we will pull back to Havana and make them dig us out."

Salazar did not like what he was hearing. What was happening to the glory that was Spain? "And what will our navy be doing during all of this?"

"Not much of anything, I'm afraid," said Villate. "Even though we are reasonably certain that the American transports have left port and are on their way, we will wait for proof. Sadly, it turns out that our two so-called battleships are inferior to any of the three armored cruisers that the Americans bought from the British. It is rumored that the American ships have also bought the new Armstrong breech-loading cannons from the British. Therefore, the Navy will avoid battle until the last moment. Worse, the Navy doesn't know what to protect, either. Nor can they send our small fleet out to intercept them. The ocean is too vast and they could easily miss the American ships. They too will wait for the Americans to arrive and then help us dislodge them."

"What about the French?" Salazar asked. "Weren't they going to help us by providing us with ships?"

"They were," said Villate, "but the French are too busy being French. They are equivocating and will likely not sell us anything until the war is over."

Salazar was aghast. What was he hearing? "Sirs, are you implying that we will lose this war?"

Villate shrugged. "Who knows what might happen when armies actually start fighting, so, yes, we might lose this war. And before you argue that premise, let me remind you that there are many who blame your impetuous actions for causing it in the first place. There are those both here and in Madrid who would have shipped you to the United States to be tried by them if their request for your extradition hadn't been such an arrogant demand. If it is forced upon us as a condition of ending a war that is unfavorable to Spain, we will happily trade you for peace.

"Therefore," Villate continued, "I strongly suggest that, if we are not victorious, you manage to get yourself killed in battle. If that happens, we will put up an appropriate statue celebrating your heroism." That last comment was said with a sneer. Salazar's ability to avoid battle was a strong rumor.

Weyler stood and walked to a large map of Cuba that had been pinned to a wall. "We will concede the point that Matanzas is an attractive and likely target, Major. We will assign two regiments of militia to support you. Along with your existing unit, you will have two thousand men. Do not promote yourself. You will still be a major although you will command what amounts to a brigade. You will take charge of defending Matanzas. You will not have enough men to stop an invasion, but we hope you can at least slow them down."

"I will do more than that," Salazar said fervently. "I will kill them."

For the first several days, the trip from the Chesapeake and down the Atlantic coast had been pleasant. Even though most of the soldiers had never been out to sea and the majority of them had gotten seasick, the nausea passed fairly quickly.

But then came the storm. It appeared as a line of black clouds on the horizon that crept inexorably and threateningly towards them. As it overwhelmed the host of transports, the waves became choppy and intense and the ship seemed to vibrate from the impacts. Captain Janson quickly ordered everyone not involved in working the ship to go below where there was relative safety from the threat of being swept overboard.

As the wind-whipped seas attacked the *Aurora*, everyone again became ill. Ryder had hoped to be able to control his heaving stomach, but he lost. He made it to his cramped quarters and vomited into a bucket. The stench of hundreds of others doing that same thing made him even more nauseous. Soon, the transport was wallowing in the vomit of hundreds of men. Worse, Ryder quickly realized there was no place to empty the damn bucket.

Somehow it became night and still the storm lashed at them. Finally and just about dawn, he felt the winds slackening. A sailor looked in on Ryder and barely stifled a grin. The bucket had spilled and there was caked vomit on his uniform. Had the sailor laughed, Ryder was certain he would have killed him. If he'd been able to stand up, that is.

"Colonel, the skipper wants you on deck."

Ryder groaned. "Tell him I'd like to be buried on land and not at sea, or is there something else he'd like to discuss."

Now the sailor did grin, but shut it down quickly. "Sir, he thinks there's a Spanish gunboat bearing down on us."

On deck, the seas were still heavy but it no longer mattered. Any stomach problems quickly disappeared when Ryder saw the small but lethal-looking vessel heading in their direction. The invasion fleet had been scattered by the storm and only a few ships were visible, and none of them were American warships. They were sheep without a shepherd.

Janson handed over his telescope. "I did some study-ing of Spanish ships after signing on with the Navy, and

I've also been to Havana on a few occasions. The Spanish have a number of gunboats like the one bearing down on us and they're designed to intercept smugglers. They're not very large, maybe sixty feet, and they have a crew of about thirty. Most of them carry four small cannons, two on each side, along with some swivel guns that are murderous at close range. They have very limited coal capacity so that means we must be fairly close to Cuba. Either that or those bastards were using their sails to conserve fuel. Oh yes, they can do at least a couple of knots faster than we can."

Ryder returned the telescope. "What do you suggest?"

"Barring a miracle, Colonel, we cannot outrun them, although we will continue to flee with the hope that one of our missing escorts will discover us. Realistically, we have but two choices. We can surrender or we can fight."

Ryder idly reached for his sidearm, then remembered it was still in his small cabin. "What's your preference?"

"This ship is my livelihood and the crew are my friends, at least most of them. If we surrender, the ship is forfeit and we will be put in prison for God knows how long, doubtless until the end of the war and that could be years. Hell, they might even ship us to Spain for the Inquisition to play with. They say it doesn't exist anymore, but I don't quite believe it. I've always wanted to be taller, but not because of the rack. And I sure as hell don't want to be burned at the stake."

"Damn it, Skipper, that's if they don't kill us outright like they did the men of the *Eldorado*," snapped a sailor who'd been standing close by.

"A good point," said Janson, "In fact, that Spaniard coming at us might just be the one who butchered those boys."

"That leaves fighting," said Ryder. "I have more than four hundred men wondering what we're going to do and there is a Gatling gun in the hold. May I suggest bringing it on deck and then use your men's skills to tie it down so we can swing it from one side of the ship to the other? I will also bring up about fifty of my best shots and have them ready as well."

Janson laughed. "You didn't look like the type who surrendered easily."

It took the better part of an hour to haul the gun on deck, secure it, and cover it with a tarpaulin. Shooters were given rifles and assigned spots on the deck. Until the Spaniard came close enough, they were to remain hidden.

"I've never seen a Gatling," Janson said.

"The Navy has a number of them. We use them to repel potential boarders. The Army has a small number but hasn't quite figured out how to use them. The French and Germans have their own variants and used them to slaughter each other in their last war."

The enemy gunboat was much closer than before. Ryder didn't need a telescope to make out the men lining her hull. If his ideas didn't work, he and his soldiers could be slaughtered.

"Captain, what guns do they have?"

"Like I said, they have four cannons, six- or nine-pounders, and they are likely very old. However, they are better than what we have, which is nothing. I don't believe they have a bow-chaser, which means they'll have to come alongside to use their guns."

"What's their range?"

"On a good day, maybe a mile, mile and a half. But they're riding low in the water so their effective range will be much less than that. Add to that the fact that the seas are still running and that the Spaniards are notoriously bad shooters, they'll have to get really close to stand a chance of hitting us."

Ryder felt a twinge of hope. Maybe this could be pulled off after all. Slowly but surely, the gunboat continued to gain on them. A puff of smoke erupted from her bow. "Just a signal gun, Colonel. He wants us to heave to. I suggest we ignore him."

The gunboat was a half mile of her port side when it finally ran parallel to the *Aurora*. The two gunports were open and the guns were run out. Janson looked through his telescope and shook his head. "I think those cannons were with the original Armada," he sniffed.

One of the guns fired, and the shell splashed in front of them and short. A moment later and the second gun fired. The shell hit just in front of their bow, showering them with water.

"Shit," said Janson, "they're either better than I thought or they're damn lucky."

The gunboat closed the range until they were only a couple of hundred yards away. The guns fired again and one shell smashed into the *Aurora*'s wooden hull. They could hear cries and screams from below. Ryder hoped they were screams of fear and not pain.

"Now!" yelled Ryder. Soldiers whipped the tarp off the Gatling while others raised up to fire their rifles. "Gatling crew," he reminded them, "sweep the deck and bridge. Riflemen, aim for the gunports and keep firing into them. It doesn't matter if you can see anyone or not. Just keep shooting."

Noise and smoke wreathed the *Aurora* as the Americans blazed away. It was hard to see what effect the shooting was having on the smaller Spanish boat, but it did look like she was pulling away and starting to wallow. White smoke came from her engine and she began to slow down. Better, it looked like no one was controlling her.

Janson was astonished. "Jesus, Colonel, I think we actually may have hurt the bastard."

He had no sooner said that when the gunboat blew up before their eyes. Parts of the gunboat along with bodies flew through the air. In only a few seconds the sea was clear. All that remained was debris and a few heads bobbing in the water.

Janson ordered the *Aurora* about to pick up survivors. They found five, but two died of their wounds within minutes. One of the survivors was the captain, who was pathetically grateful to be saved.

Janson grabbed Ryder's arm. "Look over there. Another ship and this time it's one of ours." It was the Navy's steam sloop *Powhatan*. "About time they showed up. Now let's get to Cuba before something else goes wrong."

"Good God, Haney, what the hell are you doing here?"

Diego Valdez looked confused while Haney laughed. "I might ask the same thing about you, Kendrick. What the hell are you doing in Havana?"

"At this point, Sergeant, it's been sincerely recommended that I depart before getting shot or hanged. I was told to come to this barn and that I'd meet two men who'd take me to where I would meet up with the American invasion force. If you're not aware, we're in a barn on the estate of one Gilberto Salazar, and he's the son-of-a-bitching prick who murdered the men on the *Eldorado*."

"Jesus, Kendrick, you do hang around with good company."

At that moment, Juana entered the barn. She had heard the comments. "When you are through with this pleasant reunion, may I suggest you take the horses you are going to pretend to steal and ride as far away from here as possible? Gilberto the prick, as you call him, is now in Havana and closeted with generals Weyler and Villate and will be home fairly soon along with several men of his guard. He will not get what he wishes from the generals, so he will be in an even fouler temper than usual. He will not hurt me," at least not very much, she thought, "but he would possibly kill any or all of you. He would take great pleasure in making your deaths take an eternity. So for God's sake, hurry."

Juana wheeled and returned to the main house. Kendrick thought she might have been crying. "Skinny, nasty thing, isn't she?" Haney commented.

"She's a lot better than that," Kendrick said. Haney caught the wistful look in the other man's eyes and smiled to himself. He thought he understood. Kendrick clearly had feelings for the hard-looking woman. Maybe she was more than she seemed.

"You want me to kill her husband?" Haney asked.

Kendrick was shocked at the thought—and at his reaction. Yes, it would be lovely if Gilberto Salazar somehow found himself dead. "Not today," he said as he reluctantly declined the offer. But maybe some nice sunny day in the future, he thought.

Valdez brought out three saddled horses. Haney

examined them and said they were superb mounts. "Señor Salazar has only the best," Valdez said with mock solemnity.

They mounted and rode away. It was fifty miles to Matanzas and the roads were poor. It would take them at least a day, maybe more if they had to evade Spanish patrols.

"We will ride slowly and carefully," said Valdez. "Haste will attract attention and we do not want that. I will ride behind you as befits a loyal and faithful ignorant Cuban servant. Once away from the city, I will try to make contact with my people. Sergeant Haney, I assume that you want to go back to Matanzas, where I picked you up."

Haney smiled. It was good to be back on a horse, particularly a superb one. Only steal the best, he thought, and then wondered if it actually was stealing since the angry woman had told them to take the horses.

"Matanzas it is, Diego. Just try not to kill anyone on the way."

The storm that had scattered the American transports and warships made it impossible for a coordinated landing to occur at Matanzas. The chaotic situation confronted the American command with a dilemma. If they waited offshore for the rest of the ships to arrive, there was the real possibility that the Spanish army would appear in force and the landing be bloodily repulsed. Go in too soon and the American army might be defeated in detail before if got organized.

What forced the decision was the fact that the Spanish navy was out there someplace. Nobody was certain whether their two battleships had left Havana or not. Nobody wanted Spanish wolves in among the helpless transports, and there was less than total confidence that the escorts could defeat the enemy before they inflicted severe casualties among the heavily laden transports. The U.S. Army would, therefore, land everything it had as quickly as it could and hope the rest of the ships showed up soon.

As the *Aurora* eased its way into the crowded bay and anchored, Janson took in the scene and smiled grimly. "We were damned lucky, you know. One shell in the right place and we would have had a hold full of dead and wounded."

Ryder agreed. How could he not? The one Spanish shell that had penetrated the *Aurora* had injured four soldiers but only one of them seriously. Most of the screaming and hollering had come from men who were shut up in a dark and nearly airless hold. They'd been scared out of their wits and panicked.

Janson continued. "Just like the Spanish gunboat, we're a wooden ship and a fire could have started that would have killed a lot of people. I made a comment about surrendering and being taken to Havana, but it later occurred to me that the Spaniards might have thought it expedient to sink the ship. In that case, almost all of us would have drowned."

Ryder hadn't thought of it that way. "Obviously you're telling me we didn't have enough lifeboats."

"Who does? Even ships carrying a large number of passengers don't have anywhere near enough lifeboats, and until just recently, the *Aurora* didn't carry passengers. The *Aurora* has enough for her crew and that's all. No matter what I would have tried, most of your men would have drowned."

With most of his men disembarked and the ship in a safe anchorage, Ryder had himself rowed to shore. It took a while to find anything resembling a headquarters, but he finally located General Terry who, as usual, looked overwhelmed and distraught.

"About time you got here, Colonel, although I should first congratulate you on destroying that Spanish ship. Excellent job. Lord only knows how many of our men you saved. You and Captain Janson will get medals and commendations. The word's going around the beach and people think you're a hero again."

"I was just trying to stay alive, sir."

"And that's excellent motivation, Colonel. Now here's what I want you to do. Despite the fact that only one of your battalions has been landed, I want you to proceed as quickly as you can and seize Mount Haney."

"Mount what?"

"Yes, Ryder, your beloved Sergeant Major Haney returned a few hours ago with a detachment of Cuban rebels who can help us, and a reporter named Kendrick who will likely be a royal pain in the ass. Haney said that the little hill he named for himself dominates the area and should be occupied as soon as possible. He thinks, and I agree, that if the Spanish occupy it in strength, we will have to attack and force them off, and that will cost many casualties. Much better if we make them do the attacking."

"Where's Haney now?"

"With your men and hopefully getting them organized."

Ryder found Haney and four companies of confused infantry waiting orders. Haney had already told them to fill their canteens with water and their pouches with ammunition. Ryder guessed it to be a couple of miles to the hill and, although it didn't look like a difficult climb, he knew better.

By the time they reached the base of the hill, they were drenched with sweat and gasping for breath. The oppressive Cuban heat had quickly sapped their energy. He was about to call a halt when one of the Cuban rebels came and said that a Spanish force was approaching the other side of the hill.

Shit, Ryder thought. "Everybody up and move out. Last one to the top of the hill gets busted to private."

"What if you're already a private?" someone yelled.

Ryder laughed despite his discomfort. "Master Sergeant Haney will think of something, won't you?"

"Damn right, sir. Now get off your asses and up that fucking hill!"

It was steeper than it looked and far more humid than it had been on the beach. Even Ryder was exhausted and there were far too many contenders for last man for Haney to count even if he had wanted to. By the time they reached the crest and were able to start downhill, a number of soldiers were gasping and actually crawling on their hands and knees. All were filthy and covered with mud and bugs.

"Ration the water," Ryder ordered, even though he knew it was futile. Men were already swallowing heavily from the little bit they had in their canteens.

Ryder looked for the military crest, the point beneath the actual crest and the most effective spot to place their defenses. He was about to order a patrol farther downhill when shots rang out. Puffs of smoke showed from trees only a little more than a hundred yards away. Brief flashes of white Spanish uniforms could be seen through the foliage. Without orders, his men dropped to the ground and returned fire. More Spaniards could be seen joining the first group and he realized that they'd made the top first by only a few moments.

Someone screamed. One of his soldiers had been hit. Haney dropped down beside Ryder. "I don't think there's all that many of them, sir. I think if we rush them all shooting and screaming they'll run away. At any rate, clearing the hill's a lot better than sitting here and shooting at each other."

"Agreed," said Ryder. He sent runners to the company commanders and impatiently bided his time until he got word that everyone understood.

Now came the truly dangerous part, he thought. "What the hell," he said to no one in particular. He stood and blew hard on a whistle. Responses came from either side of him and he could sense rather than see several hundred soldiers emerging and moving forward.

Ryder drew his pistol and waved it, "Faster, men, faster! And yell, damn it!"

Four hundred men screeched and hollered and ran towards the Spanish, shooting as they went. The Spanish returned fire raggedly and a couple of his men fell. In seconds, though, they were in the Spanish position. There were indeed not that many of them and they were retreating as quickly as they could from the insane Yankees. One turned and fired his rifle. The shot seemed to whistle just above Ryder's head. Ryder paused, steadied his shaking arm and emptied his revolver at the man, who grabbed his head and fell backwards.

It was over. Haney reported one dead and three

wounded among the American force. Ryder swallowed. These were the first casualties the First Maryland Volunteers had suffered in combat. They wouldn't be the last.

Ryder walked to the man he'd shot. One bullet had entered the man's left eye and another had plowed through his chest. Either could have killed the Spaniard, not that it mattered. Ryder thought the man looked about thirty and wondered if he had a family. He ordered himself to stop thinking like that. It wasn't the first time he'd caused men to die.

A corporal came up and said that a larger enemy force was approaching the hill but appeared to have stopped well out of range. Ryder took his binoculars and found the enemy. It looked like at least a battalion of Spaniards and, yes, they were pausing. It didn't look like they were in any great hurry to take their turn storming Mount Haney.

Ryder gave orders to form a perimeter and dig in as best they could. The men needed no urging and a rough barricade and shallow trench quickly appeared.

A short while later, Major Barnes arrived. He was leading a column of huffing infantry. "I got the second battalion and the third is getting organized. They'll be along shortly."

"Excellent, Major. Now send men back to bring up as much water as they can carry. Then we set up a steady stream of supplies from the bay to here. I also want patrols out to learn just what the damned Spanish are up to."

Haney knelt down and handed him a canteen. Ryder took a swallow and nearly choked. "What the hell is this?"

"Irish whisky, sir. I save it for special occasions and I think this warrants it. We just won the first round of fighting between them and us and the men are right proud."

Ryder laughed, agreed, and took another swallow, this time more slowly. They'd only won a skirmish against an outnumbered handful of Spanish, but, yes, it did feel good and so did the whisky. Better, he still had half a canteen full of water to drink after he had another swallow of Haney's whisky.

◆ Chapter 7 ◆

IT TOOK WHAT SEEMED LIKE AN ETERNITY TO ARRIVE
in St. Augustine. To say that the train line from
Charleston to St. Augustine was inadequate was a
gross understatement. The gauge was narrow and the
tracks and rail bed in such bad shape that the train
could only crawl along lest it shake the tracks apart.

The detachment of doctors and nurses working
under the flag of the Red Cross had been jammed
into passenger cars that moved slowly through the
humid Florida heat. It had been so hot inside the
cars that a couple of them had passed out. Even
though it was clear that efforts were being made to
improve the tracks, the ongoing construction further
hampered travel.

During one stop, Clara Barton gathered her flock
in a local church. There were about fifty of them.
Sarah and Ruth hung back, aware that their presence depended solely on how Miss Barton felt about
enthusiastic volunteers who lacked professional training.

There were some nurses who thought the two women had bought their way into the program and, to a large extent, they were right.

"We need to go to Cuba," Barton announced.

"I need a bath," muttered Ruth. Sarah agreed wholeheartedly. Sanitation had been miserable. They'd joked that the hogs on farms they'd passed had sneered at them.

Barton continued. "Towards that end, I have been petitioning and arguing with people in Washington and they have finally agreed. We will go to Cuba."

This was met with applause and cheers. "However," she said, "it will have to wait until the Army has moved farther inland so we can set up a hospital in relative safety. That should only be a couple of days. In the meantime, we will move by ship to Key West where, I've been told, the conditions are even more primitive there than they have been."

"I think I will take off all my clothes and jump into the ocean," said Ruth as they left the church.

"An excellent idea if we can manage to not get arrested," Sarah said.

"Try not to do that," said Miss Barton, startling them. They had not heard her come up behind them. "I will need all my nurses. More importantly, the telegraph cable between Key West and Matanzas is now operational. Apparently someone in the government with half a brain had a ship laying cable for several days prior to the attack. Since the ship was showing British colors, the Spaniards left her alone."

She handed Sarah a piece of paper. "This is an article sent north to the *Washington Post*. I believe the gentleman in question is an acquaintance of yours and that you are related to people in the First Maryland. You are to be congratulated." She said and walked away.

"FAMED INDIAN FIGHTER LEADS CHARGE UP CUBAN MOUNTAIN, by James Kendrick," the article proclaimed.

"Oh my God," Sarah exclaimed.

It read, "*Colonel Martin Ryder commander of the vaunted First Maryland Volunteers and considered by some to be one of the true heroes of the Battle of the Little Big Horn, led a charge by his regiment up the slopes of an enemy-occupied mountain overlooking and threatening the American landings below at Matanzas.*

"*Braving heavy enemy fire, Ryder and the rest of the regiment attacked the Spaniards, causing numerous enemy casualties and driving them off the peak of the mount. The fighting was intense and sometimes hand to hand. Shortly after taking the high point, the Spaniards counter-attacked and were driven off, again with heavy casualties.*

"*The position has been named Mount Haney in honor of a senior sergeant who recognized the importance of the site and urged the attack.*"

Sarah breathed deeply. She didn't know whether to be afraid or relieved. Yes, Martin was safe, but did he have to put himself in harm's way? Of course, she thought, that's what soldiers did.

"I think I would like something strong, like a brandy or a whisky," Sarah said.

Ruth smiled. "Since women are not allowed alone in a bar, I'll get one of the doctors to purchase a bottle for us and we can drink it in our room. We'll drink and you can dream about your precious Martin while

I try to figure out how to get that lovely Sergeant Haney into my bed. Mount Haney? Perhaps Sergeant Haney would like to mount me. I'd also like to know how the devil he got a mountain named after him."

Custer wadded the newspaper and threw it across their White House bedroom. "Why the bloody hell does this Ryder person keep coming back to haunt me and why is Kendrick standing beside him again?"

Libbie put down the brush she was using on her long and rich reddish-brown hair. She checked the brush for anything gray and found nothing. "George, don't let it get to you. The Army has just won a great victory. Who cares who commanded it? You're the president, the commander in chief. You're the one who'll reap the glory. Maybe Martin Ryder will be able to parlay this into a general's star and a seat in Congress, but that's about it. And as to Kendrick, he's a reporter, nothing more. When the war is over, you will review the troops in the victory parade down Pennsylvania Avenue and they will all salute you as their leader, their commander in chief. Perhaps you will even pin a medal on Ryder's chest. But don't forget, this is your war and it'll be your victory."

"You're right," he grumbled. "But I should be there."

Libbie sighed. "And you know all the reasons you can't. Congress would go into a state of shock, for one thing, if you ever left the country. They wouldn't know what to do without your presence. It simply isn't done."

He sat down heavily on a chair by the bed. "Someday it will be done and I wouldn't mind being the first to do it. If I went to Cuba it wouldn't be as if I went to the moon. The last I checked, the telegram works quite well, thank you. The troops in Cuba need me, damn it. I am their commander in chief. I should be there."

"The Army is in good hands, George, even if the hands belong to Nelson Miles. In the meantime, dear husband, you will be the president who expands the United States beyond its continental boundaries. You will be the one who adds Cuba and Puerto Rico to our country as colonies. This will be the beginning of a true American empire."

Custer laughed harshly. "That is, if Congress lets me."

She stiffened. "What are you talking about?"

Custer was delighted to know something she didn't. He had picked up on information that Libbie had not. "J. Warren Kiefer, our beloved Speaker of the House, has informed me that there is resistance in Congress to annexing Cuba. The American people are thrilled that we are going to throw out the Spanish, but they do not want to control Cuba in perpetuity. There will be a bill introduced limiting our involvement to three years. After that, the dark-skinned people of Cuba will have their freedom. I don't understand Kiefer's lack of support. He's a fellow Republican. He should support the cause of expansion and not try to contain it."

She jumped to her feet, her face red with anger. "That's absurd! The Cuban people are no more ready to govern themselves than I am to fly. What does Blaine have to say?"

"Our equally beloved secretary of state, the man who would like to succeed me as president, is just as appalled as you are. It seems that everybody wants a good, cheap victory, but nobody wants the cost of governing such a large territory for anything but a minimal length of time. Blaine has been talking with Cuban rebels and he is certain that they have been visiting congressmen and even giving speeches across the U.S. They have convinced a large number of people that the honorable thing to do would be to liberate them, train them, and then leave as quickly as possible."

Libbie was flushed with anger. "What about Puerto Rico?"

Custer shrugged. "Nobody much cares. It's small enough, so I guess it can remain ours."

"Wonderful!," she snarled and threw her hairbrush across the room. "If Congress has its way, our great American overseas empire will consist of one small, shitty island."

Maria Vasquez stayed for a week at Luis' shop. The first few days she spent eating everything in sight and also reveling in the fact that she was not in the concentration camp. When she apologized to Luis for eating so much of his food, he simply laughed at her and told her he knew how to get more. After that she began to wonder just what was going to happen in the future.

"Don't worry," said Luis dismissively. "Everything is under control. In a few days you will be sent to Matanzas where you will help a rebel leader named Diego Valdez. He knows of you and that you are smart and cunning. Do you speak English, by the way?"

"A little. I suppose I could get by."

"Even better, but try to improve on it."

"But how will I get out of Havana? Aren't the authorities looking for me?"

Luis laughed so hard she thought he'd have a heart attack. "No, Maria, they are not looking for you. In fact, the camps are so disorganized that they don't know that you even exist. All they are saying is that a prostitute sneaked up on a guard and injured him severely before robbing him."

Maria didn't know if she was disappointed or thrilled. "You mean I didn't kill the fat pig?"

"No, although rumor has it that he might yet die. They say he has a fractured skull. Even if he does recover, he might never be the same."

"What about the other soldier, the one who was going to try to go second?" And he would have, she thought. She would have been in no position to cry out or otherwise try to stop them. It was a given that she would never have received any of the food that she'd been promised. She had taken a terrible chance and had won, at least for now.

Luis laughed again, displaying the fact that he had no teeth. "Both of them have been broken to the rank of private for their stupidity. If this Ramon leaves the hospital, he will likely be discharged so he can beg on the streets. The other man, Carlos, has already been stripped of what rank he had and been sent to the front lines at Matanzas. By the way, with the gate unguarded, a number of other Cubans also escaped. You did very well, Maria."

Maria beamed. "Thank you, but when I get to Matanzas and this Diego Valdez, I would like to do better. Much better."

◆   ◆   ◆

"Water, water everywhere and not a drop to drink," muttered Ryder. "Does anyone know who was in charge of planning this operation? If you do, let me know so I can kill him."

The entire First Maryland was now on the hill known throughout the army as Mount Haney. The regiment was well dug in and vegetation had been cleared away to provide fields of fire. It was a good, strong point except for some serious shortages.

"We need water," said Ryder. "We can't drink that stinking piss that's in the swamps and streams around us, and we sure as hell can't drink the salt water in the bay. Some of the men *have,* and they are sicker than dogs."

At Ryder's direction, the men had begun filtering what passed for fresh water through layers of cloth to purge it of the crawly critters that infested it. It was slow and tedious, but did seem to provide some relief.

"I just wonder why the locals don't get sick?" asked Barnes. "Next time one of us sees a doctor, or a nurse like my sister, we should ask them, although I think it's Darwinian."

"What do you mean?"

"Maybe all the Cubans who are susceptible to getting sick and dying are already dead and the ones left are those naturally selected to survive? For some reason, the Cubans are immune to what makes us sick. Maybe it has something to do with skin color. Maybe God made black people immune because they are so primitive. Hell, maybe they haven't fully evolved."

Ryder shook his head. "Lord, what a lovely thought. That means we are condemned to a weeding out of epic proportions. It may be that more of us will die from illness than fighting, if you are right. Sadly, that outcome is not very far-fetched. If you read the casualty reports from the Civil War it happened a lot."

Barnes lit a cigar and blew the smoke in the general direction of the foliage that surrounded them. He'd noticed that some of the bugs that seemed to be staring at them didn't like it, which was fine by him. "Along with water, we also need food, ammunition, and anything else that makes sense to send to an army that's invading a foreign land."

General Miles had been complaining loudly that all the first invasion fleet had brought was manpower and enough ammunition to fight one battle. They had enough tins of food to last a couple of more days, but, after that, the men would start going hungry. The only local crop was sugar cane. It was totally useless as a food. The local Cubans had small farms and grew a few vegetables, but not in sufficient quantity to feed the army, which had now grown to fifteen thousand souls. The locals had also prudently departed with their livestock, which deprived the army of another source of food.

Nor had the army yet moved inland. General Miles was waiting for the arrival of a second transport fleet that would bring, along with an additional ten thousand men, some hoped-for supplies.

Barnes had not agreed with that plan. "Instead of sitting here on our asses, we should be moving inland and planning to strike at the Spanish. Instead, we wait here for them to hit us."

Ryder decided not to criticize his commanding officer in front of a subordinate even though he was seriously thinking of marrying said subordinate's sister. His thoughts quickly went to his and Sarah's last few hours together. They had not consummated their relationship, but their kissing and caressing had been incredibly torrid and passionate. It had been a most pleasant reminder that the lovely young widow was not a shy and innocent virgin.

Get back to reality, he commanded himself. There were good reasons for the Army's waiting. First, little more than half the army had arrived and, as already noted, it was terribly short of supplies. According to intelligence, the Spanish in Havana outnumbered them at least three to one and were entrenched in strong fortifications. It was generally felt that any American attacking force would be cut to shreds. Ryder was beginning to wonder if the entire invasion stood any chance of success. Some soldiers were already calling the expedition Custer's Folly.

Gunfire could be heard in the distance. Both sides had patrols out along with the rebels who were aiding the Americans. Contact was inevitable and sometimes bloody.

Someone shouted that men were approaching. He could see them through his binoculars. They were Cuban rebels, about a dozen of them. As they got closer, word was given that they should be allowed to pass.

Ryder grinned on seeing that their leader was Diego Valdez, who saluted and waved expansively. "Colonel Ryder, I bring you two things. First there is a wagon approaching and on it are a number of barrels of water. It will taste like guano, which is bird shit, but it will quench your thirst and not kill you."

"Bless you, Captain Valdez." Valdez laughed at the rank he'd been given. "And what's the second thing?"

"The Spanish have finally stirred themselves and a very large column is on its way to Matanzas."

Gilberto Salazar had been angered at his regiment's poor performance in trying to push the Americans off the hill overlooking Matanzas. His men had moved too slowly and tentatively, thus permitting a large American force to move onto the high ground and chase them off.

It was equally perplexing that General Weyler didn't seem to care. Weyler commanded a mixed Spanish and Cuban force of about twenty-five thousand men that was moving exquisitely slowly towards Matanzas. It was almost as if the fire-breathing general didn't want to fight the Americans. Impossible, he thought. Every Spaniard must feel that his honor had been impugned by the presence of the Americans.

Nor had his departure from his home in Havana been pleasant. Juana had been her usual bitchy self and had scarcely deigned to say goodbye. Helga had serviced him with typical German efficiency, satisfying him physically but not emotionally. Damn it to hell, he thought, he was going off to war. He deserved better from his women.

At Weyler's command, he'd pulled his main force back about five miles from the Americans. He kept patrols out and there were constant brushes with the Americans and their rebel allies. Finally, after several days, General Weyler arrived with a strong escort. The main army was strung out behind him.

Weyler insisted on going close enough to see the American lines. "They are formidable," he said on seeing the hills scarred by earthworks. "It will cost us a lot in Spanish blood, but with courage and God's help we will throw them into the ocean."

A puff of smoke emerged from the highest American held hill. A few seconds later, a cannon shell exploded several hundred yards in front of them. Weyler laughed. "Was that a gentlemanly warning to come no closer or were they panicked by the sight of us? I rather think the former, don't you, Major?"

"Perhaps they will run when they see our army formed up to attack."

"That would be nice, but it will not happen."

"May I ask when we will attack?"

"When we are ready, Major, and not sooner," Weyler said stiffly. He did not like the implied criticism. "However, I will say it will take at least a week for this sinfully slow army to arrive and get into position. Then we will have to bombard the Americans before we attack. A bombardment will likely cause very few American casualties, but to attack without one would dishearten our troops."

Salazar thought that many of Weyler's soldiers already looked disheartened but kept still. The general must know what kind of men he was leading. He wondered if King Alfonso did and what his royal majesty truly thought of this endeavor.

Then it occurred to him—was the Spanish army merely going through the motions? Would they simply fire a few rounds and retreat to Havana, leaving the rest of the island to the Americans? To run and hide before a smaller American army would be humiliating.

Weyler looked at him carefully. "If I am reading your mind, Salazar, you are concerned that we will depart for Havana after firing a few rounds to satisfy our honor. Do not be concerned. Once we are in place, we will attack and press the attack with vigor. Our goal will be to push the bastards into the ocean."

Even though the army had not moved very far inland, Clara Barton thought it prudent for her medical staff to move to Cuba in anticipation of the fighting and not as a response to it. She and her volunteers were well aware that this would be dangerous, but she was proud that they all understood the risks and accepted them. It was the best—perhaps only—way they could treat the freshly wounded.

Their small steamer moved into the calm blue waters of Matanzas Bay and anchored. It was plainly marked as a Red Cross vessel and its arrival stirred a great deal of curiosity. The regular military establishment medical personnel resented the presence of the Red Cross. They considered it an insult to their skills and felt that the Red Cross was saying that their abilities were somehow inadequate. Miss Barton seemed to agree with that assessment, although she did not quite come out and say it.

The doctors and nurses disembarked onto a handful of lifeboats and small sailboats. Thus, Sarah, Ruth, and the other nurses found themselves together. A couple of sailors had commenced rowing them to the shore only fifty yards away when one of the nurses shrieked and laughed. Sarah turned and laughed herself. A throng of soldiers was swimming and bathing in the water and every last one was buck naked.

"Ladies, don't look," commanded Barton.

"It's a little too late," said Ruth. "Besides, we'll see much more of the male anatomy when we start treating them."

"True enough," said Barton. Sarah thought her eyes were twinkling with uncharacteristic humor.

The men noticed them and most ran howling and laughing to the shore like little kids caught doing something naughty. A few, however, stood proudly and displayed themselves until they were yelled at by their officers.

"Recognize Martin in that mob?" Ruth asked and this time Clara Barton did smile. Sarah simply stuck out her tongue in response.

Moments after landing, they were met by a thoroughly upset and embarrassed Major General Nelson Miles. "Please accept my apologies, ladies, I had no idea you were coming. If I had, I would have seen to it that my men behaved themselves."

"I assure you no one was hurt, either physically or emotionally," Barton responded, "so let us get on with our work."

Miles assigned a captain to find them a place to pitch their tents and sent a detail to help them. Sarah smiled at the captain. "I have relatives and friends with the First Maryland. Can you tell me where they are?"

He paused and thought for a moment before pointing to a hill a couple of miles away. "I believe they are up there, ma'am. That is what is called Mount Haney."

The hill, or mount, was mostly covered with lush foliage. She could see places where it had been cleared and indentations in the ground that she assumed were trenches. Martin Ryder was up there, only a few miles away, a decent walk on a pleasant afternoon. Perhaps she could get word to him or her brother that they had arrived.

Something boomed and they froze. The captain was perplexed. "It would appear that the boys up there on the hill have found something worth shooting at," he said genially.

Diego Valdez and a score of Cuban insurgents lay in the thick brush that lined the narrow dirt road from Havana. They were several miles inland from the American perimeter and only a few yards from the road. Concealed by the shadows and the foliage, they were invisible. Diego had more men close by, but these were the only ones with rifles, and many of those were relics from wars gone by. A couple of his men had flintlocks that had been used against the English more than a century past. The lack of weapons was a problem that *had* to be solved.

The Spanish column was long and thin, and moved very slowly. The Spanish troops looked worn down by the heat and uninterested in the whole venture. They slouched and held their rifles any way they wished and few officers were in view. Invariably, breaks in the column occurred and Valdez watched for an opportunity. There. A squad was sauntering along as if they were on the way to Sunday Mass. For just a moment, no other Spaniards could be seen.

"Now!" he screamed and his men surged forward, shooting and howling. Several of the Spaniards fell and their screams added to the din. With their rifles empty, the rebels fell on the survivors with machetes, hacking and chopping. A couple of the Spaniards fought back, but most fell in the first wave. Then it was the turn of the survivors to fall and die in bloody piles. It was over in a few seconds. A couple of Spaniards had managed to run and Diego could hear orders being given to the rest of the column, still invisible from around the turn in the road.

"Take their rifles and ammunition, and you have ten seconds to strip off their uniforms."

His men went to it with a will. It took less than ten seconds to get rifles, ammunition, and uniform shirts from the dead and wounded. They stripped the pants off over the boots, which they left on the dead men's bodies. It would take too much time to pull them off. Besides, most of his men had spent their lives barefoot and the soles of their feet were like stones. They gathered their plunder and ran into the brush. In seconds, they were hidden and safe. The Spanish might send a patrol, but it would find nothing. Diego's men played this game far too well and for far too long. Now, they not only had more weapons, but a number of useable Spanish uniforms. He laughed. They would not become *truly* useable until his soldiers managed to get the blood off of them.

A heavily sweating soldier gave Ryder the envelope with his name written on it. The soldier was one of a number who delivered food and other items from headquarters down below the hill. Thus, it wasn't at all unusual for Ryder to get handwritten messages. There'd been talk of connecting the telegraph line to the men on Mount Haney, but it hadn't happened yet. Instead, heliographs, which reflected light and could send Morse code messages, were used to send urgent information. Clearly then, this was not urgent.

The handwriting looked vaguely familiar, but he was too tired to make any connection.

"Get yourself some water and take a ten-second break, soldier."

The trooper laughed, nodded and stepped away. Ryder noticed that he was heading directly to their small mess tent. Good man. Eat every chance you can. He looked at the envelope.

"Why don't you open it, Colonel dearest?"

"Then I won't have anything to look forward to, Sergeant Major Haney."

He tore the envelope open and gasped. It was a note from Sarah. Jesus Christ, he thought as he read it, she was *here*. How the devil had she managed that trick? He read further. She and Ruth were part of a contingent of Red Cross nurses that had just arrived. He wholeheartedly welcomed the medical aid they didn't require quite yet. The sporadic gunfire from enemy lines was proof that there would be a compelling need in the not too distant future.

As happy as he was that she was just down from the hill, he was very concerned that she was in a very dangerous position. When the Spaniards attacked, she might be in the middle of it. Would the Spaniards take into account the Red Cross emblazoned on their hospital tents? He walked to the other side of the hill and looked down onto the bay. Yes, he could see several such tents with the Red Cross vividly displayed. All right, if he could see it, so could the Spaniards. But would they honor it?

Damn it. As much as he wanted to hold her in his arms and feel her warm and clean breath on his neck, he desperately wanted her to be safe.

"Colonel, sir."

"Yes, Haney."

"Did I hear you say that Miss Holden is with Mrs. *Damon*?"

"I must have been thinking out loud, Sergeant Major, and yes, the two women have connived their way to Cuba."

Haney smiled happily. "And isn't that truly amazing, sir?"

Juana Salazar was quite pleased with herself. It was entirely possible that she had struck a blow for Cuban freedom. Better, it had been safe and easy, easy as pie, as her American lover would have said.

She could not help but wonder what James Kendrick was up to and whether or not they actually were lovers after only one night of passion together. Kendrick was doubtless a hundred times more experienced than she. Would she ever see him again? She had mentally relived their night of torrid passion a hundred times since he'd left a few days prior. He had awakened her like she'd always dreamed in a way that a lover, a knight errant, would. Of course, she'd never dreamed that her knight in shining armor would be starting to go bald and have a little paunch, but then she'd never thought she'd be thirty before even beginning to have a fulfilling sex life. On the other hand, many of her women friends admitted to not having a satisfying physical side of marriage with their husbands. She decided that she would count her blessings. If Kendrick was going to be a part of her life, well, they were going to have to deal with the fact that she was both married and a Catholic.

She would also have to go to Confession. Her confessor was her uncle, Bishop Estefan Campoy, and he would scold her and then ask why her husband did not please her. Juana would tell him the truth because that's the way she was raised and that would outrage the good bishop even more. She decided that it was about time that her uncle knew the truth about Gilberto Salazar.

Then she thought that perhaps it would be better if she waited a while before seeing her uncle in the confessional. Perhaps her husband would manage to get himself killed in the war. She could long for that but she could not, would not, pray for it. That would be a sin.

Juana presumed that Kendrick had made it safely to the American lines at Matanzas. With Diego to guide him, it should have been a simple journey. But her nation was at war, which meant that nothing was guaranteed to be easy. Her husband was out with much of the Spanish army and they were between Kendrick and the Americans. Nothing was certain in life except that she was feeling like a giddy young girl. One certainty was that she was thrilled to be able to punish both Spain and Gilberto.

Before he left, Kendrick had shown her how to get telegraph messages to the American military in the U.S. She had no idea who would actually read any of the ·information sent, and she'd been told not to send too many telegrams lest the Spanish government suddenly become curious about her change in behavior. After all, she hadn't sent more than a half dozen telegrams to the United States in the last several years.

This message was short. It was directed to a lady named Bertha Downey in New Orleans, and she assumed that Bertha didn't exist. It said that Bertha's two sisters were going to depart within a day and might make a number of stops before actually arriving at their destination. The two sisters were the pair of Spanish battleships at anchor in Havana's harbor. She had no idea where they were headed and could only inform the Americans that they were about to depart. As she watched after sending the telegram, the battleships' horns sounded stridently. Their anchors were winched up and the two ships began their stately crawl through the crowded harbor and narrow entrance and out into the Caribbean. If any American warships were watching, she didn't see them.

Matanzas was only a few hours' steaming away, if that was the ships' goal. She presumed that her message would be relayed to someone in Washington and then down to Matanzas. She'd heard that the Yanks had set up a telegraph station at their new base and hoped it was true. But then, how would they get the word out to American warships at sea?

◆ Chapter 8 ◆

A TORRENTIAL RAIN POUNDED DOWN ON THE AMERI-can army at Matanzas. Many of the soldiers didn't yet have tents, which meant they were all quickly soaked to the skin. Even though both the day and the rain were warm, they were soon chilled and shaking. Almost as bad, many of the tents the others had been issued were of poor quality and either leaked badly or were quickly torn apart by the wind.

"Damn it to hell," snarled Ryder. "I'd like to find out who's responsible for getting us this junk and make him try to live and work in it."

From his vantage point on top of the hill and through gaps in the sheets of rain he could see the damage being done to the American base. At least it looked as if the tents occupied by the Red Cross were still standing. He hadn't yet had a chance to see Sarah, and he could only hope that she was dry and safe. At least *safe*, he thought wryly. He didn't think anyone was truly dry and wouldn't be until the sun had a chance to shine for a couple of days.

"The trenches are filling with water," said Barnes.

"You look like a drowned rat," said Ryder.

"Correction, Colonel, I'm only half drowned. And may I say you don't look that great either. I've got men bailing out the trenches and even digging runoff lanes to send the water downhill, but it's pretty much a hopeless task."

"And it'll be that way until the damned rain stops. And they tell me this is just an ordinary rainstorm for this area. This is nothing like a hurricane. Hopefully, we'll be all done here when that ugly season is upon us."

Along with other officers, they'd gotten a briefing on hurricanes and what to expect. The massive storms usually arrived in the fall and the howling winds and drenching rains could easily eradicate the growing base the army had established. Caught unprepared, the army could suffer casualties greater than those suffered in battle.

"Do you really think the war will be over before hurricane season?" Barnes asked.

"Hell no, Jack. I'm just trying to keep your spirits up. It's been raining heavily for almost a day now and I'm sick and tired of it."

"And I think I hear thunder," said Barnes.

Ryder told everyone nearby to be still. Yes, it sounded like thunder. Only thing, damn it, it wasn't thunder. The Spanish navy had arrived.

Sarah and Ruth were in the tent they shared with several other nurses and huddled under a blanket as the rain pounded down on the canvas roof above them. The canvas roof leaked, but so far they'd managed to keep most of the rain off of themselves, although the ground was quickly becoming a muddy quagmire. They kept their feet tucked under themselves as they sat on Sarah's bunk. For the moment, they had the tent to themselves.

"Sarah, this is not exactly the exciting and fulfilling adventure I thought it would be. The next time I absolutely will not let you plan my vacation."

"I'm not aware that any of this was planned. On the other hand, we haven't had much to do as nurses, which is a blessing. A war without casualties is a good thing."

"That will change, I'm afraid," said Ruth.

Only a handful of soldiers and sailors had required their assistance. These were the usual broken bones that occurred when a lot of manual work was required and the workers were inexperienced and unenthusiastic. Accidents were always going to happen and some of the men were doing work that was totally unfamiliar to them. So far, only a few men had been killed. Both agreed that would change when the fighting actually started.

"Wonderful," said Ruth. "Now it's thundering."

Sarah was about to comment when an enormous explosion sent shock waves through their tent, nearly collapsing it and knocking them to the muddy ground. "What on earth was that?" she said.

Ruth had turned pale. "We're being bombarded. Christ, it's just like Paris."

Another explosion, but this one was farther away. Still, it was strong enough to finish the job of collapsing their tent. Both women crawled out from under the canvas and outside into the rain. The rain seemed to be abating, and they could see shell craters with smoke emanating from them. More shells landed and they ran towards trenches that had been dug to defend against a Spanish assault from the sea. This, they decided, qualified and they jumped in, heedless of the mud at the bottom and the fact that the trench was rapidly filling with frightened soldiers.

Along with the others, they huddled as best they could. More shells landed nearby and some were close enough to send chunks of mud raining down on them. They remained unhurt, although increasingly wet and dirty. It seemed as if the Spanish were just lobbing shells in the general direction of the American position and not aiming at anything in particular.

Sarah's only problem was that she thought one of the soldiers had his hand on her bottom and seemed to be enjoying it. This was confirmed when the man shifted his body. He got his hand under her dress and began to run his hand up her leg.

"Damn you," she said as she pulled the long pin from her hair. She quickly identified the man pawing her. He pulled his hand away and grinned happily. "Enjoy this!" she said loudly enough for him to hear as she jammed the hat pin into his thigh. The soldier bit his tongue in order to stifle a scream. Thank God for hat pins, she thought. Once again one had come to her rescue.

A fresh barrage of shells got their undivided attention. Seconds later, something huge exploded and again shook them violently.

"Oh shit, there goes our ammunition," said the man she'd just stuck.

Sarah peeked over the lip of the trench. Smoke

and flames were billowing from where a number of tents had once stood. She could see bodies lying in the mud. A number of smaller explosions followed as shells exploded. Again, they ducked down. This time she found herself on her hands and knees and with her face nearly in the muck.

There was a pause in the shelling and explosions and they all rose up. In the distance, they could see a pair of large Spanish warships heading out to sea.

As they watched, another ship approached the two Spaniards from the east. Even from a distance they could see it flew the American flag. Sadly, though, it looked like an obsolete wooden frigate from wars gone by. It fired a broadside that fell short of the two enemy ships who responded quickly. The American vessel was hit and seemed to shudder from the blows.

"Jesus," said a naval officer in the trench with them, "she's the steam frigate *Franklin*. She was obsolete when the Civil War ended. Those people are brave, but foolish."

"But they had to do something," commented Ruth. "If you haven't noticed, we don't have any big guns on shore. We're helpless."

The *Franklin* was burning. Spanish guns fired again and pieces of wood and other debris that might have been bodies flew skyward. Explosions ripped through the *Franklin*, setting more fires. Men began to jump overboard. The American ship was doomed. She turned on her side and sank slowly as water gushed through gaping holes in her hull.

Everyone was shocked to silence. Finally, Sarah spoke, "How many men were on the *Franklin*?"

"At least a couple of hundred," the officer said

sadly, "and I knew a lot of them." He smiled weakly. "I'm Ensign Paul Prentice and I was on the British ship, the *Shannon*, when she toured Havana before being turned over to our navy. I just arrived on the *Franklin*. I guess I was lucky to get off when I did."

"So where is our mighty new navy now?" Ruth said sarcastically. "I think it might have been useful."

"No idea," Prentice said sadly.

Heads were bobbing in the water and small boats were pushing off from shore to help the survivors. The Spanish ships were not going to stop and help. They had decided it was time to run. At least they weren't going to hinder rescue operations.

"It's over with," Ruth said, "unless they want to take a parting shot or two."

"Was it like this in Paris?" Sarah asked as they climbed out of the trench.

"Oh lord, it was a thousand times worse. There were hundreds, maybe thousands, of cannons firing and it went on all day and night. This was nothing compared with that, although I'm afraid there will be a number of casualties. We'd better get to the hospital and await what comes."

Prentice wished them well and walked slowly away.

When the Spanish ships began their bombardment, the enemy soldiers near Mount Haney chose that time to commence their own shooting at the Americans. The Spanish cannons were few, small, and didn't have the range. That didn't mean that Ryder's First Maryland Volunteers didn't have to pay attention. There was concern that the Spaniards would launch an attack if they thought the hill's defenders were distracted or had been drawn off to repel a potential amphibious invasion.

Ryder wouldn't let his men be distracted, although he had to grab a couple of them and bodily push them back to where they were supposed to be. They all wanted to see what was happening below in the main camp and so did Martin. Sarah was down there and he was in agony with worry for her safety. What the hell had moved her to come to Cuba?

White-clad Spanish skirmishers began to probe up the hill. Ryder had his men hold their fire until they got within a hundred yards. When the Spanish reached that point, the Americans began shooting. In seconds, concentrated rifle fire had blown them away, leaving a score of dead and wounded littering the slope. Behind the retreating survivors, he saw a larger body of soldiers, but they stopped and withdrew. The Spanish army was not ready to attack Mount Haney this rainy and miserable day.

When he was certain everything was stable, he ran to the other side of the hill and looked down. Smoke poured from where a number of shells had hit. He used his binoculars and looked at the Red Cross compound. Several tents were down and others looked damaged. Soldiers helping casualties were moving towards what remained of the Red Cross facility. He could see what looked like medical personnel helping them. Was one of them Sarah? He could only hope and pray. He hadn't prayed in a long time, but it seemed like a good idea this day. He looked out to sea where the Spanish warships were disappearing and a third ship was burning.

"Where the hell was our navy?" asked Barnes. "They should have been protecting us. Now look at all the damage and God only knows how many killed and wounded. Jesus, and look at all the ammunition that's been destroyed. We're pretty damn near helpless."

Ryder nodded agreement. "And that means we're going to both conserve what ammunition we have as well as try to gather up as much extra as we can. If the Spanish attack, we don't want to have to fight with only what the men have in their pouches. That'd last only an hour or so. Send some runners down and get more ammo before somebody figures out that most of our reserves just got blown up. We have to hold on to this high ground."

In the meantime, he thought, I've got to find out if Sarah is safe. Damn it to hell, why didn't she stay in Maryland?

Sarah vomited the first time she saw the man whose face had been destroyed. He had no eyes and the skin on his cheeks had been flayed off. He seemed to be trying to speak even though the lower part of his chin was missing as well. The result was a horrible gurgling sound.

She caught Clara Barton staring at her. "Well?"

Sarah wiped the vomit off her chin. The young American soldier in question was also missing an arm and blood bubbled out from where his chest had been crushed. Despite that, he began to thrash about on his cot. "He's going to die," she said softly.

"Why are you whispering?" asked Barton.

"Because I don't know whether or not he can hear me. The only thing we should do is give him enough morphine to make his passing painless."

"Do you know how to inject with a hypodermic?"

Sarah said that she did. She got morphine and injected it into his remaining arm. The man sighed and relaxed almost immediately. Barton nodded approvingly. "When we're through with the others, we'll come back and see how he's doing, although I'm reasonably certain he'll die shortly."

"I'm sorry I threw up."

"Nonsense. I'd have been shocked if you hadn't. And I won't be shocked if it happens again. The important thing is that you got control of yourself. This battle was just a minor bloodletting although a terrible one for this poor soldier. Things will get much worse, I'm afraid, before this war is over."

The line of wounded needing treatment was surprisingly long. If this was a minor bloodletting, Sarah thought she didn't want to see a major one. In battle there was no such thing as a peaceful death, not like most of the ones she'd seen at home. There were no gentle-faced old people lying placidly in coffins while everyone said how good they looked or how they appeared to be sleeping. Nor was this anything like the occasional badly injured people she'd helped her father treat. No, this was beyond ghastly. Worse, these were not old people. Many of the casualties were so young they hadn't begun to reach their prime, much less become aged.

The first thing the medical staff did when the wounded arrived was decide who might live and who likely would not. Sometimes it was easy. Young men who'd lost several limbs and much of their blood would likely die, like the man without a face. They were made as comfortable as possible and injected with morphine to ease their passing.

The wounded who might survive also needed that narcotic, and Sarah went around and administered it. Unlike a couple of other nurses she saw, she always washed off the needle before using it on another patient. It was her father's policy. He had read the works of Lister and Pasteur and strongly felt that cleanliness would prevent infection and gangrene. She was pleased to see that Doctor Desmond, their chief surgeon, also concurred. Some of the Army doctors dismissed such notions as foolish and time consuming. Perhaps, she thought, that was why so many of the wounded were lining up to be helped by Clara Barton and the Red Cross and not by Army doctors.

Caring for the wounded took several hours. She did not have to assist in any amputations, although she did see one poor young man having his leg sawed off just above the knee. The foot and knee had been mangled to a pulp, with pieces of white bone sticking out through the flesh. She shuddered. What the devil had she gotten herself into? She checked on the man without a face and his cot was empty. She was informed that he had died, peacefully she hoped.

"Ah, there you are," Sergeant Haney said cheerfully, ignoring the carnage around him. "I was sent down here on a fool's errand to assist one of our men who broke his leg tripping over a log. Somehow, I think the good colonel had me come here to check on you instead."

Sarah's spirits lifted. Martin was clearly safe. "Tell the good colonel that despite what you see, everything is under control."

"Truth be told, Mrs. Damon, I've seen very much worse. Compared with what I took part in as the

Civil War was ending, this is a church picnic. Sadly it'll likely be much worse before this war is over."

"Then it's good we've had a chance to practice, Sergeant, and when we're just talking like old friends and there's none of this damned rank to get in the way, do you think you could manage to call me Sarah?"

Haney grinned. "I might manage it, Sarah, but only if you tell me where I might find that statuesque paragon of Polish beauty, Ruth Holden?"

Sarah laughed and gave him directions. Haney found Ruth scrubbing the blood off her arms. Unlike Sarah, Ruth had indeed participated in a couple of amputations and stitched up some wounds herself.

"You look wonderful, Ruth."

"Go to hell, Haney. I look like a bloody monster and you know it."

She took his hand and they went outside and behind the tent. She kissed him fiercely. "Surprised?" she asked.

"Delighted, is more the word," he said and kissed her back. As his hand slid down and grasped her bottom, she pushed him away.

"This is neither the time nor the place, although I admit that helping save lives is exhilarating."

"If I find you a place, will you make the time?"

"Of course," she smiled and patted him on the cheek. "We international refugees have to stick together, don't we?"

George Armstrong Custer read the reports with dismay. "Where the hell was our navy?" he shouted. "Several hundreds dead and wounded and a warship sunk. And let's not forget the ammunition that was blown to hell."

Secretary of the Navy William Hunt was sweating and not from any heat. The United States Navy had just failed its first test in this new war. "We had knowledge that the Spanish ships were sailing, but we didn't know their destination. Attacking Matanzas certainly was one thought, but it was also deemed likely that they would strike at our second transport fleet gathering at St. Augustine. I thought it wise that we not split our major forces, which might have resulted in their two capital ships attacking and sinking one of ours. We thought the more likely target would be Florida, but we were clearly wrong. I take full responsibility for this disaster. If you want my resignation you shall have it within the hour."

Custer thought for only a second. Libbie had told him not to fire him or accept Hunt's resignation lest their political enemies claim that there was chaos in the Custer administration. Besides, there was agreement that Hunt was by far the best man to run the growing navy. Custer concurred. Hunt was too valuable. We learn from our mistakes, he thought. The Navy needed more ships.

"Sir, I do not want your resignation. What I truly want is for you to take control of your part of this war. We have three superior warships to Spain's two. We have to maneuver so that we outnumber them. Where are the Spanish ships now?"

"We don't know. They don't carry much coal, so we believe they are still in Cuban waters. Sadly, there are literally scores of places where they could hide that are close to both Havana and Matanzas and receive that coal."

Custer took a swallow of the Jim Beam bourbon he'd been favoring lately. He'd found it smoother

than the recently established Jack Daniels brand of
whisky. "And that is why every nervous Nellie along
the Atlantic coast is demanding Navy warships to protect their front lawns, and that is why Congress has
forced me to send scores of our newly commissioned
auxiliary ships to protect every little town that has a
fishing boat from a Spanish fleet that exists only in
nightmares. Jesus, what a way to run a war! When the
hell are we ever going to move out and take Havana?"

Hunt wiped his brow with a large white handkerchief.
"That cannot happen until we have sufficient forces
and sufficient supplies. The Army doesn't want to send
reinforcements until the Spanish battleships have been
either sunk or blockaded or otherwise neutralized.
Of immediate importance, the recent Spanish assault
caused an explosion that destroyed much of our reserve
ammunition. There is a real fear that an attack by the
Spanish army would find our men defenseless. That
means that the Army's first priority is ammunition, and
not reinforcements. Any move to Havana will have to
be delayed until those problems are solved."

"Shit and double shit!" Custer raged. He paced
around his office a few times, took a deep breath and
seemed to regain control. "If this situation doesn't
improve, Hunt, both of us are going to look like laughingstock jackasses. And it doesn't help that this Kendrick
asshole is down in Cuba filing stories about the Army's
bravery under adverse circumstances—circumstances
that he implies are all my fault. And once again, he's
promoted his old buddy Ryder as a hero. What the
hell, all Ryder did was beat off an ineffective probe by
a small bunch of Spanish skirmishers. It's not like he's
winning the war by himself."

Secretary of State Blaine entered unbidden and took a seat. "At least it's a small victory in a night of disasters. The public needs a hero, so let them have one. And don't forget that the first photos of the expedition will be arriving soon and many of them will be grim. The newspapers have chartered small, fast ships to take the plates from Cuba as quickly as possible so they can be developed before they rot in the heat."

Custer looked stunned by the idea of such negative publicity. "Is there any way we can stop them? We all know that a battlefield is a dismal and ugly place. If the American people see what is happening in Cuba, they may turn against the war."

For once he makes sense, thought Blaine, however futile the thought. "The last thing we want to try to do is impose censorship. That will convince our enemies that we have something to hide. We do, of course, and that is the military's incompetence, but we can't let anyone in on that little secret. In the meantime, I will be having a meeting with your esteemed political rival, Winfield Scott Hancock, on the future of Cuba if we should manage to defeat the Spaniards."

Custer poured a large splash of bourbon into his now empty glass. "And what does that fat pile of shit want?"

Blaine smiled. Custer was feeling overwhelmed and confused. He was also getting drunk. One of these days, it was inevitable that he would make an utter fool out of himself, which would leave the door to the next Republican nomination wide open to one James G. Blaine.

"Hancock will agree to change the date of our

leaving an American-occupied Cuba from three years to five years if you will consider giving him a field command should the situation warrant it."

"When hell freezes over," Custer snarled. "Wait, is he saying that Nelson Miles is going to fail?"

Blaine shrugged and Hunt looked away. "Miles has never commanded a large force in his life and he's in his fifties. Hardly ancient but he may be too old to learn."

"And Hancock isn't? Hell, he's older than Miles by a few years."

"Six or so," said Blaine, "but he's much younger in his attitude and has a world of experience."

"Which he can stuff up his ass! I'll call on him if and when the situation becomes truly desperate and not a moment sooner."

"Perhaps I can provide a hint of good news," said Hunt. "We have some naval personnel off Matanzas with a new weapon. When we find the Spanish capital ships, it is possible that we will be able to use it to sink or damage at least one of them."

Custer tried to blink away the effects of the alcohol. It didn't work. He was starting to slur his words. "What sort of weapon?"

Hunt smiled. "It's called a torpedo."

Juana never thought that her small foray into the world of military intelligence would instantly result in Spain's defeat. Instead and to her dismay, it seemed like the warning that the Spanish battleships had sailed had been misinterpreted. All Havana was cheering, drinking, and dancing in the streets. The camp of the hated gringos had been pounded into rubble and the ground soaked with gringo blood. When later word came that an American warship had been smashed to kindling by Spain's warships, the celebrations began anew. She did notice that not everyone joined in the party. Many Cubans were silent and reflective. They would revel only when the Spanish were gone.

Still, she was certain that she had done the right thing and would do it again in a heartbeat. She heard voices. Her husband was home. He opened the door to her apartment and strode in, smiling proudly.

"Victory is ours, noble wife."

"It's considered polite to knock when entering a lady's rooms."

Salazar laughed. "You are not a lady and I am too drunk to care. The Americans have been smashed. In a very short while we will launch a huge attack against them and drive them into the sea. It is my fondest hope that your lover, Kendrick, will either drown or die running and his body eaten by the land crabs. I convinced General Weyler that I had pressing business here and that the war could spare me for a few days. Therefore, here I am to dispense long overdue justice, you whore. I know you were romping in bed with that bastard Kendrick."

Juana was outraged. "How can you pretend to be betrayed when you ordered me to his room? And thank God you did. If it hadn't been for your insane wishes, I never would have known the pleasures he gave me. Pleasures, I might add, that you were incapable of providing me."

"You fucking bitch," he screamed and slapped her across the face with enough violence to split her lip. She fell to the floor and he kicked her in the stomach.

When she tried to get up, he punched her on the side of her head. He tore her dress down to her waist and squeezed her breasts until she groaned. "Did he like your tiny little tits? You're so small you're not even a woman. You must be a boy."

Juana stared in horror as he drew his sword. "I should slice you to ribbons and send you to Kendrick piece by bloody piece. But no, I am not that foolish. Your beloved uncle would condemn me and I would have to perform annoying penances. Therefore, you will live, but you will indeed know pain."

With that he began to slap her on her bare back and shoulders with the flat of the sword. She bit her lip and tried to stifle the pain but it was no use. She began to moan and then to scream.

Salazar laughed as her howls carried through the house. "Don't think for a minute that one of your more loyal servants will stop me. I sent them all away."

Despite the fact that he was not using the blade, she could feel that she'd been cut and that blood was flowing down her body. Finally, he stopped, spat on her as she cowered on the floor. He laughed at her and left.

Juana lay there and tried to gather her strength and her wits. The servants would be back shortly, but she would not call out for their help. None of them should see her like this. She pulled herself to her feet and staggered into her bathroom. The mirror showed the extent of the damage. From the neck down her body was a mass of bruises and small cuts. She was already in intense pain, but she would endure it. She had no choice if she was going to win against her husband.

Juana managed to smile even though her lip hurt

where she'd been struck. It would be swollen and discolored for a number of days, but she would explain it away as a horseback riding accident. No one would believe her, of course, but it didn't matter. Husbands beat their wives as a matter of course and it was well known that she and Gilberto were not on the best of terms. Properly combed, her hair would cover where he had struck her on the head. She carefully washed away the blood on her face and body, and then changed her dress. Her body was beginning to stiffen and ache. It would take all of her willpower to not limp or show pain, but she would not give her bastard husband or any of his friends the opportunity to gloat.

Juana realized that Gilberto hadn't accused her of spying or relaying information. The fool only thought that he'd been cuckolded, nothing more. She would have to find more information to relay to the Americans. Only this time she prayed that they would make better use of it.

Alfonso XII, King of Spain, walked through the palace garden. It should have been filled with luxuriant growth, an enormous bouquet of radiant and multicolored flowers tended by faithful servants. But no. Instead of life, everything was drab and brown, lifeless caricatures of flowers. It occurred to him that what had once been the mightiest empire on the earth couldn't even properly water a garden and keep flowers alive.

The king plucked at a dry twig and broke it. "Still nothing from the Americans? Still no indication on their part of a willingness to negotiate?"

Prime Minister Antonio Canovas stared impassively at a point over the king's shoulder. "No, majesty."

"And why not?" the king demanded. "Haven't we defeated them on land and sea?"

"Actually, sir, we've done no such thing. We gave them a bloody nose and embarrassed them, but their forces are still largely intact and growing. So too are ours," he added hastily.

The king acknowledged that fact. Another flotilla of transports had departed for Cuban waters only a couple of days earlier. It would bring an additional fifteen thousand soldiers to Cuba along with supplies of weapons and ammunition. What it could not bring was fighting spirit. The Spanish army was much like the barren garden in which he wandered.

Alfonso thought of the men in the army he'd reviewed just before they sailed away. Fifteen thousand men had been dressed in bright white uniforms and looking like soldiers, but only from a distance. Up close, their uniforms were worn and didn't quite fit. Many soldiers were old and some were astonishingly young, only boys. Nor were their weapons any better. The rifles were new enough, but he saw dirt and rust, which showed that they were not being maintained. He asked himself— what kind of soldier doesn't clean his rifle, the thing that might save his life? This war had to end before the façade of Spanish military might collapsed.

"Weyler will attack soon?" he asked.

Canovas looked uncomfortable. "General Weyler is building up his forces. It may only be fifty some miles from Havana to Matanzas, but they are diffi- cult miles and our army in Cuba is not very mobile. Cables from Havana insist that Weyler will move in a few days at the longest."

And that means two weeks, Alfonso thought. Yet

there must be a battle that would end this farce that could destroy what remained of Spain, he thought. Of course, anything resembling a Spanish victory over that bombastic fool Custer would preserve Spain for a century. He would have his clergy pray for victory. At least it would give them something to do.

◆ Chapter 9 ◆

RYDER LOOKED THROUGH HIS BINOCULARS AT THE ocean of Spanish tents that had been erected just out of the range of his few cannons. He heard a click and turned. William Pywell, Kendrick's photographer, had just taken a picture of the Spanish camp from the crest of Mount Haney. Pywell had landed by private boat the day before. He had also brought his traveling darkroom, a contraption on a carriage, and a horse to pull the thing. The pictures he'd been taking would be developed and sent to Florida the next morning. There might be a war on, but nothing would stop the men of the press. Nor were small boats like the one Pywell used bothered by the few Spanish ships cruising off Matanzas and the American coast.

"I hope that's a good one," said Ryder genially. Not only had Pywell taken photos of the Civil War, but had traveled with Custer before the Little Big Horn. He and Pywell had had a nodding acquaintance.

Pywell grinned. "It'll be as good a panorama as

Mathew Brady ever took, maybe even better since I can see and Brady can't. Poor man's just about blind, you know."

Ryder had not heard that. He thought blindness was about the worst thing that could happen to a person. "If there is a battle, will you try to photograph the action?"

"Why not?" the photographer said and shrugged. "If the sun is bright enough to freeze movement, then it'll work. The science of photography has come a long ways since the Civil War when we were afraid that all movement would wind up blurred. Of course, there also was the real fear of getting shot if we wandered too close to the fighting, which is one more reason we avoided photographing the action. No, it was better and safer to take pictures of the dead after the battle than the living during it."

Ryder thought that was prudent and wondered if he could adopt that policy as well. There was commotion on the bay side of the mountain. He recognized Haney along with another man who wore the single star of a brigadier general on his shoulders. It was Frederick Benteen and he looked exhausted from the climb. He lazily returned Ryder's salute and shook his hand.

"Colonel, you wouldn't happen to have a gin and tonic in this godforsaken place, would you?"

"Sir, if such is available, Sergeant Haney will find it for you, along with some ice."

"Give me just a few minutes, sir. The impossible often takes that long." Haney said and disappeared into one of the bunkers.

Benteen removed his hat and wiped his forehead with a handkerchief that was already soaked with sweat. "I think you already know what's going on.

But to make it official, the Army's divisions are being divided into brigades and I'm in charge of one. Your regiment's in it, of course, along with two others."

"I'm honored, although I'm just a little surprised."

"Why? Because I've been given a brigade even though everyone knows that I despise Custer's guts? I dislike him intensely for what he's said about my behavior at the Little Big Horn and he knows it. Still, he needs good officers and I think I am one."

Custer had criticized Benteen for not moving more quickly to his rescue when he'd joined up with Major Reno's forces at the now famous battle that had almost become a massacre. Custer ignored the fact that Reno outranked Benteen and came under Reno's orders on his arrival. Custer also ignored the fact that both Benteen and Reno were fighting desperately on the other side of the Little Big Horn and that Reno, the senior of the two and in command, had likely been drunk.

"At any rate," Benteen continued, "this reorganizing should make the divisions more flexible and able to respond more quickly when the Spanish attack. Their army is getting larger and larger while ours is stagnating. Allegedly we are getting reinforcements and supplies, but God only knows when."

A smiling Haney appeared beside them with two canteen cups in his hands. "As ordered, sirs. Enjoy."

Benteen and Ryder swallowed appreciatively. "May I presume you have another gin and tonic in that bunker and that it's for yourself?" asked Benteen.

"You may indeed," said Haney. "Sadly, though, that is the last of the ice."

"War is hell," muttered Ryder.

◆   ◆   ◆

Diego Valdez led his small group of "Spanish soldiers" through the vast array of tents housing the enemy army. Even though he was far from being a military professional, his inexperienced eyes could see that the Spanish army was not an elite force. They had not been stopped on entering the camp and no one had questioned them since then. Their stolen uniforms were sufficient to get them anywhere. The closest they'd come to having a problem had been when a clearly drunken captain had asked them to get him something. Diego had told the captain that they were on an errand from Colonel Juarez and the captain had sworn at them and walked away. Diego had no idea if there even *was* a Colonel Juarez.

It had been Diego's idea to check out the encampment and see what damage he and his men could do to Spain. The explosion of the American ammunition dump had given him the idea that he could do the same thing to the Spanish. Reality, however, was proving otherwise. Ammunition appeared to have been disbursed to the many units arrayed against the Americans; ergo, there would be no large and devastating explosion. It was also obvious that the Spanish were gearing up for a major attack. He hoped that the Americans were aware of that, since the large number of soldiers confronting the Americans precluded his sneaking directly through to warn them. He would have to go around the Spanish army and that would take time.

At least they'd managed to pilfer additional Spanish uniforms and this time they included a supply of boots.

He'd actually seen General Weyler and had given serious thought to killing him. Unfortunately, that would likely have resulted in his own tragic demise and that of his men, which did not appeal to any of them. They were all brave but not suicidal.

Night came and they bedded down on the ground along with thousands of others. In the morning they would leave the camp simply by marching out as if they were on some work detail. His men would not be happy that they were not able to inflict pain on the Spanish or their traitorous Cuban allies, but they would deal with it.

He was awakened by the sound of horses trotting by only a few feet away. There was enough light to see the riders' faces. With a jolt he recognized the hated Gilberto Salazar. It took all his strength to not shoot the man.

But one of his soldiers couldn't restrain himself. Diego heard a scream and a shot. Salazar and his horse went down in a heap. "Run," he yelled. The man who had fired stood with a stunned look on his face and a smoking weapon in his hands as realization of what he'd done dawned. Salazar's men turned and saw him. They fired and the soldier staggered but didn't fall.

"Stupid bastard," Diego sobbed in fury as he shot his irrational comrade in the head. He could not afford to have the fool captured and questioned.

As soldiers swarmed past him, he and the others in his group melted away, running in all directions. As he left the area, he saw men helping Salazar to his feet. He appeared hurt, but not too badly, as he was able to stand with only minimal help. The man who had fired had been a friend and fellow revolutionary for several years, but his family had been slaughtered by Salazar.

The camp was now wide awake and soldiers were milling and moving in all directions. Nobody was yet in control and soldiers were shooting wildly and at anything. A campfire had overturned and a tent was on fire. He found the outer edge of the encampment and simply departed. In a short while he was joined by a couple of his men. They were as shocked and stunned as he was. "You had to kill Jose," one of them said sadly. "He was my cousin, but he was a fool. We cannot have fools."

Ryder and his staff were transfixed by the sight below them in the Spanish camp. When the gunfire started, the sentries in both sides had sounded the alarm, sending troops into the trenches. Were the Spanish about to attack? There was no need for Ryder to sound a second alarm. His soldiers were already pouring into the trenches, rubbing the sleep from their eyes and trying to get ready for whatever the enemy might try to throw at them.

"Anybody know what the hell is going on down there?" Ryder asked. He got no response, which was what he expected. Who wanted to admit that they didn't know a damn thing? More gunfire exploded and something was on fire. Several Spanish tents were burning and the flames were spreading.

"You know what I think, sir?" said Barnes. "I think they're shooting at themselves. I think something spooked them and they've pretty well panicked."

"Makes sense," Ryder answered. "Their boys can't be any more experienced than ours." Almost every night since landing, some soldiers had fired at shadows. Some of the boys called it demon shooting or ghost attacks. Everybody's nerves were strained, what with the Spanish in plain sight but just out of range.

As if to confirm that statement, rifle fire came from another regiment on his left flank. He heard officers yelling at the men to stop shooting at shadows. At least his men had shown a semblance of fire discipline. Well, this night at least.

A cannon boomed from a Spanish battery. The shell landed hundreds of yards short of the American lines, churning up mud and vegetation. Spanish soldiers could be seen moving towards the Americans.

"Are they going to attack?"

Ryder could only watch in grim disbelief. The Spanish advance seemed confused and uncoordinated. "Give the order. Our guns can open fire when they are within range and the same with our rifles." He turned to Barnes. "I have the damndest feeling that is some kind of spontaneous eruption. If so, we're going to chase them back real fast."

Only a few hundred enemy soldiers were advancing. They were yelling and screaming. They reached the white painted stakes that Ryder's men had pounded into the ground to designate range. First, the pair of twelve-pounders on the hill fired at extreme range, hitting nothing. The Spanish soldiers wavered, but gathered their courage and advanced. American cannons fired again, this time with the shells landing in the midst of the enemy, throwing them around like toys.

"Can we use the Gatlings?" Barnes asked with almost unseemly excitement.

"No. We hold them back. They'll be our little surprise when the right time comes."

The Spanish had stopped. Officers could be seen

taking control and leading their men back to safety.
Ryder ordered everyone to cease firing.

He took a swallow of miserable tasting water from
his canteen. Now what the hell was that all about,
he wondered?

General Valeriano Weyler was livid as he left the
hospital tent and walked through the ashes of the fire.
First, a group of rebels had penetrated deep into his
encampment and then one of them had attempted to
assassinate Gilberto Salazar.

In a way, Weyler thought it was a shame that the
attacker had failed. Salazar was proving to be more
trouble than he was worth. After all, he was the man
widely given credit for starting the war in the first
place, although both he and Governor-General Villate
thought that the Americans would have found some
other reason to begin fighting. American greed and
rapacity knew no bounds. Salazar's attacker, now thoroughly dead, had mortally wounded Salazar's horse,
and the major had been thrown under the dying animal. The most serious injury to him appeared to be
a badly pulled groin muscle. The rest of his injuries
were bruises and cuts.

A groin pull could be nasty and painful and easily
take a man away from one of life's more congenial
pursuits—sex with a woman. There were rumors about
Salazar's sexual activities, but Weyler had always dismissed them. Salazar was as manly as anyone he knew
and even had a luscious and bosomy German mistress
to compensate for his shrew of a wife. He laughed
silently. If anyone could make a man's testicles wither
and blow away it would be Juana Salazar. Fairly soon,

Gilberto Salazar would be able to ride a horse but not his wife. On the other hand, he thought, laughing softly, who would want to?

Before the fire was finally put out, a score of tents had burned and a small number of men had been injured. The worst was the uncoordinated and spontaneous attack on the American positions by Cuban militia. This had resulted in a handful of dead and wounded that had been retrieved under flag of truce. During the truce, one American had yelled down, asking in Spanish just what the hell that was all about. His men did not respond, which must have told the Americans that the whole thing was a big mistake.

But now, Salazar was a kind of hero. The Americans or the rebels had struck at him specifically. Weyler had reluctantly succumbed to pressure from local Spanish and Cuban loyalists and promoted him to the temporary rank of colonel. Salazar still had close to two thousand men under his command. The loyalists had demanded a reward and he had given it to them. Salazar could be their hero.

Weyler paused and looked around. A number of soldiers were looking at him curiously. They knew that he was in charge of the army and that their lives were held in the palm of his hand. He took out his binoculars and stared at the American trenches. Blue-uniformed soldiers were moving around with impunity. He could see that they were strengthening their defenses just as he was strengthening his own. More soldiers were en route from Havana and still more were gathering around Havana from other parts of Cuba. Spain was going to take a major chance and gather almost all of her army in Cuba close to Havana in order to destroy the Americans. Only Santiago would have a strong garrison. If this meant temporarily giving control of some areas of the island to the rebels, then so be it. When Spain was victorious, the rebels could be crushed in good time.

And, he smiled, it would be a good time. Killing the enemies of Spain was the greatest of pleasures.

Once more, thought Wally Janson, as his beloved steamer, the *Aurora*, moved easily through the green ocean waters north of Cuba. Unlike the last time when cleverness and bravery were necessary to keep him from being taken prisoner, or even killed, this convoy was well protected.

At least he hoped so. Two new American cruisers, the *Atlanta* and *Chicago* led the convoy, while the third, the *Baltimore,* brought up the rear. A number of swift gunboats, recently converted from civilian use, kept the thirty or so transports in something resembling three parallel lines. Having to play by the Navy's rules chafed a lot of the civilian skippers, but Janson knew if was for their safety. Staying in order might save them in the event of an attack. Scatter and they'd be picked off like stragglers from a deer herd killed by wolves.

As before, he had a detachment of soldiers with him, only this time it was a troop of Texas cavalry and their damned horses. He thought the Texans smelled bad enough, but their horses were even worse. The Texan commander was Captain Jesse Lang, a long, lean, and deadly-looking cowboy who said he owned a ranch and other businesses outside of Dallas and that this was a great way to see some of the rest of the world. He also claimed to have fought Comanche,

Apache, and Mexicans, so a bunch of damned Spaniards would be no big thing to him.

Along with Lang's men and horses, the *Aurora* also carried a large quantity of food and ammunition. Other ships were carrying several thousand additional soldiers. Lang had brought along something that he said worked well to control cattle and ought to work deterring Spanish attackers—barbed wire. He said he'd tried to convince people in the War Department of its military potential, but they either weren't interested or were overwhelmed with ideas, many of which were crackpot notions. He insisted that his, of course, wasn't. The wire sounded intriguing to Janson, but he'd like to see it in action before endorsing it. That is, if anybody cared what he thought.

Janson's thoughts were interrupted by distant sounds. He thought he heard thunder from the east. No, it wasn't thunder; it was signal guns from other ships that were racing towards the convoy. He raised his telescope and could see a faint feather of smoke on the horizon.

"I think we've found the enemy fleet," drawled Captain Lang. He'd mounted to the small quarterdeck without permission for about the tenth time since leaving Charleston. Janson had come to realize that Texans weren't all that much on formality. But then, he'd granted that same privilege to Colonel Ryder, so what the hell.

Dark shapes appeared on the horizon, first the masts and then the bulk of the squat ships. The *Atlanta* and *Chicago* flew a number of signal pennants and then veered to meet the intruders. The *Baltimore* was coming up as well.

"Damned if we aren't about to have a naval battle,"

said Lang. "I've never seen one of them. I hope it turns out as well as the last one you had."

Janson simply nodded. He was too intent on watching the warships approaching each other on collision courses to comment further. He had, of course, told the affable captain all about his ship's encounter with the Spanish patrol boat.

"Those are the two Spanish battleships, the *Numancia* and the *Vitoria*," Janson said softly. "And the other ships are likely their smaller cruisers, the *Aragon, Castile,* and *Navarra.*"

Lang spat tobacco over the side, doubtless streaking the hull with the juice. It was something else Janson wished he wouldn't do. "You seem to know a lot about their navy."

"I thought I'd enlighten myself after they tried to kill me—something about knowing thine enemy."

The ships were now within a couple of miles of each other and commenced firing as they closed the range. Clouds of smoke obscured the warships and splashes showed where shells had missed. They were like spectators at a bad play as miss after miss raised huge splashes. It was becoming very obvious that ships moving in different directions and at varying speeds could not hit each other unless they were extremely close. The *Numancia* and the *Chicago* maneuvered to near point-blank range and fired on each other.

Shells from the *Numancia* struck first, smashing into the *Chicago* and sending debris flying, but then the *Numancia* was struck in turn by shells from the *Chicago*'s larger and more quickly reloaded guns. Still, the *Chicago* had been badly hurt and was slowing. Black smoke was pouring from her gunports.

"I think we just lost a ship," said Lang, and Janson sadly concurred. However, the *Numancia* had not escaped unscathed and the Spanish ship was taken under fire by the *Atlanta*. The *Baltimore* was also within range and began shelling the now burning *Numancia*. The enemy battleship slowed, then stopped dead in the water. The American ships moved in for the kill and *Numancia* began to sink. Scores of crewmen jumped from her.

The remaining Spanish battleship, the *Vitoria*, had turned and was steaming away.

"What the hell!" exclaimed Janson. "Look at that!" A Spanish cruiser was headed directly towards the *Baltimore*. "The son of a bitch is going to ram her."

The crew of the *Baltimore* spotted the danger and attempted to maneuver away. The smaller Spaniard matched their turns and, guns roaring, plowed into the hull of the *Baltimore*, impaling herself on the larger American ship. There was silence for a few moments, but then the Spanish ship exploded, raining fire and debris onto the American, causing numerous fires. As the *Numancia* slipped beneath the waves, the men of the *Atlanta* and *Chicago* attempted to help the *Baltimore*. What was left of the Spanish cruiser was sinking and threatening to drag the *Baltimore* down with her.

As American ships closed in to help, the *Baltimore* exploded with a deafening roar.

"Jesus," said Lang. "We're going to go and help them, aren't we?"

"Of course," said Janson. "We can't leave the living for the fish."

Janson looked around at what had once been a

well-organized convoy. Ships had scattered in all directions when the Spanish attacked and were only beginning to return. His *Aurora* was one of the closest to the site of the battle. Lifeboats were in the water and men could be seen swimming or splashing frantically, while others weren't moving. He would rescue everyone he could, American or Spanish. It didn't matter.

The *Aurora* moved slowly and carefully through the debris field. Ship's boats were lowered and crews rowed them towards scores of swimmers. Cargo nets were draped over the hull to enable the strong to climb to safety. Lang's riflemen covered them as they clambered over. "Can't be too careful," the Texan said. "Some of them damn greasers might decide to take over your little ship and run back to Cuba."

They divided the men into two groups—American and Spanish. Then they tried to help the wounded. "What about the dead?" Janson was asked.

Janson forced himself to look the few feet to the water. Bodies and chunks of meat were floating along with the current. He forced the vomit down his throat. "If it looks American, try to save it. Maybe we can identify them and contact their families."

And maybe not, he thought as one terribly mangled corpse bobbed by. Fish were already nibbling at it. He thought he saw barracuda circling from below. He visualized their razor teeth slicing through human flesh. "We'll be in Matanzas in a few hours, tomorrow at the latest," he said softly. "At least we can give them a Christian burial."

Ruth Holden padded barefoot across the small room that she and Sarah Damon shared. It had finally dawned on the military high command that Clara Barton was correct. The women nurses needed more privacy than that afforded by the canvas walls of a tent to hide them from the leering eyes of thousands of what Ruth described as horny American soldiers. Sarah had never heard the word before in that context but agreed with it. Thus, she and the ten other female nurses took over a decent-sized house in Matanzas that had been abandoned by its previous owners.

It was far from luxurious but it did afford the women a degree of privacy. Both Ruth and Sarah were dressed only in cotton shifts that left their arms bare but covered them to their knees. They were still hot and sweaty but far more comfortable than when in full attire.

A room on the first floor contained a slightly rusty metal tub, which the women filled with water from a stream that flowed into the bay, but only after first ascertaining that no military latrines were upstream. It was not luxurious bathing, and, in keeping with custom, they kept their shifts on and bathed around them. It was awkward, but it sufficed. It and the limited and bland food the Army provided were a far cry from the luxury they'd both been accustomed to. To complete the picture, there was a stinking outhouse a few yards away from the kitchen.

Ruth laughed. "This reminds me of my life as a young girl trying to escape from Poland, only it wasn't this hot."

"If you're going to reminisce, should I call you Ruta?"

Ruth shook her head sadly. "Ruth Holden is who and what I am now. Unless, of course, I change my mind once more and again decide to be Ruta Jasinski.

If I didn't think it would confuse people, I would."
She brightened. "Perhaps I'll call myself Ruta Jasinski
Holden."

Sara would not argue or tease her friend. She'd
been told all about Ruth's life before coming to the
U.S. and it wasn't pretty. The only part that was even
a bit whimsical was Ruth's selection of Holden as a
last name. It was that of a British embassy staffer in
Paris whom she found odious and boring.

"Have you heard from Haney?" Sarah asked.

Ruth, now Ruta, grinned. "It's not that far from the
top of his mountain to here. Sometimes he manages
to slip away."

"And where do you manage to find privacy?"

"In storage areas and warehouses," she said with a
knowing smile. "There are many places if you know
where to look. He knows a lot of other sergeants
and they make sure to look away when we wish to
be alone. Making love on a pile of tenting isn't the
worst thing in the world. You and your colonel should
give it a try, at least before he becomes a general."

"General? Where did you hear that?" Sarah asked,
astonished. It was the first she'd heard of any possible
promotion for Martin.

"Some sergeants gossip like old ladies," Ruta
answered. "It does seem that the higher-ranking generals are displeased with the efforts of some other
high-ranking officers. It also seems that Washington
might not be all that thrilled with the way General
Miles is leading the army and that General Terry
might be very ill. Changes could come soon, and
kindly recall that your paramour has gotten a lot of
very favorable publicity recently."

Sarah decided to send Martin a note asking about the rumored promotion. She thought about delivering it herself, but he had made it abundantly plain that he did not want her up on Mount Haney, which some were calling Haney's Hill after belatedly realizing that it wasn't all that high. Regardless, she yearned to be with him, to feel his arms around her and his hands caressing her body. She would have to figure some way to be discreetly and totally alone with him. Just a few hours would be delicious and wonderful. However, it would not be on a stack of tenting.

Sarah's thoughts were interrupted by commotion coming from outside. She and Ruta looked through a window and saw men running towards the waterfront. Someone said an American warship was coming in and it was in bad shape.

The women dressed quickly and looked through another window that faced the bay. A large warship that someone in the crowd said was the *Chicago* was steaming slowly into the bay. She was escorted by a number of other transports. The *Chicago* was listing to starboard and, as she got closer, heavy damage and evidence of fires could be seen.

Clara Barton ran to each of the women informing them of the obvious and telling them to get to the hospital. There had been a battle and there were casualties, many casualties.

Kendrick watched as the *Chicago* anchored as close to the makeshift docking facilities as it possibly could. Beside him, Pywell took pictures of the wounded battleship. Lifeboats and other small vessels began the task of getting the wounded to the hospitals. As

he walked among the wounded it occurred to him
that the mutilations suffered in land warfare were the
same as in a naval battle. Despite having seen it so
many times before, the human suffering was terribly
depressing and the stench from torn and infected flesh
and ripped bowels was almost overwhelming.

He watched as doctors and nurses went about their
grim task. That some of them were women who looked
like lovely and genteel ladies no longer surprised him.
Women were constantly disabusing the idea that they
were a frail sex that needed to be sheltered from the
world. He wondered if Juana would be able to handle
an emergency like this and decided that she would.
Not surprisingly, he hadn't heard from her. He would
have to figure out a way to get a message to her.

Clara Barton stood in front of him. "Either be
helpful or get out of the way," she demanded sternly.

Kendrick quickly decided that he would be no use
as a medico and stepped away. A civilian transport
was also disgorging wounded and unhurt and some
of each category were Spanish. The Spanish prisoners looked confused and dispirited. They also looked
harmless. Whatever fight that had been in them was
no longer there.

Someone grabbed his arm. "Hey, pal. You got any
idea where I can find an officer named Ryder?"

"Sure. He's up on that snow-covered peak called
Mount Haney. Who wants to know?"

"Jesse Lang, that's who and if that peak's snow-
covered I'm a mountain goat."

The two men introduced themselves. Kendrick
quickly realized that Lang had been an eyewitness
to the battle that saw the sinking of the *Baltimore*

and the damaging of the *Chicago*. He also realized that he probably wouldn't get access to senior Navy personnel for a while. The commanders would like to keep their losses to themselves. Too bad. He would use whatever sources he could and the hell with the Navy's secrets. Right now, it looked like the ships of the small United States Navy had been mauled.

"Lang, I'll make you a deal. I'll take you up the fearsome slopes of Mount Haney and introduce you to Colonel Ryder if you will tell me all you know about the battle that just took place."

"Sounds fair, although it might cost you a couple of drinks," Lang said. "I might just bring along the captain of the ship I came on, a man named Janson. You'll find his observations interesting as well since he actually knows which end of a ship is up."

"Excellent," said Kendrick. "Maybe the good captain can help me figure out if the United States still has a navy."

Custer was drunk, a condition that was becoming increasingly normal and a source of concern to most of his inner circle. While he had been told he should not leave the United States, there was no prohibition on his leaving the increasingly hostile confines of Washington where he was being held to account for the slow progress of the war. Thus, he had chosen to go to St. Augustine, Florida. There he could see for himself many of the efforts to maintain the Army and Navy.

For his stay, he had commandeered the elegant Markland House in St. Augustine. There, he and Libbie sought to get closer to the action and farther away from his critics. He brought with him his secretaries of War and the Navy, as well as his secretary of state. Neither man was pleased to be in a steamy Florida backwater. They felt they should be in the nation's capital where the action was and it didn't matter if they were connected to Washington by telegraph or not.

All four men sat on the veranda and sipped whisky. It was understood that Libbie Custer was just inside and would listen to everything through an open window. It served to maintain the fiction that President Custer was totally in charge instead of having a partner who might just be more than an equal. Many men, including most of those in the room, thought it was unseemly, unladylike, for a woman to be involved in the affairs of government.

"Well," Custer said, his voice slightly slurred, "who the hell won the battle?"

Secretary of the Navy Hunt put down his drink. He had scarcely touched it. "Unlike a land battle where the victor usually claims the battlefield, no one can lay claim to the ocean. However, the Spanish did depart and leave the convoy and the rest of the escorts to proceed uninterrupted to Matanzas. Therefore, it is safe to say that we were victorious."

"But we lost ships," Custer insisted. "The *Baltimore* is gone and the *Chicago* is almost destroyed. Only the *Atlanta* remains and she too was damaged. What the hell ships do we have left if that damn surviving Spanish battleship and their remaining cruisers come out to play?"

This time Hunt did take a swallow of his drink. "We have it on good authority that the remaining Spanish battleship, the *Vitoria*, is in Havana harbor where she is being watched by some of our smaller ships. The *Atlanta* is also off Havana and will engage the *Vitoria* if she tries to come out. We are confident that the *Atlanta* can handle her. Despite sensationalist rumors in the press to the contrary, the *Atlanta*'s damages were slight and she will be completely ready in a very short while. In the meantime, the *Chicago* will be temporarily repaired and then sent to Charleston for more complete repairs. Unfortunately, she will be out of the war for several months at the least."

Custer turned to his secretary of state. "Blaine, you've got to get us more ships."

Blaine shrugged. "It's not going to happen. England and France are now working together and have decided that it would be in their best interests to not play a part in this war; therefore, they will not be arming either side. Apparently they are concerned that the war between us and Spain could spread. They are also concerned that Germany might try and gobble up Spanish possessions if Spain is defeated too utterly."

"I thought we had a deal with the Brits," Custer said petulantly.

"Britannia rules the waves and Britannia waives the rules," said Blaine with a wry smile. "And British wealth rules the land the waves surround. If the British decide to renege on a deal, there's not much we can do about it except send diplomatic notes that will be read and ignored."

Hunt finished his drink and poured himself another one. It was far too hot for whisky, even on the pillared veranda of the Markland House. There was no breeze and he'd begun to sweat profusely. "Then we must go ahead with first arming merchant ships and, second, building our own battleships, no matter the cost. Unfortunately, that latter course will take time."

"And we might not have time," said Robert Lincoln. "Reports are that the Spanish will launch a massive attack against General Miles' army at almost any moment. They've moved more troops around Matanzas than we thought they would. There are enough Spaniards to overwhelm our men."

Custer stood and staggered slightly. The men could hear Libbie gasp through the open window. Fortunately, the president did not fall down. "Damn it to hell. And I'm sick and tired of reading about all these problems in the newspapers. I want someone to arrest that bastard Kendrick and send him back here to St. Augustine, and preferably in pieces."

Robert Lincoln looked away. Nobody was going to arrest Kendrick. The man was too popular with the Army for the simple reason that he reported the truth. Besides, nobody was certain where to look for the man. After his latest report of the heavy casualties suffered by the Navy, he'd decided to make himself scarce. There were even rumors that he'd fled to Havana where he had friends who would hide and protect him.

With her husband gone to the war at Matanzas and then to a hospital bed, Juana felt liberated. Gilberto's wounds weren't that serious, just debilitating. He'd dislocated his shoulder, sprained a knee and, worse, suffered a major and excruciatingly painful groin pull that, according to what she'd been told, made it almost impossible for him to sit, much less stand.

Even though her husband was generally impotent,

it pleased her that he would be useless to any other woman, even Helga, his mistress. To her astonishment, Helga felt the same way.

"He has been a pig to me, just as he has been a monster to you," Helga told her one afternoon. "He uses me and then ridicules me. He says I am fat and stupid. If I didn't need the money he gives to provide for me and my child, I would have left him a long time ago. Of course, you understand fully what kind of a man he is."

Child? Juana had no idea. "Helga, who is the father? Is it Gilberto?"

Helga thought that idea hilarious. "No, the girl's father is a merchant in Mexico City. He had been sending money, but then it stopped. He must have found out about Gilberto. So now I must work for a living and that means satisfying your husband's strange cravings."

Juana did not think Gilberto's cravings were all that strange, just nothing she wished to do with him. With Kendrick, fine, she thought and felt her cheeks flush, but not with Gilberto.

"Do you hate him enough that you would help me conspire against him?"

"With greatest pleasure," Helga said. Her cheeks shook. She'd been gaining even more weight and it wasn't flattering. Juana thought that Gilberto would soon dismiss her and look for a replacement. She shuddered. Just as long as Helga's replacement wasn't named Juana. One of her fears was that he would use his greater strength to force her to perform distasteful acts on him.

"Wonderful. I will see to it that you have funds

to provide for your daughter if you will aide me in shaming Gilberto."

Helga beamed. "What do you want me to do?"

"I have friends in the revolution who will help me get in contact with James Kendrick. Your job will be to go to the hospital and see to it that Gilberto stays there. If it looks like he will be heading home, your second job will be to warn me so that James and I can go back to our normal lives and forget we know each other."

Helga actually giggled. "And where will you and your paramour be staying and for how long?"

It was Juana's turn to smile. Actually, she was beginning to feel like a mischievous schoolgirl. "I have friends who are discreet and will provide a place. You just keep an eye on Gilberto."

"You are not ready to trust me fully, are you?"

"No."

Helga was not upset by the reply. "I wouldn't trust me either."

◆ Chapter 10 ◆

"WELL," SAID LANG, "WHAT DO YOU THINK?"

Ryder looked at the way the barbed wire encircled much of the defensive perimeter on the top of the hill. There wasn't enough to totally go around the hill's defenses without making it a fairly useless single strand fence, but what Lang had done with what little he had was impressive.

"I can't believe the Army wasn't interested. After all, similar defenses like *chevaux de frise* or *abattis* have been around for centuries," Ryder said, referring to many styles of obstacles that had been developed over time. "This is so much quicker to install and possibly more difficult to remove."

"Not only that," Lang added, "you can shoot through the stuff if it isn't too thickly stranded. I'm not trying to butter you up, but your idea of using the wire to steer any attackers towards your Gatling guns is brilliant. It's just human nature to not want to be impaled on something sharp, so, like the way water flows, the Spaniards should go to where they think there is no wire."

Ryder thought of piles of bodies stacking up in front of his guns. It was unsettling, but what was the alternative? "We need more wire, lots and lots of wire."

"It's coming, but just when I don't know."

"And you're paying for it?"

"Consider it my little contribution to the war, along with my troop of cavalry who are entirely useless on this hill."

Lang's sixty troopers had been a welcome addition to Ryder's forces. "Your horses might not have a role to play right now, but you say that your men are all excellent shots and they sure look mean as hell."

Lang agreed. "Some of the older boys fought for the Confederacy, but the younger ones just wanted to get the hell out of Texas and see at least some of the world and a part of it that is green instead of a desert, and where there's an ocean. I've got ten thousand acres of shit land that is flat and burned dry most of the time, which, I suppose, is better than having only one thousand acres of shit land. Then I'd really be poor and I'm not. You know, sometimes I wonder just why we wanted to take Texas from the Mexicans in the first place. As to my boys, they see this as maybe a once in a lifetime chance to do something exciting. That and they didn't think it would hurt none to take a few shots at Spaniards. There's no love lost between Texans and Mexicans and most of the boys don't see much difference between a Mexican and a Spaniard."

They walked the perimeter of the trenches, always keeping their heads down. The Spanish had snipers and some of them were good. To prove the point, there was the snap of a gunshot and the sound of swearing a few yards away. The sniper had missed, but the shot had come close and they weren't always that lucky. Two of his men had been wounded before everyone got the message that some Spaniards actually could shoot straight. Barnes had recalled seeing a contraption consisting of a couple of mirrors and a box that enabled spectators to see over crowds at big events. He also recalled that the Navy had some and that they were called prisms or periscopes. He had a couple constructed and they helped out a lot. The men were protected and they could still see the enemy if they started to approach.

The snipers had made it necessary to install the wire at night, when the soldiers were hidden by darkness. Ryder had his own sharpshooters and there was continuous skirmishing between the two forces.

Ryder yawned. He was exhausted. He missed Sarah. It annoyed him that his stocky gremlin of a sergeant, Haney, was finding many excuses for going into town to see his own lover. He would have to make up his own excuse. Perhaps he would raise an issue about sanitation problems and ask her for assistance resolving them. A lot of his men had come down with diarrhea recently. That, he smiled and thought, would not be a very romantic excuse. He wondered if Sarah would mind making love on a pile of tenting like Haney and Ruth did. She'd probably turn him down flat, he sighed, and she'd be right. Sarah was worthy of far better things.

"Anybody watching the weather?" asked Barnes. "We might want to take a look to the west."

The trees on the hill had obscured their view and, besides, they'd been concentrating on the barbed wire and the Spanish. A wall of dark clouds was approaching. As they watched, the wind began to pick up and heavy raindrops commenced to fall. They'd all been told that it was a couple of months before hurricane season, but that did not mean that Cuba was exempt from enormous thunderstorms.

Ryder was annoyed. "Barnes, are you telling me that nobody on the towers saw this coming?" Barnes said he'd check it out later. The lookout towers had been built on the hill to extend their view of the bay and the enemy. It was likely that the men fifty additional feet in the air didn't think a few dark clouds were very important. It was something else that would have to be corrected.

"I think it's time to batten down the hatches," Ryder said and the others began to scurry to cover. He thought about sending a warning to the army down below but realized that he had no real way of doing it. He could ring alarm bells but they were supposed to be used in the event of a Spanish attack. Ring them and the American army would run to their positions, which might not be the best idea. He decided to send a telegram from the hill to headquarters on their recently installed line and hope somebody did something about getting the men under cover. And, of course, there was always the heliograph. Maybe Kendrick would write an article about soldiers and tropical storms. The reporter had been hiding with Ryder's men on the hill.

There was a rumor that Custer, now ensconced in St. Augustine, was mad as hell and wanted Kendrick arrested. That was not going to happen. Ryder had quickly decided that he owed the man too much. Custer could find Kendrick all by himself if he wanted him that badly. Thus, Kendrick had been doing a good job of keeping himself out of sight on the hill with Ryder.

Then Ryder had another thought. When was the last time he'd seen Kendrick? He looked around, "Just where the hell is Kendrick?"

Sarah and the other nurses took shelter from the violent storm in the magnificent and elegant seventeenth-century church of San Charles de Borromeo that was now being used as their hospital. The thought of going through the downpour to their rooms was put on hold. The rain couldn't last forever, could it? No more than forty days and nights, they'd laughed. Ruth brought up the thought of thousands of American soldiers stripping off their uniforms to shower in the rain and be clean for the first time in weeks. It reminded them of the sight of soldiers bathing in the gentle surf as they landed at Matanzas.

"I hope they have enough sense to dry off when they're done. I'd hate to have them all dying of pneumonia," Sarah said.

"Be honest," said Ruth, "you'd very much like to see Martin Ryder frolicking naked in the rain and I'll bet you'd like to be with him."

Sarah agreed that she'd like to be rained upon and genuinely clean, although jumping around in a rain puddle did not seem like something they were quite ready for. She wondered if they could rig something on the flat roof of the house where they lived that they could use for real cleansing during a rainstorm instead of using water in a metal tub that came from a filthy stream. Water for drinking they boiled, but not the water for bathing.

At first she'd thought it mildly sacrilegious that
the church would be used to house the wounded but
quickly changed her mind. What could be better than
a church to help heal men's bodies as well as their
souls? Statues of the Virgin Mary and other saints
gazed benignly down on the men.

A couple of the non-Catholic chaplains and some
of the officers had complained about the overwhelmingly Catholic nature of the building and urged that
the statues and other symbols be removed or at least
covered. General Miles had sternly confronted them
and told them that what they wished was impossible
without gutting the building and offending the local
population even though those people had largely fled.
He added that when they left Matanzas, the U.S. Army
would not leave a desecrated church in its wake. The
protestors had reluctantly accepted that reasoning
and the comforting thought that they wouldn't be in
Matanzas forever.

At this time, there were very few wounded being
treated. Most of the serious casualties from earlier
fighting had been patched up and then sent by ship to
St. Augustine where there were better facilities. The
hospital ships were clearly marked with very large Red
Crosses and the Spanish government in both Havana
and Madrid had agreed to honor their safe passage
as long as no military supplies were transported. In
the event that a Spanish warship hadn't gotten the
message, ships' captains traveled with passes signed
by the Spaniards. It was an oasis of decency in an
increasingly ugly war.

At least they were dry in the church, Sarah thought.
Most of the permanent buildings in and around Matanzas

had been built of a concretelike substance the locals called adobe. Fascinating stuff, it held in the heat at night and kept buildings cooler during the day. Right now she was thankful that it kept them dry. Other than a couple of leaks in the roof, the men in their beds were comfortable and dry.

A couple of the windows had been broken during the invasion, but they'd been covered with wood planking that now served to keep out the thunderous rain. "Once again, we must contemplate building an ark," said Ruth.

"So much for a tropical paradise," added Sarah. "If this is a normal rainstorm, I wouldn't want to be here during the hurricane season. I understand the winds can blow the trees right out of the ground, just like a tornado, only cutting a much broader swath. I guess there's a lot to be said for living inland."

"Good morning, ladies," said a smiling naval Lieutenant Prentice. He'd just ducked into the hospital and was soaking wet. "Once again we meet during a rainstorm."

Sarah remembered the incident all too well. "Just as long as we don't spend the day soaking in a trench and have it followed up by gunfire."

"I have it on good authority that all of the Spanish warships, at least those that can do any real harm, are snugly berthed in Havana, and that is why I'm here. I'm working on the modification of a steamer for some very special purposes."

"And what might those be?" Ruth asked.

Prentice was about to respond when he suddenly looked distressed. "Oh dear," said Sarah, "is it possible that you've said too much already?"

Prentice looked around frantically. Had anyone else overheard him? "You're right. I have a very big mouth sometimes. It's only that what I'm doing is so remarkable that I have a hard time keeping my thoughts bottled up."

Sarah had a hard time keeping from laughing. Good grief. The young officer was still in his early twenties. How much information could he possibly possess, and how much impact could it have on the course of a war between the United States and Spain?

"Don't worry," she said. "Whatever you're doing— and we really don't know what that might be—your secret's safe with us. We have shockingly little to do with the Spanish Army, except to patch up some of their wounded and none are around at this time."

"I think I should leave," Prentice said glumly.

"It's still raining very hard," said Ruth.

Prentice shrugged. "And not likely to stop anytime soon."

The nervous young lieutenant stepped outside and headed to the bay and the spot where the *Aurora* was anchored. In only a step or two he was soaked to the skin. He wanted to kick himself. He was so proud of what he was doing with Captain Janson and the *Aurora* that he wanted to shout it to the skies. However, doing that might get him either court-martialed or killed.

For a man with a strong fast horse and good guides, the distance from Matanzas to Havana could be traveled in a day and a night. Kendrick's original idea had been to go to Cuba's capital and simply observe what was happening. However, his informers in the Spanish camp had gotten word to the American that his nemesis, Gilberto Salazar, was in a military hospital and was likely to be there for a while. Therefore, he thought it likely that Juana might be interested in having a visitor.

He knew he should not have left Ryder's camp without telling him, but he was afraid that he'd be denied permission, which he knew would be the correct thing to do. He knew too much about the American army, its position, leadership, and problems. He also knew that, if captured, he would not stand up very long under torture by the people who had invented the Spanish Inquisition. What he was doing was insane, but he wanted to see Juana and know that she was all right.

With two of Diego Valdez's men as guides they easily made their way through the Spanish army. As one laughingly said, the Spaniards had a large army but not large enough to be everywhere. Kendrick wondered if the American generals knew of the gaps in the Spanish lines. After a few miles in fields and woods, they took the miserable road to Havana and made no attempt to hide.

When he arrived at Juana's house a servant directed him elsewhere, to the house of one of her friends. Cursing, he rode the couple of miles to an elegant estate on heavily wooded grounds, where he was further directed to a small cottage several hundred yards away from the main house. He dismounted and nervously walked the few paces to the door. It had begun to rain and if nobody let him in he was going to be a soaked fool.

He knocked timidly. At first, there was no response. Then it opened and a thoroughly surprised Juana stood there, barefoot and dressed in a robe. She stared at him wide-eyed. "How did you get here so fast? I just sent the message!"

The next morning the two of them bathed, dressed, and went by carriage into Havana. They were exhausted as very little of their night in bed had been spent sleeping. Instead, they had reveled in the rediscovery of each other's bodies.

If Juana was annoyed that James wanted to take time out from their liaison to see what had changed in Havana since his last visit, she stifled the feelings. She was happy to see him, and it was clear that he felt the same way. After all, he hadn't had to seek her out in the first place. It obviously meant that he cared for her.

Kendrick took the reins of the carriage and followed Juana's directions. Again they visited one of the internment camps. There were even more prisoners jammed into it and Juana said there were still more in the others. Again the hatred in the inmate's eyes bore holes in them. "Don't they know you're on their side?" asked Kendrick.

"I hope not. If they do, then I will be useless as a rebel and will be caught by the Spanish and thrown into a dungeon. There are cells in the Castillo de la Cabaña that are centuries old and have known great filth and agony. Neither you nor I would do well in there."

He shuddered at the thought of her being violated by brutal jailers and him being tortured for information he didn't have. Once again he wondered about the wisdom of his coming to Havana.

Juana continued. "Some of us are stockpiling weapons for when the war comes here and we can liberate our own city. We have few guns, of course, so we must concentrate on giving our people machetes and spears. I just don't want to be mistaken for a Spaniard when the day of reckoning occurs."

"How will you prevent that?"

"I have no idea. When the day of reckoning arrives, I hope I will have enough time to get to the homes of rebel friends who will protect me. Certainly, one of the first targets of the rebels will be my husband and people like him and that includes the large number of American Confederates who came to Cuba after your Civil War concluded."

Kendrick understood. He had done an article on the unrepentant Confederates who'd fled to Mexico and Cuba after the end of the Civil War and the death of the Confederacy. He'd thought it ironic that people in the South had once wanted to occupy Cuba and turn it into a slave state to counterbalance the spread of Free states in the Union. A further irony was Spain's freeing of its slaves, however gradual. Where, he wondered, was someone who truly believed in the institution of slavery to go? Straight to hell seemed like a good idea.

They continued on to where they could see the main part of the harbor off the Plaza de San Francisco. They stopped and Juana pointed. "There it is, the target of the American Navy, the Spanish battleship *Vitoria*. The original idea was to have her repaired at the Arsenal on the other side of the harbor, but the ship is too large."

Kendrick noted several men taking photographs of

the *Vitoria* and the several smaller warships clustered protectively around her. "I wonder if I could get a print?"

"Why not? The pictures are for sale. It's not like the battleship's presence is a secret." She chuckled. "I will tell one of the photographers that I am a loyal Spaniard who wishes to immortalize the triumph of the Spanish Navy, and then I will buy it for you as a present."

"You're too kind," he said with a grin.

Juana put her hand on his knee and drew it up his inner thigh. "We have been riding around in this heat for long enough. The clothing I am wearing is beginning to chafe my body," she said as she glared at him sternly. "I am feeling an almost overwhelming urge to get out of them and have my body massaged."

Kendrick pretended to be shocked, "You too?"

Lang walked around the Gatling gun. It was one of an additional two brought up to the top of the hill. Until joining up with Ryder, Lang had heard of them but hadn't seen one. "What is it, fish or fowl?"

Ryder laughed softly and concurred. "I don't think anybody quite knows. The Gatling doesn't have the range of a cannon, but it's on a carriage just like it was one. Placed too far back from the fighting, it's useless. Move it too close to an enemy and their rifle-men can kill the men operating the Gatling."

"Yet you used them to kill hundreds of Sioux."

Ryder rolled his eyes, "My, how the legend has grown. It was nowhere near that many. Perhaps a couple of score both killed and wounded, but that's it. If the Sioux had wanted to take down my little detachment they could easily have spread out and overwhelmed it. I think they left because they were confused and because they didn't want to take too many casualties."

Lang nodded. "And you would have had a hell of a time swiveling the guns to meet a moving target like a bunch of Sioux on horseback."

"That's a big weakness. I think the gun should either be mounted higher and on a swivel so it can turn without chopping down the carriage's own wheels, or maybe the wheels should be smaller."

Lang continued to examine the gun. It was the first time he'd really had a chance to do so since arriving, and he found it fascinating. Along with his ranch, he owned a combination blacksmith and machine shop where he loved to tinker.

"My vote is for the smaller wheels, even though that would make it necessary to carry the gun on a wagon instead of behind pulled by horses," Lang said. "It's amazing that this damn thing has been around for twenty years and there've been no major improvements to it."

"I wouldn't say that. It's a lot better than the half dozen that General Butler bought and paid for out of his own wallet during the closing days of the Civil War, and they are certainly more reliable than what I used at the Little Big Horn. Those had a tendency to jam at the drop of a hat. Thank God they didn't or we wouldn't be standing here. These won't do that. The Navy's using them a lot because they work well on a warship, like I found out on the way here. But the Army really doesn't know what to do with them."

"The Army has a point. They are so damn big and clumsy."

"So design one that isn't. Look, I'll even give you one to work with if I think your ideas have merit. If I were you I'd hurry. I've heard through the grapevine that people like Hiram Maxim and even some inventors in Europe are working on just such a thing—a more compact and mobile machine gun."

Lang thought for a second. "And if you let me work on it and I get it patented, maybe you and I can form a company and get ourselves rich. We could call it Lang and Martin Arms. What do you think?"

Sometimes Ryder thought that he wished the Texans paid more attention to military discipline. But the men from the Lone Star State had proven themselves to be excellent fighters. One old man bragged that he had ridden with Sam Houston at the battle of San Jacinto. Martin doubted it, but hell, the guy looked old enough.

"Great idea, Captain, but first we have to defeat the damned Spaniards who are down there in plain sight. One of these days, either we or they are going to decide that we're strong enough to take on the other. This status quo situation where we're not quite at war with each other can't go on forever."

Martin took a periscope from a soldier and looked over the rampart. There was nothing to be seen. Maybe the damned Spanish snipers had taken the day off. Or maybe it was some saint's feast day. Regardless, he thought it was a hell of a way to run a war.

Major General Nelson Miles was a vain and proud man. He'd risen to the rank of brevet general in the Civil War while still a very young man and had been awarded the Medal of Honor for heroism in battle. Since the end of the Civil War, he'd distinguished himself fighting the Indians and had even supported Custer with troops after the Little Big Horn. He'd married well. His bride was related to both Senator John Sherman and General William Tecumseh Sherman.

In his early forties, he was still a young and ambitious man. He saw the invasion of Cuba with him in command as a stepping stone to greatness. The White House would be in his sights. Unfortunately, he was now assailed by personal doubts. The war was not going as hoped and there had been no great American victories.

He hated councils of war but felt the need to call one. Such councils often indicated indecisiveness on the part of the man calling it.

It was a small group that gathered in the main dining room of the Palacio de Junco in Matanzas. Until the American invasion the del Junco family had lived there. They had fled to Havana and now it was the headquarters of Nelson Miles and the American army. The room was filled with smoke. The family had left behind a number of excellent cigars that the senior officers were enjoying immensely.

Miles had divided the army into three divisions. Their commanders were John Gibbon, Alfred Terry, and George Crook. All had performed well on the frontier but Miles wasn't so sure that their successes against the Indians were transferring to success against the far more numerous and better armed Spanish. It also didn't help that all three were also major generals and ambitious as well. While Miles' orders said that he was in command of the force, he felt that the others were waiting for him to stumble.

Miles glared at them. "President Custer wants us
to attack. He doesn't seem to care that we are greatly
outnumbered and that half our army still can't tell
one end of a rifle from another. It doesn't seem to
matter to him that our three divisions have never
worked together, nor have the brigades and regiments
within them. I predict that an attack before we are
ready would result in disaster."

Gibbon glared at him. "You're sounding a lot like
McClellan in the past war. He kept seeing Confederate shadows and believed that the rebels had twice
as many men as we later found out that they did."

Terry laughed harshly. "Are you saying those are
phantoms and shadows camped around us? We have
roughly twenty-five thousand men and it is clear
that the Spanish have somewhere between fifty and
seventy-five thousand with more dribbling down those
miserable and muddy excuses for roads that lead here
from Havana."

Gibbon responded. "Oh, I agree that we are outnumbered but those are Spaniards and Cubans, gentlemen, not Confederates who were real men and real
soldiers. The Spaniards are corrupt and poorly trained
while the Cubans in their army want nothing to do
with a war against us. Custer may be right. If we
attack, they might just crumble."

"Or they might not," said a glum Crook. "If we
attack what appear to be strong positions and fail, our
army's morale will be seriously damaged and we might
be forced to withdraw from this miserable island."

"Custer would never allow it," said Miles. "He
would order us to fight to the last man, just like he
almost did against the Sioux."

"Too bad it didn't work out that way," said Terry to laughter.

"Which we just might have to," said Gibbon. "We know that our navy was badly mauled by the Spanish. Admiral Bunce says the U.S. fleet is in control and that the Spanish are bottled up in Havana. I'll be blunt—I don't totally believe him. Should it become necessary to evacuate us, who would do it? We cannot count on the Navy to get us out of here. We might have to surrender," he said with a shudder. They all recognized that such a calamity would spell an end to their careers as well as any political ambitions. That it would be a disaster for the United States was a given.

Miles stood and paced. He tugged at his uniform. He'd lost weight and it no longer fit properly. He would have to do something about that. Fortunately, there were some decent tailors in the force. He did not like appearing slovenly. It gave the men a bad impression. Maybe a Ulysses Grant could have gotten away with it, but not a Nelson Miles, he thought ruefully.

Miles continued. "Nor do we yet have enough ammunition, food, and other supplies to sustain a campaign. Even if we were to attack and somehow defeat the Spanish, what then? We would likely be too weak to move to Havana. No, we will stay here and demand supplies and reinforcements before we attack."

"Perhaps Gordon will arrive," Crook said with the hint of a sneer. Former Confederate General John Gordon was rumored to be forming a division of ex-Rebels in Georgia. The men had mixed emotions about working with Gordon. Although a skilled general and a man who had been reconstructed after the war to the point where he had served in the U.S. Senate, John B. Gordon was still a rebel and old habits and hatreds died hard. Still, if he had a division, it would be well trained and equipped and ready to fight.

General Terry coughed harshly and stood up. Miles was annoyed by the interruption until he saw that Terry's face had become pale, almost gray. Miles was suddenly concerned. "General, are you unwell?"

Terry raised his hand to say something, looked puzzled, tried to speak, and pitched forward onto the floor.

◆ **Chapter 11** ◆

WITH DOCTORS TREATING MORE CRITICAL PATIENTS
and with little doubt as to the severity of General
Terry's condition, it fell to Clara Barton to examine him
and officially pronounce him dead. She presumed that
it had been a massive and sudden heart attack and that
there was nothing anybody could have done. As his body
was taken by stretcher, scores of soldiers watched in
solemn silence. Few men had known him well if at all,
but he was one of the army's leaders, and now he was
gone. Within minutes the word had spread throughout
the camp and the men were shaken and concerned.

"After a brief ceremony, we will bury him here,"
pronounced General Miles. A small cemetery had been
started and it included a number of Navy and Army
dead. It was acknowledged that packing him in ice
and shipping his body to St. Augustine was impractical
at this time. When the war was over, perhaps then it
would be time to send his remains back to his family
in Connecticut.

Miles nodded solemnly towards the empty chair. "It may be unseemly, but we have decisions to make and they should be made promptly. I propose that General Benteen take over Terry's division. I don't believe we should wait for Custer or Sheridan to propose someone else and then wait for that person to actually arrive from Washington or even the frontier. Benteen knows the situation. I cannot imagine objections to an essential field promotion."

There was no serious disagreement. They were about to fight a campaign against Spain. They could not wait on the whims of Washington. "Then who will take over Benteen's brigade?" asked Gibbon.

"I will check with Benteen, but I rather think he will recommend Colonel Ryder. The man is skilled and experienced despite his relative youth and, along with winning some minor battles, has gotten some excellent publicity for us, which means it is highly unlikely that Custer will even think of overruling our choice."

There was mild surprise. Ryder was a West Pointer and Miles disliked West Pointers, a feeling that was reciprocated. It sometimes made for prickly relationships.

Crook managed a small laugh. "I can't imagine you being worried about the ability of a very young general."

Miles grinned and flushed. He knew he was not popular. "Sometimes younger generals are the best."

Word of Ryder's promotion had been flashed to him by heliograph from Miles' headquarters. While he was saddened by the death of General Terry, a man who had stood beside him during some dark days, he could not help but be pleased that he was now a brevet brigadier general. Only a short while ago, such an event would have been inconceivable. However, there was a dark side to his promotion. Along with the rank came responsibility for more than twenty-five hundred men in three regiments. Along with the First Maryland he now had the Second New York and the First Delaware, all volunteer units. The New York regiment was in fairly good shape but the men from Delaware would need a lot of solid training.

The first thing he did was inform Barnes that he was now acting commander of the First Maryland Volunteers. Neither Ryder nor Barnes was totally comfortable with this, but there was no immediate alternative. The battalion commanders might grumble, but Barnes had been around Ryder enough to have at least some idea how to run a regiment. Barnes had come a long way in the last few months, but it was folly to think that he could immediately be an effective regimental commander. Ryder firmly told him that he would be watching him carefully and would try to spend as much time as possible with him. Barnes understood.

As to the other two regiments, they were somewhat smaller and had officers with a modicum of experience leading their units. Ryder wasn't totally confident with either man, but these were the cards he'd been dealt. Everyone seemed competent and their men were well positioned and dug in. They ought to be able to hold off a Spanish attack.

He'd just returned to his headquarters on the hill when another message ordered him to come down. General Benteen wanted to meet with him. He borrowed a horse and rode down and into the city of Matanzas. Maybe if he was lucky he'd manage to steal a few minutes with Sarah.

Benteen surprised him by having General Miles present as well. They formally expressed confidence in his abilities to handle the situation. It was good to hear although Ryder wondered if they felt they had to compliment him. They informed him that General Terry had already been buried, which didn't surprise Ryder. There was a war on and it was very hot. His remains might be sent north in the future, assuming they could find them after a few months in Cuban ground.

Miles, who also looked so strained and gaunt that Ryder wondered about his condition, told Ryder to be on the lookout for a Spanish attack. Ryder politely said that he would and wondered just what the hell Miles thought he'd been doing since taking over Mount Haney. He noticed that Benteen turned away and stifled a grin.

The meeting was mercifully short. It was still afternoon and Ryder felt he had plenty of time to be with Sarah before it became dark. He felt he should be with his men in the event of a sneak night attack by the Spanish.

Finding her proved easier than he expected. First, he saw Ruth who directed him to a house where a stern woman told him that nurses were not allowed to associate with soldiers. She softened significantly when he reminded her that he was a general. It was the first time he'd pulled rank since his promotion, and she went upstairs to inform Sarah who was off duty and taking a nap.

She came downstairs a few minutes later. She was disheveled, pale, tired, mussed, and incredibly lovely. They fought the urge to embrace and went outside. There was no privacy there, either. Ruth took up position on his left. "I'm your chaperone," she informed them happily. "Mistress Barton insisted on it."

"Damn," said Sarah as she squeezed Martin's arm.

Ruth continued. "I could get you into the place where Haney and I enjoy ourselves; however, the stack of tents is not all that comfortable and the warehouse is appallingly hot in the afternoon. We always wait until it cools off at night."

"Good planning," Ryder said sarcastically, wondering if there was anyplace where they could find a little decent privacy.

Ruth led them to a small cottage and the three of them entered. "You cannot use the bedroom since someone else owns it. However, I feel a very strong urge to visit the kitchen and look out the window for several very long minutes. There is a lovely couch in the living room that you might find comfortable and pleasurable. You have my permission to enjoy yourselves for a few minutes. Just don't get too carried away. I might have to interrupt you and get you out of here real fast if the owner shows up."

"You're wonderful," said Sarah.

Martin looked around. The cottage was Spartan. There were no personal effects around. "Ah, whose place is this?"

Ruth smiled. "Clara Barton's"

Ensign Prentice stood behind Janson on the bridge of the *Aurora*, now temporarily renamed the *Oslo*.

Her papers showed that she was now a Norwegian merchant and she had just managed to evade the few American warships on patrol. Even if she'd been stopped, her cargo of foodstuffs was not military and, as an apparent neutral, she would likely have been permitted to go on through to Havana. If necessary, Janson would have shown his real identification, but he would not have divulged his purpose.

Prentice felt more than a few minutes trepidation as they steamed slowly through the narrow channel that led from the Caribbean to the inner harbors of Havana. He could not help but stare at the rows of guns on the battlements of the Castillo del Morro and the Castillo de la Cabaña that seemed to be staring right at him. Only a few shells would shatter their wooden-hulled ship. On the other hand, it looked like the Spanish guns were ancient and rusty. He stared though his telescope and saw no one paying attention to the *Oslo* or, for that matter, manning the guns of the two forts.

They were directed to anchor in an area of the harbor called the Ensenada de Marimelena, directly across from the downtown area of Havana and only a few hundred yards away from their target, the Spanish battleship *Vitoria*. Clustered around her were the cruisers *Aragon* and *Navarra*. Other than a much smaller cruiser and a gaggle of gunboats, this was the heart of the Spanish Navy in the New World. And, Prentice thought to himself, we are here to rip its heart out.

Spanish customs inspection had been a joke. The Spanish government was delighted to have a European ship thumb its nose at the Americans and, besides, the *Oslo*'s cargo of foodstuffs was very welcome. It was

considered hilarious to the Spaniards that the cargo
had been picked up in the U.S. and brought to Havana
for sale to America's enemy. The ship was cheerfully
waved through and cleared to unload without even a
cursory inspection.

That no one on the *Oslo* chose to take shore liberty was unusual but nothing worthy of note. They'd
informed the Spanish authorities that they would be
departing as soon as possible and likely with very
short notice. When they sensed that the American
blockaders were weak or distracted, they would run.
The Spanish authorities wished them godspeed. One
said that they were heroes and that he would have a
solemn high mass said for their safety.

Prentice, Janson, and the small crew of American
sailors who had volunteered for the mission loudly
wanted to leave Havana and allegedly make some
more money before the Americans got serious about
their half-hearted blockade. The Spanish understood
their mercantile motives.

The ship was unloaded quickly and payment in English pounds was received. As darkness fell, Prentice and
Janson stood on the bridge and looked at the *Vitoria*.
There was no attempt at secrecy on her part either.
Candles and oil lamps burned and there seemed to be
festivities ongoing. They could hear laughter and the
sound of music. Prentice thought it would be wonderful
to go on board and announce to one and all that he was
an officer in the United States Navy and he'd been sent
with terrible new weapons to sink the Spanish Navy's
only remaining major warship.

If they succeeded, they would be heroes and Prentice
openly hoped for a medal and a promotion. Janson's

hope was less dramatic. He just wanted to sink the damn enemy ship and get away. He also wanted to change the *Oslo*'s name back to the *Aurora* and get his old crew back. Those sailors remained back in St. Augustine. This was no place for civilians.

It was considered very bad luck to change a ship's name. Janson felt a cold breeze and wondered if it was the wind or his fears. Why the hell, he wondered, had he volunteered for this mission? Why had he allowed American naval engineers to modify the hull of his ship so that it now housed two large and lethal torpedoes?

General Weyler was outraged. The request from the government in Madrid, as forwarded through Havana, was almost an insult. King Alfonso XII had sent a message demanding the prompt and complete destruction of the American forces at Matanzas. The letter said that the continued American presence on Spanish soil was an intolerable insult to Spain, the situation was repugnant, and that all efforts must be expended immediately to expel the despised invaders. The implication was clear. In the opinion of the king and the government in Madrid, the Spanish army under Valeriano Weyler was doing little or nothing to resolve the grievous situation.

Vlas Villate was the governor-general of Cuba and Weyler's superior. He had been looking forward to retiring from his position in Cuba and returning to his estates in Spain. The unexpected war had intruded on his plans.

"However crudely put," Villate said, "the king has a point. This appears to be a stalemate and it cannot go on forever. The Americans must be crushed, destroyed, just as we must absolutely wipe out any vestiges of Cuban independence. Madrid cannot, however, understand why it is taking so long to move a Spanish army a mere fifty miles."

Weyler considered Villate to be both his commander and a mentor. They both felt that ruthlessness must be shown, both to the United States and to the rebels now only a few miles from where they were meeting in what had once been the home of a prosperous farmer. Nor did either man much care how many casualties were suffered by the Spanish army. The Americans must go. However, the Spanish army must be victorious in order for that to happen.

"What they don't realize is that the distance from Havana to Matanzas is the longest fifty miles in the world," Weyler said. "The road is a mud track and the army moves at a snail's pace in part because of that. There are no railroads except for those few that carried sugar products to port, and all food and ammunition must be carried by wagon or by mule. Worse, the army is an untrained mess."

"Yes, but it is the army we have and the army we must use," said Villate. "We outnumber the Americans who are just as inexperienced as we are. Many of our officers have never seen battle and even fewer of the enlisted men. However, the same must hold true for the Americans."

Weyler thought he saw an opening. "Which is why I've ordered two divisions from the Santiago garrison to be been sent north to reinforce our army at Matanzas. When they arrive, that will give us an additional twenty thousand men. Our army will total nearly a hundred thousand soldiers."

Villate shook his head. "Given the distance and, again, the state of the roads, it will be more than a month before they arrive, and they will doubtless be in terrible shape when they do. And that will mean more time for them to get ready. No, my good friend, we must show Madrid that we can fight and, if God is on our side, that we can drive the Americans into the sea." He sighed, "I long to see large numbers of American prisoners rotting in our prisons while King Alfonso piously decides their fate. Perhaps he will trade them all for President Custer? Then we can chain him and ship him to Madrid."

Weyler had to smile. "It is a compelling picture and, yes, I do see your point. I shall attack at the soonest opportunity."

"When?" Villate urged. "I must respond to the king."

Weyler stood and examined a map on the wall. The Americans held strong positions both on the hill he understood they called Mount Haney and at the opening of the Matanzas Bay. He would attack both spots. Take the foolishly named hill and guns could dominate at least part of the bay, which would drive away American shipping. Take the opening to the bay and the Americans would be trapped.

Weyler drew himself up to full attention. "We will attack in two days."

Janson and Prentice decided that the time was right. It was well after midnight, but a three-quarters moon and a cloudless sky gave them all the light they would need. The festivities on the *Vitoria* had ended and any civilians were now safely on land. This was a comfort to the two men as the idea of needlessly inflicting civilian casualties was repugnant. If necessary they would do it, but avoiding them was a fervent wish.

Better, the two small Spanish cruisers had shifted their anchorage so that getting a clear shot at the battleship was a good possibility. The *Aurora*'s anchor chains and her engine had been oiled and finely tuned so they made very little noise.

Janson signaled for all ahead slow and the *Oslo*, once again the *Aurora*, began to slowly move away from her anchorage. If anyone on shore or on the Spanish ships noticed, they didn't care. An American flag was ready to be flown as soon as Janson or Prentice gave the order. The American crewmen, most of them now grinning hugely, were dressed as American sailors and not as Norwegian merchant crewmen.

At a point they turned to starboard and began to head towards the *Vitoria*. They had informed the Spanish that they would turn towards the channel and steam through it to the ocean. At only a couple of hundred yards from the Spanish ship, Janson ordered her engines stopped. He also ordered the torpedo tubes on the hull of the ship opened. This caused the *Aurora* to wallow for a moment. The brand new Whitehead torpedoes were propelled by compressed air and had a range of three hundred yards maximum and weren't all that accurate; therefore, the Americans had to be as close as possible in order to hit their target and for the *Aurora* to stand any chance of getting away safely.

Janson nodded towards Prentice. "The honor is yours, I believe."

Prentice swallowed nervously. "Fire one," he ordered through a speaking tube. The *Aurora* shuddered as the torpedo broke free. "Fire two," he yelled, this time exultantly. The first torpedo was headed straight towards the *Vitoria* and the second quickly followed in her path.

Janson ordered the *Aurora*'s engines up to full speed and began to maneuver the ship towards and down the channel. Prentice kept an eye on the *Vitoria* as the torpedo wakes closed. He heard excited and confused yells from the enemy warship as someone spotted them. It was too late. First one and then the other struck the *Vitoria*, sending up mountains of water. The Spanish battleship shuddered and heeled over before recovering. Alarms and screams sounded.

As they headed down the channel, trumpets blared and alarm bells rang. "Fly our flag," Janson ordered and the Stars and Stripes went up at her stern.

"The *Vitoria*'s sinking," exulted Prentice. "She's actually sinking. We've done it."

Janson stole a glance. The *Vitoria* was listing heavily to port and he could see men jumping off her and into the calm warm water. Smoke was pouring out of her from down below. To his experienced eye, she was mortally wounded. The Spanish might actually salvage her someday, but it would be many months before the *Vitoria* returned to combat. "Now all we have to do is get out of here," he said grimly.

Now alert but confused, the Spanish shore batteries opened up on anything that looked like a target and that included the *Aurora*. Someone with a brain clearly realized that a ship fleeing from such a catastrophe might have had something to do with it.

Shells splashed into the water around them. Shortly, the Spanish guns got the range and cannonballs began to strike the Aurora, hulling her and smashing her. Prentice was thrown to the deck, where he lay unconscious and bleeding. A large wooden splinter had pierced Janson's shoulder and he could barely stand the pain.

"Stop engines and strike the flag," he ordered before the darkness overwhelmed him.

Lieutenant Hugo Torres of the Spanish Navy was bored and lonely. He also felt that the Spanish Navy was in such bad shape that it might not even exist in a few days. The escape of the battleship *Vitoria* from the guns of the Americans was being told as if it was a great victory when nothing could be farther from the truth. Her batteries of 6.3-inch and 5.5-inch guns were popguns when compared with the guns mounted by the ships of other modern navies. Even the few large ships possessed by the U.S. Navy outgunned the *Vitoria*. Thus, the *Vitoria* had run from the battle to the safety of Havana's harbor.

The battleship was safe but she was also locked in. As one sailor put it, she was as safe as a nun in a convent. The harbor was now her prison. Numerous American warships patrolled the entrance to the harbor. Any attempt to leave would bring them swarming. Even though all of the enemy ships outside the harbor were smaller than the *Vitoria*, there were so many of them that they would prevail. They would be like a pack of wolves tearing at a horse or a cow. At least that was what the ship's captain had declared. Torres was of the opinion that they should try to blast their way out, and that their bigger guns would prevail. However, the captain had also added that the *Vitoria* had no place to go even if she were

to win free. The only safe place for her would be
Spain and that was out of the question. It was too
far and they would never make it. With that, Torres
had to agree.

The people of Havana knew nothing of this. They
were just delighted that the mighty-looking ship was
there to protect their city.

And that was another thing that annoyed Torres.
Havana was nowhere near the cosmopolitan city he'd
thought it would be. It was small, cramped, and dirty.
Granted Madrid had her poor neighborhoods, but
Havana had so many of them! Worse, there were many
blacks and Indians and few true Spaniards. Many of
those who considered themselves noble were clearly
of mixed racial backgrounds. Madrid society would
have laughed at them.

Nor had he managed to make any headway with
the women of the town. The few really lovely ones
had already been gobbled up by the more senior and
wealthier officers. Torres' family had some money but
not enough to provide him with a lifestyle that would
impress the señoritas. There was never enough, which
was why he'd joined the Navy in the first place. He
had wanted to remove himself as a burden to his family. Well, he thought bitterly, he had indeed removed
himself. Now he might remove himself out of this life
if the *Vitoria* went to sea.

"Lieutenant, the foreign ship is moving."

Torres was about to forcefully remind the sailor
that he didn't have the watch and had only come
on deck to get out of the stifling heat below decks
when he realized that the foreign ship's behavior was
indeed strange. Was she leaving port? All the *Vitoria*'s

officers had been told that she might depart at any time. Well, he thought, this must be the time.

"Don't worry about it, sailor," he snapped.

But wait. The foreign ship was lined up as if she was planning to ram the Spaniard. There was commotion in the water on each side of the foreigner's hull.

He saw things in the water headed towards him and realized with horror that they were torpedoes.

"Alarm!" Torres screamed. "Sound the alarm."

It was too late. The torpedoes slammed into the *Vitoria*'s hull and exploded with incredible violence, actually lifting the ship out of the water for an instant. Torres felt himself being lifted into the air and thrown overboard. He landed in the water and began to thrash. Something floated by and he grabbed at it. He shrieked when he realized it was a human leg, complete with a shoe on its foot.

Crewmen were throwing themselves into the water by the score. No one was making any attempt to save the ship. No matter, he realized as he treaded water. The one remaining capital ship in the Spanish Navy was settling in the mud of Havana's harbor.

Bells and sirens were going off in the city as small boats pushed off to rescue the *Vitoria*'s crew. A few moments later, Torres was standing on a dock looking at the ruined thing that had been a proud Spanish battleship. Scores of bodies floated around her in an obscene dance. Other rescued crewmen clustered around him as if for comfort. He could not help but wonder if he was the battleship's ranking survivor. If so, he was now captain of the wreck of the *Vitoria*.

◆   ◆   ◆

Governor Villate saw the prisoners in the hospital where they'd been taken. There were only eight of them and all were injured, some very seriously. Better for his concerns, two of them were the senior officers who'd been on board the American ship.

The reports from the *Vitoria* were dismal. The battleship was resting on the muddy bottom of Havana harbor with only part of her superstructure showing. She was almost on her side and there was a pair of gaping holes in her hull. These were the results of a torpedo attack. He'd known that the English had the devices and that the inventor had been selling them to a number of nations. He wondered if Spain had any and decided it was highly unlikely. Far too modern and costly to interest the parsimonious government at Madrid, he concluded.

More important, one hundred and seven officers and men had died on the *Vitoria*. Most had been trapped belowdecks and drowned while others had been blown to pieces by the explosion. A shocking number had died in their hammocks where they'd been sleeping. The attack had been cowardly and despicable. The dead and wounded had to be avenged. Spain's honor was at stake.

As a result of the sinking, Spanish naval power in the new world was virtually nonexistent. In a short time the U.S. would have two capital ships to Spain's none, and the American smaller warships were at least as good as the less numerous Spanish vessels.

The two American officers had been brought in on stretchers. They were heavily bandaged and the younger man's legs were in splints. Villate felt like ripping the bandages from their bodies and listening to them scream.

There was a mild and intentional cough behind him. Redford Dunfield from the British Consulate and the International Red Cross had insisted on being present. Since Dunfield was British and since Great Britain was the most powerful nation in the world, his annoying request had to be honored. He was also plump, in his fifties, and exuded a sense of confidence that Villate found both condescending and annoying. He was accompanied by a newly arrived German advisor, Colonel Adolf Helmsdorf. The British consul was in civilian clothes while the German was in full uniform.

The British diplomatic presence in Havana was small. As Dunfield had mentioned several times in earlier meetings, her majesty was most parsimonious when it came to handing out diplomatic titles. Besides, the British ambassador to Spain was located in Madrid, while Havana was a backwater. The Havana consulate was more of a courtesy than anything else. In order to make ends meet, Dunfield spent most of his time working in the import-export business, where he had been successful. Unfortunately for Villate, on this day Dunfield took his consular duties very seriously. The German appeared curious but unconcerned.

The two American prisoners were unconscious and in no shape to be questioned. Villate thought they were pretending, but with Dunfield present he would let it go for another time. However, he did have Spain's pride to salve.

Villate turned on Dunfield and glared. "They will be hanged as pirates and spies."

"On what grounds?" Dunfield asked calmly but firmly. "According to her papers, their ship was a legitimate U.S. Navy warship and she was flying the

American flag when she was taken. Her officers and men are all members of the U.S. Navy; therefore, they cannot be held as pirates."

Villate felt himself turning red with frustration. "They entered the harbor flying a Norwegian flag and presented Norwegian papers. We trusted their integrity. They are *franc-tireurs*, terrorists, and, as such are subject to execution. We will hang them in such a manner that the American ships offshore can see them twist and dangle."

Helmsdorf nodded solemnly. During the Franco-Prussian war, his army had summarily executed a number of Frenchmen who were defined as terrorists. This, however, was different. For one thing, the Americans were all wearing uniforms, which was in accordance with the rules of war and legitimized their actions.

Dunfield shook his head. "According to the Geneva Convention, the officers and men of the *Aurora* were and are legitimate members of a conventional armed force and not terrorists as defined by the Convention. And may I remind you that Spain was a signatory to that agreement. Therefore, you are honor bound to adhere to its terms. You may not hang them."

I would like to shove the Geneva Accord up your ass and set it on fire, Villate thought. Rules of war, hell, he thought. War consists of killing people. There should be no rules when fighting for one's own existence. The Americans should be executed immediately. He had the feeling that the German agreed with him as well. "Are you saying it was a *ruse de guerre* and nothing more?"

"That's correct," Dunfield said, "a trick of war and,

sadly, you fell for it. These men were incredibly brave and successful and not pirates or terrorists. When they get back to their homeland, they will be feted and given medals."

"If they get back," Villate snarled. "A lot can happen to them before that. Perhaps their medical situation could take a serious change for the worse. Perhaps their wounds will become infected, causing their deaths. Perhaps such infections, instead of causing their deaths, would cause their limbs to become gangrenous and need to be amputated. Would the United States like their heroes coming home alive but without arms and legs and being carried in boxes?"

Dunfield paled and responded angrily. "I cannot recommend that you even think of committing such atrocities. In fact, I've just this instant decided that Red Cross personnel will constantly observe the American prisoners and that they will be taken to the British Consulate or some other suitable place as soon as possible, within the hour if I can arrange it."

The two men glared at each other while Helmsdorf turned away. Villate hated do-gooders. Dunfield decided to try and calm things. "Can the Americans be exchanged for Spanish prisoners?"

"I will look into it," Villate said sullenly. "However, I do not believe the Americans have taken enough of our men prisoner in this strange war to make an exchange feasible."

Villate walked over to the two inert figures. He leaned over and spat in their faces. Dunfield thought about protesting but decided he'd pushed his luck far enough.

"You can take the prisoners to wherever you wish,"

Villate said and walked away. The German followed a moment later. But first he winked at Dunfield.

Prentice had been pretending to be unconscious. He thought Janson had been as well. "Mr. Janson," he whispered, "if I heard correctly, we actually stand a chance of surviving."

"Don't get too excited," Janson whispered back. "Anything could happen. One other thing."

"What?"

"You've got spit all over your face."

The bombardment began at first light the next day. The Spanish army had brought up dozens of cannons, most of them small, and began shelling the two major locations—Mount Haney and the entrance to the bay.

With an infantry attack clearly imminent, Ryder's men manned their positions. He sent runners to ensure that his other two regiments were equally prepared. He was beginning to get a taste of higher command and he wasn't sure he liked it. All his instincts said that he should lead from the front, like a good lieutenant or captain should, but now he was a general in charge of three regiments. He could not allow himself to be shot and thus decapitate his command.

"Damn it to hell," he muttered as shells kicked up dirt on the approaches to the defenses.

"And isn't that the truth," said Haney. "And it's also the truth that the Spanish gunners are pretty miserable shots."

The Spanish were having difficulty elevating their cannons so they could hit the crest of the diminutive Mount Haney. He had given orders that his own guns should not respond or duel with the Spaniards until

and if he gave the specific command. He didn't want
to reveal their positions or let the enemy know that
he only had eight twelve-pounders to their thirty or
so guns. In order to confuse the Spanish, Ryder had
dummy gun emplacements built and painted logs
called Quaker Guns jutted out from them.

Barnes scrambled up to Ryder. "The boys are getting frustrated. They want to shoot back."

"Control yourself and your men, Jack. We'll open
fire on their infantry and not their useless cannons,
which, if you hadn't noticed, are missing us. We'll
load with grape and shrapnel, not solid shot. And
when they get close enough, we'll hit them with the
Gatlings. If they're as inexperienced as I think they
are, they'll be coming up the hill in bunches or waves
and we'll be able to hurt them badly."

Barnes turned and walked away. He gotten a few
yards when he stopped suddenly and started to return.
Haney blocked his path and glared at him. "Is whatever you need from the general really important?"

"I just wanted to know if he'd heard anything from
Sarah, or Ruth," he added after a moment.

"Worrying about them is the last thing he needs
to do now, you idiot. He has to concentrate on the
fight in front of him."

"You shouldn't call me an idiot," said a shocked
Barnes.

Haney looked around and saw that no one was
watching them. "Then don't act like one," he said as
he drove his fist hard into the other man's stomach.
Barnes doubled over and retched. Haney grabbed his
shirt and pulled him upright. "The general, bless his
heart, was indeed concerned that you might not be

ready to lead, and you are just proving his point. Now go and take control of yourself and your men and it's a damned shame you fell down like that. And just for the record, there's been no shells landing anywhere near the hospital."

A few yards away, Ryder hadn't heard a word, but figured out that Barnes had almost done something foolish. Still, sergeants should not be permitted to punch majors in the gut. He would have to punish Haney. Severely. Once the battle was over, he would have to think of something. Perhaps he'd have Haney forfeit some of his whisky. Yes, that's a very good idea.

Men began shouting. Large numbers of Spanish infantry were emerging and beginning the long climb up the hill.

◆ **Chapter 12** ◆

WITH SWORDS WAVING, SPANISH OFFICERS SHOUTED and made serious attempts to keep their men in order as they advanced towards the American lines. It was a truly impressive display as they moved out through the heavy foliage in reasonably precise lines. Unit flags flew while drums pounded, and bugles blared, all designed to bolster the bravery of the attackers and intimidate the defenders. Ryder had to admit that it worked, but only to a point.

Although he'd been in combat, it had usually consisted of skirmishes that were small, nasty, and over quickly. Even Custer's fight on the Little Big Horn had involved relatively few soldiers compared with the mass of humanity that was approaching him. This was the first time he'd seen an actual battle involving large numbers of men on each side. At one level it was thrilling; on another it was frightening. His impression was that they were all advancing to kill him. His stomach was churning and he felt a strong urge to urinate. He wondered just how his men were taking it. Probably just the way he was, he concluded.

Although seriously outnumbered, Ryder's soldiers did have the advantage of being in strong defensive positions, which gave them a sometimes false sense of security. Most of their bodies were protected, unlike those of the Spaniards who were out in the open and fully exposed. In theory, the defender had the advantage. In reality, people on both sides were going to die bloody and agonizing deaths.

As the Spanish lines reached a predetermined point, Ryder gave the order and his cannons finally began to fire. Shrapnel and grape chewed into the Spanish ranks. With his telescope he could see white uniforms turning red and bodies being ripped to shreds. Spanish officers screamed and tried to maintain order.

"It's like Pickett's Charge," said Haney, "or maybe that stupid attack at Cold Harbor."

Ryder had to wet his suddenly dry mouth before answering. "You were there?"

Haney chuckled, "Gettysburg no, but Cold Harbor, yes. I was fifteen when I stupidly lied my way into the Army. I thought it would be glamorous and glorious. Christ, was I wrong, General. I watched as an attack involving thousands of men was cut to shreds because the almighty General Ulysses S. Grant made a terrible mistake. It was just about my unit's time to go forward when someone with half a brain called off the attack. Damn, I was lucky."

"Luckier than those poor bastards," Ryder said, looking at the steadily advancing Spanish.

The Spanish formations were disintegrating into a horde as more and more shells rained down upon them. True to human nature, they sought comfort with each other and bunched up, making them even easier targets to kill. When they reached the painted markers that said they were within rifle range, close to three thousand weapons fired. Unlike slower-firing muzzle-loaders of the Civil War, modern American rifles were breech-loaders and both firepower and accuracy were greatly increased. Just as important, shooters didn't have to stand up or turn away from their targets to reload. More enemy soldiers went down like wheat being scythed. But still they came on. Some Spaniards were fleeing, but most bravely continued on.

American officers and NCOs could be heard yelling for their men to fire slowly and carefully and to aim low. There was a normal tendency to fire high and a bullet over the head went nowhere, but a bullet into the ground might just ricochet and hit something. As the Spanish reached the barbed wire, they paused, confused. They had never seen this kind of barrier before. Men behind the first ones collided with them, pushing and shoving them into the wire. The wire was a terrible thing. Spanish soldiers pulled at it and it ripped their hands to bloody shreds in the process. They tried to climb it and got stuck, tearing the flesh of their legs and bodies. They milled around and didn't know what to do.

Ryder was about to wonder where his Gatling guns were when they began adding their insane chatter to the already hideous din. Hundreds of bullets a minute ripped into the Spanish masses. Men fell and Spanish soldiers behind them tried to climb over them or use the bodies as shields. Stymied, the Spanish began aiming and firing at their tormenters, finally causing serious American casualties. Clouds of gunsmoke confused both sides. In some cases, visibility dropped to zero, but both sides still blazed away. Spanish bullets whizzed by while others smacked into the earthen embankment with a thud, and a few found flesh.

"We should be in the front line, General," Lang said.

Ryder shook his head. "Like I told you a hundred times, your men are sharpshooters and I want them where they can be best used, and not mixed in with the brawl."

"I know," said Lang. He looked like a wolf wanting to pounce.

Ryder suddenly realized that Lang was correct. The Texans should be in on the killing. "Bring your men forward now. Have them shoot into that mob but tell them to concentrate on officers and anybody who looks like he's getting through the wire."

Lang had been right. He should have used the Texans sooner and he should have had some men specializing in killing officers shooting at them in the first place. He swore at himself. He still had a lot to learn.

Soldiers in the American lines were beginning to fall. With only their heads and shoulders generally exposed, the wounds were hideous and often fatal. A couple of men broke and ran screaming for the rear. Haney shot one of them in the leg and the other got away. Ryder desperately wanted to see what was happening behind and below him with the rest of the army and Sarah, but he dared not. He had to be a strong leader for his men. He could not turn his back on the enemy no matter how badly he wanted to.

◆   ◆   ◆

"Hold," said Sergeant Kelly. "Hold until I tell you to fire."

"Why don't you wait until they are in our fucking laps, Sergeant? Or do you want us to see the whites of their eyes?"

"Why don't you just shut up, Corporal Ryan."

The howling mob of Spanish soldiers was only a couple of hundred yards away and coming fast. Ryan and Kelly were cousins who'd emigrated from Ireland a decade earlier and, even though they'd served in the army, this was their first real combat. A handful of skirmishes with Indians didn't matter, in their opinion. It was also the first time they would use the Gatling gun since that day on the Little Big Horn when they'd helped save the man who was now President of the United States from a terrible death.

They also found it amusing that the lieutenant who'd led them in their mad dash to save Custer was now their brigade leader. It was a small world, they thought every time the topic came up. It pleased them that the young general himself had recognized them and even said a few kind words to them, and laughed about shared memories.

The two cousins had left the army shortly after the Sioux had been defeated and tried several means of making a living, including working on the railroad. They'd quickly decided that building the railroads was just too damn much work. A new war, chances of promotion, and steady money had induced them to enlist in the First Maryland.

Then they had volunteered to work a Gatling gun when a couple of them were assigned to the regiment. They'd had the mistaken notion that it might keep them out of close-quarters fighting. They hadn't realized that the gun's crew was exposed to enemy artillery or sniper fire. And now a screaming horde of Spanish soldiers was only a couple of hundred yards away. Rifles and cannons were killing them and it was time for the machine guns.

"Fire!" Kelly screamed.

"About fucking time," said Ryan as he cranked the handle that fired the gun. Another soldier was in charge of feeding stick magazines filled with bullets into the gun where gravity put one in each of the revolving barrels. Still another reloaded the magazines as quickly as possible, thus keeping up a continuous rate of fire.

Kelly's job was to aim the beast and, along with a fourth soldier, manhandle it to where the torrent of bullets could do the most harm to an enemy.

Lead rained on the approaching Spaniards, knocking them down and ripping into them. Screams from the wounded and the terrified filled the air, while smoke clouds enveloped them. Bodies piled up. Some had reached the barbed wire only to find that there was little chance of getting through. Getting tangled in the wire meant death. The Spanish attack faltered and they began to fall back. Still, the bullets chased them and found them and more were killed and wounded. The Spanish did not understand their tormentors' new way of war and the retreat became a rout with wounded being trampled by the unharmed. Smoke now obscured the battlefield, so they simply fired where they thought the enemy would be. Soon, there was no enemy.

"Cease fire," Kelly ordered. The smoke thinned

and then disappeared. The hillside was blanketed with dead and wounded.

"Holy Mary," said a stunned Ryan, "what the bloody hell have we gone and done? This isn't war. This is a massacre."

He gagged as the stench from torn flesh and bowels wafted towards them and others were becoming ill as well. They had forgotten just what a large bullet could do to the human body, smashing chests and ripping off limbs. And why men who were called wounded often never returned to battle or were able to lead useful lives.

Carlos Menendez looked up at the hill and could barely see the heads and shoulders of dug in riflemen staring down at him. He was as brave a man as any Spanish soldier, but the sight shook him. After two decades in the armies of Spain and having fought in many skirmishes and a number of battles, this left him very uneasy. Yes, the army commanded by General Weyler greatly outnumbered the Yankees, but these were not the Moslem tribesmen of North Africa nor were they the Moslem Moros of the Philippines. The Moros and the tribesmen were barbarians, savages. They would castrate and flay and then burn alive anyone they caught. The Americans generated a sense of quiet and deadly efficiency, rather than the shrieking and howling of the savages who would never dream of fighting a real battle.

He'd managed to avoid fighting his fellow Spaniards in the last civil war so he had never yet fought anyone European or American. These were the feared Americans. The Yankees had beaten England and Mexico along with the savages who'd once dominated the Americas. They had even fought an incredibly brutal civil war against themselves. They were tough and hardened soldiers and, worse, held the high ground.

The Americans were in trenches and well protected while his men would be attacking in the open. Many would die and he might be one of them.

For the first time since he'd enlisted, he wondered precisely why Spain was fighting in Cuba. It was clear that the majority of the Cubans he'd met and talked to wanted nothing to do with Spain, and how could he blame them? From what he'd seen since arriving, the Spanish government in Cuba was corrupt and incompetent and brutal towards its own citizens.

Carlos was sweating profusely and not just from the combination of brutal heat and heavy uniforms. He looked at the men in his squad and saw the same fear he hoped he was hiding. He cared for his men and they needed him to be calm. He was the only one with any real combat experience, even if only against savages. The rest were virgins.

Trumpets blared and officers shouted orders. Corporal Carlos Menendez barked at his men and they formed into ranks. More trumpets sang out and they began to move forward. While the captains and lieutenants waved their swords, Carlos urged his men to yell and scream. They did and it seemed to help calm their fears, but only for a second.

Guns began to fire and men began to fall. The soldier next to him screamed and grabbed his knee. A bullet had almost taken off the lower part of his leg. Other soldiers stared at the wounded man until Carlos pushed them and got them moving forward.

Another from his squad fell, this time with a bullet in his face. Carlos did not need a doctor to tell him that the man was dead.

The attack was losing cohesion. Formations were falling apart. A terrible screeching sound was heard, followed by a rain of bullets. These must come from the Gatling guns the Americans were said to have. The officers said they were harmless and not to worry about them. But men were falling everywhere and the attack was stalling.

His lieutenant grabbed him by the shoulder. "Get those men up that hill, Corporal. That's the only way we'll survive."

Yes, he thought. Take the hill and the killing will stop. He looked for more men from his squad and saw only two. They looked at him and began running down the hill and away from the fight.

"Cowards," he screamed.

Something hit him in the leg and he fell face forward onto the ground. He tried to stand, but couldn't. He felt something sticky running down his leg. He was bleeding from his left thigh. The blood wasn't pulsing so it wasn't a serious wound, but he couldn't stand. He also couldn't go forward. Most of Spain's finest had fallen and the rest were running back to their camp. Carlos could only crawl back down the hill, hoping that the Americans didn't think killing wounded enemy soldiers was a fine sport.

They didn't, and halfway down, a couple of soldiers grabbed him by the arms and helped him to an aid station. His leg was bandaged and he was laid on the ground as the cots had been reserved for officers and the truly seriously wounded.

Two days later, his captain came to visit him. Enough of the seriously wounded had died that he now had a cot. Carlos was the only man in his squad who hadn't been either killed or very seriously wounded. The lieutenant who'd tried to get them to go forward had been shot in the stomach and had died screaming and howling the next day.

"You fought bravely, Corporal," said his captain. "I saw you through my binoculars."

Carlos wondered why the captain had been so far from the action that he needed binoculars. He kept silence.

"The doctors say you will not be fit for combat for some weeks, perhaps longer. Therefore, I am going to assign you to work with Lieutenant Flores as he works to recruit replacements."

Carlos nodded and thanked the captain. He despised working to trap innocent and not-so-innocent men into the army, but it was far better than having his body savaged by American bullets.

Sarah tried not to think. She had come to Cuba to help heal the men fighting the war and now the war was upon them in all its fury. Cannons from several directions thundered and then the clatter of rifle fire could be heard. The Spanish were attacking at the point of the bay and at the hill where Martin commanded.

"Casualties," someone yelled and the first of the mangled were led or carried in. Behind was what looked like a never-ending stream of them and the sights were worse than she had ever imagined. She wanted to scream at the sight of some of the wounds.

Men had limbs ripped off and others had been dis-emboweled, with intestines and bones clearly visible. The man with no face that she'd been afraid to treat receded into the recesses of her mind.

Clara Barton had given herself the terrible task of dividing the wounded into groups—those who could be saved by treatment, and those who should be left to die after being given enough narcotics to numb them until they slipped away quietly and peacefully.

Several priests and ministers were trying to bring solace to the wounded and sometimes it helped. Sometimes the wounded just screamed louder because they thought the presence of a churchman meant that they were going to die.

A boy on a cot close by to her was sobbing for his mother. He looked about sixteen and Miss Barton had decided that his wounds were mortal. He would never see his mother again. Sarah helped Doctor Desmond set some fractures and held a man's arm while he extracted pieces of metal from it.

The man looked up and saw Sarah. "You better run while you can," he said. His eyes were wide with fright and pain. "There's millions of them and they're gonna kill everyone. And what they'll do to the women can't be said."

She wondered if it was true. If the Spanish broke through, what would happen to them? Would the Red Cross flag be enough to save them or would a vengeful and angry Spanish army kill the wounded and then rape and murder the nurses and doctors? She'd heard that sometimes even the best of men sometimes went crazy during battle. From what she was seeing, she believed it.

A few more wounded were beginning to come down from the hill. She stole a look to see if she knew any of them. She didn't and felt a mixed sense of relief. But that didn't mean that all was well with Martin. He could still be lying up there, bloody and broken. Perhaps he was crying for her as the boy had cried for his mother. She wanted to sob but couldn't afford the luxury. The numbers of wounded were backing up.

She became aware that the firing had died down, almost stopped. There were scattered cheers off in the distance.

General Miles entered the tent and looked in on the wounded. He appeared harassed, she thought, and why not. He took off his hat and waved it, getting their attention. "We stopped them, boys. We killed a ton of them. They won't be back for a long while." With that he waved the hat once more and left the men in the tent.

A wounded man missing an arm lay on a cot beside Sarah and snorted, "At least the dumb fucker didn't ask for three cheers. I would have waved my stump instead. Oops, sorry ma'am," he said sheepishly. "I don't think I should have said that."

She smiled and gently ruffled his hair. "Soldier, I think you've earned the right to say any fucking thing you wish."

The men of Gilberto Salazar's Legion had not been called on to do anything this day. Instead, he'd leaned on his crutches and watched proudly as the Spanish army marched off in all its glory to destroy the American invaders. He'd cheered as they headed up the hill in proud ranks with flags flying and drums and bugles sounding. But then the Americans began to shoot. First the cannons tore into their ranks and then torrents of rifle and machine gun fire further decimated them. The proud ranks became a mob, but still they bravely climbed the hill. His stomach contracted and he had to stop himself from shaking with fear at the sight. He thanked Jesus and the Virgin that he had not been called upon to attack this day.

But then the advance stopped. Puzzled, Salazar aimed his binoculars and saw soldiers falling in heaps before an almost invisible barrier. What the devil? The advance was faltering and he sensed that the retreat would soon begin. This phase of the battle was over and it would be a crushing Spanish defeat. As the attackers fell back, what remained of their discipline collapsed and the Spanish withdrawal became a mob of men seeking the comfort of their earlier positions. Even officers had succumbed to the panic and were running frantically.

Salazar ground his teeth and tried not to weep. What had gone wrong? There had been so many more Spanish soldiers than American defenders and, yes, it was presumed that the attackers would suffer heavier casualties than the defending Americans. But it was also presumed that the weight of their numbers would overwhelm the American positions, however strong their positions might be.

He'd read that attacks were fragile things. Men had to agree to march into enemy fire and generally without much of a chance to return that fire. The job of the attacker was to continue to advance and make contact with an enemy who was trying to kill him, and drive that enemy away. But today, the

Spanish had been halted and, instead of simply heavy
casualties, there had been a slaughter. He found it
hard to fault the men who had suffered so much. In
a very short while there would be a truce to enable
the dead and wounded to be cleared from what had
become a field of death. He had to know what had
caused the advance to stop. He would have to swallow his many fears and go up the hill.

He confronted a frustrated General Weyler and said
that he wanted to see what had caused the attack to
fail when the truce went into effect. Swearing mightily in rage and frustration, Weyler agreed and, after
stripping off his officer's tunic and exchanging it for an
enlisted man's, Salazar limped up the hill on his cane.
He trembled with fear and wondered if he hadn't let
his passions lead him into a very bad decision. He had
reached the point where the attack had started when
yells went out that the truce was in effect. Thank God,
he thought, and walked up the rest of the hill. He was
still frightened, but he could control it.

He helped bring a couple of wounded down, which
put a lot of blood on his borrowed uniform. Good,
he thought. The next time, he went as close as possible to the high point of the attack, and got within
a few yards of what he realized was a wire barrier
with metal spikes or hooks woven into it. Of course
it had stunned and stopped the advance, he thought,
not that the attack would have gone that much farther
in the first place. The field of battle was covered with
dead and wounded Spanish soldiers. Again, he thanked
God that he had not been in the attack.

On the other side of the wire, grim and sweating American soldiers were pushing the dead who'd

made it through the wire back under it and lifting off those who'd been impaled on it. These were dropped like sacks onto the Spanish side of the wire. It felt incredibly strange to be so close to the Americans. He dared not observe too closely. Americans were watching carefully, looking for any hint of sabotage, and a couple of them were eyeing him curiously.

He'd seen what he'd wanted to. It was time to leave. A badly wounded soldier reached out and grabbed his leg and Salazar fought the urge to kick him away. Instead, he managed to get him up and, with still more difficulty, draped the soldier's arm over his shoulder. Together they limped back. When he was close enough to an aid station, he handed off his burden to another man who looked at him and shrugged. "Why did you bother, sir? This man is dead."

Through gaps in the growing clouds of white smoke Ryder could see some enemy soldiers had snuck their way through or under the wire. Next time the wire would have to be thicker, he told himself, and then wondered if there would be a next time, and if there was, where the hell would he get the additional wire?

Several Spanish soldiers appeared before him, only a few yards away from the first trench line. "Some dumb son of a bitch always gets through," snarled Haney as he shot a man.

Ryder laughed almost crazily and emptied his pistol in the direction of the attackers. He didn't hit anything, but he felt that it was the right thing to do.

Then the Spanish were gone. They had endured more than men should have to. As the firing died down, the defenders of Mount Haney could see a landscape carpeted with uniforms that had once been white and now were smeared with blood and stained with urine and feces. Already the stench was beginning to grow.

No order to cease fire was given. It was just understood. A few Spaniards cautiously stood up with their hands in the air. Some of the more lightly wounded called for help, while others just lay there and moaned. American medical personnel would care for them as soon as American soldiers were treated.

"You gonna allow for a cease fire?" asked Haney. A couple of white flags were waving from the Spanish lines, and a handful of unarmed Spanish soldiers were moving tentatively forward with palms outstretched.

Ryder checked his watch. "Give them four hours to gather their dead and wounded and only those on the other side of the wire. I want men watching the Spanish to make sure they don't try to cut the wire."

"Are you concerned that they'll find any secrets?"

"About the wire?" he said grimly. "I think they've already found out all they need to."

Kendrick's departure from Havana and the willing arms of Juana Salazar was delayed when news of the failed attack at Matanzas reached the city. Even though elated by the Spanish defeat and wanting to go where the news was, it was clearly dangerous for anyone even remotely looking like an Anglo to be on the streets of Havana. Pro-Spanish rioters roamed the streets savagely beating people indiscriminately. The government was unable to control the chaos and Kendrick wondered if they even cared. As a result, a number of Europeans had been badly hurt and at least a couple had been lynched. Establishments catering to non-Spanish had been trashed and even burned. The Havana police and militia were slowly getting the upper hand, but without much enthusiasm.

"So many stories and nowhere to send them," he said sadly.

Standing behind him, Juana slipped a bare arm around his equally bare chest and let a hand slide down his belly. Since they could not safely go out, they were spending as much time as possible in her room.

"When this war is over," she said as she fondled him, "you can write a book about your experiences as an American in Spanish Havana."

Kendrick grinned, reached back, and patted her bottom. "Can I write about this?"

"Go ahead. I no longer care what others think. On the other hand," she said with mock piety, "please change my name when you do."

Kendrick laughed hugely. Why on earth had he ever thought she was a stern and plain stick? She had blossomed into a vivacious and passionate woman. It occurred to him that she'd gained a couple of pounds since they came into each other's lives. Well, she could certainly use them. She'd told him how she'd kept herself thin in order to make herself unattractive to her husband, who was a useless lover in the first place. Not only had she not eaten much, but she had taught herself how to vomit up what she had eaten.

Before the rioting he'd gotten a British passport and been out to examine the wreck of the *Vitoria*. A helpful young lieutenant named Hugo Torres, who had survived the sinking and was now working on the wreck, told him of the horrors of the explosion caused by what was now known to be a torpedo. He called the weapon a devil's tool. He told of the panic, and the torrents of water rushing through the doomed warship and drowning scores of crewmen. Curiously, the man was not bitter.

"It was war, señor, and, obviously, I survived. If we had steamed out to duel with the Americans I might well be rotting on the bottom of the Caribbean. Instead, I was simply able to swim away from the sinking battleship. From what I've seen and heard, the American ships are bigger and better than ours, and their crews are better trained. The men under my command were the dregs of the earth who knew nothing about serving in a navy and showed no interest in learning. I will mourn for those of my friends who were killed, but I exult in the fact that I am alive."

"Will you try to raise the ship?" It was obvious from the activity that the Spanish were trying to do exactly that.

"Of course," said Torres. "If nothing else we must remove the hulk from the harbor where it is a dangerous impediment to shipping. The hole caused by the torpedo has been repaired and the next step will be to right the ship so she can be pumped out. But will she return to her place in Spain's navy? I don't think so. Her insides have been smashed by the explosion of one of her magazines and her engine has been underwater and ruined. In my opinion, she will be floated so she can be dragged out of the way or, when the war ceases, sent farther out into the ocean where she can be sunk in deep water."

Torres made the sign of the cross. "Perhaps we will be able to recover the bodies of the missing and give them a mass and a Christian burial."

"How many missing are there?"

"Six or eight, depending on which doctor you talk to. I suggest you go to the morgue and see them trying to assemble body parts into whole persons. I do not envy them their task, but honor says it must be done."

Kendrick had thanked him for his perspective and the young lieutenant had laughed. "By the way, señor, I've been to England and your British accent is as awful as anyone I have ever heard."

He and Juana had laughed over that incident and decided that he would not go out without Juana to translate for him. Nor would they emerge from their cocoon until the fighting in the streets stopped. Filing the story of his examination of the *Vitoria's* hulk would wait. Smoke continued to pour skyward from a number of sites in the beleaguered city. Perhaps the U.S. wouldn't have to storm Havana. Perhaps they could let the Spanish destroy the city for them.

Ryder called an informal council of his advisors. They included Lang, Barnes, and Haney. Rank wasn't one of the reasons for inclusion. He wanted intelligent opinions. In only a short while, the lean Texan had proven himself as a leader, while Haney always had been. As to Barnes, the acting regimental commander still had to prove himself as a leader, but certainly had the brains.

"This place stinks," said Lang, "and not just because we haven't bathed in a month of Sundays."

Between the two armies, most of the dead had been removed, but not necessarily all of the body parts. The crabs and other scavengers were eagerly devouring what remained, but much was still rotting in the heat.

Haney grinned. "Don't fret, Captain, the stench will clear up in a couple of months."

As usual, Haney had worked wonders. Food had been brought up along with fresh water. There was no ice, however, and they drank their gin and tonics warm and with few complaints. There were no worries about the Spanish returning to the attack for a while. They had been badly mauled.

"The wire stopped them," said Lang. "What we need now is a hell of a lot more wire."

"Which has been requested," Ryder answered. "But actually getting it is not going to happen overnight. I'm also impressed with your modifications to that Gatling gun."

Lang beamed. As he'd planned, he had mounted it on a swivel and lowered the wheels. As a result he had been able to turn it in a wide swath without having to move the entire weapon, enabling him to mow down scores of Spanish. "Like I said, I'm going to patent the modifications and we'll all be rich. Well, at least I will," he added cheerfully. "Of course, I'll modify the rest of our guns free of charge."

"You're a fucking saint," said Haney.

"But they'll figure out what to do about the wire, won't they?" asked Barnes. "They aren't stupid. I'll bet they're scouring all of Cuba for wire cutters."

"That and brave soldiers willing to cut it and pull it away," added Haney. "My bet is they'll find them both and we'll all be in deep shit. Their next attack will be a real bear to stop."

Ryder smiled and added a little more gin to his

glass from the very elegant crystal decanter that Haney had somehow found and liberated. "Then we'll have to plan for that fact. Yes, the wire can be circumvented, and maybe even destroyed by cannon fire, but it will still slow them down and mess up their formations. When that happens, we will have to be stronger and more disciplined."

"And better dug in," added Barnes. "We need ditches and all kinds of barricades to stop them."

Ryder agreed, "And that, gentlemen, means that we must dig, dig, and dig some more. Where we can't get wire, we make do with interlocking tree branches and anything else that will make their lives miserable. The troops won't like working that hard, but I don't really care." He finished his drink and stood. The meeting was over. "Back to work, gentlemen."

"But I'm not a gentleman," Haney said with an evil grin.

Ryder nodded. "And you never will be."

When they left, Barnes signaled Ryder. "Can we talk privately?" he asked. Ryder nodded. He thought he knew what was coming next. "I handled myself poorly during the battle. I don't think I'm qualified to command a regiment. I'd like someone else to take over the First Maryland."

"I hope this doesn't insult you, Jack, but I agree. Things happened all too fast and you were appointed because you happened to be handy." Kind of like me getting the regiment in the first place, he thought. "With some time to think on it, I'll get somebody with more experience and you'll be back on my staff."

Barnes took a deep breath and smiled wanly. "I thank you. My sister will thank you as well."

Barnes saluted crisply and departed. Ryder walked across the hill to where he could see down onto the town and the main camp. It was easy to spot the hospital church with the Red Cross painted vividly on it. He focused his telescope on it and saw people walking about. He turned to the place where the nurses were quartered. A canvas tent or room had been built on the roof. He recalled Sarah saying something about the nurses wanting a better place to bathe. He smiled and wondered just what was going on behind that canvas barrier.

Ruth sat on a stool on the roof. She was dressed only in a thin shift that revealed everything about her body, and she had wished aloud that she was naked. It was the only way one could get truly clean, she'd said, and Sarah had agreed. However, proprieties must be observed no matter how ridiculous they might seem. Even though they were safe behind the canvas walls, they could not run the risk of some soldier or sailor seeing too much and possibly going crazy with lust. Thus, they washed and cleansed themselves as best they could and rinsed with buckets of water pumped up to the roof. The water ran down a slope on the roof and down gutters. It was a fairly ingenious operation and similar to what the soldiers also had.

Ruth finished and it was Sarah's turn. She got thoroughly wet and used some of their precious soap to wash herself under her shift. Ruth then slowly poured water over her. The feeling was exquisite and she sighed with pleasure. The great battle was now history and the situation with the wounded was stable. Ships were taking the badly wounded to Florida, while the ones who would recover shortly and be returned to duty stayed behind.

"When this is over and we go back to Maryland, I've decided that I'm going to go back to using Ruta as my name and not Ruth."

Sarah squeezed the water out of her hair. "Fine, but why?"

"Because I've suddenly realized that's who I was and who I want to be. I see Cubans bravely fighting to create a new nation. I would like to see Poland free again. I should be proud of my past. Haney is proud to be an Irishman and maybe his nation will be free as well. Someday I will write a book about my life."

Sarah laughed as they let the sun dry them. "All of it?"

"Good point. I shall do some discreet editing."

"Such as romping in the hay with Haney?"

"When I write my memoirs, I'll leave it in. He won't mind a bit. So when will you see your beloved general again?"

"Soon, I hope." So close, but so far away, she thought.

Custer read the casualty reports with dismay. Despite winning the battle, the United States Army had suffered more than a thousand casualties. The fact that the Spanish had suffered an estimated three times that many meant little. The newspapers were being highly critical of both him and the war. They were openly wondering just when the army was going to move from Matanzas, take Havana, end the fighting, and get the troops home. It was clear that a stalemate was developing. There was a growing call for a change in command. More than one was suggesting that Nelson Miles be replaced by Custer's nemesis, Winfield Scott Hancock.

At the thought of that possibility, Custer scowled. He accepted the feeling that Nelson Miles might not have been the best choice to command, but who else was there? Sheridan and Sherman had declined because of age and health, and Miles' contemporaries were as inexperienced as he. Damn it, he thought. Was he doomed to go through a progression of commanding generals as Abraham Lincoln had until he finally got lucky and settled on Ulysses Grant? Too bad Grant was dead, he laughed mirthlessly. And no way in hell was he going to offer the command of anything larger than an outhouse to Winfield Scott Hancock.

"I've got to talk to Miles. I can't sit here in Florida and twiddle my thumbs while the war is going to hell."

"You can't leave the United States," reminded Libbie. "It's the law."

Custer snorted. "Actually it's just a custom, a tradition. There's no law involved at all. I had Chief Justice Fuller check it out and he agrees. No law, just a strong tradition and custom. Unfortunately, it's one that's taken very seriously."

"Which you would be foolish to break," she said sternly. "The country is upset enough right now."

"I also had Fuller check something else, dear wife," he said smugly. "Did you know that a U.S. Navy warship is considered United States territory? No? Well it is. Thus, if I travel by warship to Cuba, technically I will still be in the United States."

"Sometimes you surprise me, George."

"I could be on, say the *Atlanta* and be just a

short distance off Cuba and talk with Miles about whatever the hell he is planning on doing and I can do so without ever leaving American soil, or, more precisely, territory."

Libbie scowled. "It could be dangerous."

"Fighting a war is dangerous. Losing one is even more dangerous. I have to know what the devil is going on and what Miles is planning to do about it. Everyone says we won a great victory. Wonderful, but why haven't we followed up on it?"

"What instructions will you leave for Mr. Arthur?"

"Nothing," he laughed. "I don't plan on telling him or anyone else. Vice President Chester Arthur and Secretary of State Blaine will be pissed, but I won't care. It won't take me long to go from Florida to Matanzas and back. I just want to get the measure of Miles before I make a decision. Maybe all Miles needs to know is that he has my support. On the other hand, maybe he just needs a good kick in the ass to get him started."

Libbie stood and looked out the window. She was clearly troubled and that was unusual for her. "Why then am I feeling so uncomfortable?"

"Maybe women are meant to worry. It's their nature. What could happen, Libbie? Hell, I'll be on a warship and surrounded by a score of cannons and a couple of hundred sailors to protect me. Like I said, what the hell could go wrong?"

Manuel Garcia loved school and learning. What he didn't like was the scrawny and opinionated old man who was their teacher. Manuel had the sneaky feeling that he now knew as much as Professor Sanchez, the old goat who tormented the students and smacked them with his ruler when they gave wrong answers. Or when they asked questions he couldn't answer. Sometimes he thought that Sanchez was a fraud. Sanchez was also in love with anything Spanish and worshipped King Alfonso. He hated the Cuban rebels and the United States with equal burning passion.

He thought it would be wonderful if the king's recruiters grabbed every young man in Cuba to fight the rebels. Saying this could have been dangerous in a village where most of the people thought it would be nice if Alfonso was trampled by a herd of pigs. Lucky for him, the villagers thought of the professor as eccentric, not harmful.

Manuel sometimes thought of complaining to his mother, but he was afraid that she would yank him from the school and the pleasures it still gave him despite Señor Sanchez's attempts to humble him. He loved learning and was confident he would outlive and outlast Professor Sanchez.

For him to fail at school would also humiliate his mother, a woman he loved dearly and who was trying so hard to raise him and educate him the right way. His father was gone, disappeared into the unforgiving ocean one day when he was fishing, so they were on their own. Manuel's mother supported them by working the fields and tending other people's houses. She had hopes that his life would be better than hers had turned out. Some days she was too exhausted to talk. No, he would not burden her with his problems. He would deal with Señor Sanchez in his own way.

Lessons were over and he walked barefoot along the dirt roads. He had one pair of shoes that were starting to pinch him. His mother laughingly despaired. "When will you ever stop growing, you naughty boy," she would say before hugging him and kissing him on the top of his head. He thought his mother was beautiful and, apparently, so did some of the men in the village. Some of the older men who'd either never married or had lost their wives would come to their home and pay court. Or at least they tried to. She always rebuffed them. She said she would consider remarrying when Manuel was grown and gone. He had mixed emotions about that. He did not want to share her, but he did not want her to waste what remained of her youth. After all, she was nearly thirty.

Right now, his main goals were to protect his mother and stay out of the Spanish Army. It was beginning to look like neither goal was achievable and that depressed him.

◆ Chapter 13 ◆

A RAID? RYDER WAS INTRIGUED. IT SURE SOUNDED good to him. It would enable his men to strike at the Spanish instead of waiting to be attacked the next time. "Exactly what sort of raid do you have in mind, Captain?"

Lang grinned happily. He was bored. The great battle was now several days past, and he was getting antsy. The victory had been intoxicating and he wanted to drink some more.

"Exactly what we'll hit remains to be seen, General. What I propose is to go out with a couple of dozen of my best men and actually see what there is to raid. Hell, our patrols have been nonexistent. All of our intelligence comes from our Cuban buddies and we should see things through our own eyes, not theirs."

"So you don't trust the Cubans?"

"Oh, some of them I trust a lot, like that Valdez fellow. If I can, I'd like to take him, or at least some of his boys, with me. It'd be kind of like when we'd go out chasing renegade Indians in Texas and we'd have some tame Apaches or Comanches working with us."

Ryder wasn't certain any of the Apache or Comanche warriors would have liked being referred to as tame, and the Cubans definitely wouldn't. "Don't call Valdez or any of his friends tame. They're likely to slice you with their tame machetes."

Lang continued, "Wouldn't think of it, General. I like my testicles right where they are. At any rate, it'd be easier to hide from the Spanish in this jungle crap that surrounds everything here. Back in Texas, anything larger than a coffee cup could be seen for miles on the barren ground."

"I seem to recall that," Ryder said, thinking of his days in the American west. "Will you be taking some of your Spanish-speaking soldiers?"

Lang nodded vigorously. "All of my men speak Spanish at least as well as I do."

Martin laughed. Lang's Spanish was very basic and largely involved food, liquor, and getting laid. "Where will you go?"

"I thought I'd try to ride parallel to that goat path that passes for a road along the coast from Matanzas to Havana, at least for a while. First, though, I'd like to make a wide patrol around the Spanish camps and see what's happening."

"When will you leave?"

Lang stood. "Do you have to ask permission from Benteen or Miles?"

"Why? Benteen would go along, but I'm not so sure about Miles. I get the feeling that he doesn't want to offend the Spanish. So we won't tell him until you come back. It's always easier to ask forgiveness than permission. By the way, please make sure to come back."

It took several days for Gilberto Salazar to get in to see General Weyler. The general was far too busy writing letters to Governor-General Villate in Havana. When received, the letters would be either rewritten by Villate or simply forwarded to Madrid, with or without comment. Weyler was also exhausted and had only managed to get a good night's sleep the night before. There had been real concern that the Americans would counterattack. He would not relax until he'd been certain that no such effort by the damned Americans was planned.

"So what did you find on your foray up the hill?" Weyler asked. His face looked puffy, like he'd just gotten out of bed. "And by the way, relax and have a seat."

Salazar sat down stiffly on a camp chair, wincing from the pain in his groin. He'd aggravated it climbing up the hill. To his annoyance, the German colonel was also present and smiling his superior smile. "As we all suspected, the Americans used barbed wire to control the attack and their Gatling guns to slaughter our men. I think it is safe to say that both came as a surprise."

"Yet neither should have. We've known all along that the Americans had Gatlings although we didn't realize they had so many up on that damned hill. Worse, none of our troops, including officers, have ever faced them. We've also known of the existence of barbed wire, although its use as a military weapon had not occurred to us. From what others have told me, our men did not know what to do when confronted with this terrible wire that not only stopped them but sliced their skin."

Salazar was mildly annoyed that others had told the general about the wire. "I was able to get within a few feet of the barrier before I decided it was prudent to leave. It is not impenetrable by any means. A determined rush could have pushed through. It would have meant that the men in front would have had their flesh cut by the wire. Those men would have had to have been extremely brave. They would have had to lie down on the wire and allow others to clamber over them and using their bodies as stepping stones. It would have been difficult, but it could have been done. Men with blankets and mattresses could have done the same thing. Further, men with simple wire cutters could have eliminated the wire. I do wonder, though, whether artillery would have destroyed it or simply rearranged it."

Weyler yawned. "I think you expect too much if you believe that men will voluntarily use their bodies to crush the wire while the hooks are digging into their flesh. And as to wire cutters, they would work but the soldiers would have to wait for the men with the cutters to finish their work. While our men were waiting for the wire to disappear, the Americans would be killing the men cutting the wire and shooting the waiting formations to pieces. And, oh yes, even with holes in the wire barrier, our formations would be reduced to the mobs we saw the other day. Do I state the problem correctly, Major?"

"Yes, sir," Salazar said glumly.

Weyler turned to the German. "Do you have anything to add, Colonel Helmsdorf?"

The German smiled. He would like to have added

that he'd seen the timid way in which Salazar had gone to the wire, but declined. "What I have seen has convinced me that the German Army must have many, many more machine guns and countless miles of barbed wire. With them, the military arts have definitely shifted to the defensive."

"Interesting," said Weyler. "However, I am too tired to discuss it now. Salazar, do you have anything else to say?"

"Only that our men will be extremely loath to attack again. The rumors are thick that the wire is ungodly and inhuman. The men are terrified of it. An attack on that hill as long as the barbed wire is in place is, in my opinion, doomed before it begins."

Weyler nodded thoughtfully, then smiled. "Then we shall not attack the wire."

If Custer was irked that the *Atlanta* was not available, he didn't show it. At least he was able to get the hell away from his detractors on the mainland. Out of sight, out of mind, he thought happily. He felt like a kid playing hooky from school. Even better, if caught no one could punish him.

The *Atlanta* was fully repaired and patrolling off the channel leading to Havana. So too were most of the other American warships, including several old steam sloops. What remained of the Spanish Navy in the Atlantic was in Havana's harbor, locked up as tight as a bunch of nuns in a convent, as Commodore Bunce had told him. He added that traveling from Florida to the coast off Matanzas would be an easy trip and wouldn't require taking a major warship away from its duties to carry the president.

So why not enjoy it, Custer had thought. Thus, he had settled on using a converted yacht named the *Dolphin*. There had been several other U.S. Navy ships of that name, the last of which was a brig that had been burned to prevent capture by the Confederates. If he thought it was a bad omen, he didn't let on.

This current version of the *Dolphin* had both sails and a steam engine. She carried a handful of small cannons and was clearly intended for escort or courier purposes only. Better for Custer, she had a large and luxurious cabin worthy of a traveling President of the United States. She was categorized as an auxiliary cruiser, which was a catchall title for a miscellaneous warship.

Custer took the long slow train to St. Augustine. Not even his position could make the iron beast go faster. The newly constructed tracks did not go all the way to Key West. Going by ship from St. Augustine was the only alternative. He would be away from the telegraph lines and out of touch for the shortest length of time.

A short and extremely fat lieutenant commander named Blondell was the *Dolphin*'s skipper. He didn't know whether to be honored that the president was on his small warship or annoyed that he'd had to give up his spacious and luxurious cabin for the duration. Regardless, the two men took an instant dislike to each other.

Custer and the *Dolphin* arrived off Matanzas without incident. The ship was expected and a couple of the small warships protecting the anchorage fired off salutes. Custer enjoyed and appreciated it but was frustrated. He was only a couple of hundred yards from Cuban soil but he had promised Libbie that he would not set foot on it. Men waved and cheered and yelled at him to come ashore. He swore and waved back.

Then it was time for a barge bringing General Miles alongside and for the general to come aboard. They spent only a few minutes on deck together. Just enough time to shake hands with everyone and wave to the crowds on the beach while a photographer snapped shots. After that, it was time for privacy. They went to Custer's cabin and took seats across from each other. Sandwiches were eaten and whisky was served. Custer and Miles had known each other and, while there was a serious lack of affection, there was mutual respect due to each other's rank. Miles' trademark handlebar mustache seemed to twitch and he blinked nervously. The general was clearly tense and stressed, which concerned Custer.

Miles spoke first. "I'm glad you're here. I just wish you could go ashore and see what's happening and what we are confronting. If you would climb to the top of Mount Haney, you'd see the Spanish army that's arrayed against us and maybe people in Washington wouldn't be asking so damn many questions. Unlike some Civil War generals who were mistaken about their enemy's strength, McClellan in particular, we truly are seriously outnumbered. Our boys are by far the better soldiers, but the Spanish have got some good ones, too. When we finally do move out of our trenches, we will be the attackers and the Spanish will deal us large numbers of casualties."

This was precisely what Custer didn't want to hear. "You have upwards of twenty-five thousand men, General. They are the best America has and they are costing a helluva lot of money to feed. What more do you need? Yes, the Navy has stopped the flow of men from Spain, but if you want a large number of reinforcements, say a hundred thousand men, that is highly unlikely to happen. The nation does not believe that a bunch of greasy Spaniards and pro-Spanish Cubans can stand up to American soldiers. And speaking of which, where the hell are our beloved Cuban allies?"

"I'm not going to say the Cubans are useless, General, but that's pretty damn close. I think there are maybe ten thousand of them scattered throughout the Matanzas area, but nobody really knows. They may or may not be led by someone named Jose Marti or maybe a guerilla named Diego Valdez. By anybody's standards, they are undisciplined and most of them have no weapons except machetes and what they've managed to steal and that includes robbing our boys. They've been fighting the Spaniards for a long time and now they expect to be able to lie down and take a nap while we do the rest of the fighting. Our boys are getting pissed off by that kind of attitude."

"Jesus," Custer muttered. He took a deep swallow of his whisky. This was more that he didn't want to hear. He began to regret not bringing either Blaine or Robert Lincoln. Hell, he at least should have brought Libbie. She would have known what to say.

"What do you want from me," Miles asked, almost plaintively. "If you want my resignation, it's yours."

Custer did, but he would not admit it. What he saw before him was a defeated man. There was no spark, no life. The always supremely confident and undeniably brave Major General Nelson Appleton Miles had been given an assignment that was too big for him. Part of Custer wanted to gloat but the practical part realized that he would have to find someone better to replace him. He refused to accept that what Miles was saying was true. He firmly believed that the American soldier was far better than the Spaniard, and that should eliminate the Spanish advantage in numbers.

Off in the distance, some cannon fire boomed. Miles informed him it was Spanish. "They do that every so often. I believe they are trying to annoy us."

"I do not want your resignation," said Custer. The look on Miles' face said that he knew it was a lie.

After some further small talk, the two men shook hands gravely and Miles departed. As the general's boat was rowed ashore, Custer had an idea. He smiled and turned to the skipper of the *Dolphin*.

"Captain Blondell, I have changed my mind. We will not depart for Florida this afternoon."

"Sir?"

Custer wrung his hands with glee. "Yes, I now have an overwhelming urge to see Havana, if only from a distance, and I want to go right now."

Blondell paled. "If we do that we are likely to arrive in the middle of the night. That could be dangerous since the fleet is not expecting us."

"Nonsense. All we have to do is show up with lights on and bells and whistles and whatever the hell you have blaring away and the Navy will realize we're harmless."

"Sir, I still say it's too dangerous."

"Are you a coward, Blondell?"

Blondell's face turned beet red. "Of course not, and I resent the implication."

"And I resent sitting here off Cuba and arguing with someone who is so junior in rank to me that I shouldn't even have to acknowledge your existence.

I know you're captain of this ship and God almighty when you're on it, but I am the president and commander in chief, and if you decline to obey me, your next command will be a very small garbage scow."

Blondell paled and swallowed. "Very well, sir. We will set off for Havana."

Another Spanish cannon fired and caused no damage, merely kicking up dirt a good two hundred yards away from the American lines. The American guns did not respond. It was as if it were beneath their dignity. Ryder gestured for Lang to have a seat in the trench. Lang was filthy and his clothes torn. He looked exhausted, but also happy.

"Make yourself comfortable, Captain, but I'm afraid that real hardships are upon us. While we have gin, we are totally out of tonic."

"There is no God," Lang sighed. "I guess I'll have to make do with gin alone. Is there any ice?"

"Curiously, yes, and thank that God you say doesn't exist for Sergeant Haney. He had our engineers develop an ice-making machine. While most of the ice goes to the hospital, some of it manages to make its way up here. Now please don't tell me that you made a complete circuit of the Spanish lines. You haven't been gone anywhere near long enough."

"Correct, General, and I came back because I found things that are both good and bad. The good is that there are more holes in the Spanish lines than I have in my socks. I believe I could take a good-sized force through them and hit them in the rear or anywhere else and cause a great deal of damage."

"Excellent."

The Spanish gun boomed again. Again the shell landed well short. Lang continued. "On the bad side, I think they are preparing to attack again, but not where they did originally. It looks like a major buildup between here on Mount Haney and the opening to the bay. If I read things correctly, I'd say they're gonna attack between those points which would take them right through the city of Matanzas itself. They take that and they can claim a major victory."

Ryder took a stick and sketched a map of the area in the dirt and eyed it thoughtfully. "If they take the city, they can place guns along the coast and control the bay. We could fire down on them part of the way, but not all, and most of our ships, being unarmored, would be loath to enter and shoot it out with shore-based cannons."

"We don't have armored ships, sir? I thought we invented the damn things."

Ryder grinned. "We did and then we forgot why. Just don't say I said that to any Navy boys you might meet. They'd likely take offence. To the best of my knowledge, the only truly armored ship we have is the *Atlanta*. When the *Chicago* comes back, which won't be for quite a while, that'll give us two. Not very impressive for a world power, is it?"

"Shit," said Lang. "What are you gonna do?"

"First I'm going to finish this drink and then I'm going to send a signal to Benteen that I'd like to come down and talk to him. Custer himself was offshore meeting with Miles and, along with giving him your report, I'd like to know what was discussed."

Lang grinned. Like everyone else, he knew all about his general and Sarah Damon. The base at Matanzas was a very small town in many ways. "Maybe I can report to Benteen myself and relieve you of the awful burden of going down there."

"Maybe you can go to hell, Captain," Ryder said without rancor.

The Spanish cannon boomed again. "Can we hit that fucker, sir? He's really getting annoying."

"Yes. He's in range of about a dozen of our guns. Why, do you want to teach him a lesson?"

"I do indeed, sir. Why not have all of our guns fire one round at the same time at him and see what happens. If we don't kill him, we should scare the shit out of him."

"I like the way you think, Captain Lang. You are one nasty son of a bitch."

Clemente Cisneros liked to complain that he was proof that the Spanish Navy was totally fossilized, even though he wasn't absolutely certain what the word meant. He thought it had to do with something turning to stone and that was an apt description of the current state of the once proud Spanish Navy.

A small thin man descended from minor nobility, he had made the navy his career. He was now forty-five years old and a lieutenant commander. He lacked political connections in Madrid so it was unlikely that he would rise above his current rank. This lack further hurt his chances because the Spanish Navy was small and getting smaller. It would be even more difficult for him if Spain lost the current war with the arrogant United States. That he might be discharged and left on the beach depressed him mightily. He longed to do something that would attract the attention of the leaders in Madrid.

After commanding a couple of patrol craft during his career, he had been appointed captain of the seven-hundred-ton gunboat, the *Marques del Duero*. She was a mere one-tenth the size of a modern major warship and doubtless represented the pinnacle of his career. While small, his ship was far from helpless, carrying one 6.3-inch gun and a pair of 4.7s. She also had a crew of a hundred men whom he'd trained hard. He was also a fair man and his men had responded. He was proud of them. The *Duero* was ready to fight.

This night, however, she would be one of a number of decoys. The *Duero's* problem was her speed. On a good day, she could do only ten knots and she hadn't had many good days lately. Her engine kept acting up and her hull was fouled. She was scheduled for a refit, but she was way down the list and, besides, the mechanics in Cuba were largely incompetent. At times Cisneros thought he would be better off running under her schooner-rigged sails than counting on her temperamental engines.

Still, Cisneros had to admit that the Spanish Navy's plan for this night had considerable merit. Two good-sized cruisers and one smaller one were languishing in Havana harbor with nothing to do since the sinking of the *Vitoria* in the harbor by some incredibly brave Americans. He'd been to visit the captured American officers and, since he spoke excellent English, had had an interesting conversation. He now knew more about torpedoes then he ever cared to. At first he'd thought that the Americans had talked too much, but then realized that the information was in the newspapers.

Spanish intelligence also said that the American warship, the *Chicago*, had been sufficiently repaired to enable her to join the *Atlanta* in blockading Havana. If the remnants of the Spanish fleet were to escape, it had to be soon. Thus, he'd been given the extremely temporary rank of commodore and would lead a dozen armed merchantmen out in an attack designed to distract the *Atlanta* and other ships while the Spanish cruisers escaped to the high seas where they could commence terrorizing American merchant ships. As commerce raiders, it was believed that they could cause damage far beyond their size.

He wished for a cloudier night, but it wasn't granted. There were gaps in the clouds where stars could be seen twinkling and providing visibility for the Americans. At least the moon wasn't full. He hoped it was dark enough for him to succeed in his purpose. With his cruiser in the lead, the Spanish decoy fleet steamed out and, as soon as they were close enough to the Americans to be seen, they opened fire with their smaller guns. The Americans immediately went to battle stations while the decoys charged bravely towards them. Cisneros could only hope that the three larger cruisers, the *Aragon*, *Castile*, and *Velasco*, were escaping during the confusion he believed he was creating. Some of his ships would die and he prayed that their deaths would not be in vain.

They were soon within range of the Americans and the enemy gunnery began to tell. One of the decoys was quickly set on fire and sinking, while another was dead in the water. An American gun fired a shell that landed within feet of the *Duero*, raising a geyser of water and splashing a torrent of spray and shell fragments on her deck. A couple of his men were down. Enough, Cisneros thought, and gave the order to withdraw. They'd had their moment of glory.

He smiled. Even if the Spanish warships hadn't gotten away, it had been extremely pleasant to yank on Uncle Sam's beard. Indeed, it looked like the American ships were all steaming west, doubtless chasing the Spanish squadron that they'd belatedly spotted. He hoped his compatriots got away. It was all in God's hands.

Wait. There was a strange ship in view and approaching. It was almost within range. Better, it was not very large and, since he knew all of the Spanish warships, it had to be an American. They would not have to skulk back to Havana after only a pretense at battle.

A moment later and his three guns opened fire on the mystery ship.

Captain Blondell was aghast. The night was ablaze with cannon fire. It looked like he had taken the *Dolphin* into a major battle. Cannons were firing in all directions and it was clear that the Spanish fleet was trying to sortie from Havana.

As Custer had ordered, he'd brought the *Dolphin* towards the blockading Americans and without any attempt at subterfuge. Against his better judgment, ships lights were on and horns blared. When the battle began, he was only a mile or two away from the *Atlanta* and the others. When the firing began, he darkened the ship and prudently took it away. He did not want to be confused with a Spaniard. Even Custer, a man he was firmly convinced was a fool, concurred. In fact, he seemed shaken by the sudden turn of events.

Suddenly, the dark shape of another ship was visible only a couple of hundred yards away. Where the devil had that ship come from, he wondered. Before he could answer his own question, the other ship opened fire. A shell ripped into the forward hull of the *Dolphin*, filling the air with splinters that cut down several of his crew, leaving them as bloody ruins on the deck. A second shot again hulled her and she began to list almost immediately. The converted yacht didn't stand a chance against her unknown and far stronger attacker. When a third shell ripped into her, Blondell screamed the order to abandon ship. He didn't know who the mystery ship was or whether she was Spanish or American. He only knew that this ass of a President of the United States was about to get him and everyone else on the *Dolphin* killed if he didn't act quickly.

Fires had begun on his first and doubtless only command. Blondell hoped that his tormenter could see that he was abandoning her and no longer represented a threat.

If she ever had been, he thought angrily.

Blondell made sure everyone alive was off the ship before climbing down the short distance to a lifeboat. It was jammed with men and he sniffed when he saw that George Armstrong Custer was one of them. Idiot, he thought. Why the devil hadn't he been among the dead?

"What now, Captain Blondell?" Custer asked.

I think I'll throw you overboard, that's what's now, Blondell thought. "What we are going to do, President Custer, is float around until dawn and then hope and pray that we are found by an American ship and not by a Spaniard."

With the sea largely illuminated by the false dawn, Cisneros was able to see that the American warships

had departed. He concluded that they were doubtless chasing the Spanish cruisers that were trying
desperately to escape. The Americans had positioned
their ships to prevent an escape to the east, towards
Matanzas, where they might bombard the army. This
left an opportunity to race west and possibly escape
by hiding in the many coves and inlets that nature
had carved out of the Cuban shore.

The light also showed the wreckage of several of
his ad hoc flotilla that hadn't made it back to Havana.
With the Yanks gone, Cisneros determined to search
for survivors and rescue them before the sharks could
assault them. He felt it was the least he could do for
the brave souls he'd had the honor to lead.

Floating debris was plentiful, as were the pitiful
remains of some of his little flotilla's sailors. He was
just about to return to Havana when a lookout spied
what looked like two lifeboats lashed together and riding low in the water. They steamed slowly and carefully
in that direction. They were farther from shore than
Cisneros would have liked and, even though none of
the American warships were currently in view, they
could return at any time.

Fortune smiled on him and the men in the boats.
Better, as he pulled the *Duero* alongside, he could
see that the dozen men staring at him with expressions ranging between apathy, fear, and anger, were all
Americans. He exulted. This meant that the fighting
hadn't been all one-sided. A scout ship from Havana
told him he'd already been commended for his brave
efforts in attacking the American fleet, and now he'd
be bringing in a handful of American prisoners. Quite
likely the Americans had come from that ship he had

fired on during the night. Perhaps another commendation would be in order and, just perhaps, another promotion would no longer be such an impossibility.

The Americans were pulled out of their floundering boats and, while armed guards watched, their hands and feet were bound. He would take no chances on their trying to take over his ship. They would fail, of course, but some of his men might die in the attempt. He had to make haste. The Americans could return at any moment. His lookouts were scanning the horizon for any telltale signs of smoke.

As they approached the entrance to Havana's harbor and safety, Cisneros asked if any of the prisoners was the captain.

"I am, or was," responded a plump man. "I am Commander William Blondell, captain of the United States Navy Auxiliary Cruiser *Dolphin*. As we are your prisoners, I would like to remind you that you are required to treat us in accordance with the Geneva Convention."

Cisneros bristled at the slur on his honor. "I am well aware of my obligations according to the Convention, and I assure you that no harm will come to you. You will be taken to Havana and held until either exchanged or the war ends."

Blondell and the others appeared to understand. One man with long and graying blond hair, however, seemed confused. Perhaps he'd been hit on the head, Cisneros thought. Then he had another thought that jarred him. The man looked so very familiar. It dawned on him and he grinned from ear to ear. The promotion would be his.

He walked over and shook the man's hand. "Welcome to Spanish Cuba, President Custer."

◆ Chapter 14 ◆

IT HAD COMMENCED RAINING HEAVILY AGAIN, TURNING the ground into a quagmire. Both Ryder and Benteen were covered with mud from their knees down. "Is the weather better up there on Mount Haney?" General Benteen asked.

Ryder sipped some coffee and didn't grimace. Surprisingly, it wasn't bad. It was strong and very hot, and that's what counted. "Sadly, no. Most of the men feel we're just that much closer to the rain clouds."

"What a wonderful vision. At any rate, Ryder, we're not here to discuss the weather. I did discuss your thoughts with General Miles and, to put it bluntly, he totally disagrees with what Captain Lang found and what you believe. I disagreed with Miles and let's just say we had a very spirited discussion on the matter. He is convinced that any Spanish attack will consist of another assault on your position or on the entrance to the bay, or even both. He told me it didn't really matter since he didn't think the Spanish have the stomach for another attack on anything, at least not for a long while. When I suggested that we should attack since the Spaniards are such weaklings, I thought he'd throw me out of his office."

Ryder was puzzled. "I thought that Miles' meeting with Custer had resulted in his agreeing to attack?"

"So did I, but he's apparently having second thoughts with Custer on his way back to Florida, which is another concern. He was supposed to go to Key West and then to St. Augustine, and there's been no report of his arrival. He should have gotten there by now. One of our gunboat captains reported that he thought he saw the president's ship heading north towards Havana. Going off on a run like that would be just like Custer. He was always too impetuous for his own good."

"And it would be dangerous," added Ryder. They had just gotten reports that the Spanish Navy had tried to escape from Havana and that there had been a major naval battle. Reports were inconclusive, but it did seem that several vessels had been sunk. "Christ, what if the president had been swept up in that mess?"

Benteen grimaced. "If Custer's dead it means that Chester A. Arthur is now the President of the United States. If Custer is missing or a prisoner, I don't know what the hell happens next. Jesus, what a mess."

Governor-General Villate looked with delight on the blanket-covered man who slept soundly. If he'd been a cat, the general thought, he would have purred.

The man below him seemed unaware that he was chained to the cot. Villate coughed loudly and the man stirred. He winced with pain. The doctors said his ankle was badly sprained and his body was covered with cuts and bruises.

Villate smiled. "Good afternoon, President Custer. May I cordially welcome you to Cuba?"

Custer glared at him. "You may cordially go to hell. You may also remove these goddamn chains. Where do you think I'd run with a bad ankle?"

"We'll talk about removing your shackles later," Villate responded coldly. "In the meantime, you are my prisoner and I will treat with you in any manner I wish."

"As long as it is in accordance with the Geneva Convention," said British Consul Redford Dunfield. To Villate's dismay, he'd again shown up to interfere with Villate's pleasure. Dunfield then introduced himself to Custer, who grunted and nodded.

Dunfield smiled and continued. "I don't think I have to remind you that President Custer is the head of the United States government and must be treated in accordance with his rank."

Villate laughed. The situation was still too priceless for him to get really angry. "When we hang him, I promise to use a new rope."

Dunfield was mildly amused as well. Custer was not. Dunfield could see a flicker of concern. Would the Spanish truly consider hanging him? The thought clearly concerned him.

Villate continued. "You may not like the arrangements," he said to Dunfield, "but I am not going to put him in a position where his countrymen might try to free him. As you see, he is in a private cell here in the Morro Castle. Rescuing him would be a fruitless and costly endeavor. Besides, we would kill him to prevent that from happening."

"It would not be necessary to keep him here. If you continue to do so, you will risk the anger of the international community. Heads of state are kept in far better circumstances than this. I can guarantee you that Her Majesty's government will not be happy if this situation continues."

"He needs medical help," Villate said, exaggerating Custer's condition. He was conscious that he was about to lose another argument with the damned Englishman. "What do you propose?" he asked resignedly.

"I have an estate on the outskirts of town. You know it and you've been there. It's practically a fortress. I propose that General Custer be moved there and protected, guarded if you will, by a good battalion of your finest and most loyal troops. I further propose that photographs be taken of the president showing that he is being well kept, and that he be able to communicate with his government."

"Perhaps he will ask them to surrender," Villate sneered.

"The hell I will," said Custer, "and quit talking around me."

"Again, kindly recall that you are a prisoner," said Villate. An idea had formed and he loved the thought of it. "We will announce to the world that we hold you and that you require medical attention. This will mean that you will remain here for at least a couple of days until we can make arrangements to move you to Señor Dunfield's estate. Except for proving your existence and relative well-being, you will remain incommunicado."

Custer's eyes burned with anger. "Bastard." Villate laughed again.

◆　　◆　　◆

The news hit the American forces at Matanzas like a thunderbolt. They got the telegram from Florida at almost the same time that the Spanish soldiers did. These began celebrating wildly, cheering and firing their weapons into the air. Some actually had fireworks and sent rockets into the air.

"The dumb son of a bitch has gone and done it again," said General Benteen. "Jesus Christ, what the hell kind of mess has Custer gotten him and us into now? And do the damn Spaniards expect us to surrender?"

Ryder decided to remain silent. He'd been down again from the hill for yet another meeting and had found the time for a few moments of delicious privacy with Sarah. He was aware that his lips were bruised from the intensity of their kisses and that his uniform was rumpled. He didn't give a damn and it was obvious that Custer's fate was far more important than his being disheveled.

Benteen continued. "On the other hand, some might view this as an opportunity. Who knows what the powers in Washington will decide on as a course of action? My guess is that they will do absolutely nothing for the short term."

"That would be my guess as well," Ryder said. "Have we heard anything from the Spanish as to what they might want for Custer's return?"

"Not a peep. Although I would guess that they would insist on our leaving Cuba as one condition, which won't happen. That would be the same as admitting defeat. We would never be able to field an army to invade Cuba again. Ryder, what's your sense of the morale of the troops?"

Ryder shrugged. "I haven't had all that much time to talk with people, but my immediate sense is that of confusion. Everybody's wondering just how the hell did the president manage to get captured at sea when everybody says we rule the waves? I have heard a couple of voices say that we might be better off with new leadership and that a new leader might replace General Miles."

Benteen grinned wickedly. "I'll forget you said that."

"Much appreciated. Otherwise, I have the feeling that the men will survive quite nicely without President Custer and that they'd like to get this war over. Do you think the Spanish will want to work out an exchange for him?"

Benteen guffawed. "Exchange him for what? We won't have to do that. I've got this feeling that the Spaniards will throw him back after putting up with him for a few months."

Juana kissed her good friend Mercedes de Milan on her heavily rouged cheeks. The older woman gave her a warm hug in return. "How are things with your lover in my little cottage?" the sixty-year-old widow asked.

"Amazingly well, thank you. I have never known such happiness. I almost don't know what to do about it."

"Then enjoy yourself as I have enjoyed all of my lovers."

"And how many have there been, dear Mercedes?"

She waved her hand. "Too many to count and I've enjoyed them all, including the one lover I have now. I will not name him because you might be shocked."

"You don't fear discovery?"

"I used to, of course, but not much anymore. I am

a widow and I can pretty much do what I want. You, on the other hand, are married to a man who, while a fool and a brute, might be a dangerous fool and an even more dangerous brute. But don't let danger hold you back. Even if you cuckold your husband, the worst he could do is beat you and divorce you and then you would be free. I am also protected by my bodyguards who are very loyal. You've met my chief guard, haven't you?"

Juana smiled and nodded. Hector Rojas was a giant of a man who worshipped Mercedes. Rumors said that Rojas had killed many times in his life. She wondered if Hector ever shared Mercedes' bed.

Mercedes reached over and handed Juana a cigarillo. The two women enjoyed a few puffs of the expensive tobacco before Mercedes continued. "Danger makes love affairs even more splendid. I remember one time when I was seated on a raised wooden bench in a stadium watching some dismal musical performance in a very dark night. I was about to doze off when I felt the light pressure of someone caressing my inner calf."

Juana laughed, "Oh my."

"Oh my, indeed. I truly didn't know what to do as his hand delicately slid its way up my calf to my thigh and then to that wonderful soft spot that men love so much. I had to bite my lip to keep from crying out as he gently and exquisitely manipulated me and totally aroused me. A couple of times I groaned and my aunt looked at me curiously. I gestured that I was having some trouble with my stomach and she let it go. The erotic game lasted quite some time and, finally, I felt him slide one of my garters down. And then he disappeared. At least I hoped the bold rogue was a he."

Juana was almost convulsing with laughter. "Well, was it a he?"

"Yes," said Mercedes, smiling at the memory. "The next day, a handsome young man I didn't know came to me with a package. It contained my garter and he cheerfully admitted to both fondling me and removing it. I rewarded him by taking him into my boudoir and insisting that he put it on my leg, but not until that was all I was wearing."

"How wonderful."

"Not really. It turned out that he was much more facile with his hands than with any other part of his body. But it was an exciting few weeks until I grew tired of him. That was some years ago and the poor dear is back in Spain and doubtless growing fat. But hearing me talk is not why you came to see me, is it? What do you and your American lover want that I can provide?"

"He would like access to Custer for the purpose of doing an interview. I've known that your current lover is Mr. Dunfield, the British Consul, and since President Custer will soon be ensconced at Mr. Dunfield's villa, James and I thought it could be something that you would be able to arrange."

Mercedes was mildly surprised that her secret was no secret at all. She laughed again, "Why not?"

"Well, am I now the President of the United States or not?"

The question came from Chester A. Arthur, the stocky fifty-three-year-old Vice President of the United States. According to the Constitution, he was the man next in line for the presidency on the death of the president. The question he asked was one that no one was quite ready to answer. While the death of a president was covered and understood, the question of a president being incapacitated because he was a prisoner of war was not. Presidential incapacity for various reasons had caused confusion in the past and was doing so now.

"My husband is still alive and as long as he breathes, he is the president," Libbie Custer practically snarled.

The others in the president's office simply looked away at the outburst. Arthur, however, was not deterred.

"Madam, as much as I sympathize with your predicament, I must remind you that you have no official position in this matter or, for that matter, at this meeting. You are here as a courtesy. I must also remind you that the government of the United States must continue to run, and that is why we have met here today. The idea of President Custer being shackled in Havana is repugnant, but it is occurring and we can do nothing about it. Your husband may be helpless but we must not be. We haven't that luxury."

A tear trickled down Libbie Custer's cheek. Word had reached them that photographs of President Custer, in chains and in a cell, had made it to Key West and were on their way north. That they would appear in newspapers throughout the world was understood. Custer's shame had become America's shame.

"I do wonder just how he managed to get himself captured," said Arthur. "There are so many conflicting stories."

"And all of them are irrelevant to the situation," said Secretary of State Blaine. "Congress can investigate to its heart's content when this war is over and crucify those responsible, but, as you said, Mr. Arthur, we have a country and a war to run."

"What about getting my husband back?" Libbie stood and practically shrieked.

"I'm sorry," said Blaine as she sat down, "but we've heard nothing from the Spanish regarding a reasonable price to pay for him. All we've heard are rumors that would involve our leaving Cuba and signing a treaty in which we would promise never to invade again. We would also agree to pay Spain an enormous financial indemnity. I must add that we have no leverage whatsoever."

"And that can never happen," added Arthur. "It would be a humiliation almost too great for our nation and our party to bear, which is why we must decide just who is running the country in Custer's absence and continue on with the war. I have taken the liberty of checking with Chief Justice Fuller and he is of the opinion that the Constitution does not really cover this sort of exigency. He does feel that naming an acting president for the duration of the emergency would be appropriate. And obviously, that acting president would be me."

Libbie Custer was shaking and again on the verge of hysterics. "You would take away his office?"

Blaine was getting annoyed. "Madam, he isn't here and he isn't likely to return anytime soon. And I must again remind you that you are present as a courtesy. You hold no office, either elected or appointed. If you keep this up, I can assure you that we will meet without you and outside of the White House."

Blaine was further annoyed by the fact that Custer's foolishness might have propelled Chester Arthur into the White House, and not just as an acting president. He had been hoping that Custer's incompetence would lead to his not being renominated by the Republican Party in the next election. In that case, he, James G. Blaine, would be honored if they turned to him as their candidate. If Arthur was to turn Custer's mess into something resembling a victory for himself, he would be a formidable force and might just take that nomination away from him. Blaine could only seethe and plot. Nor could he change the fact that, as vice president *or* acting president, Chester A. Arthur was in charge.

"What is the Army going to do?" Blaine asked of Secretary of War Robert Lincoln.

"Right now, they are waiting for the next Spanish attack," Lincoln answered. "General Miles is of the opinion that it will come soon and will be a repeat of the attacks on the entrance to the bay and that hill called Mount Haney. I do know that all of his generals do not agree with him. They feel it will come between those two points in an attempt to split the army."

"And Miles has decided otherwise?" Arthur asked.

"Yes."

"Jesus," said the Vice President. "I can only hope he's right. What is the Navy doing, Mr. Hunt?"

Navy Secretary Hunt was not happy. "Havana is blockaded, but the three Spanish cruisers that escaped have not been located. They could be in any one or more of hundreds of coves and bays. I do not, however, think that they have sailed far or towards the United States. For one thing, they don't carry enough coal. For another, they just aren't all that big and danger- ous. Nor can they risk incurring even the slightest damage since there is no place they can be repaired. Even so, their existence is scaring the bejeezus out of everyone on the East Coast. We have several dozen armed and hastily armored converted merchant ships outside our major ports. The Navy is confident that they will not be needed, but their presence helps keep the population happy."

Blaine shook his head sadly. "In short, we have the makings of a stalemate."

Lincoln disagreed. "Not really. Our army cannot sit there forever. It has to be supplied and reinforced and, all the while, the fever season is coming. All the Spanish have to do is wait and our army might just be destroyed by sickness."

"Jesus," said Arthur. "We have got to get Miles and the army moving."

"And I don't know if Miles is the man to do it," said Lincoln and the others nodded agreement, even a solemn Libbie Custer.

The heavy-set Arthur stood and walked ponderously to a window overlooking the lawn. "If Miles cannot drive the army to Havana, we must find a general who can, even if that means thinking the unthinkable."

Libbie Custer paled. "No. You can't be serious. It's bad enough that George is a prisoner of the Spanish, but now you would kill him?"

Ryder's headquarters bunker had become a very substantial dwelling. He now had a solid roof and gutters for drainage. Of course, he made sure that all of his men had similar amenities before his was completed. The amount of barbed wire surrounding the hill had more than tripled. Ships from New

Orleans and Galveston had brought in miles of it. He was confident that the wire and the other improvements that had been made to the defenses on Mount Haney would make a Spanish assault a very bloody one. Curiously, not all the other senior officers were supporters of using barbed wire because they thought it might detract from their soldier's offensive fighting spirit. Their loss, Ryder thought, and he then commandeered their share of the wire. If they wouldn't use it, he would.

Many of the same officers who hated wire also hated machine guns because they encouraged soldiers to use up too much ammunition too quickly. Ryder wondered if they'd forgotten that the purpose of a war was to kill the enemy.

He hated the thought of his men becoming stagnant, but they had done pretty much all they could do without unduly endangering themselves. War against Spain had become exceedingly boring. Now he could sneak down and see Sarah on a reasonably regular basis, confident that he would be informed in plenty of time to react against anything the Spaniards might try. They could even go for walks. Other nurses had also established relationships and Haney was still seeing Ruth, who had begun calling herself Ruta. Some of the soldiers were obviously envious, but there was nothing he could do about that. He was not going to ignore Sarah.

A few civilians had tried to return to Matanzas, but the army was discouraging their presence. Too many of them could be spies.

His regimental commanders were good, and Sarah's brother was settling in his true position as a staff officer. Ryder sometimes mentally kicked himself for thinking that Jack Barnes had been ready to command a regiment.

If he needed someone to do some fighting, he always had Lang and Haney, along with the Cuban leader, Diego Valdez. The Cuban had at least a thousand men under his command and seemed content to place himself more or less under Ryder's leadership. Leadership, Ryder thought, not command. No one commanded Valdez, not even the vivacious young lady who was now his mistress, a young widow named Maria Vasquez.

Haney entered and sat down, "Anything new on Custer, General?"

"Of course not, Sergeant, and stop asking silly questions. When something happens, you'll know it well before anyone else."

Haney ignored the jab. "And that means that Nelson Miles is paralyzed, doesn't it? The army isn't going to move. We're just going to sit here until either the Spanish overwhelm us or the fevers kill us or both. I thought that Custer had stiffened his spine, but I guess getting captured put a stop to all that."

Ryder laughed harshly. "It might be getting worse. My scouts say that the Spanish are really building up their strength something fierce and will be ready to attack us in a matter of days."

"And Miles still won't reinforce the center? That's crazy."

"Don't call your commanding general crazy. He might be, but you don't say it, especially where somebody might hear you. According to Benteen, Miles feels he doesn't have enough men to cover everything. It's about five miles from the opening of the bay to where we are sitting and he feels that's too far, especially when you consider that he'd have to defend both sides of the bay."

"Makes sense," the sergeant admitted reluctantly.

"So, Benteen has decided that this moldy lump of mud that's been named after your worthless ass shall be transformed into a citadel. He just informed me that he wants storerooms for food and ammunition and more bunkers for additional soldiers. If we're pushed away from the bay, he doesn't want us starving to death or having to throw rocks at the Spaniards. He feels another two thousand men can strengthen this place. He also said he wants a fresh water well dug and seemed shocked when I told him we'd already done it."

"What about nurses?" Haney asked softly. Ryder was about to say something when he recalled that the sergeant was still very close to Ruta Holden, perhaps just as close as he was to Sarah. No, he thought, they weren't just as close. He hadn't gotten Sarah to bed yet, much less made love on a stack of dusty and uncomfortable tents.

"When the time comes, Sergeant, we will do what we have to, even if that includes sending you down the hill on an errand of mercy to save the wounded and the people who take care of them."

Haney nodded and then grinned. "That works fine for me."

Kendrick felt incredibly nervous. Not only was the house where Custer was being kept surrounded by Spanish soldiers, but it was less than a mile from the massive Castillo del Principe, the ominous fortification that had been built nearly a century before. The Principe was the anchor in the reconstructed fortifications protecting Havana and one of several similar but smaller forts in a loose ring around Havana. Kendrick quietly wondered just how the American Army would storm these forts, assuming, of course, that the army ever got off its collective butt and made it to Havana.

Dunfield lived in a Mediterranean-style villa that was not unusual for the Caribbean. Square outer walls built with stone and with few windows made it look like a fortress and Kendrick realized that's what it could become in a matter of minutes. At the moment, it was a prison as well as a home. The four walls surrounded an inner courtyard in which fountains sprayed water and colorful flowers brightened the scene. It was as if the outer world didn't exist.

Kendrick was informed that Custer was being kept in a suite of rooms on the second floor. Somewhat gratuitously, he was informed that the window was barred and that guards were in the street below. He would have expected nothing else. He asked if he was expected and the guard, a fat corporal, simply shrugged. He didn't know and didn't care. Kendrick asked how Custer was doing.

"He eats, sleeps, shits, and takes walks in the courtyard," the corporal said.

"Has he said anything to you?"

The corporal shook his head. "He is a rude bastard."

"Then he hasn't changed at all," Kendrick said and the guard, surprised at the candor, actually laughed.

When Kendrick went to open the door, the guard grabbed his arm and halted him. He searched him for weapons, even taking a small pocket knife with a

Red Cross on it that he'd bought years ago in Switzerland. He was assured that it would be returned to him when he left. Kendrick had his doubts.

"Please leave the door open, Señor Kendrick. Otherwise we will not interfere with you or listen to your conversation."

Kendrick thanked the man and tipped him a couple of American dollars, which further improved the corporal's disposition.

Kendrick entered the suite and blinked in the darkness. "Jesus Christ," came a familiar voice. "Just when I thought I'd gotten far enough away from you, you pop up again. What the hell have I done to deserve this?"

"Mr. President, you have been a very bad boy and it's cost me a lot to get to see you in person."

There was a bottle of Bacardi Rum in Custer's hand and an empty one was on the floor. It was apparent that the president was in no condition to escape even if his prison was wide open.

"This stuff isn't bad, Kendrick, you should try it."

"Some other day, perhaps. So, how are you doing? How are they treating you?"

"Well enough," Custer said and took a long swallow. "Now, how is my war coming? Has Miles attacked? The sooner he punches through, the sooner I can get the hell out of this glorified prison and go back to running the country."

"I regret to inform you that Miles appears to have lost what courage you thought you gave him. The army isn't moving and he is simply waiting for the next Spanish attack."

"Damn him. What are they doing in Washington?"

"From what I've been able to discern, they are trying to figure out who is in charge in your absence. Chester Arthur is the favorite and he will likely go for a change in command. It might not be somebody you like."

Kendrick had heard no such information. What he was saying had the feel of logic, so he felt comfortable fibbing to Custer. To his surprise, Custer did not seem upset. "There's not much I can do about that, is there? My one and only goal is to get back to the States and Libbie and take over again. Then I can run any bastard I don't like out of town. Until then, I am totally irrelevant. It's like I actually had been killed at the Little Big Horn and sometimes I wish I had."

Good luck with taking over if he ever did return, thought Kendrick. "Tell me about how you got caught. Commander Blondell and his crew have been exchanged and he's told everyone that you ordered him to go to Havana against his wishes and that your getting captured is all your fault. Any comment?"

A shrug and another swallow followed by a belch. "Blondell's a fat little prick but he's right. I wanted to see Havana and I made him do it. I couldn't lie about it if I wanted to."

"Do you favor signing a treaty of peace unfavorable to the U.S. in order to get you out of here?"

"Fuck no. I'm desperate, not crazy. Besides, I'm in no position to dictate any peace terms and no way could I have unfavorable terms ratified by the Senate."

Kendrick was mildly surprised at Custer's coherent understanding of the situation. "So you're willing to stay here for a very long time if necessary?"

"Willing? Hell, Kendrick, I most certainly am *not*

willing. On the other hand I have to recognize reality.
I'm not going anyplace until there is peace. The next
time you slip out of here and back to our lines, you
let Libbie, Blaine, Arthur, and anyone else know that
I will not be bought and sold like a bushel of corn."

Kendrick said that he would do just that. He did
not inform Custer that he had no plans to leave
Havana in the immediate future. No, this is where
the big story would be. Either the U.S. would win
and Havana would be conquered, or Spain would win
and the Spanish empire would be rejuvenated. He
would write up his interview and then type it. Juana
had access to a new Remington Typewriter and he
had taught himself how to use it. The story would
be placed in a British diplomatic pouch and go by
ship to Florida.

"Besides freeing you, Mr. President, is there anything else I can do?"

Custer eyed the now empty Bacardi bottle. He
threw it in a wastebasket. "Yes. I've decided I really
don't like this shit. See if you can get me a few dozen
cases of bourbon to tide me over until the war ends."

Chester Arthur, James Blaine, and the others,
including Libbie Custer, did not like referring to
themselves as a "junta" or a "cabal" as some of the
Washington and New York newspapers were doing.
Those terms had sinister undertones and what they
were doing was both legal and public, and, of course,
necessary. The United States had to be governed and
continue to run.

And add to that the fact that the public was outraged by the way the war was going and the situation

was volatile. Marches had taken place in a number of cities as pro-war and anti-war adherents shouted their opinions. Groups carrying banners paraded and shouted. No one was shocked to see numbers of women involved in the marching. The women wanted the war over and their men returned home. On a number of occasions, the marches had become violent and more than a dozen had been killed rioting in New York and Boston.

"I wish Kendrick had kept the interview quiet," Blaine muttered. "At least until we could have read it first and been prepared for the uproar."

Kendrick's interview with Custer had become public. It had been sold to scores of newspapers, garnering the reporter large amounts of money and several book offers. He was becoming rich in absentia and would be given a hero's welcome when he too returned home.

"He's a reporter," said Arthur, "what the devil did you expect? Actually, reporters are the devil, or at least people who have sold their souls to the devil."

Blaine didn't think that the comment was funny at all. "The President of the United States is sitting there drunk as a lord while a prisoner of the Spanish. He says he has no confidence in the commanding general, and would like someone to send him some Kentucky bourbon. Jesus, what the hell is this country coming to?"

"At least he's alive and well," responded Libbie Custer in a soft and muted voice that was totally uncharacteristic of her. Her eyes were sunken and her complexion gray. She looked like a woman in mourning, which she was. She was slowly becoming reconciled to the inescapable fact that her beloved husband would not be returning for quite a while. And worse, when he did return, scorn would be heaped upon him. As president, Custer had committed several unforgivable sins. He had left the country and the public was not accepting the theory that he had still been in the United States by virtue of being on the *Dolphin*. His political enemies had argued that the *Dolphin* had been in Spanish or Cuban waters and could not have been in sovereign American territory. Legally, they might be wrong, but the public's ire was up. Then, Custer had managed to get himself captured and was being held in a Havana prison and appeared to be spending his time in a drunken stupor. The shame to the United States was almost palpable.

George Armstrong Custer's rash and idiotic behavior had embarrassed the United States in the eyes of the world. In Kendrick's article, the president had said that he wanted to return so he could again take over. The consensus was that he was deluding himself.

Libbie stood. "It would have been far better if he had been killed at the Little Big Horn. At least then he would have died a hero instead of rotting in a prison. Custer's Last Stand would have been on a hill in the Dakotas with a gun in his hand, and not on a couch in a Havana apartment with a bottle of rum in his hand."

With that, she sobbed and swept out of the room.

"I generally find it hard feeling sorry for her," said Arthur. "She's always been conniving on her husband's behalf and now it's come back to hit her in the face."

Blaine simply nodded. He too had written off President Custer as a serious contender for the presidency the next election. He'd begun thinking that he could stymie Chester Arthur's ambitions at the next

Republican convention if he could get Libbie Custer on his side. For the first time in her life, the marvelously attractive and sensuous woman was scared and vulnerable. Better, she was a sympathetic presence. She didn't have to denounce her dunce of a husband, merely announce how much she was depending on James G. Blaine to lead the country out of this terrible dilemma. President Custer might be despised by the public, but his grieving almost-widow could strike a sympathetic chord among delegates at the next Republican Convention.

Blaine was reasonably happily married to his wife Harriet, but he would not be above seducing Libbie Custer if it could help his political ambitions. Nor did the seduction have to be in the physical sense, although that would be marvelous. Many times he had imagined her naked and beneath him. He thought that many in Washington had imagined the same thing. No, all he had to do was get her under his control and get her to speak and act as he wished her to. Who knows, he thought, she might actually be a widow in the very near future.

A very young aide entered bearing a message. He looked in confusion as to who should get it. As Blaine seethed, Arthur waved the boy over and took the paper, again taking command. The vice president read it and nodded. He looked at his pocket watch. "It is nearly noon and word has been received that the Spanish are again attacking our positions in force."

"Damn it to hell," said Blaine.

"I have also been informed that General Sheridan along with former General Winfield Scott Hancock will be arriving shortly."

Blaine was astonished. "Who the devil invited them?"

Arthur smiled tolerantly. "As Commanding General of the United States Army, I don't believe that Philip Sheridan requires an invitation to give us his sage advice and counsel. However and to set your mind at ease, I requested both men to come here. As to Hancock's being present, I'm certain you can guess why."

Maria Garcia watched in horror as the ragged column of fifty or so dusty soldiers and conscripts came down the path towards her house. Others in her small village had already run inside and closed their doors. They would watch through the openings in the walls that they called windows, but they would not interfere. That would be pointless and dangerous.

The Spaniards' presence could mean only one thing. Her only surviving son, her baby, was going to be taken away and turned into a soldier. For an instant she thought about telling Manuel to run like the wind and hide. But where would he go? The soldiers were already fanning out as if expecting the sixteen-year-old boy to flee. It was apparent that the Spanish soldiers had done this before. Nor could she ask help from his father. He was dead and she was alone.

A heavyset corporal walked up to her. He was sweating profusely but kept his uniform buttoned in an attempt to look professional. "Please tell Manuel Garcia to come out and bring with him what belongings he wishes to take with him. He is about to have the honor of becoming a soldier of Spain."

"What honor?" she snapped. "You will have him fighting his fellow Cubans or, worse, the Americans. If you take him I will never see him again."

The corporal looked genuinely saddened. "Señora, no one can tell what might happen in time of war. All I do know is that he is to become a soldier of Spain and he will be one of many to be on the lookout for an American landing."

"And what will he do if they come, throw rocks at them? Are you going to teach him to shoot a gun, fire a cannon?" She reached out and tugged at his arm. "Corporal, if you leave without him, tonight I will let you come to my bed."

The corporal blinked. Señora Garcia was a fine looking and mature woman with a full ripe figure. She breathed deeply and he thought her breasts would rip through the fabric of her blouse and her nipples, clearly outlined, seemed to be calling to him.

"I would dearly love to, kind lady, but the lieutenant who is picking his nose and riding that horse is an ass and he will not let that happen. Your son is coming with us. If he decides to run, we have dogs that will run him down and tear at his flesh. Is that what you wish?"

It was not. She sagged and called her son out on the handful of planks that served as a porch. The boy emerged and blinked in the sunlight. He was tall for his age but very thin. The others in the column looked on, bored. They had seen this vignette play out many times before.

Maria put her hand on her son's shoulder and squeezed. "I want you to get your best clothing. There is no point in your going off to war looking like someone who has already lost one."

The boy nodded and started to turn away. The corporal stopped him. "Do not do that, señora. Dress him in rags, the dirtiest clothes you can find. Otherwise, anything he has that is worth something will be stolen before tomorrow's dawn."

"He's right," said the boy, finally speaking. "And I will not wear shoes or boots. My feet are tough enough to handle the roads."

"Can you read or write?" asked the corporal.

"Yes," he said.

"Excellent. Then I will tell the lieutenant that you would make a fine clerk. He has been looking for one for a while. Only don't let him put his hand on your ass, unless, of course, you like that sort of thing."

It didn't take long for Manuel to gather his meager possessions and join the straggly column. Maria waved the corporal over. "Will he be able to send letters?"

The corporal nodded solemnly. His heart was not in these actions which were little more than kidnappings. "He will write, and I will ensure that they are mailed properly. I will do everything I can to also ensure his safety."

"What is your name, Corporal?"

"Carlos Menendez, señora, and I have been a soldier of Spain for almost twenty years. I became a soldier because there was no other route open to me, just as there isn't now for your son. I was ragged and hungry and now I have at least the semblance of a uniform although the food has been lacking lately."

"Is this what you enlisted to do?"

"No, señora, I wanted to be a soldier, not a thief of children."

"Then why don't you desert and join the rebels?"

Menendez looked around to see if anyone was paying any attention to him. They weren't. "Because

I am Spanish and the rebels would likely chop me into little pieces before I had a chance to explain myself. But trust me, I will do what I can to protect your boy. The army is building a small fort at Santa Cruz del Norte. It is where the lieutenant will put him and where he will be the lieutenant's clerk. It will be well away from any battlefield."

Maria nodded gratefully and lightly rested her hand on his arm. "Then show up here shortly after dark and bring some rum and a loaf of bread. Despite the uniform you wear, you appear to be a decent man and I will need some comforting this night, perhaps a lot of comforting."

◆ Chapter 15 ◆

WHEN THE FIRST SHELL SMASHED THROUGH THE wall of the army's hospital in the church of San Charles de Borromeo, Sarah's first thought was that a horrible mistake had been made. Artillery shells had been known to go in wrong directions. Perhaps, she thought, this was the case. No one would intentionally bombard a church or a hospital, would they?

When the second and third shells slammed into the building, sending glass and plaster along with chunks of stone raining down on them, the nurses realized it was no mistake.

As always, Clara Barton took charge. "Gather everyone and everything you can carry and get down to the waterfront."

No one needed urging. Shells were falling all around the hospital and smashing into other buildings. Men were running for their lives to find safety in trenches, while horses screamed in panic. One was hit and disemboweled by a shell. It howled like a demon on fire before it died.

There were only a dozen or so patients in the hospital and most of these were able to get out under their own power. The handful remaining were helped or carried by staff and volunteers out to the trenches.

"I'm getting very tired of this," said Ruta as she settled into the relative safety of the trench's earthen walls.

"I'm not arguing with you," Sarah responded. Her arms were full of medical supplies.

A company of soldiers ran past them and inland in the general direction of the front. Rifle fire, along with the incessant cannonading, had commenced. The war had finally come to them.

Clara Barton jumped into the trench with them. "We are going to split up. I'm going to take half of my people up to the entrance to the bay, while you, Ruta, will take the remainder towards Mount Haney."

"Then we're losing, aren't we?" asked Sarah.

"Indeed and quite badly. The Spanish are attacking all along the line, but it does look like they are concentrating on splitting our forces in half." Barton smiled briefly. "And yes, it does look like your General Ryder was correct after all, not that it matters right now. Our job is to get the wounded taken care of and our own people into places of safety."

With that, Barton clambered out of the trench with surprising alacrity and, hunched over, ran away with several of her medical personnel.

Ruta was the natural leader of the others. She got all of the remaining medical personnel and the handful of wounded out of the trench and towards the waterfront. Along the way, they passed another company-sized unit of American infantry running towards the sound of gunfire that appeared to be much closer.

As they inched towards what they hoped would be safety, numbers of soldiers suddenly swarmed passed them, running the other direction. Their officers screamed at them to form up and get ready to fight, but too many were wide-eyed with terror.

Ruta grabbed Sarah's arm. "Look over there."

Sarah did as she was told and gasped in shock. A mob of several hundred Spanish soldiers was heading towards them. They were howling and screaming in insane fury. They had broken through the despised Americans, and their bloodlust was up. If the nurses didn't hurry, they'd wind up as prisoners if they were lucky. The Spanish could easily simply rape them and butcher them in their insane fury. Even the best and most disciplined soldiers could lose their minds in battle and the Spanish were neither the best nor the most disciplined. In the distance, they could see other waves of Spaniards heading towards other targets. The sounds of the battle were overwhelming and terrifying.

"Run!" yelled Sarah. The women dropped everything. They hiked up their skirts and ran as fast as they could. Bullets whizzed and pinged around them. One of the nurses screamed and fell over. Her arm was twisted and bleeding.

"Carry her," ordered Ruta. There was no time for a tourniquet. If she bled to death there was nothing they could do.

Another nurse fell over. The top of her head was gone. This cannot be happening, thought Sarah. We're nurses. We aren't soldiers. The Geneva Convention is supposed to protect us. How could human beings do such terrible things to each other? This was far worse than anything she'd yet seen.

The Spanish were only a little more than a hundred yards away when several of them buckled and fell. A number of Americans in wide-brimmed cowboy hats pushed by the nurses, knelt, and continued to fire. Each bullet seemed to strike a Spaniard, with the officers being the favored targets.

The Spanish lost their enthusiasm and took cover. "Now follow me," said Haney, "and don't look back or delay or anything. Just run like your bloomers are on fire."

Despite the insanity of the situation, Sarah found herself laughing. My bloomers cannot be on fire, she thought. I'm not wearing bloomers.

They ran for a couple of hundred yards and then paused. The soldiers who'd saved them were identified as Texans by Haney, who said that they were really good shots. They moved through gaps in barbed wire and were then escorted over trenches that were filled with American soldiers. More Americans moved through the defenses and to safety. Cannons fired over their heads and they heard the chatter of Gatling guns. Sarah took a moment to see what was happening and wished she hadn't. Shells were exploding over and within the Spanish ranks, shredding and dismembering bodies. War is hell and never forget that awful fact, she reminded herself.

An American gunboat in the bay found that the Spanish were within range and added to the thunderous din with her cannons. The air was filled with smoke and debris. The nurses were walking now and not running. Their breath still came in gasps. They were exhausted, both emotionally and physically. "There are eight of us," said Ruta, "and that includes Nurse Atkins who probably will lose her arm. Carmody is dead and there will be no attempt to retrieve her body. Perhaps it can be done if a flag of truce is initiated. Otherwise, we will not risk anyone."

The nurses were moved into a sandbagged bunker where they could rest. Sarah thought she had seen Martin farther up on the hill, but she wasn't certain. The sound of gunfire came from the inland side of the hill as well. She was certain that Martin was far too busy to check on her. He would find her in due course. In the meantime they would all rest and figure out where they could set up a hospital where the Spanish wouldn't destroy it.

Colonel Gilberto Salazar still walked with difficulty. The wound to his groin was healing but exquisitely slowly. As the men of his Legion moved up the hill that both sides were now calling Mount Haney, he was forced to fall behind. He didn't mind that at all. Let other brave fools get killed.

His attack was going to fail and in that failure lay success. It was conceded that the American fortifications on Mount Haney were too strong to take by storm. They would require a steady and deadly pounding by heavy artillery the Spanish Army didn't have. These would have to be followed by a further assault by huge numbers of well-trained infantry, which Spain also did not have. No, the job of his Legion was to demonstrate and pretend to attack, holding the Americans in position so that the main force under

General Weyler could storm through the American center and split the Yankee force in half.

For this demonstration, Salazar had been given command of four other regiments, all understrength and poorly trained. Since he didn't want his own men killed in a useless gesture, he had the new regiments lead while his legion acted as a tactical reserve. As the soldiers neared the hated barbed wire, American rifles and machine guns opened up. Only a few cannons fired at them and it occurred to him that the American defenders were shifting their cannons to better cover the attack on their middle.

Soldiers fell in heaps, but not his best men. When it was apparent that the attack was not going to succeed, he ordered them all to lie prone and shoot at the entrenched Americans. Even this was futile. After only a few minutes, his men began to fall back. Some of the officers tried to stop them, but too many joined in the retreat.

Cowardly bastards, he cursed, conveniently ignoring the fact that he'd held back. Finally, a message arrived authorizing the retreat that was already occurring. It said that the attack on the middle was a complete success and that hundreds, if not thousands, of Americans were dead, wounded, or captured.

Even though they were retreating, all around him men were cheering. They had singed the beard of Uncle Sam, and better, Salazar hadn't gotten hurt. Another messenger brought him word that General Weyler was very pleased with the way his men had pinned down the Americans on the hill and kept them from counterattacking. Weyler confirmed Salazar's rank as colonel. No longer was he a temporary colonel.

Perhaps even his scrawny slut of a wife would be proud of him.

As he headed back to his quarters, he noticed that he wasn't limping as much. Tonight he would go into the village where Helga was ensconced. He smiled at the thought of her servicing his manhood with her marvelous lips. Thank God he could be certain of her loyalty and love towards him. He could count on her, not like his cold bitch of a wife. Helga was a hundred times more woman than Juana, and if that American reporter wanted to fuck her, well he could have her. Salazar laughed as he wondered if Kendrick's cock would freeze inside her and fall off. He thought it more than likely.

It was almost dawn before Ryder felt confident enough in the security of his men's position to take a break and lie down. He'd been up almost all night shifting men and units into positions and helping sight cannons so they could fire down into the newly developing Spanish lines below Mount Haney. At dawn a truce would be in effect to help gather up the dead and wounded from both sides. The cries and moans coming from the wounded tore at all of them, but they were gradually fading away as men either died of their wounds or were carried away by comrades taking advantage of the darkness and an unofficial truce to sneak out and help them.

Ryder slipped out of his tunic and shirt and managed to wipe himself somewhat clean with a rag and a pitcher of water. He closed his eyes and immediately went to sleep. When he awoke, it was midday and he cursed angrily.

"You shouldn't talk like that," said Sarah as she pushed him back on the cot. "The world did not end while you were resting. Your soldiers will get the wrong idea and think you're a violent man who likes to swear. Everything's under control, Martin. Both sides are licking their wounds."

He looked around and continued to wake up. They were in the back room of his quarters and a blanket had been hung to give him some privacy from the office part. "We shouldn't be alone like this."

"I'm a nurse and Ruta's just outside with a couple of other nurses. The wounded are all taken care of, so don't worry about your men being neglected. They will think I'm treating you for some malady or minor injury. And besides, we don't have enough privacy to really get into trouble. By the way, you look terrible. You won't be too much use to your men if you're too sick and hungry to lead them."

"Do you really believe that?"

"Not for one second. Now be still and kiss me."

He pulled her down to him and they kissed hungrily, passionately. When she finally pulled back, she looked down on him with tenderness and sadness. "I'm going to shock you, Martin. I want to go someplace lovely and private and make love to you and it won't matter if we're married or not. I've decided that life is too short and death too violent and close by to waste on ceremonials."

"Funny, but I was thinking pretty much the same thing. I wasn't shocked, though. Frankly, I'm delighted."

She poured some water into a bowl and began to clean off his chest and arms. "You're filthy and this water isn't that much cleaner."

"I just tried to clean up," he said.

She left and returned with a fresh pitcher. "With what? Mud? You need to get used to doing a better job if you want to get me in your bed. I will not have a filthy lover."

"I'll work on it," he said and gasped. He was becoming thoroughly aroused as she rinsed off his bare chest. From the way Sarah was biting her lip, he thought that she was too. "Perhaps you could just come here several times a day and take care of my personal hygiene needs."

She laughed. "It appears that your needs have nothing to do with hygiene. Speaking of which, have you noticed how dirty and tattered my nurse's uniform is? Of course you have. Now look at this." She pulled her dress up well above her knees. He wanted to gape at her lovely and shapely legs but he couldn't. The dark stockings she was wearing were torn almost to shreds. "All of us are wearing clothing that is at least as bad as this."

Martin sat up. The romantic interlude was over, at least for the moment. "I've seen beggars who were better dressed. What do you want me to do?"

"Unless you can get us ladies some appropriate women's wear, we would like you to order the quartermaster to issue us men's uniforms, size small, very small if they have any such thing. If not, we will tailor what we can get to our needs."

"It's irregular, but so is the idea of having you here in the first place. Consider it done. But what will Clara Barton think?"

She leaned down and kissed him longingly, for a moment letting her tongue wander with his. "I don't much care what Clara Barton thinks," she said when they broke and could talk. "She can solve her own problems."

Sarah ran her hand down his chest and stomach and lightly over his pants and the very obvious swelling hiding beneath the cloth. "Just remember, my very dear General, that the suddenly lusty Widow Damon needs you and craves you very much, so stay safe."

Pleased and confident, Winfield Scott Hancock, former major general in the Union Army and 1880 Democratic candidate for President of the United States, formally presented himself to Blaine, Arthur, and the others. Libbie Custer was not present. She could not bear to be in the same room as the man who had run against her beloved husband and had almost beaten him. Left unsaid was the thought that a President Hancock wouldn't have gotten the U.S. in the terrible mess that the war in Cuba had become.

Lieutenant General Philip Sheridan accompanied him. It was not lost on the attendees that Hancock looked far more fit and trim and healthy than Sheridan, who was seven years his junior.

"Don't we have any young generals?" sneered Blaine.

"No we don't," Sheridan said blandly, "and therein lies the curse of the peacetime army—and navy I might add. During war, merit and survival are rewarded and cream rises to the top. In peacetime, rank freezes, even fossilizes. Just about every general we currently have in the Army achieved that rank during the Civil War, and that tragic event ended more than sixteen years ago."

"And as I can still talk and walk, I decline to be referred to as a fossil," answered a smiling Hancock. He was in a confident and ebullient mood. He was about to be honored and vindicated by his political enemies. "I may be many years older than Nelson Miles, but in many ways I am very much younger than he."

Even Blaine had to agree with that assessment. "Have you come to be America's savior, Mister Hancock?"

Hancock refused to be insulted by Blaine's not referring to him as "General." Even though he was a civilian, he was entitled to the courtesy. "I don't think America needs a savior, sir, but the war in Cuba certainly does."

Vice President Arthur decided it was time to end the pettiness. Blaine was beginning to annoy him. "Agreed. Now, General Hancock, what can you bring to the table?"

Hancock took a deep breath. "It's been a long time since I led men in battle, but I am confident I can rally the troops and conclude the war with an American victory."

Even Blaine had to nod agreement. Few could not recall Hancock's taking control of the Union lines at the Battle of Gettysburg and stabilizing them before he was terribly wounded. That wound still troubled him and on occasion caused him great pain. There were those who thought that it had been Hancock and not Meade who had won that climactic battle.

"What do you need for victory?" Arthur asked in a soft voice.

"I need rank sufficient to the task. Reinstate me, but as a lieutenant general. That will make me second to General Sheridan but above anyone in command in Cuba, which will eliminate conflicts."

"Agreed," said Arthur and the others nodded.

"General Miles is correct. We need more men. There are two more divisions in training and I want them immediately. General Gordon's division and General Chamberlain's must be on the move to Cuba as soon as humanly possible."

There was silence but no disagreement. John Gordon's men were all Southerners, and there had been resistance to having former Confederates fighting as a unit. But Hancock was popular in the South. He'd been fairly lenient to Southerners during the Reconstruction period. His detractors had said he had been too lenient on the former and largely unrepentant rebels. No matter, he would have Gordon's Division.

Joshua Chamberlain's division of volunteers primarily came from Maine, New Hampshire, and Vermont. In an exquisite irony, it had been Brevet Major General Chamberlain who had been tasked with receiving the surrender of Robert E. Lee's troops at Appomattox. The Confederate general tasked with surrendering the Army of Northern Virginia had been John Gordon. Chamberlain had won Gordon's and the rest of the Confederates' respect by ordering his men to salute the rebels as they marched past and laid down their arms. After the war, Gordon had become very controversial. Even though he denied it, rumors said he had been in charge of the Ku Klux Klan.

On the other hand, John Gordon had been elected to the U.S. Senate.

"I understand that Joshua Chamberlain's in poor health," said Arthur.

Sheridan chuckled. "You tell him. The man's insistent. He feels that serving as a general in the Civil War, being awarded the Medal of Honor and later becoming governor of Maine, and still later president of Bowdoin College entitle him to consideration, and I agree."

Between Gordon and Chamberlain, they could bring another fifteen to twenty thousand men to the battle. Would they be enough to win? That would be up to Lieutenant General Hancock.

"We are in agreement?" asked Sheridan and all said yes.

Even Blaine seemed pleased. "Well, General Hancock, how soon will your men commence arriving at Matanzas?"

Hancock smiled widely, "Events will transpire very soon, gentlemen."

Phil Sheridan turned away and smiled. He and Hancock had discussed strategy for the coming campaign. No reinforcements would be landing at Matanzas. For the time being, Nelson Miles, with help from the Navy, would be on his own in defending his two perimeters at that dismal Cuban port.

"I think I've done this before," sighed Wally Janson as he looked over the gathering host of ships anchored off Charleston, South Carolina, "Although maybe it was in another and more pleasant life."

The transports were all shapes and sizes and of varying speeds. Someone had the bright idea of breaking them into two groups—the slower ships in one and the faster in another, since a convoy would be held to the speed of its slowest member. A rough estimate had more than two hundred vessels clustered off Charleston. In a very short while they would commence loading two divisions of infantry and all their supplies.

Lieutenant Junior Grade Paul Prentice smiled tolerantly. He'd heard the comments several times in the last couple of days. Along with the other survivors from the ill-fated *Aurora*, he and Janson had been exchanged for an equivalent number of Spanish prisoners. Treated as heroes for their role in sinking the Spanish battleship *Vitoria*, the U.S. Navy had offered the older Janson command of a newly commissioned gunboat, which he promptly named the *Orion*. He didn't ask if the Navy already had plans for the name. As a sailor, he had a deep affection for the constellations. The two men had been awarded the Medal of Honor for sinking the Spanish battleship.

The *Orion* displaced about twelve hundred tons and was armed with a pair of six-inch guns, along with a handful of nine- and twelve-pound cannons. Armor plating had been attached to her sides and around her bridge, which affected her speed and maneuverability. She was a deadly force even though no one would ever call her an ironclad. With luck, the light armor would deflect bullets or shrapnel and small cannon shells, but would be useless against the shells from bigger weapons. The *Orion* would choose her fights carefully. Spain might have lost her two battleships, but her remaining cruisers would be more than a match for Janson's ship.

Janson was her skipper, while Prentice was on board as a supernumerary. The leg he'd broken when captured hadn't completely healed and he was on crutches. He would not be able to return to active duty until he was fully well. In the meantime, Janson needed assistance to function as a real naval officer. Janson's commission would last for the duration of the war and it was presumed that the *Orion* would be signed over to his ownership as partial compensation for the loss of the *Aurora*.

The *Orion* was one of two score similar ships that had been hastily pressed into service in the rapidly expanding navy. All had been converted from merchantmen. Small and lethal, they would protect the gathering armada from the few remaining Spanish warships if they should venture out from where they were hiding. The Navy was building a number of real armored cruisers that would be substantially better than the powerful *Atlanta*, which was patrolling off Charleston and no longer on duty at Havana. The new ships would not be ready for a year of two. The newspapers had called the situation a shame and heaped more blame on President Custer. Both Prentice and Janson were inclined to agree with the assessment, as was most of the population of the United States.

"The first time I left on a mission like this, it was from Baltimore," Janson mused out loud. "At least we're a few hundred miles closer to Cuba than we were that first time, which will make it easier on all the troops who'll be jammed in the holds of all those ships. Did I ever tell you how we were attacked by a Spanish gunboat and how that young Colonel Ryder figured out how to sink it? I like to think that fight was part of why he got promoted to general."

"Only about a hundred times," Prentice said tolerantly. "This Ryder must be a hell of a general. Not all generals and admirals are willing to fight. A lot of them simply want to make speeches and look good in their uniforms."

"Lieutenant, you are wise beyond your years."

"Skipper, have you learned our final destination?"

Janson's eyes widened in surprise, "Are you telling me it's not Matanzas?"

"All I'm saying is that I keep hearing rumors. I also understand that the Army is going to undergo a major reorganization now that Hancock's in charge. I keep hearing that someone named Couch is going to be named to an important position. The name's familiar, but I don't know why."

Janson yawned. It was good to have someone he could talk to without having to worry about little things like rank. "Paul, I'm sure they'll tell us when they decide it's important enough. For your information, Darius Couch was a Union general, but I don't recall all that much about him. Wait, I do recall one thing. He likes to pronounce his name Coach instead of Couch. I guess he doesn't want to be compared to a piece of furniture."

Darius N. Couch, recently returned to the army as a major general in command of the newly designated Second Corps, was looking for redemption. He was sixty years old and every day he recalled how he had failed his country at the battle of Chancellorsville in the spring of 1863. In his mind he had let the very real chance of defeating or even destroying Lee's Army of Northern Virginia slip through his normally very capable hands. Had he acted decisively, how many lives could have been saved, how many thousands of families would not still be in mourning? He could only wonder and mourn for himself and the faceless others. Unlike the more powerfully built Hancock, Couch

was small and slight and subject to bouts of ill health.
Couch had also been decorated for gallantry in the
Mexican War, at the battle of Buena Vista.

"I won't let you down," he said solemnly.

Hancock nodded. "I know."

"Not like Chancellorsville."

Hancock understood the man's frustration. At Chancellorsville, the terribly overmatched Joe Hooker had
been the victim of a surprise attack by Lee. The
much larger Union Army had been pushed back
into a defensive perimeter. Still, they were in good
shape until Hooker had been wounded, struck on the
head by falling debris. As he was taken to the rear,
Hooker ordered Couch, his second in command, to
retreat. There were vehement arguments both for and
against obeying that order. Couch felt that Lee had
done all he could and was ripe for a counterattack.
Hooker, concussed and confused, insisted on ordering
a retreat and was taken away by ambulance, leaving
Couch in temporary command of the massive Army
of the Potomac.

"I obeyed the orders of an injured and confused
man who, quite likely, wasn't right in the head. I
should have seized control and fought Lee. We could
have whipped him. We could have shortened the
war, maybe even ended it. It sickens me every time
I think of it."

Hancock smiled. Couch had obeyed orders and that
had absolved him from any blame for the defeat at
Chancellorsville. However, Couch was right. Sometimes
orders are meant to be ignored. "Well, now you get
to fight Weyler, and I want you to fight him all the
way to Havana."

Couch could not bring himself to smile in return. "Neither I nor the Second Corps will let you down, General Hancock." Then he did smile briefly. "Of course I do not envy you having to work with General Miles. If he were in my command, I would likely have to kill him."

Hancock laughed. He was pleased with his decision to bring Couch back to the colors. Although another of what James G. Blaine annoyingly referred to as an older general, it was clear that Couch was full of fight and wanted to purge himself of history. He would command the newly created Second Corps, which consisted of Gordon's and Chamberlain's divisions. The two subordinate generals had met a few days earlier and politely recalled previous incidents including the surrender at Appomattox. Although they would never be close friends, both Couch and Hancock were convinced that they would both cooperate and obey. Second Corps was in good hands and would operate independently of First Corps.

That left First Corps, which, until it was just recently designated, was the entire American army in Cuba. First Corps was in Nelson Miles' hands and would remain so. Hancock would be with Miles and oversee the touchy and vain little man's actions. Miles would not be happy, but that was none of Hancock's concern. First Corps consisted of three divisions—Benteen's, Gibbon's, and Crook's. Altogether, the two army corps totaled nearly forty thousand men. It was the largest American army to take the field since the Civil War. If it was defeated, the whole idea of a war against Spain would result in nothing more than a bloody humiliation for the United States.

Therefore, Hancock thought as he left the conference with Couch, I will not be defeated.

Therefore again, he concluded, I must get to Matanzas as soon as possible. He would travel on the steam sloop *Enterprise*, while Couch would have his temporary headquarters on the *Atlanta*.

◆ Chapter 16 ◆

MAJOR GENERAL BENTEEN MADE HIMSELF AS COM-
fortable as possible in Ryder's bunker. He had
just finished a circuit of the new lines of defenses
on and around Mount Haney. These now included
extensive trench lines for the rest of his division and
not only Ryder's brigade. The defenses ran from the
waterfront on both sides of the hill and around it.
They were several lines deep and Benteen was pleased.

"No fortress is ever impregnable, Martin, but you've
done a great job. Of course, you had me alongside
to help you," he added with a grin.

Ryder shook his head and ignored the good-natured
jibe. "We only lack two things, General, food and water.
There are enough of us to hold off the Spaniards and
we have enough ammunition to fight a number of
battles, but we might just die of starvation or thirst
while carrying loaded weapons."

The crushing Spanish attack on the city of Matanzas
had resulted in the loss of much of their supplies. As

the men retreated to Haney and the entrance to the
bay, they'd carried with them as much ammunition
as possible. This meant leaving stockpiles of food for
the Spanish to plunder. Nor was their water situation
much better. The men around Haney now numbered
more than eight thousand and, while water was available, it came in a literal trickle from the wells already
dug. These had been adequate for Ryder's brigade, but
not for an entire division and a number of refugees.
The Spanish, sensing the situation, had attempted to
divert the few streams that ran close to the American
lines. They'd only partly succeeded, but it did mean
an inadequate supply for cooking and sanitation.

The two generals were alone. This was a conversation, not a conference. "How's Miles taking his demo-
tion?" asked Ryder.

"Outwardly, he appears to be controlling his anger.
Inwardly, I think he's relieved. Commanding an independent army this size was too much for him. When
Hancock and the Second Corps arrive, he'll still have
an important role to play, but he won't be responsible
for the major decisions. Miles is a brave man and a
good fighter, but he was put in water too deep for him
and that was Custer's fault. He should have chosen
the best man under any circumstances, not the best
from a small pool of choices that he alone created.
He should have left politics out of it."

"What president could have done that?" Ryder
grumbled.

"No one that I know of," Benteen admitted with
a smile.

Several cannons boomed from the American positions. The taking of Matanzas had not presented the

Spanish with the complete victory they'd wanted. Cannons from Mount Haney and from the mouth of the bay covered most of the distance between the two points, which kept the Spanish from fortifying what they'd taken. Word had come that, after recovering the dead and wounded under yet another flag of truce, the Spanish had apologized for bombarding the hospital. They claimed that they'd been told that the church had been fortified. The apology had been accepted even though no one believed it. The Red Cross symbol had been prominently displayed on all sides of the building.

Benteen continued. "I also like the way you've established tracks and trails so you can move your big guns and your Gatlings quickly. You mass those things against a Spanish attack and the greasers won't like it."

Ryder wanted to light a cigar, but he only had a couple left and didn't feel like sharing them with Benteen. "The Spanish don't like being called greasers."

"Who cares what the Spanish think?"

"One more question. When Hancock arrives with an additional fifteen thousand or so men, where the hell are we supposed to put them?"

Benteen sighed, "Beats the hell out of me, Martin. Now be a good boy and give me one of those cigars you're hiding, because I'm not leaving until I get one."

Hector Rojas was a big man in many ways. Physically huge, he was an important part of Mercedes de Milan's household. In many ways he was its leader, and not just because he occasionally shared his mistress's bed. He was far smarter than his brutish looks, which sometimes fooled people, often to their permanent loss.

Nor was Hector the jealous type. He knew his place. He fully accepted that Mercedes' current number-one lover was the British diplomat, Redford Dunfield. This slightly surprised him because Dunfield seemed to be more than a little effeminate. Perhaps he had hidden skills or more subtle ways of satisfying Mercedes, he thought with a smile. No matter. Mercedes de Milan was approaching old age with ill grace and fear and this had made her sexually insatiable. She was deathly afraid that no one would want her when her looks faded. When Dunfield or a predecessor was not available to serve her, Rojas was. She also tipped well after each session and, as a result, he'd accumulated a significant amount of money.

One of his duties was to ensure that all was safe and secure in the de Milan compound. Hector knew that the two lovers who occupied the cottage were in danger from the skinny woman's husband, Gilberto Salazar. On occasion Rojas had walked by the cottage and seen them naked through a window. Juana Salazar did not arouse him although he conceded that she would do in a pinch. She was just too thin for his tastes.

Regardless, she and her American lover were Mercedes' guests and were to be protected. Hector liked to wander the compound at odd times just to see what might be afoot. By staggering his patrols, he hoped to confuse anyone who might want to break in and harm the lovers. It also kept his other guards on their toes.

This night was cloudy and there were few shadows. In a couple of hours, false dawn would rise. He was reacting to information from an informer in Salazar's legion that there would be an attempt on the lives of the two guests. The darkness smelled of danger and that excited him. He moved around the compound's perimeter with surprising grace and silence. He liked to think of himself as a large predator cat like the pictures of lions and leopards he'd seen in books in Mercedes' extensive library.

Hearing something, he paused. The compound was close enough to the city to pick up numerous background noises. There was a pattern to these sounds, even when punctuated by the odd shout or scream, or the occasional gunshot. What he was listening for was the sound of footfalls, or bushes and leaves being brushed against by something that shouldn't be there. He knew enough to identify and ignore the sounds of dogs or cats or even rodents. They did not concern him.

He heard something once more and froze. He heard it again and decided it wasn't an animal, at least not a four-legged one. He moved stealthily towards the sound, keeping it between him and the cottage. As he generally did, he had a large hammer in his hand and he handled it like a twig. One side was flat for pounding, while the other was wedge-shaped and good for crushing. He had a knife and a pistol in his belt, but his usual weapon of choice was the hammer. A gun made too much noise, and a knife was messy and often did not kill or even disable immediately. Even slicing a man's throat did not necessarily bring immediate death. The victim could flop and make noises for some time and be bleeding all over the place.

However, even a glancing blow from the hammer would shatter bones and cause shock, while a direct blow was usually fatal, at least when he swung it with blinding speed.

Rojas smelled blood. He moved cautiously and found the body of one of his guards. He swore softly. The boy had only been fifteen and now he was dead. He had volunteered to be a guard to prove his manhood and earn a little extra money and now he was dead. His head had been bashed in and his throat had been skillfully sliced open.

Rojas smiled tightly and moved closer to the lovers' cottage. The two men he'd sensed and now could see were concentrating on their approach to the cottage and paying no attention to what was happening behind them. Fools, he thought. As he stalked them he noted that each had a revolver in his waistband. Dangerous fools, he amended. He could call the alarm and others would come to his aid, but that would take a few precious minutes during which he could be shot. No, he would solve this himself and there would be no gunfire.

The two intruders were so preoccupied that he got within a few feet of them before he launched his bulk at them with fearful speed. He struck the first with the hammer and the man's skull shattered with a sickening sound, like a melon dropping on cement. He whirled and struck at the second man who was only beginning to turn with a look of puzzlement on his face. The hammer struck him between the eyes, killing him instantly.

Rojas breathed deeply and looked around. He had disturbed no one. He threw the bodies over his shoulder, walked to the stable and dumped them into a cart. After covering the corpses with a blanket and some straw he walked to the main house and entered through the servant's entrance. He was pleased to see that the Englishman was not present. That made things so much simpler.

He entered Mercedes' bedroom and awakened her. She was used to the touch of his hand and did not startle. As usual, she had been sleeping naked and made no effort to more fully cover what he had seen so many times before. Nor was she shocked by what he told her. An attack on the lovers had been expected.

"What will you do with the bodies?"

"At dawn, when the curfew is over, I will take them a few miles out of town and dump them in a field. It will be a while before anyone notices them, if ever, and by then they will be unrecognizable. Not even their mothers will know them."

Mercedes shuddered at the thought of the intruders being eaten by birds and animals and insects and bloated by the sun, but it had to be done. Other things had to be done as well. She could not allow Gilberto Salazar or his men to enter her property and murder people. He had crossed a line.

She handed him a corner of the light blanket that only partly covered her. He grinned and gently pulled it off her. Her beauty might be fading, but she was still highly desirable.

She smiled and held out her hand. He grasped it and she pulled him down to her. She had never had sex with a man who had just killed on her behalf and it thoroughly excited her. "You have done so very well, Hector Rojas, that I think you deserve a very great reward."

◆   ◆   ◆

Jesus, thought Kendrick. He was too stunned to return to bed where Juana slept peacefully. He hadn't been able to sleep and had gone to a window simply to look around. Even though he loved Juana and loved being with her, he was getting bored and needed to get near where the story and the action were. Thus, he'd seen the two men approaching. He'd been about to awaken Juana and make a run for the main house when a massive bulk had surged over the intruders like a wave, knocking them down with wickedly fast swings of a hammer. He recognized Rojas by his size. He'd seen the man around many times. Kendrick had kept on cordial terms with him and was now very thankful he had.

Kendrick also understood what would happen to the bodies. They would disappear and never be found. He would have to find a way of thanking Rojas. He had a feeling that both Rojas and Mercedes would deny that anything like what he'd seen had ever happened and he was fine with that. Still, he had to let them know of his appreciation. Rojas had just saved his and Juana's lives.

He walked softly back to bed, although he wondered if he would ever be able to get to sleep again. Next, he wondered if they should move to a more secure location. But to where, he wondered. If he could get the two of them back to the American lines, perhaps they'd be safe there. But maybe they'd be safe nowhere with Gilberto Salazar still in the picture. How could the man be so jealous of him when he'd thrown Juana at him? The man was mad, that was why. After hating and discarding Juana, he was now obsessed with no one else possessing her.

Perhaps they should move to the main house. There wouldn't be as much privacy, but they would be safer. No, he had to find a better, safer place for them. He could not leave Havana until the war was over. The story of a lifetime, maybe several lifetimes, was unfolding before his eyes. Word had come that the relief force had sailed from Charleston and the people of the city of Havana were tense and confused. Either Cuba was going to be free of Spain or the United States was going to suffer an ignominious defeat. Either way, he would be in Havana.

Ruta looked at the fresh grave. The mound of raw earth was the final resting place of Nurse Ethel Carmody. Her shattered and nearly headless body had been recovered during a truce and quickly buried. She was the first of the volunteer nurses to die. With the exception of Nurse Atkins who had lost her arm, none of the others had even been wounded. Bumps, cuts and bruises, yes, but nothing serious had occurred to them.

"Doctor Desmond gave a wonderful eulogy for her, didn't he?" commented Ruta. Desmond had moved from the head of the bay to Mount Haney. It was a clear indication that a major Spanish move was likely.

"Too bad so much of what he said wasn't true," said Sarah.

Ruta agreed. "I know. He said she was a marvelous nurse, which she wasn't, and a gentle, loving human being who was cherished by everyone, which she also wasn't. Too bad I couldn't believe a word of what he said. Carmody was a wretched person."

"Never speak ill of the dead," said Sarah. "No

matter how miserable they were in their lifetimes, they were always faithful husbands and wives, loving brothers and sisters, and devoted friends. Eulogies are never about the truth."

Ruta laughed bitterly. "My father beat us with his fists and a cane he kept for that purpose, and his brother tried to rape me. I told my father about his brother and dear father said I must be lying. He beat me again for slandering his dear brother. I hope both of them are dead and burning in hell. That would be my eulogy."

"I had an uncle who kept trying to run his hands up my dress," said Sarah. "I told my father and he beat him up very badly. It slowed him down but didn't stop him. I just learned to be more agile. He died a couple of years ago. Everyone cried and said what a saint he'd been in life. I felt like desecrating his grave. I was going to go to his grave at night and urinate on it. I couldn't because I was afraid of cemeteries in the night."

Ruta agreed. "I think we all have eulogies we'd like to give, but won't. Carmody wasn't perfect, but she was here and she was trying her best."

Sarah agreed. "On the other hand, Nurse Carmody didn't deserve to die like she did. There's going to be at least one more battle and it's entirely possible that some of us might fall. Martin says there's no way the Spanish can make any guarantees about our safety. We are all jammed in so close here that there is no real safety. We've dug caves and bunkers and all that means is that we might be buried alive during a bombardment."

Ruta sighed. "You are so cheerful today. You and

Martin need to be alone for a few minutes to calm yourselves down like Haney and I have been."

Sarah was astonished. "Have you really managed to be alone with your beloved sergeant up here on this wretched hill? Where on earth did you ever find the time and space for such an encounter?"

Ruta grinned wickedly. "If you have the time you can always find the space. And it doesn't have to take all that much time. And we'd better get used to not having much space. When the relief army gets here, our forces will almost double. As they say, one should make hay while the sun shines."

Sarah laughed and made a note to seek out Martin. There was a pause in the fighting as the two sides shifted and jockeyed for advantage. Perhaps they could find a few moments to be alone before Matanzas was even more jammed with American soldiers.

But then she had a thought and she recalled what Martin had said. He had wondered aloud just why everyone thought the relief army was coming to Matanzas.

General Weyler rode down the line to meet with his senior field officers and made the dramatic announcement that the American reinforcements were on their way. "Our future is spelled out for us. If Cuba is to remain Spanish, then the American force at Matanzas must be expelled. We must defeat the Americans before their reinforcements can land and the two groups unite. We will attack in overwhelming force and ferocity and destroy them."

He paused dramatically and looked at the assembly. "For King and Spain," he yelled dramatically. "For King and Spain," several score voices echoed.

It did not escape Weyler's notice that not everyone had cheered and some of those had been lacking in enthusiasm and lustiness. They were clearly horrified at the thought of again attacking the wire and the machine guns. The guns and the wire had neutralized Spain's advantage in numbers.

Weyler departed and the group disbanded to return to their units and inspire them to make the ultimate sacrifice required in storming the American fortifications. Gilberto Salazar, however, had that and other things on his mind. Clearly, the two men he'd sent to kill Juana and Kendrick had failed. Either that or they'd taken the money he'd given them in advance and disappeared, which he considered unlikely. He hadn't given them all that much money. The bulk of the cash was to be their reward when they were successful. Therefore, they had lost in an encounter with whoever was protecting the slut and her lover, and he assumed that it had been Mercedes' tame bear of a man named Hector Rojas.

It infuriated him that, with the Americans approaching the horizon, there wouldn't be another opportunity to kill them until the battle and perhaps the war was decided. The bitch would continue to live and spread her skinny legs for Kendrick. Sometimes he recalled that he had started the farce, but he dismissed it. No wife of his would have taken him seriously when he told her to sleep with another man. No, he had been betrayed by her and her lover.

Gilberto had a most pleasant thought. When he was victorious and a hero, he would kill Kendrick with his bare hands and then turn Juana over to his troops and the hell with her uncle the bishop. He was going to burn in hell for all he'd done so what did offending a prince of the church matter?

George Armstrong Custer took a last sad look at the bottle of rum. There was about an inch in the bottom and instead of swallowing it, he poured it out a window and onto some flowers, belatedly wondering if the alcohol would kill the flowers. In a way he was grateful nobody had been able to get him any bourbon. It would have been wasted. The decision to stop drinking might have been even more difficult.

The imprisoned President of the United States had had an epiphany. The Army was going to free him and it didn't matter if Winfield Scott Hancock was its commander or not. He was going to be rescued and he didn't want to be a drunken, dirty sot when it happened. He'd also been having that dream where the Sioux had killed him. He'd been waking up in a soaking sweat and a couple of times he thought he'd screamed out loud. If he stopped drinking himself into a stupor, perhaps the dream would go away.

"I'm done feeling sorry for myself," he said to his British host.

"I was wondering when that would happen," Redford Dunfield said with a smile. "And trust me, I didn't begrudge you one bit for wondering just what the devil had happened to put you in such a predicament."

"I want to be ready and armed when Hancock arrives with his army. We can at least meet as equals." Well, almost, he thought. "I am greatly concerned that the Spanish will attempt to move me when that time comes and hold me hostage elsewhere. I cannot permit that to happen, at least not without a hell of a fight; hence the need for at least one weapon, several if you have them."

"And some clean clothes," Dunfield said drily. "Quite honestly, you look like hell and you stink to high heaven."

Custer flushed. He'd already taken stock of himself in a mirror. "Indeed, and I'd like the use of either a razor or the services of a barber if you won't trust me with anything sharp. And yes, I would like to take a bath as well."

Dunfield made a mock bow that Custer ignored. "I will send you a barber and not because I don't trust you. I'm afraid that your hands are a bit shaky and you might just slice yourself to ribbons. I will also send you my tailor with instructions to clothe you appropriately, but not too expensively. I'm sure you're aware that Her Majesty Queen Victoria is quite close with her money."

"I will be thankful for whatever you can provide."

"Since you're returning to mankind, do you desire female companionship?"

Custer flushed. "Indeed, but unless you can transport Libbie down to me, I don't think I wish to chance it." No, he thought, power corrupts and I've certainly been corrupted in the past, but not now. "Thank you, but no thank you."

"By the way, two other people will be moving in and will be under guard but they will not be prisoners. One is Juana Salazar and the second man you know, James Kendrick. I know you despise him, but try to be nice to each other while you're under my roof."

Custer smiled wanly. "I know my place. When this is all over, I reserve the right to strangle him."

On the other hand, Custer thought, if he sees how

I am now and how heroically I behave during the coming battle, perhaps he can be a tool in getting back my reputation.

Two admirals commanded the massive fleet heading to Cuba and Janson thought that was at least one too many. Prentice had laughed and agreed.

In overall command was the aging David Dixon Porter. At seventy, he had served with Farragut and Grant during the Civil War. Totally professional, he had made many enemies by insisting on high standards by all ranks. He was well organized and considered a fighter. His organizational skills were on display as the great host of ships made it down the Atlantic coast towards Cuba. Porter's skills were augmented by those of the much younger Admiral Pierce Crosby. Crosby was in charge of shepherding the civilian transports with a minimum of confusion and had managed to do so. Porter kept control of the warships and directed gunboats and patrol vessels out every time a strange sail or mast or puff of smoke was seen.

As night fell, each ship was required to show oil lamps as running lights to prevent collisions and ships getting lost. Of course, each morning still brought its number of strays, which the smaller warships like the *Orion* dutifully rounded up. Since they functioned as shepherds, Janson had gotten in the habit of referring to their civilian charges as lambs.

"What we really need," said Janson, "is a kind of telegraph between ships. Using signal flags and sending Morse code by signal lamp is just too inaccurate and prone to error. And the range is too damn limited, too."

Prentice laughed. "You're right, but you'd need a

really long cord for telegraph between ships. I don't doubt that something will be invented to make it happen, but not on this trip. By the way, shouldn't we be nearing Matanzas by now?"

Janson conceded the point about the wire and agreed that Cuba should be just over the horizon. The *Orion* was in the fleet's van and the men had bets as to when Cuba would be sighted and who would be the first sailor to do so. Sailors, he concluded, would bet on damn near anything.

"Land ho!" a lookout cried and a number of men cheered while others grumbled. Money changed hands as the men lined the rail to see the faint smudge on the horizon.

"Damn it to hell," muttered Janson. "Either we're lost or we're not headed for Matanzas."

"Could it be Havana?" asked an equally puzzled Prentice. "But it sure doesn't look like Havana."

Janson yelled to his crew, asking if anyone recognized their landfall. One young sailor timidly raised his hand. "Sir, it sort of looks like Santa Cruz del Norte."

"And just what the hell is Santa Cruz del Norte?" Janson asked with a smile.

The sailor responded, "Captain, it's a shitty little fishing village just about halfway between Matanzas and Havana."

"Oh my God," said Prentice, awed by the apparent strategy. "If we land here, we'll have an army that can either march on Havana or attack the Spaniard's rear at Matanzas."

Manuel Garcia had been inducted only two weeks earlier and had been given a uniform that didn't fit and a rifle he had never fired. For that matter, he'd never fired a gun of any kind in his young life. Nor had he ever worn shoes on his sturdy, hardened feet.

He was near the small town of Santa Cruz del Norte, which was only a few miles from his home and his mother. He and a handful of others were commanded by his former schoolteacher, who was as confused and puzzled as everyone. The erstwhile soldiers had serious doubts about the teacher. They wondered if he wasn't senile. Manuel wondered that as well. As Manuel's teacher, he had professed his love for Spain and his willingness to die for her. Now he didn't seem so sure of himself.

They had dug what someone referred to as a redoubt, but it was only a low earth-walled fort that faced the sea. A small cannon had been found and placed in it to threaten the ocean. That there were no shells or ammunition didn't seem to concern anyone. Finally, the very young and junior Spanish officer who commanded them showed up with a dozen men along with small amount of ammunition. He pronounced himself pleased and told everyone that they could easily hold off the approaching American hordes if the Yanks should have the balls to show themselves. The men with the lieutenant were regulars and they openly sneered at Manual's militia.

The announcement horrified Manuel. He knew there was a war on, but he had understood that the fighting was a score of miles away. That was also too close, but the front seemed stable, so people had learned to live and let live. What else could they do? They were pawns. He'd given thought to joining the rebels, but hadn't worked up the nerve. If caught, he'd be hanged or shot. Now, with Americans possibly approaching, he wondered if he had the nerve to desert. He reminded himself that deserters were also either hanged or shot.

At least Corporal Menendez had kept his word. Manuel had worked as a clerk for the lieutenant up until the last couple of days. With the Americans believed to be on the way, clerking could wait. A letter from his mother implied that she and the corporal had become close. He had mixed emotions about that. He wanted his mother to be happy, but he wanted his mother to himself. Of course, he realized, there was little he could do about it at this time.

Only a couple of days later, Manuel and the others awakened to a nightmare. All the ships in the world were approaching his little fort. The lieutenant screamed and they all grabbed their rifles. One went off accidentally and the lieutenant screamed again. Manuel rubbed his eyes. The nightmare would not go away. He could see the guns of the giant warships and it looked like they were all turned towards him.

The American ships closed to within range of their mighty guns and opened fire. The sound was deafening and the shells exploded around their little fort. The first barrage hit nothing and killed no one. The lieutenant stood on the wall and yelled defiance at the Americans. He was hysterical and white froth came from his mouth.

Small boats filled with soldiers were being rowed towards the shore. Manuel counted his bullets—twelve. With twelve rounds he was supposed to hold off the Yankee hordes? He laughed harshly and realized he was growing up too fast.

The American guns fired again and this time they struck. The lieutenant disappeared in a spray of pink mist and pieces of bone. Manuel screamed and huddled on the ground. Another shell struck the cannon, sending it tumbling over. It landed on a Spaniard who began screaming at the top of his lungs. His screams lasted only a few seconds before they ended in a gurgle.

It occurred to Manuel that it would be safe to flee while the Yankees reloaded. Yes, it was time.

"Run," he screamed as he got to his feet. He jumped over the low wall at the rear of the fort and ran for his life. The rest of the tiny garrison ran with him. None of them had their rifles and they frantically tore at their uniforms. In seconds they were almost naked. He would get clothes from his mother and hide in the bushes until the war passed him.

He laughed when he saw that his old teacher was buck naked and running faster than any of them.

Major General Darius Couch stepped more nimbly out of the small boat and into the ankle deep water than he thought he would. The idea of leading an army once again was exhilarating. He felt at least ten years younger than his actual age.

The bombardment of the pitiful shore defenses had been violent but short. The little earthen-walled fort almost seemed to disappear under the impact. The men of Gordon's division had landed in reasonably good order and were moving inward towards the road that connected Matanzas with Havana. Chamberlain's troops would land shortly. He would soon have a full fifteen thousand men to hurl at the enemy's rear. It would be like Chancellorsville again, except that he would play the role of Stonewall Jackson and not the inept Joe Hooker. He reminded himself not to get shot by his own men like Jackson had.

The landing had been well organized and had gone off almost without a hitch. Only a couple of boats had capsized and spilled their passengers and only a handful of the passengers had drowned. It was regrettable, a tragedy, but a necessary price to pay. He thought it was a shame that so few people, including sailors who should know better, knew how to swim.

Couch's attack would not be as sudden and dramatic as when Jackson's force fell on an unsuspecting Union flank and destroyed it. No, he could easily imagine scores of messengers heading to General Weyler at Matanzas with the terrible news that a large new enemy was in his rear. Other messengers would be riding to inform Villate in Havana. He assumed that the Spanish had telegraph lines operating between Havana and Matanzas. If the lines existed, the American army would be able to cut the one that ran parallel to the road running from Matanzas to Havana. Weyler would have to contend with the fact that, in order to fight the new American army, he would have to pull men away from the siege lines at Matanzas. If that happened, he was confident that Nelson Miles, spurred on by Hancock, would launch his own counterattack, hopefully catching the Spanish in a pincers.

There had been serious discussions about what should be the main thrust of the American invasion. Some advisors had said they should strike directly towards Havana, the head of the Spanish snake. Hancock had been adamant. Their goal was the destruction of Weyler's army. Hadn't they learned anything,

Hancock had wondered out loud, from the Civil War? While generals on both sides had striven to conquer capitals, large cities, and vast tracts of land, only Grant and Sherman had understood that you won a war by destroying the enemy's ability to fight and today that meant killing Weyler's army. Havana, like Washington or Richmond, would always be there.

There was another real fear. On hearing that an enemy was behind him, it was possible, even likely, that Weyler would attack Matanzas with a desperate fury. The smaller American force could be overwhelmed and massacred. Worse, thousands of Americans could wind up as prisoners.

The Second Corps had to get there in a hurry. So too did the Navy. Already empty American transports were heading back to Florida where they would reload with more men and supplies. In the meantime, he would request Admiral Dixon to send a number of his smaller gunboats east to Matanzas where their guns might help blunt a Spanish attack.

Manuel Garcia leaned on his shovel and contemplated his miserable fate and the likelihood that God hated him. What made him think that he could simply run away from the Spanish Army? He hadn't gotten more than a couple of miles from the smoldering and bloody ruins of the fort at Santa Cruz del Norte before he'd been captured by a Spanish patrol. His protestations that he was fleeing for his life and simply looking to rejoin his unit were laughed at for the lies they were. He had wanted to find his way home and hide under his bed until this miserable war was over. The Spanish took him and his old teacher to Havana where justice was meted out. The old man was hanged. Manuel had watched in horror as his teacher's skinny legs kicked and his feet scraped at the earth that was cruelly and tantalizingly barely beneath his reach. His face turned black and his eyes almost bugged out of their sockets while he danced. The soldiers had laughed hysterically as he both emptied his bowels and ejaculated before he died. Manuel had despised Professor Sanchez, but he did not deserve to be murdered.

"That one burst of pleasure will have to last him for all eternity," said a skinny sergeant. "You, however, will have a choice. You can choose to be hanged and dance just like your old friend did or you can join a labor battalion."

There was no real choice. He joined the battalion. He even thought that he'd be safer than in an army unit since he wouldn't be involved in any fighting. Events had proven him wrong in that regard as well. He and a number of boys his age and younger in the battalion were out in the open while the shelling occurred. They had dug slit trenches to dive in to if the shelling got too bad, but their overseers generally jumped in first and told the laborers to keep working. When the shelling got bad, the boys lay on the ground and whimpered, or ignored the orders and simply piled in.

When it was safe enough to continue, their eyes were greeted with more scenes of death and destruction. While it was evident that the Americans wanted only to destroy fortifications, their shells sometimes landed in nearby buildings, killing and maiming. He was beginning to grow used to the sight of dismembered bodies and the sounds of the screaming wounded and that frightened him. He never wanted to get accustomed to his new nightmare life.

Their sergeant, a fat pig who said he was from Barcelona and thereby superior to mere Cubans, screamed and ordered them back to work. Manuel and the other boys fantasized about driving one of their shovels up his ass. Along with being a pig, the sergeant was also a coward. Even when the bombardment was clearly not in their area, he was always the first one into a trench.

An explosion ripped through the nearby fortress of Castillo del Principe. The massive and oddly shaped stone structure jutted out from the Spanish defenses and, as someone had explained, was designed to provide flanking fire against an attacking enemy. Manual thought that was funny. The century-old stone structure would be a pile of rubble before long and the Americans would simply either ignore it or walk over what would soon be a jumble of rocks. Once, Manuel had been an unsophisticated farm boy. Now he was learning more about the world and war than he ever wanted to or thought possible.

Another explosion sent him reeling. For a moment he thought he was dead, but then he realized he was choking on dust. Dead men don't choke, he told himself. He managed to get to a standing position. Several bodies lay near him along with a number of bloody body parts and other chunks of human meat. He gagged. He recognized the fat sergeant from Barcelona by his head. The rest of his body was nowhere to be seen. A couple of his young coworkers grabbed him and dragged him away while yelling at him. He had a hard time hearing but he understood their meaning if not their words. Flee, they were saying. Run for your life.

Manuel's shovel had been broken by the blast, but the blade and a decent portion of the shaft remained. He reached down and grabbed it. If all else failed, it would serve as some kind of weapon.

"Grab your tools," he yelled at them. The boys nodded their comprehension and grabbed shovels and anything else that could be used to defend themselves. When they were armed, they were all looking at him. By virtue of giving an order that made sense, he had just become their leader.

He and the others headed into the city, looking for Spanish patrols to avoid. They wanted to flee to the Americans but that would involve going through Spanish lines where they would likely be shot as the deserters they were.

Manuel wanted to cry. He wanted to go home to his mother. Did that make him a coward? If it did, he was not concerned. This was not his war and all he wanted was to leave Havana. And he certainly did not want to be responsible for a pack of boys as young as he.

◆ Chapter 17 ◆

THE FIRE FROM THE SPANISH LINES WAS DEAFENING and overwhelming, causing everyone to keep their heads down as bullets and shells flew overhead or thudded into the American barricades and trenches. At the moment, the Spanish were making no attempt to attack. They were using their cannons and thousands of riflemen to provide covering fire for the soldiers who were creeping up towards the hated barbed wire.

Martin only let a handful of his men expose themselves to enemy bullets, and those were his invaluable sharpshooters. The Spanish were pushing pieces of wood and anything else that would stop or deflect a bullet ahead of each crawling soldier, which made them very hard to hit. What they were about to do was painfully obvious, but not even machine gun fire appeared to hit enough of them to stop or deter them.

"We knew they'd figure out something," said Benteen. "I just didn't think it would be this simple."

When they were close enough to the wire, Spanish soldiers would quickly stand and hurl a grappling hook into the wire. Most of the time it held and a trailing rope was pulled on by Spaniards who yanked the poles holding the wire from the ground. The wire was then dragged back to the Spanish lines. The wall of wire was being systematically dismantled.

"At least they've told us exactly where they're going to attack," Ryder said. "Now I can place my guns with a degree of confidence."

Benteen muttered something obscene that Martin didn't think warranted a reply. A two-hundred-yard breach in the barbed wire was almost completed. To stop an attack, he'd jammed in almost his entire brigade and Benteen had placed another behind it. Six Gatling guns were arrayed along with a number of cannons loaded with grape and shrapnel. Lang's work in making the machine guns more portable was proving its worth.

On the other hand, he fervently wished that Sarah and the others were safe in Florida instead of less than a hundred yards behind him. Women should not be in battle, especially women who were dressed in men's uniforms. If the position was overwhelmed, would the Spanish even recognize the nurses as women until after it was too late? And what would happen to them if they did? One of Valdez's Cuban rebels said that the Spanish considered a woman in man's clothing to be a whore and that she would likely be treated as one.

Trumpets sounded from below and thousands of voices roared their defiance. They signaled that it was time for the assault. A horde of Spaniards emerged from the ground. They'd gotten much closer than Ryder had believed they could. American rifles and machine guns ripped through them. They fell by the score, but kept coming. His cannon fired grape and shrapnel and shredded still more bodies. These too fell and the dead and wounded began to pile up. The smoke was blowing downhill and hiding the Spanish from Ryder's men. The Americans fired into the clouds and hoped they hit something. His men had to expose themselves in order to fire and they were falling. Some screamed, but far too many simply lay ominously still where they lay in crumpled bloody heaps in their trenches.

His men were falling back from their first trench line and tumbling into the second. He had intended to stay farther back from the front than he'd done during the first attack, but the Spaniards were getting closer and closer to his position. He ordered his men to fix bayonets. Ryder heard the fire of heavy guns coming from his rear. Shells far larger than those from his field guns landed among the Spaniards still climbing the hill.

"What the hell?" Ryder wondered. A few moments later, a breathless Major Barnes flopped down.

"The Navy's arrived. There are gunboats in the bay, and it looks like one of our bigger sloops is shelling the Spaniards by the bay's opening."

More shells landed, further shredding the Spanish attack. The enemy paused, seemed confused and dispirited, and then began to drift back. In another minute and another volley, the backward drift became a run. The Spaniards were fleeing.

"We should attack," said Barnes.

Ryder shook his head. "Until and if we can contact

the Navy about our intentions, we're better off staying right here. We wouldn't want to get killed by our own people, would we?"

Barnes response was a sudden shriek. Ryder turned. Barnes' right hand was a pulpy mass below his wrist. Bones and tendons were clearly visible and he was bleeding profusely. Hands grabbed him and a rough tourniquet was applied above his elbow. He stopped screaming and his face turned a pasty white. His eyes were blank and rolling back in his head. He dropped to his knees and fell backwards.

"Get him to the rear," yelled Haney. Soldiers quickly complied. Ryder could only shake his head. Sarah was going to be horribly shocked and stunned when she saw her brother and there was nothing he could do. His job was where he was, on the top of a hill looking down as the Spaniards slowly withdrew.

"The Navy's ceased fire," said Benteen. His cheek had been sliced open and the wound made him talk funny. "The Spanish are almost out of the ships' range anyhow. We will advance."

Whistles and bugles blew. The men of Ryder's brigade moved cautiously out of their trenches and down the slope. They walked gingerly through the ground that was blanketed with dead and wounded. They tried very hard to not step on a wounded man or a corpse, but there were places where the Spanish casualties were piled so deeply that it was impossible. Some of the dead groaned as they were stepped on, giving the illusion that they were still alive. They weren't. It was air being expelled from their dead lungs. Some of the wounded screamed, but there was nothing the Americans could do for them.

They kept an eye out for any wounded Spaniard who wanted to take an American with him before he died. None did, and they walked through the charnel house and into the Spanish camp. Only a few more wounded lay there along with several dozen enemy soldiers who stood with their hands up.

"Now what, General?" asked Lang.

Ryder looked around and picked out a good defensive position. "We stop here and get organized, maybe figure out how many men we've got left and, oh yeah, get some food, water, and ammunition."

"What do we do about cleaning up the battlefield? We should do something before all those bodies begin to stink to high heaven," Lang said.

The several dozen surrendering Spaniards had become a couple of hundred with more giving up every minute. Ryder agreed with Lang. There already was a stench coming from the battlefield as ripped bodies, blood, and torn entrails along with the usual smells of sweat, piss, and shit began to heat up. Some bodies were beginning to bloat.

Martin waved in the general direction of the prisoners. "We'll let them collect and bury their comrades. They can take any wounded back to our hospitals."

Haney was beside him. "Want me to go and check on Major Barnes?"

Ryder nodded. "And everyone else." Haney understood. It was a given that he would check on Sarah and Ruta as well. Martin would have to find a way to see Sarah and comfort her. Barnes' hand was clearly gone, and a wound like the one he'd gotten could easily get infected and prove fatal. Damn it to hell.

◆   ◆   ◆

Gilberto Salazar stopped running after about a mile. He could still see the damned hill in the distance and the many tiny dots that were American soldiers emerging from their trenches. He had led his men as close as possible for his own safety until they were able to throw their grappling hooks and begin to drag down the wire. At that point he had stopped and gradually fallen back. The hooks had been his idea and his men had been ordered to be a major part of the effort. They had performed nobly and bravely, but now most of them were dead or wounded.

Salazar counted the men gathered around him. There were just under a hundred and some of them were wounded and would play no further role in the fighting. His brave legion had been bled out of existence. He wanted to weep from frustration and bitterness, but would not permit himself to show weakness.

The failure of the attack wasn't his fault. The damned American warships had shown up just as the Spanish army was about to destroy the enemy. There had also been rumors of a large American landing to their rear that had arrived at about the same time. This had caused fear and confusion. The ferocious American defense, combined with the presence of the warships and a possible enemy force in their rear had proven disastrous to the fighting spirit of the Spanish army. They had broken and run. The Spanish army had collapsed.

Salazar recognized an aide from Weyler's staff. The man was wide-eyed and looked as if he was about to panic. Salazar grabbed his arm. "Do you have orders for us?"

The aide looked surprised, then suddenly pleased as he saw that it was Salazar. "Yes. I have been ordered

to find you. All units are to take the roads to Havana.
The Americans have landed in great force at Santa Cruz
del Norte. Reports say there are a hundred thousand of
them and that they are heading here. General Weyler
says we must flee to Havana before we are destroyed."

Sarah wiped her brother's forehead with a damp
cloth. He was unconscious and could only moan,
although she sensed that he was comforted by the feel.
She wore a smock over her cut-down soldier's uniform
and she, the smock, and her uniform were covered
with drying blood and gore. She'd managed to keep
her hands reasonably clean and had done her best to
avoid infecting Jack and anyone else she'd treated.

"I'm sorry," said Doctor Desmond. He too was
covered with the blood of soldiers and his eyes were
red-ringed with exhaustion. "We tried to save as
much of his right arm as possible, but his hand was
destroyed along with some of the bone above his wrist.
With luck he'll make it, but he will need help until
he learns to function with only one hand."

"He was right-handed," she said numbly. "What will
he do without a right hand?" Desmond didn't hear
her. He had gone on to another patient.

At least the killing had stopped, she thought, if
only for a moment. The sounds of battle had faded
to nothing. Martin and the army were off the hill and
advancing inland. The combined might of the United
States Army and Navy had won a great victory. So
why were all of these people moaning and screaming,
and why were there those hideous mounds of white
limbs outside where flies were gathering by the millions to feast on them?

Nothing she'd seen or done before had prepared her for these sights and smells. Ruta was beside her. "Was it like this in Paris?" Sarah asked.

Ruta was just as filthy and exhausted. "Believe it or not, it was worse. At least we're not starving as well."

A soldier howled in indescribable agony. Someone said they were running out of ether. Ruta grabbed her arm. "We have to get back to help the others. You can either help your brother or mourn him later, Sarah. There's nothing you can do for him right now."

She agreed. Helping others to live was her duty. There truly was nothing more she could do for Jack. His fate was out of her control. She looked across and saw that Martin had come up the hill and was checking on some wounded soldiers. He looked up and caught her eye. He nodded grimly and walked over. They would not embrace in the hospital. Instead, they let their hands touch. She quickly explained about her brother and he responded that he knew, that he'd seen him get shot and that Jack was fortunate to be alive.

"I wonder if he'll feel that way later," she said. Martin said nothing.

A general was approaching them. "Jesus," he said. "It's Hancock."

Ryder snapped to attention and saluted. Hancock returned the gesture and shook Martin's hand. "Benteen says your men were magnificent. But what about your brigade's casualties?"

Ryder took a deep breath. "In rough numbers, two hundred dead and three hundred wounded. Considering the brigade was under-strength, that's about twenty per cent of our men."

Even though the numbers were nothing like what

Hancock had seen at Gettysburg and elsewhere, they were brutal enough and typical of other units. They could not afford to lose men at that rate. The roughly forty thousand men now in Cuba were just about all there was. Even if he could somehow conjure up a larger army, he would have enormous difficulties supplying it.

"We will not chase them," Hancock said, "at least not right away. We must rest our men and get them resupplied. When that happens we will move towards Havana along the coast road. I'm sure the Spanish will be setting up roadblocks and strong points to slow us and bleed us."

"If you get help from the guerillas, General, perhaps you can bypass them, maybe even attack them in the rear."

Hancock scowled. "I was told that the guerillas were unreliable, that they were little more than bandits."

"General, may I ask who told you that?"

Hancock looked away. "Why, it was our secretary of state, James G. Blaine. He said they were thieves who would steal everything that wasn't nailed down. And if they succeeded in gaining independence, that there would be a massacre of innocents that would eclipse anything that had happened elsewhere, even in Haiti. He said he'd spoken with some of their leaders and said they were a bunch of liars as well."

"Sir, some are liars and thieves, but I've been working with a group that has been extremely helpful. They've scouted for us, carried messages, and ambushed small Spanish units. They've even managed to go in and out of Havana almost at will. They cannot stand up to the Spanish army in a traditional battle. They don't have the weapons, the training, or the leadership. But they can guide us and will fight for us. Actually they're fighting for themselves, since they are convinced that they will be independent when all of this is over."

"I don't know about independence," said Hancock. "That will be decided by the president, whoever he is, along with Congress. However, we do need good scouts who can fight. I've seen the maps of Cuba and, for all intents and purposes, they are utterly useless. They show no roads in the interior and that cannot be true, so, yes, I will gratefully accept their help."

Hancock patted Ryder on the shoulder and smiled. "In the meantime, look to your wounded and bury your dead. And don't forget to talk to that lovely young woman who's been staring at us."

The last thing in the world Governor-General Vlas Villate needed was an uninvited visitor from the Vatican. His once large army was in disarray and falling back as best it could to relative safety behind the impressive but still incomplete defenses of Havana. The Americans had begun their advance and, although moving slowly, appeared unstoppable. His army would fight them, and slow them along the road, but most of the army was demoralized and confused. A number of men and officers had not yet arrived from Matanzas, and that included his field commander, General Valeriano Weyler.

"Admit him," Villate snarled to a secretary who scurried to an anteroom. He returned in a minute and announced the presence of Monsignor Eugenio Bernardi. The monsignor was short and plump, leading

Villate to guess that the man had taken no vow that would result in his missing meals. Celibacy too was probably honored in the breach, as it was with so many priests.

They shook hands formally and Villate offered wine, which the priest eagerly accepted. "I represent Rome," he said a trifle pompously.

"And what does Rome say?" Villate responded sarcastically.

Bernardi either ignored the jibe or it went over his head. "His Holiness, Pope Leo XIII, is very concerned about the war with the United States. As you are well aware, the Holy Father is also very worried about the role of the papacy in a changing and modern world. While not espousing certain liberal tendencies, he wants the role of the pope to be important and relevant in the world. He realizes that the many new nations in the world, and that includes the United States, will never be as influenced by the Church as they might have been in the past. However, he does wish the Holy See to take and maintain a leadership role. Therefore, he wishes this war concluded quickly and he does wish the United States defeated."

"As do I, Monsignor," Villate said with a hint of exasperation. "But pray tell me, how does the pope wish me to bring this to fruition?"

"The United States is growing and with it the curses of Protestantism, secularism, and democracy. We cannot hope to defeat Protestantism, while the thought of democracy is frightening to the Church. Should democracy take hold in a Catholic land like Cuba, then the island might well be lost to the faith. It will be even more tragic if secularism were to become the law of the land as it is in the United States. The Church must remain as the established church in Cuba, and that can only occur with Spain as its governor. Cuba, therefore, must be defended to the last. I should mention that King Alfonso agrees with that assessment."

Villate stood and walked around his office. Bernardi remained seated, a slight that Villate chose to ignore. "And what material aid will the pope provide?" Villate asked with unconcealed anger. "The Holy Father no longer possesses even the limited military resources of the Papal States. He is confined to the Vatican. I need soldiers, weapons, and ammunition, and I wouldn't mind having a number of modern warships either. Please do not say that you will keep us in your prayers. There are enough people praying for our victory and still the Americans are advancing after defeating the best that Spain has."

Bernardi nodded smugly. "Sir, I have it on good authority that a relief army will soon be brought by a Spanish fleet."

Villate could not help himself. He laughed out loud, startling the priest. "Spare me, Monsignor, and do not insult me. Just this morning I received a cable from our beloved King Alfonso. In it he reiterated that there would be no relief and that the Spanish forces in Cuba are on their own."

Now Bernardi appeared shaken. "That is not what I understood when I left Rome."

"I don't know your sources, but perhaps they also believe in fairy tales. Unfortunately, what I just told you is the truth. However, I have a wonderful idea, Monsignor, and it is one that the Holy Father should appreciate. There are many, many priests in and around Havana, far more than our poor city needs. You will gather them up and issue them weapons so they can fight the enemy, smiting him hip and thigh."

"You should not mock the desires of the Holy Father."

"I am not mocking, Monsignor. I am very serious. In fact, I am deadly serious. If the priests will not fight, then organize them into labor battalions that can work building the defenses of Havana. And that would include nuns as well. From what I've seen, many of them can use the exercise."

A captain entered the room, earning glares from both men. He handed Villate a note, which he quickly read. "Well, well, I do have a bit of good news, although it is far from anything that will ensure victory. It appears that General Weyler and several thousand of his men have managed to find their way back to Havana and even now are entering the city."

"Praise the Lord."

Praise the Lord, indeed, Villate, thought as the pudgy little prelate departed after swallowing the last of the wine. He didn't even give the governor-general his blessing. Villate wondered just how many priests and nuns would show up to fight or form labor battalions. Not many he thought. On the other hand, Weyler's return, along with at least part of his army, meant that he might have enough men to defeat an American attack. If he could turn the war into a siege for Havana, perhaps he could bleed the Americans. Perhaps also, the fevers would strike the damn Yankees and kill them all. The next time he saw Monsignor Bernardi, he would request that the overweight prelate pray for just that. Maybe he would ask that the priest go on a fast for victory, and that thought made him smile.

Kendrick's skin had been darkened by oils and his head was completely shaven. Juana thought he looked like a bald pirate. Kendrick thought he looked like a complete ass. The disguise, rude as it was, would enable him to wander the streets of Havana without being noticed. Looking like he did, he was almost invisible in the crowds. He also carried a pistol in a holster under his shirt and a dagger in his boot. The attempt on their lives by Gilberto Salazar's two assassins was fresh in his mind. He had the vague but comforting feeling that one of Rojas' men was following him and protecting him from a distance.

The disaster at Matanzas had stunned the population of Havana, many of whom were very pro-Spanish. They were appalled at the thought of an American victory and the possible installation of the rebels as the new government. They could see their comfortable and centuries-old way of life disintegrating. Those who claimed Spanish heritage and nobility could see exile at best if the Americans won and a terrible death if the mob did.

Kendrick's only fear was that someone would want to talk to him. His Spanish had improved dramatically, but he still spoke it like a foreigner. He carried identification that said he was a laborer for Dunfield and an immigrant from Argentina. Nobody, however, seemed the slightest bit interested in him. Nobody even looked when he walked to the edge of the water and stared at the recovery work being done on the hulk of the *Vitoria*. Somebody had finally realized that the ruined battleship carried a number of heavy guns that could be put to good use on the walls of Havana. Credit for the effort was being given to a naval officer named Cisneros. Kendrick recalled that he was the man who'd actually captured Custer. The shells too would be salvaged, but the powder was soaked and useless unless the Spaniards could figure out some way of drying it out.

The thought of those six- and five-inch guns being turned against American soldiers chilled him. Did General Hancock know, and, if not, how would he get word to him?

Chilling too was the thought of having dinner with George Armstrong Custer. Although sobered and cleaned up, the President of the United States was still a boor. He seemed to think that the world awaited his resurrection, and was in an exultant mood as the American army progressed towards Havana. Kendrick would take mental notes and write what he hoped would be a fair and impartial report.

As he returned and began the long walk back, a column of soldiers marched by. He used the word "marched" loosely. They were in ragged formation, looked exhausted and, worse for Spain, appeared defeated. He quickly realized that these were the latest to make it back from Matanzas.

As they column trudged by, he estimated their numbers at several thousand and wondered if there were other columns or if this was all that remained of the Matanzas army. There was a scattering of cheers as General Weyler rode by on an old horse. Kendrick stiffened with surprise as he saw the man riding directly behind Weyler. It was Gilberto Salazar. He fumed. Of course the son of a bitch would survive the disaster at Matanzas. Now he and Juana would have to be doubly, trebly, careful. Maybe he could get her out of the city and down to the American lines.

Maybe he could grow wings and fly.

Sarah took off the filthy smock that she wore over her army uniform and held it under the water of the stream that flowed into the bay. The dried blood and other matter loosened and fell away, staining the water a vile shade of pink. She shook the cloth and the water reddened more. She kept squeezing and shaking until nothing more came off. Satisfied that she'd done the best she could, she wrung it out and hung it over a branch. The day was hot and not overly humid, and it should dry quickly.

She sensed rather than heard or saw Martin standing behind her. "Do you always watch a lady doing her laundry?"

"Every chance I get. Now, are you going to jump in that stream or not?"

"Don't tempt me. I'm filthy, body and soul. I would sell everything I own for a bath. On second thought, I think I *will* jump in."

She didn't actually jump. Rather, she took off her shoes and stockings, stepped into the clear running water and sat down. "This is wonderful. Care to join me?"

Martin laughed. "The minute I do, General Hancock will come strolling by or Benteen will call for an immediate meeting."

"Turn around and watch out for me," she ordered. She slipped the military tunic up and washed underneath as best she could. She then did the same for her trousers, lowering them down to her ankles and letting the fresh water do its magic.

A couple of moments later she straightened her clothes and stood up. Her clothes were soaking wet, but they would quickly dry. In the meantime, being cold was a delicious feeling.

"Did you peek?"

"Only a little," he admitted with a smile. "The water distorted the picture. From what I did see, however, you are lovely."

"Swine," she said gently. "When are you leaving for Havana?"

"In about an hour. The First Maryland and the rest of my brigade will bring up the rear, at least for a while. Both Benteen and Hancock have been showering me with compliments, which means I'll be moving up to the front in a little while."

"I prefer you at the rear. At least there it's a little safer."

"What about you?"

"The entire medical contingent will be moving out by ship to either Santa Cruz del Norte or Santa Maria del Mar, which is even closer to Havana."

Martin whistled in surprise. "Somebody's optimistic. We haven't taken del Mar yet."

"All generals should be optimists, Martin. At any rate, our seriously wounded are en route to Florida and the more lightly wounded are being returned to limited duty. In a little while, Matanzas and all the killing done there will be but a fading memory."

"I don't think so," he corrected. "Too many dead and wounded to make it simply go away. Granted the fighting here pales in comparison with the great battles of the Civil War, but there has been some nasty bloodletting here at Matanzas." He mentally kicked himself as he thought of her brother.

Sarah saw and understood the expression on Martin's face. "Don't worry about Jack. My brother is improving and even coming to grips with the fact of his lost hand. He told me that now he'll never have to work hard again in his life, and that all of the young ladies in Washington will throw themselves at him because he's a heroic wounded veteran."

"Would you throw yourself at me if I was wounded?"

"I thought I already had. You had a number of cuts and bruises when I saw you in your tent."

"Which is nothing compared with what others, like your brother, are having to endure," he said grimly.

Sarah shuddered and Martin held her arm. He was still afraid to show too much affection where others might see them. Then he decided, the hell with it, and held her tightly to him. He simply didn't care if anybody noticed. Nor did she. She held him tightly and wept. Her body convulsed against his and he wanted to sweep her up and take her away to someplace safe.

She pushed him away. "We shouldn't have done that," she said as she dried her eyes with a handkerchief that was none too clean. "On the other hand, I truly don't care what other people think. Do you want me to report us to General Hancock? Perhaps he'll send us back to the States in disgrace. I think I might like that."

The roadblock was primitive but strong. Spanish soldiers were arrayed on either side of the narrow dirt road and heavily dug in. They were also well camouflaged and hidden by thick brush. An advancing force would have to be within a couple of hundred yards before they would be seen. Assuming, that is, that the Spanish troops had enough discipline to stay still, thought Diego Valdez. His lover, Maria Vasquez, had scouted them and estimated their number at about five hundred—a battalion, nothing more, and they had no cannons. Still, they could inflict casualties on his allies, the Americans, if they were not forewarned. He'd already sent a couple of runners back to the leading American commander, a General Chamberlain. The American had the reputation of being a canny veteran and one who would not reject advice from a mere Cuban. Too many Americans would, he thought ruefully.

There. He could see the head of the American column. Skirmishers and scouts led it, looking and probing for an enemy. Diego smiled. Even if he hadn't warned them, the Americans were ready.

Blue-coated soldiers advanced and moved out onto the fields that led to the Spaniards who were still hidden but would have to emerge to fight. Diego wondered at the idiocy of the Spanish wearing white to go to war. Of course, the Americans wearing blue wasn't all that much smarter. Both sides were a long ways from invisible. He had about a hundred men and they were all dressed in rags that had faded to the color of the earth.

He watched in approval as two American cannons were wheeled into position. From their flags, he discerned that a brigade was arrayed behind them. Good. The messages had gotten through. Someone in the Spanish lines must be swearing at his bad fortune.

The cannons fired and after a couple of ranging shots, shells began to land in the Spanish defenses, shredding trees and shrubs, and destroying the Spanish trenches and barricades. Something exploded in the Spanish lines and he could hear the screams of the wounded. The bombardment lasted about half an hour and then the Americans began to move towards what Diego could see were shattered Spanish ranks. The Spaniards were melting away. Officers frantically tried to stop them, but it was like stopping the rain. Outgunned and outnumbered, the Spanish had no more fight in them.

Valdez turned to where his men were waiting and watching. Less than two hundred yards away, the Spaniards were streaming down the road. His men were grinning expectantly.

"Well, what are you waiting for?" he laughed. "Kill them. Only remember to take prisoners. The Americans don't like it when we massacre all our enemies, no matter how much they deserve it."

His men howled their pleasure and began firing into the fleeing Spaniards, many of whom were their Cuban brethren. Tough, he thought. Even though they were likely unwilling conscripts, they were still the enemy. The fight for a free Cuba had long ago become the worst kind of civil war.

Some Spaniards tried to fire back at their new tormentors, but when a few were cut down, the others began to back away. His men hadn't practiced enough to be good shots, but they still caused damage and these Spanish began to run. All control and discipline had been lost.

"Chase them," Valdez howled and his men surged forward screaming. Because of a chronic shortage of

ammunition, rebel General Gomez had urged his men
to fire one shot and then run at the Spaniards with
their machetes. They'd done it before and the effect
on the Spaniards was shattering. Nobody wanted to
be chopped to pieces.

The remaining Spanish soldiers dropped their arms
and held up their hands, screaming for mercy. A few
of Diego's soldiers forgot their orders and shot and
hacked at their enemies until he and his few officers
got control. He counted casualties. Of his men, there
were four wounded and none seriously. A score of
Spanish were dead and a number of others were
wounded. The Americans had seen the fighting and
had stopped their own firing.

He pointed at the bodies of those who'd been
slaughtered. "Drag those away and hide them. I don't
want the Americans thinking that we're a bunch of
savages."

Valdez's men laughed as if he'd just said the fun-
niest thing in the world. A few moments later, the
American General Chamberlain, a pale man with a
drooping mustache, shook his hand and congratulated
him on a job well done.

When the general disappeared, he took Maria's
hand and smiled at her. Tonight they would make
desperate love on a blanket a little ways away from
his camp. He had promised her that he would liberate and destroy the despicable concentration camps
like the one she'd escaped from.

Secretary of State James G. Blaine could see all his
ambitions for the presidency and the existence of an
overseas American Empire being flushed ignominiously

down the toilet. He looked into the sad eyes of Libbie Custer and wished he truly could reach out and comfort her. Sadly, she had made it clear to one and all that she was totally dedicated to rescuing her husband and resuming their lives together. Not that he would have tried, of course, but she was so achingly lovely. Whatever had she seen in her impetuous husband? He banished the thoughts from his brain. He was married and loved his wife. He would only see the White House when he was a guest, as he was now.

"I do understand the irony, Mr. Blaine. When my husband is rescued it will be because of the efforts of his main political rivals, Winfield Scott Hancock and Chester A. Arthur. And I do understand that it might propel either Hancock or Arthur into the White House. According to the newspapers, Hancock has skillfully merged both former Union and Confederate soldiers into one army, a remarkable achievement. It also appears that he will be besieging Havana in short order. However, he doesn't have enough men to properly invest Havana, and he will not get any significant reinforcements."

Blaine nodded and put down his tea. They were in her private residence in the White House. The servants were present but discreetly out of hearing. "All of which means that this war could drag on and on," he said. "Sooner or later, Hancock must either storm the city or wait for his men to catch the fever and die. Fortunately, the fevers have not been severe this year, at least not yet."

"At least we have taken Puerto Rico without serious incident."

Marine Commandant Colonel Charles G. McCawley

had scraped together the equivalent of a regiment from various ships' crews and, along with fresh enlistments, had landed outside San Juan while under the cover of American gunboats. The conquest had been almost totally bloodless, with only one Marine killed and four wounded. McCawley and the Marines were the nation's newest heroes. Perhaps a score of Spaniards had fallen in the conquest of Puerto Rico.

"And, dear lady, the Marines will soon reembark and be sent to Cuba. They will be replaced in Puerto Rico by our militia who will do nothing more than occupy that peaceful and lovely little place. There is the remote possibility that we will be able to gather up the equivalent of another brigade by combining the Marines and a Negro cavalry regiment. The cavalry will fight dismounted, of course. Barring a miracle, we will not be able to ship and supply very many horses. Or men, for that matter."

"Yet we must win. Or do you feel constrained because of the actions of Congress?"

Blaine tried to hide his annoyance but failed. Cuban rebel spokesman Fidel Cardanzo had spoken with him on several occasions about his visions for the future of Cuba and they did not include a new Cuba as a permanent province or territory of the United States. No, the Cuban rebels wanted independence and they wanted it immediately. The idea of turning over such an island jewel as Cuba to the rag-tag and largely black rebels disgusted him. They needed much more help before they could rule a country on their own.

As usual, Congress was confused with some members wanting a permanent takeover of the Spanish possession, while others said that the U.S. should maintain sovereignty over the island for a set amount of time, approximately four years after victory. This seemed to be the idea that, in some form, would carry. Cardanzo and the rebels would protest, but if there was a date certain by which the U.S. would leave, then perhaps they would be satisfied. The Cuban rebels' leader, Jose Marti, had spent a considerable amount of time wooing various members of Congress and had largely succeeded. Cuba would not be a permanent part of an American empire, and that infuriated Blaine.

At a slightly different level, there were negotiations with Cardanzo regarding giving American merchants preferred status when Cuba was liberated. Additionally, the U.S. Navy required land for bases and coaling stations when the war was finally concluded. Cardanzo, speaking for Jose Marti and others, had made it clear that using Havana for anything other than the incidental presence of American warships was not negotiable. Other sites, however, were acceptable as potential permanent bases. Matanzas was an obvious locale, but there were thoughts that Santiago, on the other side and east of Havana, would be better. The farther away from Havana the better, they said. Out of sight, out of mind with the American fleet, went the thought.

There were rumors of a superb anchorage to the east of Santiago at a place called Guantanamo. That had to be checked out. In a few years, only American footholds would remain in Cuba.

Libbie smiled tolerantly. "You are a very unhappy man, and that is a shame. I am truly sorry that you will not see the presidency in this lifetime."

Blaine smiled bleakly. She was lying through her

teeth. She was thrilled that his ambitions had been thwarted. And to think he once thought of her as a potential ally. He stood, leaned over, and kissed her hand. "Perhaps I shall be reincarnated as a Roman emperor and could rule by decree. Perhaps that is truly more my style."

The meeting between Gilberto Salazar and Monsignor Bernardi had been tense. The governor-general had given them their orders, however, and they were determined to carry them out. Salazar's legion, now down to only a hundred men, would be reconstituted by volunteers called to action by the rabid exhortations of Bernardi.

The small Italian priest had a booming voice and the wild eyes of a fanatic. He called upon the faithful to rise up and drive the Protestant invaders out of Cuba, totally ignoring the fact that many of the Americans were Catholics, especially those from Ireland. He raged that the Americans would destroy statues of the Virgin and sexually assault nuns. His speeches were given as sermons during Mass, or in parks or on street corners. Wherever anyone gathered in the name of Jesus, he said, there he would preach. To his own annoyance, he was only moderately successful, and primarily because most of the men now in Havana were already in a military unit. Those few who weren't in the army tended to be too old, too young, or too infirm.

With considerable effort, the two men managed to gather up enough men to bring Salazar's Legion up to a thousand men, although many were not prime soldier material. Arming them was not a problem. The land outside Havana was littered with abandoned rifles as a large part of the army had thrown them away and simply disappeared.

Regardless of their physical limitations, the new recruits burned with zeal. They wanted nothing more than to hurl themselves at either the Americans or the Cuban rebels, and if they were killed in the effort, even better. They yearned to be martyrs.

On reviewing them, Governor-General Villate had said that their intensity reminded him of some Moslem sects he'd fought against while commanding Spanish forces in Africa. Martyrdom, he'd said, was a Moslem goal that they cherished. Salazar had no idea what sects he was talking about. If his recruits wanted to kill themselves for the glory of God while he got the glory of victory, then that was wonderful. Salazar wanted victory and survival. Martyrdom was for fools.

◆ Chapter 18 ◆

RYDER STIFFENED AND CAME TO ATTENTION WHEN
he saw General Hancock approaching. As always,
the commander of the U.S. forces in Cuba was impec-
cably dressed, which made Martin feel more than a little
dirty since his uniform hadn't been cleaned in a while.
To make matters worse, he and Lang had just spent
some time crawling on their bellies to get a good look
at the Spanish defenses. A very solemn Nelson Miles
followed Hancock. It looked to Ryder that Miles still
hadn't gotten over being supplanted as commander of
the American forces. Generals Crook and Gibbon lagged
behind, amiably talking to each other.

The grueling advance from Matanzas to the outskirts of Havana was finally over. It had taken two
long weeks to get the army out of its original base
and down the narrow and inadequate coastal road. At
spots, the road had been little more than a trail and
the Spaniards had set a number of ambushes. These
had either been brushed aside or there had been some

brief but serious fighting. Regardless, it had taken time and blood to move the fifty or so miles to Havana.

Hancock returned Martin's salute. "Good to see you, but I thought I'd be meeting with Benteen."

"He's sick, General. He asked me to fill in for him."

Hancock shrugged as if to say it wasn't all that important who he met with. "How ill is he? Please tell me it's not the fever."

For some reason, the dreaded fevers had not hit the American army in force, at least not yet. Both sides were holding their breath, awaiting the murderous and mysterious disease that most people thought was caused by breathing the dank and stinking swampy air. Some thought the fever was caused by tiny, invisible organisms called germs, but there was disagreement about that theory. Ryder briefly wondered what Sarah or her father thought about the idea of germs.

"Apparently it's not the fever, General. The doctors think it's something he ate and he should be up in a few days."

"What do you think?"

"I don't think the doctors have a clue as to what's wrong with him. All anyone knows is that he can only get out of bed to crap and puke. Since we've broken out of Matanzas, there's a lot of commerce between us and sympathetic locals and that includes eating some pretty strange and spicy food."

Hancock laughed. "Then we'll let him rest and purge himself of his sins. Come with me, I want to talk with you."

With Hancock leading, they walked to a slight rise where they could view the raw scars that were the earthen Spanish embankments that ran from the

Caribbean to Havana's inner harbor. Through their tele-
scopes they could see that the enemy ramparts bristled
with armed men as the American army deployed for
a battle that was not going to come this day. Behind
the Spanish walls, and out of artillery range, a number
of wooden observation towers had been built.

"Are you impressed?" Hancock asked.

"Not really," said Martin. "It's a far cry from the
triple walls of ancient Byzantium that I'd read about
or even the Confederate works at Petersburg, and I
did see what's left of those. With enough guns and
time we could pound the place to pieces even though
they still outnumber us."

"But that would take far too long and we don't
have the time. Despite the fact that we are landing
and installing howitzers and heavy mortars to bombard the fortifications, we must bring things to a
head before this degenerates into a long and fruitless
siege. Remember that Byzantium wasn't taken for a
thousand years and Petersburg's siege lasted about a
year. No, there will be no lengthy siege. We cannot
afford it. The American people want this war over."

Ryder wondered just why he and the absent Benteen
had been being singled out but kept quiet. He looked
skyward to where an American observation balloon
looked down on Havana from several hundred feet
above the ground. The brave soul in the balloon had
a much better view of Havana than did the Spaniards
in their wooden towers.

Hancock shielded his eyes and also looked at the
contraption. "Is it true that a photographer is up there?"

Ryder grinned. "The estimable William Pywell is
indeed up there. He's trying to get panoramic pictures

of the coming battle. So far the gondola has jiggled too
much to get a good clear photo of anything. I spoke
to him last night and he says today will be his last try.
After that, he may try building his own observation
tower. He hopes that it will be a steadier platform."

"All journalists and photographers are crazy, Martin,
only you didn't hear that from me."

An explosion boomed and they all turned to watch a
mortar shell arc high into the sky and fall behind the
walls of Havana. A second later, the shell exploded,
sending a cloud of debris into the air.

"A ranging shot," sniffed Hancock. "I very much
doubt that it hit anything important. Tell me, Martin,
have you ever seen a Masai warrior kill a lion?"

"Can't say as I have, sir."

"Well, neither have I. But I do have it on good
authority that a young Masai warrior is sent out onto
the African plains or veldt armed with only a short
stabbing spear and a pair of huge balls between his
legs. It's a rite of passage and they must kill a lion
with nothing but their cunning and that little spear
in order to become a warrior. They stalk the beast,
get very close, and ram the spear into the heart of
the lion, killing him instantly. At least that's the plan.
A miss, of course, could prove fatal to the hunter as
the lion is not likely to allow the young lad a second
chance."

A second shell crashed and exploded. Martin wondered just where the general's musings were going.
He did have the uncomfortable feeling that they
might involve him.

Hancock saw the dismay on Ryder's face and smiled.
"Don't worry. I have no intention of sending anyone

out to storm Havana with a small spear. What I *do* want is to attack and go straight for the heart. They have too many men for us to attack at more than one point and be successful. The Spanish may be poorly led and poorly trained, but even inferior soldiers might do well if ensconced behind the perceived security of a wall. Ergo, we must get them *away* from that wall. What I propose to do is to launch a violent attack at a narrow point, like a spear, break through, and wreak havoc in their rear. It would be somewhat like Alexander the Great did in his battles against larger enemy armies—go for the heart or, if you wish, the jugular."

Ryder smiled wanly. "And I presume this involves me."

"Indeed. Unfortunately, it is the price of your successes. The attack will be spearheaded by Benteen's division and further led by your brigade. I am confident that you will succeed. You have proven yourself a skillful and resourceful leader and fighter. I am also confident that you will plan well and accomplish all this with a minimum of casualties."

By way of emphasis, another mortar landed behind the enemy lines. This time something other than the shell exploded, and men all around began to cheer as clouds and flames billowed. "Probably ammunition," said Hancock and then looked sheepish. What else could it have been?

Hancock continued. "It will take a couple of weeks to gather our forces and we will try to confuse the Spanish by first shelling various places along the line. While I would never underestimate an enemy, I am confident that Generals Weyler and Villate are under orders from Havana to defend everything. If they do that, of course, they will wind up defending nothing."

Ryder wondered just how Hancock was so certain about the orders Villate and Weyler had. Spies must be everywhere, he concluded.

Hancock continued, "What I plan to do is build a rail line that largely parallels their defenses and move cannons up and down it by way of trains, even firing big guns from the rail cars. With luck, that'll keep the Spaniards chasing their tails. Then we stop when and where we wish and your men get to lead the attack. Tell me, General, do you have any thoughts as to how you will get your men safely over those walls?"

Ryder smiled grimly. "Frankly, sir, I'd been thinking along those lines and I do have some ideas."

Hancock smiled. "I'm not surprised. Well then, why not firm them up and then we'll talk again. By the way, when the time for the big attack comes, you will not be alone. There will be additional mischief afoot. The Navy insists on coming along for the ride and causing at worst a major distraction that will further confuse and demoralize our enemies."

Hancock turned and saw Ruta Holden standing a short distance away. She looked worried. She was also wearing a brightly colored full-length skirt instead of the cut-down man's uniform the nurses had been wearing.

The general nodded and smiled affably at her. "Ryder, did you know that churchmen up in the states are outraged that female nurses would dare to go to war wearing men's clothing? They say it's lewd and licentious and that only whores would dress as men. Of course, they don't give a fig that it's the best, most efficient and even most decent way for a woman to treat a wounded patient. They cannot imagine that a man who's been seriously wounded would have priorities other than getting a stiff dick and having it serviced. Lord, what fools some mortals be."

Ryder laughed. Again leaving the confines of Matanzas had paid dividends. The women were actually able to shop in area villages and get women's clothing. Sarah had purchased several brightly colored Cuban-style dresses, and he thought she looked marvelous in them and much more carnal than when she'd been wearing a man's army uniform.

"Ryder, why don't you go and see what that poor woman wants. It doubtless has something to do with your betrothed. You and that other nurse are betrothed, aren't you?"

Damn, Ryder thought again. Does everyone know about our private lives? "General, I sure as hell hope so."

At Ruta's urging, Martin immediately went to Sarah. He found her in the back of one of the hospital tents and sitting among piles of supplies. Her face was red and it was obvious she had been crying.

Martin sat down beside her and held her hand. She immediately grabbed his with both of hers, pressing hard with surprising strength. "I may be losing my brother. He may be dead as we speak."

"What happened?"

"What almost always happens when one is wounded on a battlefield. Despite everyone's best efforts, his wound became infected. I got a telegram that said he's on his way to Washington where my father can pick him up and give him the personal and sanitary care he couldn't get in an Army hospital."

Ryder couldn't argue with her assessment of the Army's hospitals. So many doctors were little more than well-intended butchers for whom sanitation was still an undefined word. "Are you going to go to be with him?"

Tears began to spill down her cheeks. "What, and leave you to get into trouble? No. Even though I would like to be at his side, the situation is what I said. He may already be dead. Or he may be recovering, in which case my trip would have been just as futile. My place is here, with you and with the damned army and all the new wounded I'm going to see."

Ruta was at her accustomed place blocking the entrance to the storeroom. Her back was turned to them, not that he cared if she saw them together. She was, however, preventing anyone else from seeing them. He put his arm around Sarah's shoulder and pulled her to him. He kissed her gently and planned to stop with that, but she suddenly returned his kiss with an almost savage fervor. Wonderful, he thought, and returned the favor, matching kiss for kiss until they were gasping.

She pushed him back and smiled. Her concerns about her brother were clearly fading. "We have to find a better place to meet than army supply facilities."

"A bedroom would be nice. By the way, General Hancock referred to us as betrothed. Are we betrothed?"

"Yes, Martin, a bedroom would be ideal and, yes, we are betrothed. I was hoping to wait until we got back to the States before either getting married or consummating our relationship, but I wonder if that is the best course of action. Perhaps we should look into finding someone who would marry us. However, and even though I am only a nominal Protestant like you, I don't think I want us to be married by a Catholic priest. And further, I don't want our honeymoon to be in a warehouse unless it's a very nice warehouse."

"I understand."

She stood and straightened her dress. Somehow it had ridden up above her lovely knees. "Good. I feel better now knowing that our wedding is in your capable hands." She smiled and tenderly kissed him one more time. "Now you have two assignments. You must plan both your battle and our wedding. Good luck, dearest."

Yes, he thought, and he knew which will be the more difficult—the wedding.

Kendrick stood on the second floor balcony of Dunfield's home and stared into the distance where clouds of smoke and fire were being swept by the wind. Small groups of Spanish soldiers ran down the streets. They were out of control and had begun looting and beating civilians. Dunfield had hired a number of men to protect his property and they were heavily armed and visible. The mobs prudently looked for easier pickings. It disturbed Kendrick that somewhere out in the city was Juana's husband, leading a band of men reputed to be religious fanatics and quite violent. They hadn't yet made a move towards Dunfield's estate and Kendrick wondered if it was because of Dunfield's British connections or because the place was a fortress. Kendrick didn't doubt that Salazar would eventually make a move.

Behind him and prudently indoors where the mob

couldn't see him, Custer was crowing that the army had finally arrived and was going to rescue him and restore him to the presidency. It could be, Kendrick admitted. But was putting Custer back in the White House the wisest course of action? Yet, what other course of action was there? As long as he lived, Custer was the President of the United States and Chester Arthur was only the acting president. But what if he didn't live, Kendrick thought and quickly banished it.

He had another thought and decided to ask the question he'd been deferring.

"Mr. President, just who started this bloody war?"

Custer blinked in surprise and laughed when he realized the implications of the question. "Are you accusing me of being so duplicitous as to have caused the massacre on that ship? Not a chance. I may be a merciless bastard and my wife a skilled conniver and Blaine a lying snake, but neither of us betrayed the *Eldorado* and caused that massacre. I'll admit that we gave it some thought, but we found out that the Spanish already knew everything about the ship, including its crew, cargo, and destination. Hell, they even knew you were going to be on board. What we really thought would happen was that everybody would be taken prisoner, tried, found guilty, and sentenced. Then they would be sent to a jail until ransomed or something diplomatic occurred. Maybe the *Eldorado*'s captain would have been hanged and maybe one or two rebel leaders as well, but that's the cruel price of a failed rebellion. I have no idea what would have happened to you, but I did think your exalted status as a journalist would have provided you with a degree of safety."

"But you did nothing to stop it."

1882 ◆ CUSTER IN CHAINS 389

"We didn't find out that the *Eldorado* was actually going to be intercepted until it had sailed. By then it was far too late."

"Then who did tell?"

"Who knows and who cares and why the hell should we have had any concerns?" Custer responded. "Everyone on that ship was a volunteer, including you. For all I know it was those American daredevils who wanted to conquer Cuba for their own purposes or even the Cuban rebels who caused the massacre in an attempt to drag us into their damn war. If that's the case, they succeeded beyond their wildest expectations."

Custer lit up a cigar and drew contentedly. "Personally, I think there were so many leaks in the *Eldorado* enterprise that it would be impossible to trace and identify the source for that damned book you're so hell bent on writing."

Kendrick laughed and lit up his own cigar. In deference to Custer's newfound sobriety, he was deferring having a drink until later. He and Juana would have at least a couple before retiring to bed and yet another evening of frolicking. Juana was bent on purging herself of years of sexual restrictions and repressions and Kendrick would be there to help her. Custer was right about the book, however. He had enough material to fill a couple of manuscripts. All he had to do was survive this coming battle and get the hell out of Cuba and to New York.

General Weyler stepped into Villate's office and closed the door behind him. The window was open and the smoke from numerous fires wafted in. Rifle shots rattled in the distance. "The city is clearly going to hell, General," he said as he sat down in the chair in front of Villate's large and ornate desk. "So is Cuba, for that matter."

Villate shrugged off his concerns. "We will regain control of Havana in a few hours. In the meantime, we will let the soldiers work off their anger at having been so thoroughly defeated and forced to retreat to this last bastion of the Spanish empire in the Atlantic."

Weyler kept his face expressionless. Villate's comments were a not very subtle criticism of his handling of the American landings at Matanzas. Cables from Madrid had been received from an angry king and prime minister. How could a Spanish army that outnumbered the Americans by so many have been forced back to a small perimeter around Havana? How indeed, Weyler kept wondering. By rights, the smaller American army should have been pushed into the sea where thousands of American soldiers would have drowned. Worse, nearly every garrison in Cuba, including the large one at Santiago, was also under siege by the Cuban rebels who were growing in number and aggressiveness with each passing day.

The answer to the failure at Matanzas was quite simple. Many of the enlisted men in the Spanish army didn't want to fight. Consisting in one part of Cuban conscripts and another part of Spanish conscripts, there was little motivation to engage the Americans. The Cuban conscripts either wanted to go home, or desert and join the rebels, while the Spanish enlisted men were homesick for Spain and had no idea why on earth they were fighting a war thousands of miles away in Cuba. The officer corps and the noncommissioned officers were made of sterner stuff, at least most of them.

Weyler wondered what the German observer, Helmsdorf, was thinking and sending to Berlin either in diplomatic pouches or via coded telegrams. The German's attitude towards him was arrogant and condescending. It was almost as if he was saying that any German general could have better handled the fighting. He thought ruefully that Helmsdorf's unspoken thoughts might have merit.

Weyler decided to respond to Villate's comments. "The army will fight well behind the walls of Havana. However, if those walls are breached, I am not confident of anything. The entire army might collapse. I would like to repeat my earlier request that a second line of fortifications be built behind the first one."

Villate shook his head angrily. "I said no before and I'm saying it again. If we build a second line it will be the same as admitting that we cannot hold the first. The already demoralized army might, as you suggest, collapse entirely. I would prefer that we attack. I suggest that we organize elite forces and send them out in raids. That will buoy up the confidence of the people and the army."

"It will be done," Weyler said. He liked the idea of keeping the Americans off balance. "On a slightly different topic, how long can we hold out and what plans does Madrid have for us? And when will Madrid send us reinforcements?"

Villate laughed loudly enough that people working and talking outside his office were suddenly silent. "They will not send us shit. We are totally on our own. We must defend ourselves so vigorously that the Americans will either withdraw or decide to negotiate an honorable end to this war. For instance, in return for sending them both Custer and that idiot Salazar so they can hang him, they might be induced to leave."

"General, do you really believe that?"

"Of course not," Villate snapped. "In the meantime, we will make do with what we have. If you haven't noticed, I've expelled many thousands of civilians who are of no military use to us. Those are the women and children and the men who are too young or too old to fight. Spanish women are being permitted to stay, of course. We cannot allow noble Spanish ladies to be abused by either the Americans or the rebels. The useless ones were simply taking up valuable space and eating irreplaceable food. As a result, we can last for about four months before starvation sets in. That assumes, of course, that the fools who are burning the city don't destroy our food reserves as well. I've also closed the concentration camps and sent the inmates off any way they wish."

"What about our ammunition?"

"That depends on how hard and long we have to fight. We have enough for several large battles, but that's it. Once it's gone, it's gone, and it does not look like our good friends in the navy will be able to break the American blockade and deliver more to us."

Weyler was saddened. "So, unless something dramatic happens, in a few months we will be starving and weaponless."

Villate shook his head angrily. "Welcome to the modern Spanish empire in the New World."

Haney stood beside Diego Valdez and looked at the mass of humanity penned up in a large field and loosely guarded by poorly armed Cuban rebels. He

estimated at least ten thousand people were milling around. Almost all of them looked confused and
dispirited, and many were bruised and injured. They
all looked dirty and hungry. These were the human
refuse that Villate had cast out to either fend for
themselves or be fed by the American army.

"Diego, my friend, just what the hell do you plan
on doing with these poor people?"

"We will separate the wheat from the chaff. I have
my women searching the women from Havana for any
hidden weapons or anything else that might identify
them as spies. Maria Vasquez leads that effort."

Haney leered. "What about prostitutes?"

Valdez chuckled. "Those we let go right away. They
help the economy."

Several brothels had sprung up around the American army and so far Hancock had done nothing
to stop prostitution beyond ordering the whores to
stay out of sight. Also, numbers of Cuban women
had taken up informal relationships with American
soldiers. It was the way of war as it had been since
time immemorial.

"And the men?" Haney asked.

"Notice please, that there are very few men of
military age in the camp. It appears that Villate and
Weyler are keeping them back in Havana. If they are
not drafted into the army, they will be used as laborers to help shore up the city's defenses. Of course,
they'll be working right where we're shelling the city.
The poor bastards will be lucky to survive the war.
If we don't kill them, the Spanish will work them to
death. I would say they will treat them like dogs, but
dogs might have a better chance."

"Helluva thing," Haney said. "No wonder the Cubans want the Spanish gone."

"And you Yankees gone, too," Valdez said with a chuckle. Haney knew the man well enough to know that he wasn't kidding.

Custer stared at the man in disbelief. "You bastard! What are you doing here? Have you come here to gloat? Wasn't it enough that you captured me?"

Spanish Navy Commander Clemente Cisneros bowed. They were alone in the privacy of Custer's apartment. "I am here to do no such thing. Quite frankly, President Custer, I am here to protect you. You may not be aware, but my little warship has been stripped of its guns so that those weapons can be incorporated into the defenses of Havana. While I regret the move, I recognize its necessity. My ship would have been devoured by your navy's larger warships as little more than a snack. Or haven't you noticed that every day there are at least a dozen American ships just off the entrance to the harbor and just out of range of our shore guns."

"I hadn't really noticed," Custer admitted reluctantly. "The land war outside my door has me fully occupied."

Cisneros continued. "Only a handful of the American ships are true warships. The vast majority of them are converted civilian ships. Some armor plating has been added and guns have been installed. They would not stand up to a modern capital ship for even a minute. However, they are better than what Spain has to send against them and there are so many of them. If you were to look farther out to the ocean you would see an additional score of them more distantly ringing the entrance to Havana's harbor."

"Am I supposed to feel sorry for you, Commander? Well, I don't. If you hadn't captured me, I might be in Washington directing this war instead of sitting on my ass as a prisoner in Havana."

"And if it hadn't been for me, you might also have been swept out to sea where your bones would be lying on the bottom in the mud after the fish got through stripping the flesh from them. No, President Custer, I saved your life."

Custer reluctantly conceded the point. "I suppose you're right. The lifeboat was leaking and Captain Blondell probably couldn't have found the outer ring of a bathtub without someone to guide him, much less a safe shore. And that brings us back to the beginning. What the hell are you doing here?"

Cisneros had discussed matters with Blondell before the man's exchange and had far greater confidence in the captain of the *Dolphin* than did Custer. Now was, however, no time for argument.

"It has been determined that all soldiers should man the parapets against you gringos. It has also been determined that my sailors are not soldiers; therefore, they would be useless in a land battle. It was suggested that they be used to guard Havana's treasures, such as the Cathedral San Cristobal. Our duties include protecting this building, which, along with housing you, is also the home of the British Consul in Havana."

"So you are now my jailer?"

"I prefer to think of myself as your host. But let me assure you that while I will do everything in my power to protect you, I will also do everything I can to prevent you from escaping to your fellow Americans and that includes shooting you if it becomes necessary. We would aim to wound, of course, but my men are not such great shots, and that means you could easily get killed if you were to attempt something foolish. Right now, you are a valuable bargaining chip. When a peace is negotiated, you will be an important part of it."

Custer watched as several of Cisneros' men walked through the building. They carried rifles and had cut-lasses in scabbards slung over their shoulders. They looked well trained and hardened. They saw Cisneros and grinned happily. The inept soldiers who had been protecting him had been replaced by men who would do their duty and, if he judged things correctly, the sailors were devoted to Cisneros.

Custer smiled ingratiatingly and held out his hand, which the other man took. "Will you be staying for dinner?" he asked.

◆ Chapter 19 ◆

THE LARGE, SQUAT SIEGE MORTAR HAD FIRST BEEN used in the Civil War in the long fight for Petersburg, Virginia, but age did not diminish its effectiveness. It could hurl a ninety-pound shell nearly a mile and a half and, hidden behind its own earthen walls, it was almost impervious to the light enemy fire directed at it and its sisters.

"Beautiful thing isn't it?" asked a gaunt General Benteen as he leaned on his cane. He was out of breath and he cursed the illness that had weakened him so much. "That damn big gun of ours can't be killed unless the Spanish are dumb enough to run out and attack it. On the other hand," he said thoughtfully, "I wouldn't put it past them. They haven't fired their cannons very much at all, which tells me that they don't have a lot of ammunition and certainly none to spare for shooting at targets they can't hit."

The illness that had attacked Benteen was abating, but he was still weak and had lost a lot of weight.

The doctors were mystified as to what had hit him. They blamed it on bad air, spiders, bad food, and bad luck. Sarah had told Martin that the general had very likely drunk some very bad water. Benteen did not think it was possible, since, as he joked, he only drank alcohol and never water. But, since he was recovering, everyone was willing to let the doctors figure out what had happened.

"Shouldn't you be resting?" Ryder asked.

"Go to hell, Martin. You just want my job. A couple more promotions and you'll be in charge of this whole army."

"Which is just about the last thing I want," Ryder responded. "I'm not certain I'm ready to command a brigade, much less a division and certainly not an army."

Benteen laughed. "Incompetence never stopped other people from rising to high office. Just look at your history and think of how many of Lincoln's generals failed before he found Grant. And Grant was a virtual nobody before the Civil War. Just like you. Maybe you'll be this war's Grant."

"As long as I'm not the next war's Custer," said Ryder.

Ryder helped the other man up a low rise. The mortar was about to fire and it was time to get out of the way. Older cannons had a bad habit of exploding and spraying chunks of hot metal all around at the oddest times, killing anyone who happened to be in their way. There was no reason for anyone not directly connected with firing the massive weapon to be out in the open.

Ryder continued, "For me to be this war's Grant, it'd have to last three or four years like the last one. It ain't gonna happen, General."

"One can only hope you're right," said Benteen a

second before the charge exploded and sent the shell arcing high into the air. They followed it with their eyes and watched as it landed and exploded beyond the city's walls. This time there was no secondary explosion.

"I guess we just dug up some dirt," laughed Benteen. "According to the boys in the balloons, the Spanish have gotten smart and have pulled back their troops. They're sitting safely a quarter of a mile away from the walls. When they think we're gonna attack, they'll run back to their firing platforms and try to kill us."

Since Ryder was going to command the attack, the picture he envisioned was not a pretty one. "Perhaps we should fake an attack. Then, when they've all returned to their positions, start firing at them. Wouldn't that be a nasty surprise?"

Benteen watched as the mortar's crew reloaded. "The real surprise would be if General Hancock hasn't already thought of it, Martin."

Bishop Estefan Campoy looked fondly at the conflicted woman sitting across the room from him. He loved her like the daughter he would never have and he ached at the thought of her being in so much emotional pain. To his eternal regret, he had been one of many friends and relatives who had urged, even coerced, plain and innocent young Juana into marrying Gilberto Salazar.

"Will you hear my confession, Uncle?"

Unabashedly, he wiped away a tear. "No," he said softly, "and you know why."

"Yes, but let me hear it from you."

Campoy sighed. This was the first time he had seen Juana since she'd run away with the American reporter. He couldn't bring himself to visit her in the home of Mercedes de la Pena, a woman of loose morals he considered complicit in Juana's sins. There would have been too much public scandal. But now she was in the British Consulate and that provided a form of cover. He could always claim official Church business. That no one would believe him was irrelevant.

He wiped away another tear. Why was life so unfair? Juana was a good woman who deserved so much better. "I can hear your confession and counsel you as I have so many times in the past, but I cannot give you absolution for the obvious reason that you are not in the slightest bit sorry for your sin."

Juana smiled and her face lit up. "Nor will I ever be, Uncle. But where is it written that I must stay married to a monster, a man who beats his wife and tortures innocent people, and a man who murders innocent men and women? I think that is the greater sin. Worse, he may even have created this foul war."

He had heard the same question from others and sometimes he did doubt the Church's reasoning. There was nothing he could do about it, however. "Both the laws of the Church and the laws of Spain prohibit divorce. And even if you and Mr. Kendrick were to flee to the United States, you would find that you were still bound by many of those same laws. Divorce in Cuba is impossible and almost so in the U.S."

Juana stood and brought the bishop some brandy. "Then what about an annulment?"

"On what grounds, and please don't tell me you've never consummated your marriage."

"For all intents and purposes, we haven't, and don't look so shocked, dear Uncle. Surely you've heard rumors about his strange and exotic preferences. And even if we *did* consummate our marriage, the last time he took me to his bed and tried was a number of years ago. He has effectively abandoned me."

The bishop swirled his brandy and took a sip. "This is outstanding brandy. Are you trying to coerce me?"

"Of course," she smiled warmly.

"Does anyone else know enough about the details of your marriage to be able to testify under oath in a Church court or in a Spanish court?"

Her face fell. "No."

"And while he may be a murderer and a fool and a deviant to some, he is a hero to others. He was even wounded in battle, was he not?"

Juana laughed hugely, surprising the bishop. "Uncle, he fell off his horse and ruptured himself, which, while painful, is hardly a war wound. Yes, he has been in battle, but did you notice that he always survives unscathed while many of his men are slaughtered? His actions are hardly heroic."

Campoy smiled. Ruptured? How delicious. "Juana, would you be willing to say that you are frigid and have refused him his rights as a husband?"

Juana thought for only a second. "Of course," she said. "It would only be part of a lie since he hasn't asked in so long. If he had, I would have rejected him outright, especially after he betrayed me to his mistresses. I only wish that his latest, Helga, was still in Havana. We had come to an accommodation and I believe she would have supported me."

Campoy gestured and received some more brandy. "I don't know how you would explain away your sexual frolics in the home of Mercedes de la Pena or here in the estate of Mr. Dunfield. These are hardly the actions of a frigid woman."

"Are you saying I can't be selectively frigid? I think you would find many women are that way. You'd know that if you'd been listening more closely during confessions instead of dozing off."

Campoy laughed and stood. It was time to go. "I will think on what you are saying. I cannot hear your confession and give you absolution, but I can give you and your barbarian Protestant lover my personal prayers and blessings, and I do. In the meantime, I will try to help you find a way out of your dilemma. But first, I have a different task. There is a matter of church and state I must discuss with our beloved governor-general. This war is bringing out the worst in people and now I am finding that there are quite a few more bad priests than I ever thought. Almost all of my clergy are good people and it is deeply disturbing when I find that a handful have betrayed the laws of God and man."

"Well then, Uncle, may I pray that my husband dies in battle? Heroically, of course."

Campoy winced. "That thought is most un-Christian and un-Catholic. And besides, be careful what you wish for, it might come true." Although, he thought, it would be a fitting end to their problems, even ones she didn't know existed.

Juana kissed him on the cheek and led him to the door. She looked around the outside and determined that Cisneros' guards were in place and that there was no danger to her or to the bishop. She didn't think that Salazar would strike at a man of God like her uncle, but who knew what he was capable of.

◆   ◆   ◆

Ryder was jarred awake by the sound of gunfire, punctuated by screams and yells. Bugles and drums added to the din as the alarm was sounded. But why, he wondered as he pulled on his pants? According to the clock on his stand, it was three in the morning.

Haney burst in. "It's a raid, General. The goddamn Spanish are trying to destroy our guns. They've hit General Gibbon's division with a large force and they seem to be causing a lot of damage."

Ryder thought quickly. Gibbons' division was to his brigade's right as he faced the Spanish lines and, he thought with sudden horror, the hospital where Sarah worked was directly behind it.

All over the area, his men were rousing. He quickly ordered one of his three regiments to maintain their forward positions facing the Spanish and ordered the other two to prepare for a flanking attack against the Spaniards. None of this would occur instantly. The men, dragged from their sleep, were forming up as quickly as they could, but they would have to advance as entire major units and not as small groups that would be cut to pieces by the Spanish.

If Haney was right, and he usually was, this was only a raid, which meant that the attackers would withdraw fairly soon. It could not be a major attack since the observers in the balloons would have caught the movement of large numbers of enemy troops towards the area. This meant that the Spanish would retreat fairly soon but after they had spiked cannons, destroyed ammunition and other supplies, and caused as much mischief as they could.

After what seemed an eternity, his two remaining regiments moved towards the fight. They kept their order and moved slowly so as to avoid shooting fellow American soldiers. After only a couple of hundred yards, they saw numbers of Spaniards pulling back and firing at them and at other advancing Americans. Ryder's soldiers returned fire. Because of the darkness, almost all shooting was wild and inaccurate. Even when a target appeared, the flash of gunfire and smoke temporarily blinded the shooters.

Fires from burning supplies and small explosions punctuated the night, further destroying soldiers' vision. Ryder caught up with an outraged Gibbon. "Somebody's going to be crucified for letting them get on top of us like this," he raged. Ryder had the sneaking thought that it might have been Gibbon's men who were responsible, but prudently kept quiet.

They soon came upon the first Spanish dead. Someone had gotten smart, Ryder thought. The soldiers weren't dressed in their white uniforms. Instead, they were wearing what looked like dark blue. Their faces had been smeared with dirt to make them even more difficult to spot. Still, wide-awake sentries should have caught them before they got as far as they did.

Ryder stayed close to General Gibbon and heard that a number of cannons had been spiked. While Gibbon swore colorfully, another messenger said that the Spanish had done a poor job of disabling the guns and that they all would be back in working order in a few hours.

"Thank heaven for small favors," Gibbon snarled. "It was just a raid and they botched it. This'll be embarrassing, but I'll get over it. Hell, I didn't have that much of a career left anyhow."

Ryder tried to force another concern out of his

mind. Sarah and the hospital were fairly close and looked like they were directly in the path of the Spanish assault. Some tents were burning, but he couldn't tell what they had been. He looked for Haney and couldn't find him. Good. The man had probably slipped away to find out what had happened to Ruta and, at the same time, Sarah.

Sarah and several others, including Ruta, had been sleeping soundly when the shooting started. Their first reaction was the same as everyone's—shock that the gunfire was so close, and then horror that it was getting closer. Something was clearly, horribly, wrong.

She and the others slipped robes over their ankle-length nightgowns and put on their shoes. If they had to flee they would be ready to escape. They were wrong. There would be no escape. Minutes later, Spanish soldiers burst into their tent. A couple of them jeered and laughed at the disheveled nurses, but were soon silenced by a Spanish captain.

"You are nurses from the hospital, are you not?"

Sarah saw no point in lying. "Yes."

"Good. You will come with us. You are an unexpected bonus. Governor Villate will be pleased to have you working in our hospital and healing Spanish soldiers instead of aiding the gringos who have invaded our land."

Sarah started to argue and struggle, as did the others, but they were quickly knocked down and tied up. She was angry at being restrained and by the fact that the still laughing soldiers were taking the opportunity to paw her, one even slipping his hands under her nightgown.

The captain again controlled the situation, slapping the impertinent soldier who didn't seem at all abashed. "Ladies, it will go so much easier for you if you stop fighting. One way or the other, you will be going to Havana and, one way or another, you will be helping wounded Spanish soldiers."

When they hesitated, he eyed them coldly. "Perhaps I did not make myself clear. So far I have restrained my men. If you do not accept my kind invitation, I will grant them certain latitudes with you. Their favorite sport when transporting women prisoners is to hang them by their hands from the crossbar of the cart. After which, you will be stripped naked and driven all around Havana so that one and all can see your charms. The men will be posing you with your legs spread and your knees in the air, ensuring that your most private and intimate body parts are vividly displayed for admiring thousands. You will not actually be raped—I will not permit that, of course—but you will feel thoroughly violated by the time you make it to the dubious safety of a prison cell."

Sarah sagged and Ruta caught her eye. The two of them shrugged and the others nodded. "Well," Ruta said with a forced smile, "I always wanted to see Havana."

Even though there was a Red Cross flying from a flagpole outside the Spanish hospital, it bore little resemblance to the conditions in the American army. The hospital personnel they saw were poorly trained and there was little appearance of hygiene. It was as if the concept had not yet been introduced in the Spanish army.

Following their capture, the five nurses had been taken by wagon to see Governor-General Vlas Villate. They were frightened but tried not to show it. His reputation for cruelty and harshness was well known. Before being given over to Villate, Sarah had asked the captain if he really would have permitted his men to strip and display them. He'd laughed hugely, "Of course not. Spaniards are not barbarians."

Villate smiled when they were taken to his office. "You ladies are an unintended bonus. And since you are Red Cross personnel and not any part of the U.S. Army, you will be treated with utmost respect. Until and if arrangements are made for your return, you will work as you did, but in a Spanish hospital and treating Spanish wounded. I trust you will not decline the honor."

The young captain might have been making a cruel joke about mistreating them, but Villate was a monster. They would not take any chances.

Sarah forced a smile. "Then we will not consider declining. We would appreciate it if you could somehow arrange for us to receive better clothing, since we left in such a hurry."

Villate had been trying to eye their bodies through their nightgowns and whatever else they had thrown on. "You've made an excellent decision. One of the good sisters at the cathedral will see to it that you are properly dressed. Although I sincerely doubt that any of you are virgins, I believe you will make most fetching nuns."

Only a few hours later, they found themselves working under the stern supervision of one Sister Maria Magdalena, a very large woman who called herself a nurse but who knew little about the craft, and a very young Doctor Pedro Juarez. The doctor had been trying hard, but was overwhelmed by the number of wounded. His assistants were few and mostly incompetent. Thus, he welcomed the five Americans and promised them good treatment in return for good work. The nurses thought that was fair. He also said they would sleep in the convent near the cathedral for the time being.

Sister Maria, on the other hand, made it clear that she despised them. Not only were they not Catholic, but they were Americans, a nation she hated because it was filled with heretics. She made it known that she would have them whipped if they offended her, and the American women believed her.

"This is better than being kept in a dungeon," Ruta muttered and the others concurred as they dressed in religious garments. "I'm not too sure I like being dressed like a postulant or a novice nun, but this will work."

Because of language issues, they were assigned to work as a group and under Doctor Juarez. His English was basic at best and they decided to try to use Spanish as much as possible. After their time in Cuba, Sarah's Spanish had become fairly decent, and Ruta seemed to have a flair for languages. Despite their dislike for their current condition, they determined to do their best to help the hundreds of wounded who looked at them beseechingly. Their first job would be to sweep the filth off the floors and try to get the men fresh bandages and bedding. Sarah wondered what Sister Magdalena would be doing and the doctor had shaken his head and said that the real nun would be watching them.

"These are the enlisted men," Doctor Juarez said with a tinge of bitterness. "The officers have their own hospital and doctors and, yes, the best of Spanish nurses. Please do not be offended, but the officers have kept the best for themselves and left these men with the dregs."

"We are not offended," said Sarah. "And we will do our best to help these men. I can only hope, however, that none of them is returned to duty to fight against my countrymen."

"You know I cannot control that."

Ruta smiled sweetly. "Then perhaps you can grant us one other favor. Would you be able to have Sister Mary Dragon transferred elsewhere?"

Juarez smiled and rolled his eyes. "I will do my best, but there is a rumor that her far lovelier cousin is General Villate's mistress."

Fire and shells from the American guns had damaged Gilberto Salazar's estate, the place where Kendrick and Juana had cuckolded him. It enraged him. The structure was largely intact, but his home had been profaned. He would not live there again. Not only was it the place where his faithless wife had betrayed him, but it was also the place where his mistress, Helga, had plundered much of his wealth before disappearing.

He had arrived to find his two remaining servants cowering in the basement. Helga had arrived a few days earlier with several Cuban women and had taken all of his cash and anything else of value they could carry off. The servants said they had tried to stop her but that she had cursed them, threatened them, and beaten them badly. Salazar doubted their story. For

one thing, there were no bruises on them and, for
another, the two were consummate cowards and liars.

Helga had somehow managed to get from Salazar's
quarters at Matanzas to Havana ahead of the routed
army. Loaded with their loot, they had then left
Havana where he was told by an informer that she'd
found a way to take a ship to Mexico with her child.
Well, that part of his life was over. When Spain was
victorious, he would find another aristocratic woman
to service him. In the meantime, one of the servants
would do. They wouldn't like it, but they would not
protest overmuch. They would cooperate and be
rewarded or defy him and be terribly hurt.

What he would really like to do was gather his
reconstituted legion and storm the estate of the British
Consul, Redford Dunfield. Once in the villa, he would
castrate Kendrick with his sword and turn Juana over
to his men to enjoy while he watched. If Kendrick had
not bled to death, he would hack him to pieces. The
fanatic monsignor from Rome might disapprove, but he
would also understand. The woman was a sinner. She
had to be punished. Besides, Salazar thought with a
hint of whimsy, he could always go to Confession from
Monsignor Bernardi and beg forgiveness. Bernardi
would hate it, but would comply.

Salazar started as he realized that the annoying
priest was beside him. "What are you thinking of,
Colonel?" the priest asked.

"I'm thinking of a beautiful picture. In it, my whore
of a wife is burning at the stake while her shit of a
lover is being drawn and quartered."

Bernardi laughed nervously. He never knew when
his partner was kidding or not. "Your hatred of her

for her sins is compelling. However and as before, now is not the time for the luxury of a personal vendetta. First we must find ways to help Spain defend Havana and defeat the Americans. Then you can see to the painful destruction of your faithless wife and her heretic lover."

Sarah and the other American nurses had just taken up mops, brooms, and anything they could use as a weapon to wield against a furious and steadily advancing Sister Magdalena, when the door to their ward opened. To their astonishment, Governor-General Villate stood there. Beside him was a very nervous Doctor Juarez and what appeared to be a bald American man in his late thirties. He looked amused at the scenario, while Villate appeared outraged. Juarez looked like he would pass out from fear caused by being so close to the dreaded and thoroughly angry Villate.

"What the devil is going on?" Villate demanded.

Ruta stepped forward. "Do you see this bruise on my face?" she said angrily. There was indeed a red blotch on her cheek and it was turning purple. It fairly well matched one on Sister Magdalena's chin. "We are nurses, General, not cattle to be whipped and beaten. This vile creature decided we weren't working hard enough and started hitting us with her broom, and I think it's the same one she rides around on."

"You are lazy American whores and swine," snarled the nun. She turned to Villate. "This creature struck me. I am a woman of God and I demand that she be flogged within an inch of her heretical life."

Sarah laughed mockingly. "A woman of God? I can't think of a god that would have you."

When Sister Magdalena started to charge like an enraged bear, the other American nurses formed a phalanx and she paused. This gave Villate a moment to put himself between them. When he did, he looked around at the scores of wounded soldiers on their cots. They were looking at him with expressions of fear and hatred, and it dawned on him that if many of them could move, they would rise up and tear him to bloody pieces. He then wondered if they had been searched for weapons—might some of them have knives hidden in their rags? He put his hand on his pearl-handled revolver and signaled for his bodyguards to come into the ward.

Villate sighed. "The gringo who is enjoying this insane debacle is Mr. James Kendrick, an American reporter. It has been an open secret that he's been in Havana at the home of the British Consul and periodically spying on us while writing articles about your foolish President Custer. It has been decided that he will write an article about how you American nurses are caring for Spanish soldiers and becoming beloved by them and all the time being treated well by us." Sister Magdalena gasped and turned away on hearing the comments.

Kendrick? Sarah quickly recognized the name from her conversations with Martin. And this Kendrick was staying with Custer with the British Consul? How very interesting, she thought. Might she and the others manage to finesse their way into the consulate where they would be relatively safe when the battle started? But that would mean abandoning the wounded men they now thought of as their own. She would have to think on that. These poor creatures were not her enemy.

Sarah smiled warmly. "We would all be thrilled to be interviewed by the esteemed Mr. Kendrick, but not here. We would also appreciate it if he was allowed to send some personal messages to our families regarding our situation."

"Everyone in the United States is aware of your situation," Kendrick said. "But I will see to it that each of you is allowed to send personal messages to loved ones."

"But any interviews will take place here," said Villate.

"Then there will be no interviews," snapped Sarah.

"And why not?" asked a bewildered Villate.

"Because we are sick and tired of being pushed around and being treated as property instead of human beings," Ruta answered. "We were stolen like cattle, treated barbarically, and now, after our working hard to save the lives of your soldiers, you won't grant us that one little favor?"

Villate looked away. It was clear that he didn't give a damn about the lives of the Cuban peasant soldiers in the ward. He took a deep breath and turned back. "I will graciously concede. The interviews will take place in Mr. Dunfield's residence. There you will have the privacy to tell Mr. Kendrick anything you desire without having to worry about being overheard or misinterpreted."

"I will watch out for them and make sure that they say nothing that would slander Spain," said Sister Magdalena.

Before Villate could respond, Kendrick interjected. "You will do no such thing. Mr. Dunfield will not permit you to enter the consulate. Besides," he continued, "General Villate will be given copies of everything I've written before it is sent. If there are mistakes, I'm certain he will, ah, correct them."

Even Villate smiled at the blatant falsehood. By the time he read Kendrick's writings, the text would be well on its way to Washington.

Mercedes de Milan had not been feeling well. Her stomach ached and she was having trouble keeping food down, which made her crabby and irritable. One of her friends told her that her problems signaled the approach of old age. She hated the thought of aging. Just that morning she had looked in her mirror and seen new wrinkles and a few more strands of gray hair. The hair she could dye, but the wrinkles were there forever. She could hide some of them with heavy makeup, but she had seen older women using too much and ending up looking like clowns. She hated growing old and it made her short-tempered.

Even though she was uncomfortable having Gilberto Salazar in her house, she could think of no reason to deny him entrance or even be concerned about it. Yes, he was a monster who murdered his enemies, but he was also a Spanish gentleman and, yes, he had what some people considered deviant sexual appetites, but they were appetites shared and enjoyed by so many other men. And, she smiled to herself, some women as well.

She received him in her parlor. She did not sit down and she did not invite him to do so either. "To what do I owe this honor, Colonel?" she said sarcastically. Her stomach had just started cramping. "I didn't think you'd be brave enough to show yourself here since the abortive attack on this house."

Salazar smiled nervously. "That was an unfortunate

mistake. Yes, I wanted to take back my wife and yes, I wanted to punish her lover, but there was never any intent to harm anyone. My men misunderstood. They were overzealous and they have been disciplined."

Disciplined? Mercedes had seen their dead bodies. Rojas had taken her out to the place where they'd been dumped. "Then why did they carry knives and guns, Colonel?"

"Why, to protect themselves against Kendrick and your guardian, Rojas. By the way, where is the very large Hector Rojas?"

She smiled tightly. Why did he want to know? Mercedes wondered. "He is running a brief errand for me. He will return momentarily."

Salazar's eyes suddenly blazed with fury and she realized she shouldn't have admitted that Rojas had gone at all. "Why did you protect my whore of a wife?" he snarled. "I deserve to know."

Mercedes was not easily intimidated, and the pain in her stomach overwhelmed her caution, "To protect her from a pig like you."

Salazar screamed his fury and punched her with all his might in the middle of her frail chest. She staggered backwards and then fell to the floor. She gasped and lay on her back with her arms outstretched. Salazar watched in grim fascination as her eyes rolled back in her head and her arms and legs twitched uncontrollably.

In a few seconds, her twitching stopped and his nose told him that her bowels had released. Damn it, he thought, was the bitch dead? Had he killed her? He bent down and checked her pulse. It fluttered and stopped. He cursed silently. He hadn't planned to kill the old whore, but she had provoked him beyond reason. He looked around. None of the servants was present. Good. He straightened up and walked out with as much dignity as he could manage. He wanted to leave before Rojas returned. Salazar was armed, but Rojas was a killer.

As he stepped outside and into the sunlight, he realized that he might escape any scrutiny or suspicion if there was to be an investigation into the death of Mercedes de la Pena. He had hit her where no one would easily discover a mark. With only a little luck, the servants and Rojas would think the evil old woman had suffered a fatal heart attack.

Rojas was led into Mercedes' bedroom only a few minutes later. Ironically, he had seen Salazar walking down the street without a care in the world and had thought nothing of it. They'd even nodded greetings. Between sobs, the servants told him that Salazar had been alone with their mistress and that he had punched her in the chest and killed her. When Salazar had struck the fatal blow, they'd been watching through a hole in the wall designed by Mercedes for just such surveillance. Terrified, they'd kept quiet, and Salazar had left thinking his assault was a secret.

Rojas shifted Mercedes' clothing so he could see the dark blotch on her chest. Yes, he thought, such a blow could be fatal, especially to a frail old woman. He'd inflicted such blows himself with his heavy hammer and seen his younger, healthier victims die gasping for breaths that would never come. Such a blow would even stop a person's heart. Perhaps that was what happened to Mercedes.

Rojas decided that he had to leave. Even though he was innocent, he couldn't take a chance that the authorities might want a scapegoat. He went to Mercedes' room and took all the money she had in her purse and in the wall safe hidden behind an ugly painting of a bunch of flowers. He had memorized the combination after watching his mistress open it several times. He had never opened it himself until now and had no idea what he might find. To his delight he found almost twenty thousand dollars in American money and several hundred British pound notes.

Excellent, he thought. He did not want to have to take and sell jewelry that would go for a fraction of its worth and likely be identified as having belonged to his deceased mistress. He turned to the servants and told them that they could have whatever they wished and they began a mad scramble to grab anything of value including the jewelry he didn't want.

He smiled to himself. If anyone became suspicious and the servants were caught with the precious items, they would be suspected of stealing from a dead woman and not him.

But now he had a problem and it was called justice. Mercedes de la Pena had been very good to Hector Rojas. She had not deserved to be killed like Salazar had done. She should still be alive and teasing him and perhaps inviting him into her bed where he would convince her that she was still young. He would have to think what to do about Gilberto Salazar. Whatever he decided would be painful and permanent. Salazar would suffer.

◆　◆　◆

Martin had to yell to make himself heard by the five hundred men in the battalion. They were all standing casually and looking at him curiously. Nothing good ever came from being addressed en masse by a senior officer and even less so by a general.

"Congratulations, men. You all look like hell. Back home you would be arrested on sight and thrown into jail as vagrants."

The men were all wearing what a Cuban peasant revolutionary soldier would wear—ragged pants, torn shirt, sandals, and big, floppy hats.

The soldiers roared with laughter and one asked just when they would be going home so this happy event could happen. He ignored the comment. A soldier whom he knew to be a sergeant under his rags waved his hand. "General, I know you've got us wearing this stinking shit for a good reason and I know you ain't gonna tell us that reason today, but will we be able to take our real uniforms with us when we go out and do whatever you want us to do?"

"Sergeant Kelly, that is a real good and real long question," he answered. "And are all the sergeants in this man's army from Ireland?"

Kelly was a small, wiry man and he grinned impudently. "Only the good ones," he responded and was greeted with a chorus of good-natured jeers and boos. The sergeant's brogue was thick enough to cut with a knife. It told Martin that Kelly, along with so many Irishmen, had arrived fairly recently in the U.S.

Ryder held up his hands for silence and quickly got it. "Despite my rank I can say with confidence that I don't know all that is going to happen. When I do and can tell you, I will. In the meantime, don't lose the rags you've been issued today. They could wind up being very important. Oh yes, don't advertise the fact that you have them."

As the men dispersed to go back to their quarters and change into their regular uniforms, Sergeant Kelly turned to his companion and cousin from County Cork, Corporal Ryan. "Does his generalship actually expect five hundred men to keep this nonsense a secret?"

Ryan shook his head. "Not a chance," he said thoughtfully. "All this does is tell us that whatever is going to happen is going to occur soon."

"Can't argue with that reasoning," Kelly said. "And it also points out that we're going to be in disguise and try to fool the goddamn Spanish into thinking we're a bunch of raggedy-ass Cuban rebels."

"And that means we're going to be close to the front, where there is likely to be a lot of shooting. Shit."

"Ryan, do you have any of your Bushmills left? I think we're going to be in need of a drink."

"Sergeant, we finished it a long time ago. Don't you remember?"

"Of course I do. I was just hoping I was wrong. I guess we'll have to make do with that shit they call rum."

The comments about Bushmills were a joke. It and other Irish brands like Jameson were too pricy for them. They'd talked about pooling their money and buying a bottle when they got back to Baltimore. The two men had arrived from Ireland a dozen years earlier as kids and were poorer than dirt. They had been trying to work their way to respectability since then. Joining the Maryland militia a few years before had seemed like a good idea and volunteering to fight in Cuba an even better one. Hell, they were even able to shoot at people. Too bad their targets were Spanish and not English.

In the distance, the American artillery again began to fire. Ryan shook his head. "Either we attack soon or we're gonna run out of ammunition. My money's on soon. I suggest we concentrate on just how the hell we're going to drag our Gatling guns through the streets of Havana."

Lieutenant Hugo Torres watched with dismay and horror as the black fingers of smoke on the horizon separated and became warships, many warships. Soon they could see the white water at the ships' bows as they bulled their way through the sea.

As a result of surviving the sinking of the *Vitorio*, he was now second in command of the cruiser *Aragon*. It was a dubious honor at best. The ship was rusty and totally ill-maintained. Her engines sounded like they were gasping for life and he wondered if they would have to rig sails. There was little coal left in her bunkers and what they had was of poor quality. She was rated at fourteen knots, but she barely made ten during the flight from Havana. The *Aragon* was supposed to have a crew of nearly four hundred, but fewer than half that had left Havana with them. Had the others deserted?

Only if they were wise, Torres thought.

The ship carried eight eight-inch guns, which sounded impressive, but they were not in good shape and he wondered if they would even fire. No one seemed to know when they were last used. It came as no surprise to find that the ammunition was of poor quality as well.

At just over three thousand tons, the *Aragon* was the largest Spanish ship in the small squadron. As a result, she was the flagship. She was half the size of the larger American warships and totally outgunned. A battle would end in a slaughter. Even so, the newly appointed captain had just finished haranguing the crew on the virtues of dying well. At least that's what Torres thought of the speech. He said they would fight the Yankees for the glory of Spain. The previous captain had claimed he was too ill to make the escape from Havana. Torres thought their flight at night from Havana was cowardly and stupid. They had no place to go and were short on food and water as well as fuel and ammunition.

Nor could they scuttle their ships and try to make it on foot to somewhere safe. There was no safe haven. Scores of rebels were visible on the shore. He could hear their jeers and curses. They would chop to pieces anyone who came ashore.

They were doomed.

The captain waved his sword. When he stopped, Torres noticed flecks of rust on the blade. "For Spain, for King Alfonso, and for Holy Mother Church. Let us go and fight and, if need be, die as heroes."

A burly sailor stepped forward. "I do not wish to die and I certainly do not wish to die in a foolish battle that we cannot win. Today I refuse to fight."

Several junior officers moved towards the man to arrest him, but he was quickly surrounded by a several dozen other sailors who protected and cheered him. "Surrender, surrender," they chanted.

In seconds, the rest of the crew was chanting as well. The captain looked stricken. "We must fight for our honor. Look, the enemy is almost upon us."

Torres looked in the direction of the approaching Americans. They were indeed much closer and forming up to run parallel to the Spanish squadron. There was a puff of smoke from the lead warship and the shell splashed well short of the *Aragon*. It was a literal shot across their bows. In a very short while the Americans would commence firing for real and the slaughter would begin.

"Fuck our honor," yelled the sailor who was the ringleader. "Take the officers."

It happened so quickly Torres realized it must have been planned. He was grabbed and his arms pinned to his side. They took his sword and pistol.

Torres turned to the ringleader. "If you want to surrender, then someone must tell the Americans. Otherwise they will start shelling us."

"Will you do it?" asked the ringleader, suddenly concerned that the battle might start despite his fervent wishes.

Torres shook off his captors. "You may keep the pistol, but give me back my sword. It was a gift from my mother and, besides, I may have to pretend to surrender it to the Americans."

"Bastard, traitor," said the captain as Torres' sword was returned. The other officers looked away.

"He needs a swim," laughed the ringleader. Other mutineers grabbed the captain and threw him overboard. Several other officers followed.

"Don't let them drown," said Torres. "We're doing this to stop any killing."

The sailors growled, then laughed as they pulled their bedraggled skipper and the others from the drink.

Torres gave orders to the crew to lower the colors and turn the guns either down or away from the Americans. He realized that his fate had just been decided for him. He would never be able to return to Spain. He wondered if some other Spanish-speaking country in the New World could use a good naval officer.

"The *Orion* does not belong in a line of battle," Janson said. "She is not a battleship. Hell, she isn't even a real cruiser, despite what her papers say. So here we are, ready to go and fight the remnants of the Spanish Navy."

The *Orion* was the seventh in the line of American warships. Ahead of her were the heavy cruisers *Atlanta* and *Chicago* and four Civil War vintage steam sloops. The *Atlanta* was the flagship and Admiral Porter was on board her. The steam sloops were followed by a dozen auxiliary cruisers of all shapes and sizes. They were en route to the small Cuban port of Playa Colorada to the west and south of Havana. Credible intelligence said that the mere handful of Spanish ships remaining in Cuban waters were riding there at anchor. That the Spanish hadn't steamed farther away was explained by the fact that they couldn't get additional coal, or even wood to burn as fuel. To make matters worse, the friendly port of Santiago was out of their limited range. Playa Colorada was a day's worth of steaming from Havana. The Spanish squadron had gone as far as it could. The dash from Havana was over.

The Spanish ships were the cruisers *Aragon* and *Navarra* and the light cruiser *Velasco*. Two small and useless monitors were also with the cruisers. The Spanish were heavily outgunned and outnumbered. It was rumored by some that Admiral Porter wanted to destroy them in one last and glorious fleet action, while others felt that he wanted to overawe them into surrendering. Janson and Prentice hoped that inducing them to give up was the goal. Both men had seen enough death and destruction to last a lifetime.

"Spanish honor might demand a battle," mused Janson, "even if it means useless bloodshed. People get killed even in a symbolic battle."

There would be no secret arrival for the American fleet. Black smoke from burning coal poured from their stacks, signaling their presence for many miles. The two men wondered if the Spaniards would still be at Playa Colorada or if they would have fled as far as their limited supply of fuel would take them.

Signal flags flew from the *Atlanta*—enemy in sight. The crew of the *Orion* cheered. Soon the Spanish squadron—they refused to call it a fleet—was visible. At first the enemy ships looked grim and dangerous, but Prentice and Janson quickly changed their minds. The Spanish vessels were small and as they drew closer, rust could be seen on their hulls. A sailor commented that it looked like either American capital ship could swallow the Spanish ones.

"My God," said Prentice. "Is this the end of the Spanish empire in North America, a handful of small and obsolete warships? Is this pitiful remnant of a navy what is left of the nation that conquered half the world and launched the Armada against England?"

"I'm afraid so," said Janson.

As they drew closer, they could see that the ships

were anchored against the Cuban shoreline. More signals from the *Atlanta* said the American ships were to stop and hold position just out of the range of the Spanish guns. The *Atlanta* fired one gun and the shell fell well short. The miss was intentional, they realized.

"What the hell is happening?" wondered Prentice. There appeared to be fighting on board the Spanish ships and they could hear small arms fire.

Janson peered through his telescope. "It looks like the crew is trying to overpower the officers. I think what we are watching is an old-fashioned mutiny. If so, I'll bet that the crew doesn't want any more fighting, not even something symbolic."

They continued to watch as several men were thrown overboard. "Officers, I'll bet," said Janson. "I hope they can swim."

A moment later and there was loud cheering from the Spanish ships. The mutiny was over and the mutineers had won. Ropes were lowered to retrieve the officers thrown overboard. It had been a civilized mutiny.

A few moments later, a small boat was lowered from one of the enemy cruisers and rowed over to the *Atlanta*. "It looks like we are going to parlay and that is a very good sign," said Janson.

In a very short while, the boat returned to her ship. More signals flew from the *Atlanta*. "We are not to fire, repeat, not to fire," said Janson "unless, of course, the Spaniards violate the truce and fire upon us. Also, Paul, you and I are to report immediately to the flagship."

Paul was puzzled. "What kind of trouble are we in now?"

A few moments later, one small cannon was fired from the *Aragon*. There was no splash as no shell had been loaded. Spain's need for honor had just been satisfied by the firing of one unloaded gun in the general direction of the enemy. Spanish flags were dropped and the battle of Playa Colorada was over.

Janson shifted the *Orion* to a position much closer to the now anchored *Atlanta* and then the two of them went by ship's boat to the flagship. Their orders were to report immediately, so they did not have the opportunity to change into dress uniforms. It didn't matter. Admiral David Dixon Porter was preoccupied with the Spanish ships that were rocking gently at anchor only a few hundred yards away. His full beard was more white than dark and his eyes were piercing. The two men saluted and stood waiting to be acknowledged.

After a few seconds, Porter stood and returned the salute. He then extended his hand and they shook it. "I've been remiss," the admiral said. "I wanted to congratulate you on sinking that Spanish battleship, but haven't had the time. Now I can and you do have the thanks of a nation. We can be pleased that there's one less enemy battleship to contend with. Of course," he said with a tight smile, "it doesn't look like the Spanish feel like fighting anyone this day."

Porter turned and gestured to the Spanish ships where their crews lined the rails of their ships. "Look at them. They are scared to death and not of us, but of the Cubans. I just told their emissary that their surrender must be complete and unconditional and if there is any attempt to scuttle ships that are now our prizes, I will have them all cast ashore naked and unarmed so that the Cuban rebels can chop them to pieces with their machetes. I wouldn't, of course, but they don't know that. For the past week, the poor fools have been afraid to go ashore for any reason and, along with running out of fuel, are also getting hungry and thirsty. Now, you're probably wondering what this has to do with you."

"Yes, sir," said Janson, clearly awed by the intense man.

"You, Captain Janson, will return to the *Aurora*, while you, Lieutenant Prentice, will take over a score or so of men from both your ship and mine and take control of the *Aragon* as prize master. You will then take her to a spot just off Havana where she can be clearly seen. Similar crews will handle the other ships. I want the Spanish generals in Havana to see that their so-called fleet is actually in American hands. Lieutenant Prentice, you and the other prizes will sail in concert with our fleet, so you shouldn't have any worries about the Spanish prisoners trying to take control of the ship. If they do try something, you will cut them down immediately and violently. Can you do that?"

Prentice stiffened. "Yes, sir."

Porter smiled. "Captaining a near-derelict ship and a few score demoralized prisoners should be nothing to someone who helped sink a battleship, although it will look good on your record. I assume you can find Havana, can't you?"

It was Prentice's turn to smile. "With my eyes closed, sir."

"Excellent, but do try to keep them open. When you get to Havana and the Spaniards have seen the last of their fleet, you will be directed to an anchorage and the prisoners will be removed. You and the others will return to the *Orion* while the captured ships await additional crews to take them to Florida or wherever the Navy Department wants them."

"Sir, may I ask if the captured ships will become part of our navy?" asked Prentice.

"A good question, Lieutenant. On one hand, they would greatly augment our small navy, but on the other, they are not very modern ships and I hope that the United States would not pin its hopes on having them as a strong line of defense. We must build newer and better ships if we are to protect our investments in Cuba and Puerto Rico. If not, some other power is very likely to reach out with its navy and take them. Britain is just arrogant enough to do it without so much as a thank you, while France and Spain hate us."

Corporal Carlos Menendez slowly walked up the path to Rosita Garcia's small home. He had been there many times since he had taken her son. He had eaten there and shared Rosita's bed. She had proven to be a passionate joy and he was very fond of her. Tonight, as evening gathered, he thought she shared that feeling.

However, her feelings towards him soon might come to an abrupt end. She appeared on the tiny porch with a small candle in her hand and stared at him. "Where is my son?" she asked, her voice breaking.

"I don't know, Rosita. The Americans attacked at Santa Cruz and no one expected it. The place where he was working was shelled, but he did get away. But then he was captured and charged with being a deserter. The Spanish Army, my army, gave him a choice. He could work as a laborer or he could hang. He chose to work."

Rosita sagged and sat down on the ground. "Then where is he?"

Carlos sat on the ground a few feet before her. "I don't know. Where he was working was attacked. I got there afterwards and there were several bodies, but none were his." At least none that he could find, he thought. A couple were so badly mangled they could have been anybody's.

"So he has escaped and is alive?"

"Possibly. I just don't know for certain."

"And how do you know all these things, and why should I believe you?"

Carlos took a deep breath. "After twenty years as a soldier I have made many friends and I can talk with them and ask them questions. Sometimes sergeants and corporals know more than the generals."

"But you don't know where Miguel is now, do you?"

"No, but I've heard rumors that there are packs of deserters roaming Havana and that some of them are young boys. Let me rest here tonight and I will sneak back into the city tomorrow and find out some more. I am not expected back until tomorrow afternoon."

"You will not share my bed. You will sleep on the porch."

Carlos understood. He had failed her. She went inside and he curled up on the wooden porch. He was exhausted and sleep came quickly.

Two hours later she came out and nudged him with her bare foot. She was wearing only a shirt that came halfway down her muscular thighs. "I have changed my mind. I cannot sleep. I believe that you have done as much as was humanly possible, and I cannot demand more. You will come into my bed, and you will hold me, nothing else, until I fall asleep. Then, in the morning, you and I will again make love. You will go back to Havana and do everything you can to find my son."

◆ Chapter 20 ◆

BACK IN HIS TENT, MARTIN TOOK THE BRIEF LETTER
from Sarah out of his pocket and read it for the
tenth time in the last hour. She was safe and well,
which he pretty much knew. She and the others were
no longer living in the convent, which she said was
hilariously inappropriate considering her carnal long-
ings for him. Instead, their new quarters were on the
property of the British Consul, a man named Redford
Dunfield. Dunfield was complaining that his estate
was getting very crowded, what with nurses, guards,
and, of course, President Custer.

Martin refolded the letter. He sniffed it briefly,
hoping it still carried her essence. It didn't, of course,
and he hoped that no one had seen him do it. He
walked to the map of Havana that was spread out on
a table and noted the location of the British consulate. While it wasn't extremely close to where he and
his brigade would be attacking, it was close enough
to be in a danger zone. Of course, when the battle

began, everyone and everything in Havana would be in danger. But then, she might be with Custer when the attack happened. Surely the Spanish would try to protect the President of the United States. Another thought intruded and it sickened him. Would they kill Custer and everyone around him, including Sarah, Ruta, and the other nurses, rather than see him liberated?

Lieutenant Junior Grade Paul Prentice leaned against the railing of the *Orion* and stared at the Cuban shoreline through Janson's telescope. It was only a few miles away and the details stood out boldly in the early evening light. The ground sloped gently up from the beach. It was just as he recalled it. Better, he could see no sign of Spanish military activity.

Captain Janson moved alongside him. "You're not thinking of going back, are you?"

"I hope not, at least not as a spy or scout. I don't think there's too much more I can add to the information the Navy already has."

Each night for the past week, Prentice had been rowed to shore in a fishing boat. There he had met with Cuban rebels and scouted both the terrain and the Spanish fortifications. The land, he decided, contained no serious obstacles and could easily be handled, even in the dark, by well-trained and highly disciplined U.S. Army soldiers and Marines.

He had also concluded that the rumors about the Spanish defenses were correct. The larger of the two forts, known as *La Cabaña,* was poorly defended. With Cuban help, he had even penetrated the fortifications and been able to give the large numbers of cannons a quick examination. Some of the guns were as ancient as had been rumored. They were at least two centuries old and were badly rusted. A quick check of primer holes showed them clogged with rust. He reported to the Navy that he would pray for anyone who tried to use them.

This information both pleased and dismayed the higher-ups. If the guns were *that* bad, how could they be turned and used against the Spanish? The answer was simple—most of them couldn't. The American force would have to land a number of their own and that included the weapons from smaller ships like the *Orion*. Janson was highly displeased with that piece of news, but recognized that it was necessary.

"You don't have to go in with them," Janson said with a hint of sadness. He had gotten fond of the younger officer and often thought of him as the son he'd never had.

"Yes, I do," Prentice said. "I know the land and I know the people the Marines will be dealing with. Working with a stranger might lead to confusion and that would be tragic, to say the least."

Janson sniffed his reluctant agreement. "That and the fact that it will be a hell of an adventure to tell your grandchildren, provided, of course, that you don't get yourself killed during this grand adventure."

Prentice shook his head and then wondered if Janson could see the gesture in the fading light. Even though the Spanish were well aware that many ships were off shore, the *Orion* was showing no lights as darkness fell.

"I have no plans to get killed."

"Nobody ever does, Paul. But somehow it just happens during war, and usually when you least expect it."

Prentice decided to change the subject. It was getting too close to his own fears. He was no hero and had very mixed emotions about the so-called grand adventure he was about to go on. True, he had volunteered to go ashore and meet with the rebels, but only because he had dealt with some of them on a casual basis while at Mount Haney and because he spoke passable Spanish.

"When will the cargo be coming aboard?" he asked.

Janson laughed at the idea of calling a hundred Marines cargo. "I understand it'll be tomorrow night. All of which means they'll be jammed on board with us for at least a day. Well, I had more soldiers stuffed in the *Aurora* the first trip over. Of course, the *Aurora* was a larger ship. No matter, the Marines will endure it."

Prentice tried to visualize the more than two thousand Marines and Negro cavalrymen, their equipment, ammunition, and enough food to last them a week, all on board about fifty ships of varying size. Fortunately, the ships involved had all been on blockade for a couple of weeks. The Spanish were used to their presence and they had made no threatening gestures against the Spanish fortifications at the entrance to Havana's harbor.

Thanks to his efforts at patrolling and spying, the brass now knew that the enemy defenses were as decayed as the Spanish empire they represented. Would this make the invasion easier? Lord, he hoped so.

"I'm hungry," said one of the smallest boys. His name was Gilberto and he was not quite twelve years old. That was, if he knew his correct age in the first place. "We're going to starve to death, aren't we?"

"Not if I can help it," said Manuel Garcia, the erstwhile leader of the small group that was now one person smaller. Of course, he had no idea how to prevent such a fate. If the city wasn't soon liberated by the Americans and their Cuban allies, they would indeed weaken and, while they wouldn't likely die, their weaknesses would make it easier for the Spanish authorities to catch them.

After fleeing the bombardment and running into Havana, they had hidden in a number of basements, abandoned buildings, and sheds, and even slept out in the open. For food, they had scavenged through trash and stolen from homes and shops whenever possible. The last few nights, however, had been a horror. After running for their lives, they had finally found a secure place to hide while the Spanish army looked for them. They were in a mausoleum in a large cemetery near the Cathedral of San Cristobal. A couple of the coffins had broken open and they shared the space with grinning skeletons. Manuel had calmed the other boys by turning the skulls so that they looked away. He hoped he wasn't committing a sacrilege.

Tico was the smallest and youngest one, and also the most innocent and most desperate. A couple of nights earlier, they had been grubbing through the trash behind a large house when the door had suddenly opened. A priest they knew as the crazy Roman monsignor who was trying to organize soldiers to die for Spain and Christ stood in the doorway. The light behind him was blinding. The others had fled, but Tico had been transfixed and the priest had grabbed him.

"What are you doing, my son?" they'd heard the priest say in a calming voice.

When Tico explained that he was hungry, they heard the priest tell the boy to wait by the door. Amazed, they watched as the priest disappeared inside and then come back with two loaves of bread. "Take these and share them with your companions. Do it just like Jesus did with the loaves and fishes. All of you come back tomorrow, and there will be more food."

That night they gorged themselves on the bread and didn't even complain that it was a little stale. The next night they went to the back door of what they now realized was the cathedral rectory. On the stoop by the door were two more loaves of bread and a jug of something. They were about to start forward and claim their prize when Manuel told them to wait. It was too quiet.

"What if there are soldiers around, and what if it is a trap?" he asked.

"But I'm hungry," said Tico. "And besides, it was a priest who gave us the food, wasn't it? A priest wouldn't lie, would he?"

"Be patient. Let's look around first. We've got to make sure this is safe. We don't want to hang, do we?"

Even as he said it, Manuel knew he'd be lucky to spot any soldiers. It was dark and here were just too many places for them to hide. But then he smelled burning tobacco along with the stench of human sweat. There were men close by and almost all of the men in Havana were soldiers. He was about to tell the boys to return to their latest hideout in a basement when he realized that Tico had ignored his orders and was walking cautiously up to the irresistible food.

"No," he hissed, but Tico either couldn't or wouldn't hear.

The boy reached the bread and was bending down

to pick it up when doors opened and soldiers flooded out. At the same time, the rectory door opened and the crazy priest came out screaming. "You were to wait for all of them, you fools, not just this little wretch."

Manuel heard swearing and obscenities from the soldiers as poor little Tico wriggled and writhed helplessly in their grasp.

"Over there," the priest yelled and pointed in Manuel's direction. They had been spotted. "Catch the bastard deserters."

The remaining boys ran for their lives. The soldiers were older and stronger, but the boys were motivated by fear. The boys also by now knew the streets and alleys very well. They darted in and out of darkened paths and managed to stay just out of the grasp of the soldiers. One by one, the soldiers gave up, doubled over and gasping for breath. The boys were totally exhausted as well. A couple of them *had* been grabbed at by the soldiers, and Manuel had been staggered by a strong hand on his ankle when a soldier threw himself at him. He'd screamed and kicked himself free.

"We cannot go back to where we were or where we've ever been," Manuel said as his breath calmed and he got control of his fears. "Tico will talk and they will be waiting for us."

"Tico is brave," one of the other boys said, his stammer betraying his own fear.

Manuel again realized he was too wise for his years. He remembered his schoolteacher being beaten and hanged by the Spanish. "Yes, Tico is brave and, yes, Tico is strong. But the Spanish are stronger and they will break him and make him talk. Trust me, they will break him. Everyone will break sooner or later."

"What will we do?"

Manuel managed a smile. He had been thinking along the lines of desperation when it came to hiding places and had seen the mausoleums in the cemetery. "I think I know of a final resting place for us," he said.

The next evening they found Tico. He had been beaten, whipped, and there were burns all over his small naked body. He was hanging by the neck from the limb of a tree. They also found evidence that soldiers had found many of their earlier hiding places. Sadly, they knew that Tico had been brave but had ultimately talked.

Poor foolish boy, Manuel thought. At least he had found out the name of the priest who had betrayed them. His name was Bernardi and he was indeed evil. And evil had to be crushed.

It was raining again and they couldn't see the Spanish watchtowers. On the other hand, Ryder thought, the observation balloons were safely tethered to the ground. They now had three of the balloons and, as a number of soldiers said, were useless as tits on a boar in the rain.

"Maybe we won't have to wear those stupid Cuban costumes," muttered Lang.

"You look great in one," said Ryder.

"I would say something really appropriate, but you are a general."

"Good thinking. You may still have to wear those stupid outfits, but you're right to look at the bright side. The rain is hiding all of our movements. Of course, it's also hiding theirs from us. Once again, the blind are leading the blind."

"I thought that was standard Army procedure," Lang said with a smile.

"I don't think the army has a standard procedure for invading a foreign country."

"Not just to change the subject, General, but is it true that we'll be the first to enter Havana?"

Ryder knew he should keep quiet, but rumors were rife and Lang was a trusted advisor and a damn good leader. "I would be very surprised if we weren't. Unless, of course, my well-laid plans don't work and we're all killed. In that case, we won't be the first into Havana."

"Ah, a happy thought, sir. But I have a question— what are the plans for liberating the president and, ah, all those other people with him?"

Ryder smiled. The other people in question were the nurses, although it was understood that other important personages were staying with the British consul. "Lang, you are the soul of discretion. What on earth are you possibly thinking?"

Lang pulled out two Cuban cigars and handed one to Ryder. Cigars were another luxury available now that the army had burst out of its lines at Matanzas. The two men lit up and puffed contentedly for a moment.

"Well, General, once upon a while ago, I led a raid against the Spanish. Then, just a short while ago, they raided our lines. Since it appears we're playing tit for tat, I feel it's time to tat their tit. In other words, I think it's time we raided their asses and made them squeal."

Ryder blew a perfect smoke ring and watched as it drifted across to the other side of the tent. "I like the thought, but there's very little chance of success right now. And if you did launch a raid, it would give away the fact that we are planning a major attack."

Lang nearly choked on his cigar. "General, don't you think they know what we're up to, at least in a basic sense? Besides, I have no plans to raid before the attack. My plan, such as it is now, will be to launch a raid during the attack when everybody and his brother will be fighting the main battle."

Ryder blew another ring and decided he was getting really good at it. "Are you thinking of a flying column or a forlorn hope?" he asked, referring to sometimes desperate attacks of the past.

"Forlorn hope my ass, General. I plan on doing nothing forlorn. I plan on surviving and getting a medal pinned on my chest by representatives of a grateful nation and I won't even care if that representative is that asshole, Custer."

"If you can pull it off, Captain, a lot of people will be eternally grateful, although maybe not some people in Washington. How far along are your plans?"

Lang grinned. "They're getting there. In the meantime, since rank has its privileges, may I assume that you have something stronger than warm water in this tent?"

Monsignor Bernardi entered the office of Governor-General Villate with a feeling of trepidation. He had been doing God's work and was proud of his efforts. There was concern, however, that others might not see it in that light. The weak and the misguided always misunderstood him and the need to take strong measures against those who would defy the Church. He was also less than thrilled to find Bishop Campoy present as well. Campoy was not one of his supporters. He believed in accommodation, while Bernardi believed in confrontation with the Devil and the destruction of God's enemies.

He was invited to be seated but was offered nothing in the way of refreshments. That did not bode well. The bishop was clearly uncomfortable. "Your zeal is causing problems for both the Church and Cuba," he said.

"I find that hard to believe, sir. I am working for God and Spain. I have recruited, trained, and armed a force of men that will be instrumental in pushing back the Americans, as well as for keeping Cuba part of Spain and in the bosom of Our Holy Mother Church."

Campoy shook his head. "And for that you needed to *kill* that boy?"

Which boy? wondered Bernardi. There had been more than a few. Then he recalled. "The person you refer to as a boy was a deserter. He and a pack of other young wolves are living in the streets of Havana by stealing and thumbing their noses at the government and the church. We meted out justice."

Campoy continued. "Did justice include torturing that boy? He could not have been older than ten. I saw his body. He had been whipped and his flesh was covered with burns. Why did that happen? Why in the name of God did you think such atrocities were necessary?"

Bernardi was undeterred. "We were trying to find out where the others in the pack of devils were hiding. We did, of course, but it took a while to pry the information from him. He was a stubborn little savage."

Villate leaned forward. He smelled the monsignor's

blood in the water and it pleased him. "By that time, I assume that the others in the pack of devils had already left that place if indeed they ever returned to it. Am I not correct?"

"You are," Bernardi admitted grudgingly. "And you are also correct that we have no idea where they are right now."

"How many men have deserted your legion because of this murder?" Villate asked.

"A few," Bernardi said softly and after a moment's hesitation.

"A few?" snapped Villate. "The true number is more like fifty and you know it. Fifty men have either disappeared into the slums of Havana or have gone over to the rebels. And how many others disapprove but have not deserted but will no longer fight as hard as they had been willing to for God and King. What you did was distasteful even to those extremely devout Catholics you and Salazar have recruited."

"It was justice," Bernardi responded sullenly. "And justice is sometimes very harsh."

The bishop shook his head. "Justice, Monsignor, consists of a trial and an appropriate punishment, but only if the accused is found guilty according to the laws of Spain. There was no trial, only a punishment. What you did was little more than a lynching and it was made worse because you implied that the church supported your actions."

"I am authorized to defend the faith against its enemies," Bernardi snapped. "You've seen my credentials from Rome."

Bishop Campoy smiled coldly. "Really? Both the Spanish government and the Vatican have had many

more important things to do than verify your credentials, but we finally did get a response to our cables.
Neither His Holiness nor anyone else in the Vatican
acknowledges any association with you. We were told
that you were a wide-eyed radical priest who opposed
reforms the Pope was trying to institute. They said
that whatever credentials you showed indicating otherwise are fraudulent. We accept that you are indeed
a monsignor, but you do not represent the will of
Pope Leo XIII."

Bernardi started to sputter. "I represent the wishes
of many Roman Catholics in opposing the spread of
heresy by any means necessary."

"Have you considered that Spain might lose this
war?" Villate asked. "We are indeed losing it right
now. Our army is penned in and our fleet has been
destroyed. The enemy is getting stronger while we
grow weaker. When the war ends, the Americans will
demand their pound of flesh and that includes Gilberto
Salazar. If your people commit further atrocities, that
pound of flesh may include you as well. Salazar will
be given more justice by the Americans than you gave
that boy. Salazar will likely be sent to either Washington or New York and put on trial for the murders of
those men on the *Eldorado* and then hanged. If you
are still alive and here in Havana, you may also be
tried for the murder of that boy. Perhaps one or two
of those fifty new deserters who will no longer be on
hand to defend us will testify against you. Did you
know, by the way, that the boy had been sodomized
as well as beaten?"

Campoy was shocked. "Dear God."

"I had nothing to do with that," Bernardi insisted.

"Perhaps not directly," said Campoy, "but you could be guilty of negligence, which is both a crime and a sin."

Bernardi looked at the two men. "I know what you're doing," he said. "You're trying to cover yourselves for the time when the Americans take over Havana."

To his surprise, Villate laughed. "Of course, you fool. I do not wish to be hanged by either the United States for atrocities, or by our weak King Alfonso for having lost his precious Cuba. If you are thinking that you will be blamed at least in part for the debacle that is coming, then you are absolutely correct. I strongly urge you, if you wish to survive, to change your way of doing things. In short, no more executions. At least none without my express permission."

"I understand," said Bernardi.

Campoy leaned forward. "And if you have them on you, I will take those so-called credentials."

"A fleet," Secretary of State James Blaine exulted. "We've captured a bloody fleet. Now we can go on and take more of Spain's decaying empire."

The telegram from Cuba had just come in announcing that five Spanish cruisers were now in American hands. The public, of course, had found out about it too. There were no secrets in Washington and newspapers were already trumpeting the news that a Spanish fleet in Cuba had surrendered to an American fleet. The battle had been brief and there had been no American casualties, which made the triumph even more exciting. All throughout the nation's capital, church bells were ringing and throngs of people were gathering around the White House. Fireworks displays were planned for the evening in Washington,

New York, and other major cities. More than a victory, it was a hope that the now heartily disliked war would soon be over. The Washington *Post* said that an American noose was tightening around the throats of Spain and Cuba. Blaine thought the prose was too florid but otherwise liked the sentiments.

Blaine and the others were in Blaine's office in the State, War, and Navy Building just west of the White House. Blaine, along with Vice President Chester Arthur and the secretaries of the Navy and War, had chosen this site for their meeting to avoid the annoying presence of Libbie Custer. Her demands for negotiating or winning the release of her husband were becoming more and more strident, and there were growing concerns about her mental stability.

"Five small ships is hardly a fleet," said Arthur drily. "And besides, what other Spanish properties would you wish us to annex?"

"The Philippines and Guam come to mind," Blaine said cheerfully. "Without a navy, the Spaniards can't very well defend them from us, can they?"

"Nor could we hold them, even if we managed to take them," responded Naval Secretary William Hunt. "Those lands are thousands of miles away and have been under Spanish rule for centuries. We would have to send our ships halfway around the world on a journey that could take as long as four months each way. You forget that almost all of our warships are in the Atlantic, and not the Pacific. Maybe someday we'll build a canal across the Isthmus of Panama, but right now that's nothing more than an engineer's fantasy."

Arthur agreed with Hunt. "If we send what navy we have across the Pacific, we would have no ships here to protect us from European predators. England could take the Philippines from us in an instant, while France could exact a bloody vengeance if she so wished. We are a long ways from being a great power, although having a modern navy would be a major step forward."

"So too would a canal across the Isthmus," said Hunt.

Blaine was forced to agree, but he had further grand ideas. "Then we must have a two-ocean navy. If Great Britain can have a navy scattered all over the earth, then we surely must be able to have real squadrons in both oceans and not the handful of relics we currently possess. Gentlemen, we are entering into a new era of American power. If we are going to be a serious player on the world stage, then we must possess the tools."

"Don't you mean props?" the vice president chided gently. "All of that will cost money. If our new colonies turn out to be a fiscal drain, the voters will turn against us in a heartbeat."

Secretary of War Lincoln added. "We are already paying a price. More than a thousand of our young men are dead with at least twice that many wounded, and the fever season is just beginning. I will grant you that these numbers are tiny in comparison with the great battles of Gettysburg, Shiloh, and elsewhere, but those were many years ago and today's numbers represent real people whose death must mean something in order to be justified."

"A price must be paid for an empire," said Blaine dismissively. "But what if I suggest a free entry to our Pacific empire? I'm thinking, of course about Hawaii. It's been said that the islands are incredibly lovely, but they are ruled by a backward tribal hierarchy. We have a treaty with them that grants the islands favored status for trading, but the Americans who have settled there have been agitating for something better. I suggest we give them their wishes. I also suggest that we take the islands before someone else does."

Hunt smiled. Such a bloodless conquest would legitimize his plans for an expanded navy. "We could take the islands with the small and old warships we have out there, and utilize only a regiment or two of volunteers from California to overwhelm the island-ers. Then, of course, we would need to establish and maintain bases in or around their major city, Honolulu. I understand there are marvelous anchorages avail-able. I think Hawaii would definitely be a start in the Pacific and, better, I do not believe Hawaii has any history of fever."

Blaine was pleased. A mere dot on the map of the world was better than no dot on the map. He would get the United States a foothold in the vast Pacific and Hunt would get further justification for his improved navy.

The usually ill-tempered Nelson Miles angrily pushed the piece of paper across the table to General Hancock. General Couch, who had already read it, showed no expression. He already had a fair idea what Hancock's decision would be.

Miles, however, wanted his thoughts heard. "Clara Barton may be the closest thing we have to an Ameri-can saint, but the idea that we would send aid to the enemy is preposterous. I acknowledge that they are only asking for ether and other medical supplies and not weapons, but any Spanish soldier healed through the use of an anesthetic could soon be fighting against us."

"I disagree with that assumption," said Couch. "Any soldier operated on now is not going to be fighting us for a goodly long time, if ever, given the terrible wounds that modern weapons can inflict. Giving them medical supplies now is something that might just serve us well in a postwar environment. A little mercy shown now could pay dividends down the road."

General Hancock had been astonished to receive a letter from Clara Barton reminding him that the Red Cross was an international organization and that the United States was honor and treaty bound to adhere to the terms of the Geneva Convention. While sending medical supplies to an enemy to treat their wounded was not specifically mentioned, she firmly felt that it fell within its terms.

Hancock took the letter and handed it to an aide. "I'm not surprised they are suffering shortages. Our blockade and siege have been fairly effective. Some food might be smuggled in, but not ether or other medications. Therefore, we shall supply it to them. According to Miss Barton's letter, they have enough for only a week or so. I propose that we agree to send them some in just about a week."

Nelson Miles blinked and smiled tightly as the implications behind Hancock's statement sunk in. "A lot could change in a week. The whole world could have been changed, at least their world."

Haney and Lang crawled the half mile from the American works to the Spanish fortifications in nervous silence. If the intelligence that the Spaniards had pulled back was inaccurate, they could be met with a murderous torrent of bullets. At best, they could be allowed to proceed and then be taken prisoner. Neither fate seemed particularly attractive.

Shells had cratered the ground, which gave them some cover as they snuck forward. Each foot gained brought them closer to either safety or tragedy. Even though each man wanted to say or whisper something, they knew better. Adding to their concerns was the fervent wish that their artillerymen understood their orders and were not going to fire. They hadn't shelled the Spanish for the last several days as a deliberate ploy to make the Spanish think that this was a safe sector. Just not too safe with a shell or two every now and then to keep them on their toes. Haney and Lang just hoped that the gunners remembered the schedule.

They were only a few feet away from the defensive crest. There were no sounds, although they thought they could smell tobacco being smoked. Lang and Haney shrugged and slithered over and into a Spanish trench. It was empty and they exhaled a sigh of relief. Someone coughed, but it wasn't close by. Even so, the trench wasn't totally empty. The Spanish had left a few troops behind to watch the Americans. They would have to avoid detection if the plan was to succeed. They could not alarm the Spanish and send them rushing back to their trenches before the Americans attacked. This foray was only to determine if the Spaniards actually were keeping a minimal presence at their front lines. So far that appeared to be the case.

They hunched down and looked over the embankment to the now visible city of Havana. Haney was acutely aware that Ruta was somewhere within it, along with Sarah and the other nurses. His eyes could see people moving around in the distance, but in no great numbers and with no sense of urgency. Numerous cook fires were burning. There was the smell of smoke and some of it came from charred buildings. Even though there was laughter and some drunken idiot was singing badly, the Spanish were mostly asleep. They wouldn't stay that way much longer, he thought happily, and this night could be the last full night that Havana was under Spain's flag.

An hour later they were back in their own lines; exhausted and dirty, but safe. "Well?" asked Ryder.

"There can't be more than a handful of them in their forward trenches," Haney said as he guzzled water. "We can take them out easily."

Lang nodded agreement. "When will we begin bombarding again?"

"Just about right now," said Ryder. A moment later, American mortars lifted shells towards the enemy.

◆ Chapter 21 ◆

LIEUTENANT PRENTICE ENVIED THE MARINES AND sometimes wished he was one. Lean, hard, and disciplined, they epitomized what a fighting man should be. He imagined them as Spartan warriors or Roman legionnaires. The hundred Marines crowding the deck of the *Orion* looked like they could lick a force ten times their size. The dismounted Negro cavalrymen on other ships looked equally fierce and professional, but they were Army and his heart was with the Navy.

The Marines could also row their own boats, while the cavalrymen needed help. The sailors on other ships cheerfully complained that the black soldiers couldn't row across a bathtub. They prudently said this out of the hearing of the Buffalo Soldiers of the Ninth U.S. Cavalry. The name had been given to them by the Indian tribes they had fought.

Fifty-six-year-old Colonel Charles G. McCawley commanded the six hundred Marines who would lead the assault, which thoroughly annoyed the soldiers, who felt that they should go first. They did, however, understand the realities of the situation. The Marines were good with boats, while the soldiers were not. The Marines would go in first with the dismounted cavalry following quickly. Prentice would go with the Marine colonel.

Boats were lowered and filled with Marines who wore dark uniforms and had blackened their faces. The Negro cavalrymen jeered that they needed no such assistance to be hidden in the dark, causing obscenities to fly back and forth.

The Marines rowed steadily and surely to the shore. Their landing point was lit by men with candles and lanterns and they were just north of the almost star-shaped fort called Morro Castle. It was assumed that the men in the various units would get mixed up; therefore, there would be no time-consuming attempt to sort people out. Under the command of McCawley and others the men poured out the boats as soon as the wooden hulls scraped the shore.

Prentice jumped out, took a few steps in the hip-deep water and stumbled. His revolver was now wet and all that he could count on was a cutlass. He cursed and pushed his way through the water to the shore. The colonel had arrived well ahead of anyone else. "Hurry up, Prentice; we won't be waiting for you."

Yes, they would, he thought. He was the one who knew where they were going. He was the one who had been scouting out the terrain. He took the lead with a grinning McCawley just a step behind. The colonel was exulting in the fact that his Marines would be fighting as a unit, and not as small units on board warships.

Prentice quickly found the path that would lead them to the Morro Castle. It and La Cabaña guarded the half of the entrance to Havana's harbor that was across from the city itself. The Negro cavalry would attack the more sprawling fortress of La Cabaña.

"Faster," the colonel ordered and the men responded. Prentice had figured it as a two-mile jog from the beach. The big threat, of course, was discovery. That it would happen was inevitable. Discovered too soon, and the enemy could be pouring rifle and cannon fire into the helpless ranks of Americans. As they ran past houses and cottages, people awakened. Windows were opened and, in some cases, people stepped outside to see what was happening. When they saw an army passing, most of them prudently went indoors, while others ran away from both the soldiers and the fort. In a few cases, Spanish-speaking soldiers angrily told people to go inside their houses and hide.

After an eternity, the ramparts were in sight. There was no apparent activity. Whatever noise the column had made, it had not been enough to rouse the garrison that Prentice knew was small and poorly led. Prentice led men to where he'd spotted a gate. It was shut, of course. The colonel signaled and a handful of men raced towards it and confirmed that it was shut firmly. Prentice found himself holding his breath while the men fiddled with the explosives they'd brought. They lit the fuse and ran as fast as they could.

Just then, they were spotted and Spanish voices called out a challenge. "Too late," McCawley said with a grin. A second later and a blast ripped the gate apart. The Marines didn't wait to see if the way inside was clear, they just ran screaming towards the smoking void and disappeared inside. Prentice followed on their heels, nearly stumbling over debris.

The Spanish fought, many of them with screaming desperation. There were but a hundred of them at most while more than six hundred Americans were in their midst, shooting them and stabbing them with bayonets. An unarmed Spaniard lunged at Prentice who hacked at him with his cutlass. The man screamed and fell to his knees as blood gushed from his shoulder. "I surrender," he sobbed in Spanish. Prentice kicked him to the ground and continued on.

Resistance crumbled. Many Spaniards surrendered, while others ran out into the darkness. A fire was burning and some ammunition was exploding, but the Americans quickly solved those problems. Farther down, Prentice could hear similar fighting raging as the Buffalo Soldiers clawed their way inside La Cabaña. Prentice was confident that they would succeed. That garrison too was small and poorly armed. The incompetent Spanish leadership had left the back door to Havana wide open.

Prentice joined a group that was examining the numerous cannons that faced the entrance to the harbor. Across the channel was the small fort of La Punta. He wondered what its garrison was thinking as smoke and gunfire erupted from the two larger forts that were to have protected the city. American ships would have had to run that deadly gauntlet if they had tried to force their way in. As soon as it was determined which of the Spanish guns were useable, they would commence bombarding La Punta and targets of opportunity.

In a very short while they concluded that only about

half of the cannons were safe enough to use and many of them could only be used with reduced charges.

While Marines struggled with the captured cannons, and others were dragged up the trail from the ships, Prentice wondered about the man he'd chopped with his cutlass. Dreading what he would see, he found his way back to where he'd left the Spaniard. The man lay on the ground with his mouth open and his eyes glazed over. Blood had coagulated on his wound and was turning black. Flies were swarming in their hundreds. Prentice made it to a wall before vomiting.

"Your first, Lieutenant?" asked a Marine corporal. His arm was in a sling. Prentice looked to see if the man was being smart and saw sympathy instead of sarcasm.

Paul wiped his mouth with his sleeve. "This is the first time I ever killed anyone directly. When you fire a cannon you usually don't see the results. Worse, he wasn't even armed, although he was lunging at me."

The corporal nodded. "That means he was trying to kill you, so what you did was war and self-defense. Maybe it's better when we kill from a distance. I really don't want to look into the whites of their eyes. It becomes just too damn personal."

Prentice agreed and vomited a second time.

Governor-General Vlas Villate was awakened by the sound of thunder and the distant muted crackling of gunfire. He swung his bare legs out of the bed, as always careful to not awaken the stocky Cuban woman who was his current mistress. She wasn't all that attractive but she fucked like a tigress and made no demands on him. Her cousin was that demon of a nun named Magdalena. He often wondered what that not very holy woman thought of her cousin screwing the governor of Cuba. Jealousy, he thought. In his opinion, celibacy was the most idiotic thing the Catholic Church had ever invented. Only a fool would deprive himself or herself of the joys of sex.

He shuffled to a window that pointed to the American lines and heard nothing. Shit, he thought, that meant that the sounds were coming from the channel.

Clad only in his nightshirt, he walked to another window. From this he could see out towards the entrance of the harbor. Since the siege had commenced, he had begun sleeping in the security of the fortress known as Real Fueza. Over two hundred years old, it had been obsolete the day it was built because it was set too far back from the channel to defend it. It was just another ancient piece of stupidity from Madrid. Until tonight, however, its history meant little. This night, Real Fueza made a splendid observation tower with a great view of the other side of the channel. As he watched, an explosion ripped through La Cabaña, sending flames and smoke into the sky. Morro Castle was already burning. He grabbed a telescope and thought he could see people running around. They looked like ants that had been spilled from their hill.

An aide rushed in and paused, dismayed at seeing his governor in his night clothes. "Don't gawk, you fool. Who is in charge of the forts on the other side of the channel?"

"The Navy, sir."

Villate sagged. "And we don't have a damned navy anymore, do we? Does that mean that no one is in charge over there?"

The aide prudently decided not to answer. "Never

mind, damn it. Sound the alarm. Where there is one attack, there will likely be two." Or three, or four, he thought angrily. "Sound bells, trumpets, bang pots and pans, and anything that will make noise. It may be too late for those people across the channel, but we will be ready. And oh yes, get me my damned uniform."

Madrid, he realized, wouldn't give a stinking damn who was supposed to be in charge of those forts. They would only note that one Vlas Villate was governor-general of Cuba, and that all responsibility for what was looking more and more like a catastrophic defeat rested on his broad soldiers. He should have made certain that there was better control of the forts and that troops were out patrolling. The bastards in Madrid would have his head for this. He thought briefly of the money he'd siphoned from government funds and into accounts in Argentina and Brazil. There was more than enough to live comfortably for the rest of his life. He would not go back to Spain for court martial and everlasting shame.

Nor would he take the Cuban woman with him. She was stirring and looking at him solemnly. He would be able to do much better wherever he went. He was confident that his second in command, Weyler, had also invested prudently in his future and would not be returning to Spain except, of course, to tell King Alfonso how badly Vlas Villate had fought this war. Villate chuckled softly. It was nothing more than what he would do himself.

His real fear was that he would be captured by the Cuban rebels who hated him with a fiery passion. They would delight in cutting chunks from his large body and feeding them to the dogs while he watched and screamed. And yes, he would scream. Anyone would.

If this battle was going to end as badly as he thought it might, it was time to complete his prudent arrangements and to leave. Before that, he thought happily, he would order that stupid Monsignor Bernardi to put himself and his legion of fanatics in the forefront of the battle. And Gilberto Salazar could be there as well. After all, it had been Salazar's monumental stupidity that had started this war. Salazar was going to cost Spain the island of Cuba and himself, Vlas Villate, his reputation.

Tomorrow—assuming there was a tomorrow—he would move his headquarters to some place that wouldn't look like a military installation and thus attract cannon fire from the American warships that were sure to charge down the channel and into Havana harbor with their guns blazing.

His aide returned with a uniform in his arms. He dismissed the man and began to dress himself. Always go to war with your pants on, he reminded himself.

Lang and Haney again crawled towards the enemy works. This time they trailed a rope and every fifty yards behind them another American soldier used it as a guide to lead him.

For a second time in as many nights, they reached their goal safely. They huddled in the Spanish trench and waited for the others. An impatient Haney jerked on the rope in a futile attempt to get the others to hurry. It took nearly a precious hour to get the equivalent of a platoon ready to fan out and kill sentries. As this was happening, still more Americans clambered in. No one was surprised that Ryder was among them.

"I thought that generals were too important to go on raids like this?" Haney said.

Ryder smiled in the night. "How come you're not out taking care of Spaniards?"

"Lang informed him I was too damned clumsy," he sniffed. "Once upon a time I could sneak up on a wide awake rabbit in the daylight while I was wearing cowbells, but I guess those days are gone forever."

"Just as well, Sergeant Major. I need you here with me."

A few moments later, two of Lang's men, one coming from each direction, returned to say that the battlement had been cleared for more than a hundred yards each way and that the safe distance was increasing.

Ryder acknowledged the information. "Sergeant Major, I just decided that I no longer need you with me. I want you to get back to the brigade as fast as you can and tell them to run up here quickly and not to worry about making noise. Then send a message to Benteen asking him to have the rest of the division to move up as well. Quickly would be greatly appreciated," he added.

A moment after Haney departed, Lang reappeared. His Bowie knife had blood drying on it. "Man's best friend is not always a dog," he said as he poured water from his canteen on it and wiped off the blade. "Sometimes a good knife is even better."

"How many did you have to kill?"

"Only a couple," he answered. "Most of them surrendered right away when we burst in among them. They were scattered in groups of no more than three. They weren't very well organized or attentive, for that matter. Most of them were sound asleep."

More men began to arrive. In short order, he had a full battalion of the First Maryland in position with more arriving each moment.

"It looks like something's burning," said Lang. "Smells like it, too."

Through the darkness they could see smoke arising from just past the city where the channel to the ocean was. "General, in a few seconds I think that all hell is going to break loose."

Ryder agreed. He grabbed some junior officers to act as couriers. "All three of you are to run like hell." He selected one lieutenant and told him to tell the other battalion commanders to drop any thoughts of secrecy and get their men to him and in position immediately. To the second, he requested that division artillery begin bombarding Spanish positions, also immediately. The third he had deliver a message to General Benteen. "My respects to the general and he might want to consider bringing up the rest of the division even faster than I originally requested. Tell him that the city is about to explode and that things are likely to get very hot in a very short while."

As the men scooted off, bells, bugles, and rifle fire came from Havana. Ryder recalled that the Navy was supposed to provide a diversion. Then he wondered whether his attack was to be a diversion for the Navy. Either way, a major battle was brewing.

"Jesus Christ," said Lang. "Look what the cat dragged in."

"At your service," said photographer William Pywell. "The sun is going to rise shortly and this will be a lovely spot to place a camera."

Ryder shook his head. "It would be an even lovelier spot for a Gatling gun."

◆   ◆   ◆

Everyone at British Consul Redford Dunfield's extensive home was suddenly awakened by the alarms going off all over the city. Custer had been roused from his sleep by the familiar sound of gunfire and was already dressed when everyone gathered in the main dining area. A slightly sleepy Spanish navy Commander Clemente Cisneros addressed them.

"This may be a false alarm, but I think not. It appears that the Americans have either forced the channel or somehow stormed the forts across the channel. Either way they are now able to bombard the city. It may well be that a major infantry attack will soon be launched against Havana."

"We must get to the hospital immediately," Sarah announced. "If you are correct, there will be many wounded to care for."

"Your devotion to your duty is praiseworthy," Cisneros said, "but I cannot allow it. My orders are to keep all of you safe and sending you out into what might be the midst of a climactic battle for Havana is not keeping you safe. With or without your permission, you will remain here."

Sarah was aghast. "Then who will care for the wounded?"

"They will have to fend for themselves until and if it is safe. I cannot run the risk of any of you getting hurt."

"I assume that your soulful concern applies to me as well," said a clearly annoyed President Custer.

"Frankly, sir, I don't much care what happens to you, but my government does. Therefore I am required to protect you from both yourself and the numerous enemies outside the walls of this place who would like to see you dead. Or perhaps they would like to hold you hostage for a large cash ransom and safe passage somewhere."

"Would Villate or Weyler sink so low as to do that?" Custer asked.

Cisneros laughed harshly. "Most people would do just about anything to save their lives, don't you think?"

"What about me?" asked Kendrick. "I'm a reporter. I have a right and an obligation to observe and write about the coming battle."

"I applaud your devotion to your duty and the next book you plan to write, but kindly recall that you have enemies outside these walls who would dearly love to see you dead. Your lovely Juana would be most upset with me if that were to happen; therefore, it will not happen. You will remain here and safely out of the reach of Gilberto Salazar."

Custer was incredulous. "You would order your men to fire on other Spaniards?"

"If those so-called Spaniards were to attack this place they would be violating their orders as well as what passes for international law. This is the British Consulate, not some tavern. If anyone attacks, they will have become rebels and criminals and, yes, we will fight them."

"I'm relieved for Juana's sake," said Kendrick, "but I would still like to report on what I can see with my own eyes. I could use runners, but I don't like to do that."

"Perhaps you would rather get shot by either Salazar's men or some trigger-happy Spanish recruit who has been poorly trained and barely knows how to fire his rifle."

"Good point," Kendrick muttered. "I'll stay put." At least, he thought, until he could figure a way out that would also be reasonably safe.

"Put your back into it, you lazy Irishman." Sweat was pouring down Sergeant Kelly's face. "If the bloody general would mind getting us some bloody help pulling this dead rhinoceros, maybe we could actually move a lot faster. Kindly recall, General, that this beastie was designed to be pulled by horses and not people."

Benteen laughed. Kelly was one of his favorite NCOs. "So we don't have horses but we do have ignorant Irish mules." He turned to a number of men who had been doing little more than gawk. "All of you, grab ropes, grab anything and pull and pull fast. I want those guns in position in minutes, not hours."

More hands did help and the column of Gatling guns gained speed. Kelly took a deep breath and yelled for the men to move faster. Benteen helped by telling them all to run, which made Kelly swear loudly.

Kelly understood fully. The machine guns had to be in place before the Spanish swarmed out of their lines and towards the outnumbered Americans. This time there was no barbed wire or trenches to halt them. The hell being rained down on them by American cannons would hinder but would not stop the massed enemy. Only rifle fire and the precious Gatlings could.

Lang had done a masterful job of modifying them. The wheels were smaller and lower, which meant that the guns, now mounted on a swivel, could fire over them. Unfortunately, it also meant that the guns were harder to pull and, since horses were in short supply in Cuba, manpower was essential to move the weapons.

"Hurry up, Kelly, the war's not going to wait for you to get out of bed and start moving."

"Haney," he gasped, "you may be bigger than me and have a couple more stripes on your sleeve, but, so help me God, I am going to kill your ass, you fucking shanty Irish bastard."

"Quit fighting, children," Ryder said as he grabbed a rope and joined in the effort. "Just a few more yards and you'll be done and can start killing Spaniards."

Haney shook his head. "Generals aren't supposed to be pulling tow ropes."

Ryder ignored him and, along with other men, manhandled the first gun into position. The next five followed in short order. Tow ropes were dropped and metal shields were put in place. The shields were another of Lang's ideas. Nobody in the Army's hierarchy could decide whether the machine guns were fish or fowl, cannons or rifles. Set too far back from the front lines, they were wildly inaccurate. Closer to the enemy, they were murderously effective but the crews were vulnerable to sniper fire or even massed rifle fire. The shields would provide a degree of protection for the four-man crews.

"Jesus," exclaimed Haney, "it looks like someone kicked over an anthill."

As the dawn was rising, the Spanish lines were erupting with men forming up for the attack. They poured out of the ruined buildings and into the narrow streets. The artillery was raining down on them and killing them by the score, but there were thousands of them and more forming up to attack with every minute.

"When should I open fire?" yelled Kelly.

"Now!" answered Ryder.

Five guns were in place with more arriving. Every machine gun the army had was going to support the attack. The weapons began to fire, and their demonic chatter was deafening.

Bullets fired from an extreme range rained down on the Spaniards, dropping still more of them. They were too far off for anything resembling aimed bullets, but were within killing range. To Ryder it reminded him of the time he'd fired on the Sioux at the Little Big Horn, only this time the Spanish were more numerous and farther away. The guns could not miss. They almost certainly had to hit something in the mass of humanity. The guns were more accurate than rifle fire. Even the most experienced soldier might just fire into the ground or in the air or worse, not fire at all in his fear. The Gatlings were handled by teams of men who supported each other and saw to it that the stream of bullets was not only fired, but that shots landed where they were intended. The result was carnage.

Trumpets blared and the Spaniards surged forward. It was like the attacks on Mount Haney, only this time on a level plain with no barbed wire to separate the two sides. Gunners made adjustments and riflemen fired. Smoke obscured the battlefield as the two forces closed.

Ryder pulled out his revolver and unsheathed his sword. He tried to remember the last time he had even practiced with a sword. He was more likely to kill himself with it than a Spaniard.

The Spaniards were emerging through the battle-smoke. They were screaming as if Satan was behind them. They were fighting for their lives.

So too, however, were the Americans. The machine guns were now firing point-blank at waist level. Each gun was on a swivel, which meant that each gun could spray bullets in nearly a one hundred and eighty degree arc.

Ryder threw down his sword and took a second revolver from a fallen soldier. The Spaniards were firing back and too many of his men were falling. Something hit him hard in the chest and he fell back, staggered. A Spaniard was directly in front of him and Ryder managed to shoot him. He lurched to his feet and quickly checked for blood. Amazingly, there wasn't very much at all. Maybe it wasn't a bullet that had hit him.

The battle was now between brave men on one side and brave men supported by cold and deadly technology on the other. Technology won. The Spaniards began to fall back just as reinforcements from the rest of Benteen's division along with soldiers from Gibbon's division filled the gaps caused by casualties.

Ryder's arm was grabbed. "You all right, Ryder?" It was General Hancock. Ryder looked down. A stream of blood was visible on his shirt.

"You shouldn't be up here," said Ryder. Each breath was painful and he wondered if whatever had struck him hadn't broken a rib.

"Go back and have that wound taken care of," said Hancock.

"I'll leave when you do, General." Hancock laughed harshly and went on to another part of the battle.

The smoke was clearing and the Spaniards were retreating slowly and stubbornly. By companies and then by battalions, the American army began to move after them. Orders were not necessary. The Spaniards would be pushed and pushed hard until they surrendered or died.

Ryder looked around anxiously. Where the hell was Lang? The Texan had a job to do with his flying column.

The monsignor howled with joy. "We are to join the attack. By the Blessed Virgin we shall prevail."

Gilberto Salazar was less than enthused but realized he had to obey the direct orders just received from Villate. The breach in Havana's defenses had to be closed regardless the cost and it made perfectly good sense to send in the monsignor's fanatics. The artillery barrage had been terrifying and from what he could see through gaps in the battle smoke, the infantry assault was wavering. The Americans must have a hundred Gatling guns, he decided, and all of them would be aimed at his body.

"Forward," screamed Bernardi, "forward for Spain and Jesus and the Blessed Virgin."

The men of the legion moved to the attack. Salazar noted that some were less enthusiastic than others. He understood them. Salazar tried to hold back, but the press of bodies propelled him onward. He wanted to run and hide but could not be seen as a coward. He had to do something, however, to get out of this terrible fight. A few yards ahead of him, the crazy monsignor was screaming and waving what looked like a sword. Where the devil had the fool gotten a sword, Salazar wondered.

And what the hell did he plan on doing with it?

Salazar stumbled over a dead soldier and fell on his

face. He looked up in time to see Bernardi's body con-
vulse as machine gun bullets ripped through it. Salazar
laughed hysterically. The madman deserved to die, but
he, Gilberto Salazar, did not. He had a task to complete.

Salazar found a piece of a brick with a sharp edge
and gouged it into his scalp and forehead. Like all head
wounds, it quickly gushed blood that covered his face
and made it look like he'd been horribly wounded.

He pretended to stagger to his feet. The remnants
of his legion were fleeing. He joined them. Once again
he was a wounded hero who would save what was left
of his command. He would gather them and do what
he truly wanted to do—take revenge on Juana and her
bastard of an American lover. In the meantime, the
Americans were advancing and there was nothing he
could do about it.

This time it was the Americans who were attacking.
The siege of Havana was going to come to a conclusion this day. Carlos Menendez had been given a rifle
and a dozen raw and confused recruits to lead. He'd
protested that his leg wasn't truly healed and been
hit with the flat of a captain's sword for his efforts.

The latest attack on the American positions had
been as great a failure as the others. The machine
guns were just too deadly and too terrifying. Even he
had an almost overwhelming urge to piss.

Spanish soldiers were yelling and pointing at the
advancing Americans. They were terrified and he saw
why. The Americans were bringing their devil guns
with them. Before this, the Gatlings had sat behind
fortifications and killed from a distance. Now they
were advancing with the blue-clad infantry.

Again, the Spanish lines broke. Men ran or threw down their weapons and held up their hands in meek surrender. Carlos thought for a moment and decided on the latter. He laid down his rifle, never fired, and raised his hands. He trembled in fear as the Americans came near. Would they kill him? It could even happen by accident. What if a foolish Spaniard decided to shoot an American? The Yanks would be furious and doubtless massacre prisoners.

To his astonishment, the Americans swept by with barely a glance. A few seconds later, he and the others were ordered by gestures to head out of Havana. It dawned on him that the Yanks weren't interested in keeping and feeding prisoners and that he would be on his own. He had his cane to help him walk and he would head back to Manuel Garcia's lovely mother. But first he had to find the damned boy.

The boys huddled in the crypt. The skulls of its occupants and assorted other bones no longer bothered them. They were terrified of the man-made thunder that was coming ever closer. Another had joined them. They had been adopted by a small thin dog that they fed with scraps, which was something they felt was hilarious. They too were existing on scraps. The dog wagged its tail and licked their hands. Its love, even if motivated by food, gave them something they could focus on besides their perilous condition.

They originally considered naming the dog Tico after their dead comrade, but decided to name it Alfonso after their dog of a king who had gotten them into all this trouble. They would find another way to honor Tico. Manuel thought it was sad that they didn't even

know Tico's last name or where he came from. They
also hoped that the little priest who had murdered
their friend would burn in Hell.

The dog sniffed the powdery bones and decided they
were too dry to provide any sustenance. Manuel thought
it was nice that the little dog did not have an appetite
for humans, although he would have understood if it
had. If starvation will make a man do crazy things like
Tico did, then what would it do to an animal.

He didn't want to know. He'd heard that there were
such things as cannibals that willingly ate human flesh
and was beginning to understand them.

The earthshaking thunder of the cannons had been
joined by the rattle of small-arms fire that was getting
ever closer. Their time of reckoning was coming and
they were terrified. They huddled together and even
the dog picked up on their fears, pressing against them
and shaking as much as they did. Manuel wondered
if they had anything that could pass as a white flag
so they could at least attempt to surrender. To their
horror, they heard footsteps all around the crypt. They
also realized that the sound of gunfire was fading.

"Leave your weapons in there and come out with
your hands up," The command was shouted in poor
but understandable Spanish. "We know that you're
in there. Come out right now or we start shooting."

They looked at each other and quickly decided to
comply. They yelled that they were coming out and
staggered into the sunlight where they were confronted
by a number of hairy, dirty giants in dressed in blue
who had rifles pointed at them. They were the first
Americans they had ever seen. All their hands were
up with the exception of Manuel who held the dog

in his arms. The frightened animal had peed on him but Manuel didn't care.

"Children, who are you and what are you doing in there?" asked the same man who had ordered them to leave the place of death. His voice was sad and no longer fearsome and he lowered his rifle. "Are you Spanish soldiers?"

Manuel decided that honesty was probably the best policy. "They tried to make us soldiers, but we left them. We didn't want to fight anyone." He tried not to sob but couldn't help himself. The others were crying as well. The dog whimpered and looked confused.

The blue giant translated for his companions who laughed softly. One reached down and petted Alfonso, who licked the giant's hand. "You were wise to desert," said the man who understood Spanish. "Spaniards are dying by the thousands. Little boys should not be fighting machine guns."

Manual wasn't certain what machine guns were but had heard about them. He understood that they were something terrible.

"What do you boys want to do now?" the soldier asked.

Manuel couldn't help another tear from forming and running down his filthy cheek. The others were sobbing as well. "Sir, we want to go home."

One of the soldiers looked away after hearing the translation while another took out part of a loaf of bread, broke off a piece and gave it to the dog who gulped it. Then he saw how the boys looked longingly at the bread, laughed, and brought out a much larger part of a loaf and gave it to Manuel, who thanked him and broke it into roughly equal pieces.

The American gestured towards the road. Large numbers of people were filing down it and all were headed in the same direction, the country. "Mix in with those people and go outside the city. You have no weapons and you look harmless, so it's not likely that anyone will stop you. After that you're on your own. Do you know where your home is?"

Manuel nodded proudly. "I am from Santa Cruz del Norte. My mother has a house there and she will take care of us. We will go there until I can find a way to get my friends to their real homes."

"Your mother will be very proud of you," the American said. He pushed some more food their way and the other soldiers contributed as well. They would eat well this day. The giant American ruffled Manuel's hair. "Travel safely."

They walked for an entire day and were well out of the city and the column of refugees was thinning. They were hungry again and thirsty. Some people were looking carefully at the people in the column as if they wanted to find someone who was lost. He shrugged. All he wanted to do was find his way home.

He gasped as a large hand came down on his shoulder. "You are a difficult young man to find."

"Corporal Menendez, what are you doing here?"

"I am not a corporal any more. I am only Carlos Menendez and I am a farmer. I was looking for a young boy to take back to his mother. Now it looks like I have found several lost boys and a skinny dog. I think she will be very happy to see you, all of you." He handed them a canteen. "Now drink some water and gather your strength."

◆　◆　◆

Cisneros prided himself on being a good naval officer and one who prepared for contingencies. Thus, he was shocked when Salazar's soldiers entered the British Consulate through a rear door he didn't know existed. For the last moments of his life, he ruefully admitted that warships don't have rear entrances.

Convinced that the consulate's inhabitants were the enemies of Spain, the remnants of Salazar's and Monsignor Bernardi's troops poured in, fired wildly at shadows or anything that moved. They rushed forward and then opened the double front door, letting in more of their men. Cisneros' men shot down a number of the attackers, but there were too many of them already in the building. Outraged and desperate, Cisneros led a charge against Salazar and his men. Cisneros knew that Salazar had caused this war and this calamity for Spain and he wanted justice for his country.

While Cisneros' men hesitated for an instant before shooting their fellow countrymen, Salazar's fanatic troops had no such reservations. Without orders and while Salazar hid behind a wall, they poured a volley into the sailors. Cisneros fell with a bullet in his head and several in his chest. Their leader gone, the remaining sailors ran outside and fled into the city.

Salazar was about to lead a search for Kendrick and Juana when more gunfire hit his men from a room off their left. Enraged, Salazar dropped to the floor and fired through the doorway and heard screams. He looked in and saw several bodies and a number of women cowering on the floor. He quickly satisfied himself that none of the women was Juana and that Kendrick was not among the dead or dying. That meant that they had escaped during the confusion.

A dark-haired nurse knelt by one of the fallen men. She was British or American by her looks. The woman looked up at him, her eyes filled with anger. "Do you realize what you have just done?"

Salazar laughed. There was no longer any threat to worry about. "I have defended Spain's honor and now I will go and defend mine."

Sarah now recognized him from the pictures she'd seen. "Gilberto Salazar, not only did you start this war, but you just shot the President of the United States."

◆ Chapter 22 ◆

LANG'S INTENDED LIGHTNING THRUST TOWARDS THE British Consulate had confronted reality. The old streets of Havana were filled with retreating Spanish soldiers who were fighting each other as well as Cuban rebels. Black smoke filled the air and hot ashes from burning homes and buildings fell on them. Lang thought that the city of Havana was burning and being turned to cinders just as ancient Rome had been destroyed under Nero.

Lang's men moved as a compact mass towards what they felt was the right direction. The streets were narrow and congested and, even with Diego Valdez and a score of his men to help, they got lost a couple of times. Some roads were little more than alleys. Several times they were confronted by groups of Spanish soldiers who, on seeing the disciplined Americans, melted away. Only one time did a Spaniard open fire on them and he was cut down in a barrage of gunfire. Lang commented that moving through

Havana was like swimming upstream against a school of desperate fish.

The Spanish were fighting the Cubans and the Americans, and the Cubans were fighting each other as the last act of a brutal civil war played out in the blood-soaked streets. Several times, Valdez and his men had to be restrained from exacting brutal revenge against their oppressors. Valdez's mistress, Maria, accompanied him and tried to act as a calming influence. As a result, atrocities were at a minimum.

Many Spaniards wished to surrender, but accepting their surrender was not the purpose of Lang's column. Their goal was the British Consulate and the rescue of President George Armstrong Custer. That Custer was imprisoned with other Americans who were far more popular and personally more important to Lang and the other Americans was irrelevant. They had a task assigned to them.

They passed the smashed and smoldering fortress of Castillo del Principe. Ahead they could see the spires of the Cathedral of San Cristobal. Smoke was swirling around it as well. "My world is burning," said Valdez. Maria caught up with them and held Valdez's arm.

"You'll have a long time to rebuild it," answered Lang.

Lang signaled a halt. Ahead of them was their goal, the large enclave that was the British Consulate and the home of Redford Dunfield. The massive wooden doors were open and smoke was pouring from a number of windows. Bloody bodies were strewn around the outside of what had been a magnificent estate.

They moved cautiously to the main entrance and walked in, their weapons at the ready. They passed more bodies as they entered the central courtyard. There was silence. Lang wondered if the place had been abandoned. If so, where the devil was Custer?

"Hello," Lang hollered. "Anybody home?" he added and immediately felt foolish for saying that. A couple of his men snickered nervously, and he silenced them with a glare.

Valdez yelled something in Spanish and there was still silence. "This is the United States Army," Lang added. "Come out. You are safe."

There was a rustling noise followed by a woman's voice. "Is that you, Captain Lang?"

Lang breathed a sigh of relief. "Yes, it is, Mrs. Damon, although I regret to inform you that neither your general nor Sergeant Haney are with us."

Sarah and Ruta emerged from a hallway. They were filthy and bruised and their clothing was torn. Each was carrying a rifle and had a pistol stuck in their waistbands.

"I hope you have a doctor with you. President Custer was badly wounded in the fighting. I'm afraid he might die."

General Weyler had a hard time finding the current headquarters of Governor-General Villate as he had moved it several times in response to changing threats from both the Americans and the Cuban insurgents. Finally, he located it in a small abandoned hotel. A number of staff officers were wandering around in confusion. They looked lost and thoroughly dispirited. Weyler grabbed the arm of a captain he knew was an aide to Villate.

"Captain Avila, where the hell is the general?"

The captain laughed harshly. "How the devil would I know? I haven't seen him in hours. It is my firm belief, General Weyler, that the bird has flown and is now on the high seas and headed for some other country that will give him and his money sanctuary."

Weyler grabbed the Avila by the collar. "Are you saying that he has deserted his post?"

Avila laughed, almost hysterically. His world was crashing around him. "Yes, General. Tell me, do you see him around? No, and nobody has, like I said, for some time. The last time I did see him he had several foot lockers and other pieces of luggage ready to be loaded onto a waiting carriage. I thought he was merely moving his quarters again, but he had already told me that he would not return to Spain in disgrace for losing Cuba where he would have to endure a court martial and possibly a hanging. Even if he wasn't hanged, he would suffer eternal shame and disgrace. I believe those boxes and luggage contained money and securities to help him set up a new and prosperous life in another country. I have been looking at some of Villate's correspondence and I now know that he had been in contact with a man who owned a fishing boat. I do not believe that the American Navy would concern itself with such an insignificant craft if he should try to flee in it."

Weyler could see Avila's logic. "Then we won't even consider him."

"With respects, General Weyler, I believe that you are the next senior officer. Therefore, the command of the armies and government of Cuba now rests on your shoulders."

Villate, you bastard, Weyler thought, but then

smiled. The old man had done him a favor. Yes, he would likely have to surrender, but the shame would be Villate's and not his. There would be an inquiry in Madrid where scorn would be heaped on Villate's absent head. He, Valeriano Weyler, would be found guilty of nothing more than inheriting Villate's mess. He would show how he had fought bravely but had been betrayed by his leader. He would survive and likely be given an even more important command by a grateful Spain and king.

"Get me any senior officers you can find. We have to begin negotiating an end to this war."

Against the advice of his staff, Ryder had entered Havana. He had gotten word that President Custer had been shot and that Sarah, Ruta, and the others were safe. Although he was not the slightest bit fond of Custer, he could not bring himself to wish ill to the foolish man. He had sent a doctor on ahead with orders to get to the consulate as quickly as possible. As to his responsibilities, he still had a brigade to coordinate as it moved deeper and deeper into the mass of buildings, many of them burning, that was Havana.

The news that a Spaniard had shot Custer had spread rapidly throughout the army. It angered the American soldiers, who were fighting even more ferociously than before. Rifle fire and Gatling guns were destroying any resistance that the Spanish could manage. If something didn't happen, the battle could turn into a massacre as other American forces had penetrated other parts of Havana's defenses. Pywell took picture after picture and Martin wondered how many of them would turn out. Enough, he hoped, so that the world would see the carnage.

Whenever they could, soldiers yelled in Spanish for the enemy to surrender. They were told that they would be protected and treated well. They were told that they would be sent home if that was their wish. It was beginning to work. Numbers of Spanish soldiers had thrown down their rifles and begun walking towards them with their hands up. Their expressions said that they were terrified they would be murdered by the American soldiers. Numerous white flags were waving from windows as well as by individual soldiers. Ryder gave the order to cease fire and an uneasy silence descended. Without being ordered, Spanish soldiers lay down their arms and nervously stepped away.

Whole units had begun surrendering. Spanish officers willingly took charge and organized a parade of disconsolate and unarmed men heading out of Havana. Ryder had no idea where they would go and didn't give a damn. He was, however, shocked at how many there were. Hopefully, there were too many for the Cuban rebels to massacre. He hoped somebody was taking charge of protecting the prisoners from any attempt at massacre.

"Haney, with decent training and leadership, they could have either held out forever or chewed us to little pieces."

"Thank God, St. Patrick, and Richard Gatling for saving us," Haney said. "Now, General dearest, let's find that damned consulate."

Before they could advance further, a Spanish captain waving a white flag approached them nervously. "Are you a senior officer?" he asked.

Before Ryder could answer, Haney stepped in front of him, and snapped to attention and glared at the poor man. "I am an aide to General Martin Ryder. Who the devil are you?"

The captain looked like he was going to cry. "I am Captain Joaquin Avila, the senior aide to General Valeriano Weyler who is now the governor-general of Cuba. My general would like to find a senior officer to accept the surrender of all the Spanish forces in Cuba."

Ryder's mind reeled. From Hancock on down they had thought that the Spanish would be forced to surrender Havana, but this man had just said that Weyler was willing to surrender all of Cuba. Jesus. He turned to a young American officer who was watching and listening with his mouth open. "Lieutenant, run back to where the field telegraph reaches and send messages to Generals Hancock, Benteen, and Miles. Tell them that Weyler wishes to surrender all of Cuba and not just Havana. Tell them that I am going to accept that surrender on their behalf and order a cease-fire to take affect at least in my area."

Prentice had managed to cadge a lift back to the *Orion* where Janson's ship was in line to enter the confines of Havana's harbor. Gunfire from the Spanish side of the narrow channel had been reduced to sporadic small arms fire. To further protect the lightly armored auxiliary cruiser, Janson had the port side of the hull draped in wooden planks to help keep bullets from piercing the *Orion's* thin hull.

A pair of Gatling guns had been mounted on the port side as well, and bursts of bullets had silenced almost all of the remaining enemy gunners. In his opinion, it was indeed becoming the age of the machine gun.

Prentice fully understood the difficulty of moving a large and cumbersome machine gun while under fire. Mounting guns on a stable but moveable plat- form such as a ship was an ideal use of the deadly weapons. Not only could the guns rake enemy posi- tions, but they could also be used effectively against attacks by small boats.

"In for a penny," said Janson as the ship entered the narrow channel. Buildings and fortifications on both sides were smoking and some were in flames. Prentice held his breath as they moved slowly through what was clearly the most dangerous part of their journey.

Then the channel widened and they emerged into the harbor. "Dante's Inferno," said Prentice.

"If Dante wrote about a city on fire, then you're right."

Clouds of smoke partly obscured the sunlight and made them choke. Prentice hoped he wasn't choking on ashes from human flesh, then decided there wasn't much he could do about it. He had come a long way in the last few months and wasn't certain he liked the trip. It had been one thing to sink an enemy gunboat and then a battleship, but killing that man in the Span- ish fort had been difficult to deal with, even though the man had been attacking him and it had occurred so quickly. He would never get over the look on the man's face as he lay there mortally wounded from Prentice's sword stroke. Now it was terrible to watch a proud and ancient city burning to death.

Large numbers of small boats sailed or steamed past them, clearly trying to escape to the open sea. "I

suppose we should try to stop them," said Janson, "but
there are so damn many of them. Besides, the admiral
doesn't seem too concerned, so why should we?"

"Oh my God," Prentice exclaimed. "Look at that!"

Many of the buildings lining the once beautiful waterfront were burning, and the streets were
packed with Spanish soldiers. Most of them were
without weapons, while others threw their rifles into
the harbor. Some were waving white flags and others
simply waving their arms in a frantic attempt to show
that they were harmless. A soldier fell into the water,
pushed by those behind him. More followed. Only a
couple surfaced.

"We could kill a thousand with one volley," said
Janson. "Unless given a direct order from Admiral
Porter I will not fire, and perhaps not even then. It
would be like slaughtering sheep or chickens."

Signal flags fluttered from the flagship. Prentice
interpreted. "We are to anchor but keep up steam.
No small boats will be allowed near us. I guess that's
in case they try to rush us and overwhelm us."

"Makes sense. Somehow, though, I don't think the
good admiral expected this sort of reception. Nope, I'll
bet you a dollar that the old war dog expected to fight
his way in and may just be a little disappointed, just
like he might have been when the Spanish squadron
surrendered without a fight."

Prentice laughed softly. "Skipper, I'm not the slightest bit disappointed."

Salazar's legion now consisted of himself and two
very nervous soldiers. He was convinced that they
would run at the first chance, so he kept his revolver

out and watched them carefully. He would not put it past them to attack him and rob him.

He had given considerable thought to where Juana and Kendrick would go and decided there was only one logical conclusion. With escape through the crumbling Spanish lines and out to the Americans still impractical because of ongoing fighting, that left only the residence of Juana's uncle, the esteemed Bishop Estefan Campoy.

Salazar pounded on the door of the bishop's residence and it was opened fairly quickly. The bishop stood before him, his arms folded across his chest. "You may not enter here."

Salazar growled and pushed the cleric aside. Campoy again tried to stop him and Salazar knocked him down. When Campoy got to his feet, his face was bloodied. "You have struck a man of the cloth. You have committed a grievous sin."

Salazar laughed. "Add it to the list."

Campoy tried to block Salazar's entrance to the kitchen. Juana and Kendrick stood against a wall. They looked almost resigned to their fate. Kendrick had armed himself with a kitchen knife, which Salazar thought was hilarious.

Salazar howled with glee and aimed his pistol at them. "You are going to die."

"No," said the bishop. "If you shoot them you will be guilty of the crime of murder. I will testify at your trial and you will hang."

"No, Bishop, that simply will not happen," Salazar said. "Don't you think I planned for this eventuality? I knew they would come running to you if they got out of the consulate. Now I am going to kill them and when they are dead I will fall on my knees and beg you to hear my confession. As a good priest, you will be obliged to do so and then confession of my crime will be protected by the seal of the confessional. You will not be permitted to testify against me according to the rules of Holy Mother Church."

Campoy groaned. "Don't do it," he pleaded. "Don't kill them."

Salazar pushed the bishop aside. Neither Kendrick nor Juana moved, which puzzled him. They even seemed to be looking over his shoulder. At what? Did they see God? Perhaps they were paralyzed with fright? He raised his right arm, but his right arm wouldn't respond. Seconds later, torrents of pain overwhelmed him and he dropped to his knees. The pistol dropped uselessly to the floor. Instinctively, he tried to reach it with his left hand, but he felt something smash into that shoulder as well. He howled and he fell onto his back. He looked up and saw a demon.

"Why did you have to kill her?" Hector Rojas asked in a flat, dull voice. His large hammer hung loosely from the leather loop around his hand.

The agony from the broken bones in Salazar's shoulders made speech almost impossible. "Get me a doctor," he managed to gasp.

"No doctor," Rojas said calmly. He swung the hammer and smashed Salazar's left kneecap. "Again, why did you kill her?"

"She angered me," Salazar managed to gasp through his agonies. "She said I wasn't a man." He looked wildly for the two men who were supposed to protect him. They weren't around. Either they'd fled or Rojas had killed them. The bishop was standing with Juana and Kendrick.

"She was right. You aren't a man," Rojas said as he swung the hammer and destroyed Salazar's right knee-cap, causing his incoherent screams to reach an even higher crescendo. "Mercedes was a wonderful woman. She was kind and thoughtful, and you killed her like she was a bug. She should be alive and you should not be. I am going to correct at least part of that."

Rojas swung the hammer again and brought it down on Salazar's skull, smashing it. Rojas could hear Juana vomiting and the bishop praying. He wiped the mess that had been Salazar's brains off of the hammer and turned to the bishop. "I have killed a helpless man and I want you to hear my confession."

Campoy swallowed. "With pleasure. We will go into the other room and you will confess this and any other sins you might have committed. Your penance will be light because you have killed a monster. When that is done, perhaps we can discuss your taking employment with me. You would be in charge of protecting the cathedral and all its valuables."

Rojas smiled. He would have a good job along with all the wealth that he had taken. "I would like that."

The bishop continued. "I have seen Mercedes' will and she has left a goodly part of it to you. You took care of her and she will take care of you."

Rojas nodded. He wondered if the bishop suspected that he had looted money from Mercedes' safe. Ah well.

Juana was wide-eyed and stunned at the turn of events, and Kendrick wasn't in much better shape. Campoy took both of Juana's hands in his and smiled with genuine joy. "My dearest niece, it very much looks like you are now a widow. All of our wishes and prayers have come true. If you want to marry this fire-breathing pagan, I will dispense with any formalities and marry you right after I hear this other gentleman's confession."

Juana smiled and grabbed Kendrick's arm. "The pagan and I would like that very much."

Campoy hugged her. "After the nuptials I would strongly urge you to leave Cuba as quickly as you can. The fever season is coming and I don't know how well the Americans are prepared for it."

"You can count on it," said Kendrick. "I have a book to write."

◆ Chapter 23 ◆

SURGEON GENERAL REAR ADMIRAL JOHN B. HAMILTON had a sterling reputation as an administrator, doctor, and reformer. Thus, his opinions were highly regarded and the handful of high-ranking listeners sitting at the table with him was extremely attentive.

"Mr. President, Mr. Secretary of State, and the Secretaries of War and the Navy," he began as if giving a lecture, "I wish I had better news for you but I don't. Despite our best efforts, we still have no firm idea what causes yellow fever, how to prevent it, and how to cure it. And all this is despite offering a ten thousand dollar reward to the person who finds the cause and cure. As a result, of course, we've been inundated by suggestions that were both plausible and insane."

"I can only imagine," said President Chester Arthur. "But do any of them have merit? We have had thousands of men go down with the fever and, while many have recovered or are recovering, others have died and the disease has become a catastrophe."

"Well, sir, we have pretty well laid to rest the twin ideas that Negro soldiers are immune to it or that it is caused by breathing bad air. We are now of the opinion that it is caused by germs and not by bad air. Since Negro soldiers have also caught the fever, we know that they are not inherently immune because of their African heritage. It is small consolation, but Spanish soldiers are suffering just as badly."

Blaine shook his head angrily. "I don't give a damn about Spanish soldiers. I want our boys protected from this scourge."

President Arthur turned away. All across the country blame for the disease was falling on Blaine for being such a strong supporter and instigator of the war. He was being pilloried in newspapers and on the floor of Congress as the man who had caused the deaths of so many young men. The American people were better able to handle wounds and deaths in battle than they were from disease. That there had been enormous numbers of fatalities during previous wars was ignored for the simple reason that the war in Cuba was a foreign war in a strange and foreign land. What are we doing there? This was a simple question that was being asked loudly and often. Why had we gone in in the first place, and why don't we just get the hell out and leave Cuba for the Cubans?

"Are there any serious leads?" asked Arthur.

"A Cuban doctor named Carlos Finlay seems to think the disease is caused by and spread by mosquitoes. Perhaps the mosquitoes carry germs that pass into the human bloodstream much in the manner that rats carried plague-infected fleas that bit people and spread that disease. Right now the idea of mosquitoes as a source is as good an idea as anyone else has."

Blaine showed his disbelief. "Even if true, how does one eliminate mosquitoes? Hopefully not one at a time," he snorted contemptuously.

Hamilton showed his frustration. "Of course not! The obvious tactic is to find out how and where the little creatures live and breed and stamp out those places, and this is what we are now doing. To the best of our knowledge, they live in swamps and stagnant water and there are literally tens of thousands of potential breeding spots in Cuba. Unfortunately, it will take a long while to determine if the efforts to clean up the breeding grounds will be successful. It should also be noted that the fever does not attack people in colder climes, which lends some credence to the mosquito theory."

"In the meantime," Arthur said sadly, "our boys are sickening and dying."

"Sadly, sir, these things take time and sometimes lots of time and with no guarantee whatsoever that we are on the right track."

"What can we do?" Blaine said sadly.

Admiral Hamilton shook his head sadly. "The only feasible thing we can do now is see to it that our boys get to colder weather as soon as possible."

King Alfonso XII sagged back in his chair. He felt ill. He had turned the offending telegram face down so he wouldn't have to look at it, would not have to confront the disaster it represented. The Spanish forces in all of Cuba had surrendered to the Americans.

Even those divisions far away had been ordered to surrender by General Weyler.

There was no way to keep the tragedy a secret. The cable had arrived without being encoded. Now all of Madrid was aware that Cuba, the jewel of the empire that had been Spanish for nearly four hundred years, had been surrendered. And worse, it had been surrendered to those that the Holy Mother Church still referred to as heretics. Outside the palace there was rioting and buildings were being burned. Alfonso wondered if there would be a thirteenth Alfonso or would he be the end of the imperial line.

Prime Minister Canovas was pale with disbelief. "We outnumbered them, we sent a fleet, we had good generals. I don't understand this."

Former Prime Minister Praxedes was blunt. "We sent an army of conscripts that was poorly trained and inadequately armed and led. We then sent them thousands of miles away from their homes to fight a war they didn't understand. The soldiers sympathized with the rebels and didn't want to fight. That we outnumbered the Americans is irrelevant. How many times have you seen a small vicious dog beat a larger dog in a fight?"

"We're talking about armies, not dogs," Canovas said angrily.

"Spain will become a second-rate power," said the king.

"With profoundest respects," said Praxedes, "Spain began to become a second-rate power when the Armada was destroyed in the sixteenth century. The collapse was completed during the Napoleonic wars. We are a second-rate power, and if we don't do something to prevent a further brutal collapse, Spain will become a total irrelevancy in the world of nations."

"What would you have me do?" asked the king.

Praxedes answered. "We must accept the fact that our empire is largely gone. We have lost Cuba and Puerto Rico. We must negotiate the best treaty we can with the United States. All that we have left are the Philippine Islands and a few specks of land in the Pacific along with our territories in North Africa. If the Americans desire them, they can take the Philippines from us without any effort whatsoever. Those islands are again in a state of rebellion and we will not be able to crush it. We do not have an army, and even if we did, we have almost no navy; therefore, we would have no way of sending it to the Philippines."

"What do you propose?" asked a despondent Canovas.

"That we sell everything to the Americans," Praxedes answered. "They can claim Cuba and Puerto Rico by right of conquest, and we will not be able to hold on to the Philippines. If the Americans want them, they can take them at any time. So too can the British and the Germans. I've received a telegram from a friend of mine in Berlin saying that there is pressure on the Kaiser to annex the islands. I suggest we take whatever we can get for the remnants of our overseas empire and begin to rebuild."

Alfonso smiled wryly. "Then we will offer the Philippines to the highest bidder. And God help the winner. He will have to fight the rebels."

◆ Epilog ◆

SARAH WALKED BAREFOOT THROUGH THE COOL WATER. Even though the water in the pond only came up to her calves, it was marvelously refreshing. The weather in Maryland this summer morning was seasonably warm and promised to get hot. She had stripped off her outer clothing and enjoyed the play of the breeze against her body.

"You're beautiful," said Martin. "Come down to me and we'll make another baby." Like Sarah, Martin was dressed in his underclothing. They were far enough away from the main house and hidden by trees and bushes to be unconcerned about privacy.

"Baby number one is only six months old and I am not yet ready for a second. Young Martin Junior is more than enough." Young Martin's birth had been difficult and there were serious doubts as to whether they should have another. "And I am truly thankful that Jack and his fiancée are back in the house watching him. I would love to see him change a diaper with only one arm. You have enough trouble with two."

"We could use one of Doctor Condom's magic devices," he pleaded.

"All right," she relented with a warm smile. She got a condom from her handbag, affixed it to his manhood, and, after a few moments of exquisitely tender foreplay, lowered herself onto his body.

When they were done, she smiled, kissed him gently, and lay beside him. "That was much better than on a pile of tents," she said and the two of them laughed. It was their personal joke and they hoped they never stopped thinking it was funny. "Are you still not going to Washington for the dedication?"

"I'll stay here with you if you don't mind. The deification of the late George Armstrong Custer is a little too much to stomach. I prefer what Kendrick wrote in his book."

On the blanket beside them lay the book in question. The title was *George Armstrong Custer—Fool or Hero?* by James Kendrick. The subtitle said that Kendrick had been with Custer from the Little Big Horn to his admittedly tragic death from his wounds in Havana. The book was a runaway bestseller and had made a fortune for James Kendrick. He and his Cuban wife were being lionized in New York.

Sarah and Martin agreed with Kendrick's conclusions regarding Custer. He had been brave to the point of recklessness, but he had not been a fool. He simply had too much confidence in his ability to accomplish any goal. As a result, he had involved the United States in the most controversial war in its history.

Alongside that book was another book. This was a collection of photos by the photographer, William Pywell. The graphic pictures of so many dead and wounded were a further condemnation of the late Custer and what many felt was his unnecessary war. Pywell had even managed to get some clear action shots of soldiers advancing, fighting, and being killed.

An equestrian statue to Custer was to be dedicated on the Mall in front of the Capitol Building. He would be on a mighty stallion and waving a sabre. Some of the critics said that he should be facing backwards since he had been such a horse's ass. They were in a minority. Most of the country thought he was a hero and a martyr, although a deeply flawed one.

Libbie Custer would be there along with many in the government including President Chester Arthur. Libbie had become a recluse and a gaunt and graying shadow of her once dynamic self. She clearly blamed her husband's death on her machinations on his behalf. Some of her friends thought she was losing her mind. After the ceremony she would return to her home in Monroe, Michigan.

When Martin resigned his commission, he had almost totally severed himself from the Army. As he'd explained to Sarah, the Army would contract in size and he would once again be either a captain or, if the Army threw him a bone, a major. He would then be doomed to spending the next twenty years in crude frontier outposts, all the while begging for promotion to lieutenant colonel. Sarah said she would go wherever he went, but he would not burden her with that kind of life. No, his military career was over. As he told her and anyone else who asked, it had been wonderful being a general, but he would never again achieve that rank. Nelson Miles was the Army's commanding general.

As her husband, Martin was learning the ins and

outs of her business investments and finding that he was as good at it as she. They would be good partners in commerce as well as in bed.

The loss of so many good men in Cuba was a constant source of sadness and disgust. Almost two thousand Americans had died in combat and another five thousand were in their graves as a result of the fevers that finally struck both armies with savage ferocity. Nor did the fever respect rank. Hancock had died, along with Benteen and Crooks. Even so, there would still not be openings for a too-young brigadier in a shrunken army. Seniority would again rule.

One result of the devastating disease was that Cuba was virtually unoccupied by the American military. The Cubans had won. The United States had taken Hawaii as a consolation prize and had purchased the Philippines from Spain for a nominal sum. Martin and many others wondered if this had been a wise decision.

"Martin, I did tell you that Ruta and her stable-boy lover were coming over this evening, didn't I?"

Martin guffawed. Haney and Ruta would never commit to being married. They had made that abundantly clear. He had a job allegedly administering her horses. This gave him a cottage on her property and access to the main house anytime they wished and to hell with what anyone else thought.

"Sarah, this is not a bad life. Perhaps we should spend the rest of the day here and make love a few more times."

"Perhaps indeed," she said with a smile as she watched the clouds move majestically overhead. The clouds were white and fluffy. There were no storm clouds on the horizon. At least not yet.

PRAISE FOR BEN BOVA

WHERE SCIENCE FICTION MEETS SCIENCE FACT

About the award-winning stories and novels of Ben Bova:
"Technically accurate and absorbing . . ."   —*Kirkus*

"[Bova is] the science fiction author who will have the greatest effect on the world."   —*Ray Bradbury*

"A masterful storyteller"   —*Vector*

"Gives a good read while turning your eyes to what might be in the not so distant future, just like Clarke and Asimov used to do so well."   —*SFX*

About Mars, Inc., by Ben Bova:
". . . perfectly enjoyable as an SF book (could Bova write anything that wasn't enjoyable?), Mars, Inc. has that torn-from-the-headline vibe that's obviously intended for a larger audience. . . . the bottom line? Mars, Inc. has inspiration, excitement, thrills, romance, a dash of satire—and is a good, fun read. . . ."
—*Analog*

"The Hugo winner returns to his most popular subject: the quest for Mars."   —*Publishers Weekly*

". . . escapist fantasy for rocket scientists and space engineers, those dreaming of these kinds of missions. Yet Bova's story is rigorously realistic. . . . a fun read showing you do not need car chases or shootouts to deliver a fast-paced and exciting story."
—*Daily News of Galveston County*